BRING ME NEAR

MARGUERITE MARTIN GRAY

Cover designed by Roseanna White.

Celebrate Lit Publishing

www.celebratelitpublishing.com

ISBN: 978-0-9995370-4-6

To My Sisters,
Sarah Pleasant
Christine Choice
Charlotte Lucy
Not many people are blessed with three loving sisters. You inspire and challenge me.
The Martin girls, we will always be, from cradle to grave.
God knew I needed each of you in my life.
Thank you. This is your story too.

CHAPTER 1

Charles Town, South Carolina
       December 31, 1774

Louis Lestarjette paused with his hands on the hard-cherry wood armoire doors, depending on the strength of the massive piece of furniture to hold him upright. The slight pounding of a headache reminded him of the task before him.

Meet at the Exchange at eleven.

He was to come alone. The note had not been signed. Christopher Gadsden, his friend and business partner, had told him he'd receive an opportunity to help the cause. Since he trusted Christopher, he did not second-guess whether he should meet tonight. Nothing could keep him away. He needed to know how to protect Elizabeth from the turmoil brewing. It wasn't a matter of trust, for he could trust her with anything. The dilemma dealt with if he should bring more worry into her life before he knew the details. *Please understand my secrecy, Elizabeth.* He had the feeling it wouldn't be the last time.

He should be upstairs crawling into bed beside Elizabeth, welcoming in the New Year with her in his arms. A few minutes earlier, she had put their infant daughter to bed. Now, she waited.

1

Louis climbed the stairs with heavy feet and stood in the doorway of the nursery. Elizabeth adjusted the blanket on Harriet's body and softly whispered "sweet dreams." She smiled at Louis and took his hand as she passed into the hallway.

"All the activity exhausted the little thing. Her first party." She tried to hide a yawn beneath her fingers.

"It's almost ten o'clock. I think you need to take advantage of Harriet's fatigue."

Louis regarded his wife preparing for bed, craving to share with her every detail of Christopher's involvement with new schemes. Secrets he had to keep for now. If she knew what he hid from her, her desire to go with him would win out. He let her continue her routine while he concocted an excuse for his absence. He needed tonight, a chance to figure out if he could do this. Or could he choose a way out?

Elizabeth sat at her dressing table and unlaced her half-boots. "Perhaps you are right. I am rather exhausted. Will you join me?" She pulled his cravat down, bringing his head close for a kiss.

"In a little while." He shuffled his feet. "I need to finish some correspondence. I'll come up soon." He kissed her. Should he reveal his confidences now? Perhaps he should just stay. The note dictated they'd understand if he didn't attend tonight.

Elizabeth pushed away from his close embrace and her blue-gray eyes melted his resolve a bit. "Louis, are you all right? That was a very long kiss, not that I minded."

"Happy New Year." He brushed her cheek, locked in her gaze. He closed his eyes, gaining strength without her long lashes, silky hair loose down her back, and kissable lips begging him to reconsider. "Good night, my dear." He turned and headed downstairs to the library. The tick-tock of the mantel clock counted off the minutes. The beating of his heart and the pounding of his head melded with the rhythm.

At a quarter until eleven, he breathed a prayer, put his overcoat on, glanced up the stairs, and exited through the back door.

No one noticed him depart, and no one discerned where he was going.

The streets were not empty even at this late hour, since many revelers stayed out to see the New Year dawn. Glimpsing the fatigued citizens advancing toward home or more celebrating, Louis concurred that their decision to share a family gathering at her parents' house in lieu of a big social affair remained the right one. Louis stuffed his hands in his pockets and hunched his shoulders against the cold breeze from the river. Any other night, a lone man on the streets would be odd at this hour.

The Exchange Building loomed in front of him. He checked his pocket watch—five minutes of the hour. He traversed the length of the building and terminated at a side-garden gate.

"Mr. Lestarjette." Out of the shadows materialized Mr. William Drayton, the renowned Charles Town Loyalist turned Partisan, a prominent, vocal leader. "I'm glad you decided to meet me." Louis covered his surprise by willing his jaw in place.

They shook hands. To any bystander, they resembled friends who just met on the street.

"Thank you." Louis could no longer suppress the suspense. "I am curious, sir, about the nature of this interview."

"Naturally. I know you have a wife and baby to attend, so I'll get to the point. We, that is South Carolina and the Sons of Liberty, may need your help and availability." He bent in closer to deliver the last words. "You have come recommended by Silas Deane and John Adams. Very soon, South Carolina will set up a secret committee to perform certain tasks that cannot be outlined in detail for all to see. With your mind for business and your contacts in France, you could be an asset to this committee." Mr. Drayton stopped, either for air or for Louis' comment.

"Mr. Deane had mentioned something like this. I didn't know it would be needed so soon."

"Believe me. It is needed." Mr. Drayton pursed his lips and scratched his chin. The glow from the street lamps cast shadows across his face. "I can't tell you much more except when the time comes, secrecy will be of utmost importance."

"How is this business in Charles Town connected with Mr. Deane and Mr. Adams?" Louis asked.

"All colonies are preparing for this battle together. But it could be that the Continental Congress needs you as well." Mr. Drayton turned toward Louis and met him eye-to-eye. "If you don't wish to be involved in our activities, send me a note before our meeting on the eleventh that says you will not be able to help in the matters we discussed tonight. Otherwise, I will assume that you stand ready to assist our cause."

"You know of my commitment. Although I don't like keeping things from my wife, I'll take all matters into consideration. Thank you for your trust in me."

Mr. Drayton nodded his head. "I understand. But it is better for all concerned that it be this way." He extended his hand, ending the meeting. "Until the meeting in a few days."

"Until then." As the man's shadow merged with the night, Louis bowed his head, shrugged his shoulders, and retraced his steps. St. Michael's bells chimed in the New Year as Louis entered his library. 1775. Time had not stopped, nor had the world's groaning.

Elizabeth didn't remember what woke her from her coveted sleep. A whimper from Harriet or the walls creaking? Putting on her warm robe and slippers, she'd checked on the baby and headed downstairs to investigate.

The bells of St. Michael's announced the New Year as she raised her lamp level with her cheek. From the top of the staircase, the ribbon of pale-yellow light underneath the library door pulled her forward. Shadows crisscrossed the stream, washing the foyer with dancing patterns.

She turned the knob and pushed the door open. "Louis." He had his back to her, bending over his desk bracing himself by his outstretched arms.

He swiveled and opened his arms inviting her to tumble into his embrace. "Elizabeth, why aren't you in bed?"

"I could ask you the same question."

They both laughed, then uttered in unison, "Happy New Year."

She shivered even in his warm embrace. "1775. My imagination is crawling with questions. What are we facing?"

He kissed her forehead. "I'm convinced it will be nothing like we've experienced before. The good thing is that we have each other."

Louis turned down the lamp and led Elizabeth up the stairs to a place where conflict was banned and the new year looked bright wrapped in their love.

CHAPTER 2

*E*lizabeth ran her hands down Louis' sleeves and turned her eyes to his. He'd seen that look before. "Don't go to the meeting tonight, Louis," she pleaded, trying to deter him from the sticky business in town. "Stay home with us. Harriet hasn't seen you much this week."

Louis placed his hands gently on her shoulders letting his fingertips ease her tension. "You know I can't stay away. You don't want me to go because you want to be there, too." He tried to lighten the moment. Perhaps he guessed correctly. "Anyway, Harriet is hardly three weeks old and has eyes for only you."

A slight whimper drew Louis to Harriet's day cradle. He melted at her blue eyes, a Lestarjette trait, as they adjusted to the mid-morning light. If he could make her world as peaceful as the cool breeze playing in the sunlight for the rest of her life, he would. Therefore, he had to go to the meeting.

I must take the next step.

"What do you think, Harriet? Should I stay home to care for you?" Her tiny fingers wrapped around his. "Maybe I should." His status in life still startled him—married for over a year, a father, a successful merchant, and a ship owner. His ties went beyond these walls. How he arrived here was a mystery. All he really knew was that he had turned his decisions over to God's will.

He grinned and turned his head toward Elizabeth. "Every day decisions are being made for our future. I must be a part of the solution. You and your petticoat brigade know what's at stake here." She smiled back even as her arms crossed in annoyance. She had a strong dose of Elliott stubbornness and pride, straight from her father. Her beauty softened her sternness. Louis touched her soft loose brown curls bouncing around her face. It didn't matter if she wore the latest Parisian fashion or local homespun, he never tired of watching her, even in her annoyance with him. Did she guess that he held a secret? Would he have to be secretive in the future too? Should he tell her of his actions?

Elizabeth walked over and fidgeted with the blanket over the cradle. "Are you laughing at your female counterparts? We won't have to use our ingenious contraptions if you men can find a way to prevent these continued disagreements."

"We're working on it, but the obstacle is the British government."

"I know. Promise you'll tell me everything from tonight. Are you sure women aren't invited?"

He yearned for her to attend--the one woman who had helped him figure out where his priorities should lie. "I could sneak you in, but the crowd would dissuade you. A hundred and eighty-four delegates are expected, plus the rest of us."

"Well, Harriet and I are going to the mercantile today to visit Aunt Jeannette, and we'll see the crowds for ourselves." Already her blue eyes had closed in sleep, and Louis' finger had been released. Almost as if Harriet knew what he had to do.

"Be careful," he warned. "The streets are full of people from all over the colony."

Louis bent and kissed his spirited wife. Her cheek pressed against his palm, and she sighed. She felt the weight of the battle as much as or more than he did, for she had been attached to this land since birth. Although his commitment ran deep, two years didn't compare to a lifetime. Perhaps, he could confide in her soon.

❀

Tonight's meeting had been set back in December after electing delegates to a General Provincial Committee. Christopher had established himself as one of the leaders—a very vocal and radical one. Since Louis' main information came from his friend's viewpoint, he hoped to see for himself the views of other groups.

He couldn't shake the impulse to talk to Christopher before the meeting tonight. Ever since New Year's Eve, Louis had debated his moves within the political system. Then two days ago, Silas Deane had sent him a letter through Christopher. At first, he was confused. What was the point of involving Louis? Deane's words had left him curious but not convinced. "There is talk of a Secret Committee within the Congress becoming official in the future. I want you to be prepared. We could use a man with connections in France."

His feet moved him toward the river and Christopher's office. A few minutes would soothe his anxiety. Or send him racing in the opposite direction.

Louis tapped on the window, and Christopher motioned for him to enter. He patted his pocket where Mr. Deane's letter rested. "Good morning. Do you have a few minutes?"

His friend pointed to a leather chair in front of his desk. "I do. I'm sorry I've been so busy and missed our meeting last week."

"I know you need to prepare for tonight." He took the note out of his pocket and placed it on the desk. "As you know I received this from Silas Deane. What is the point? Why me?"

Christopher walked to the window and turned back toward Louis. "Things will begin progressing quickly, I think. I want us to be prepared. I want people that I can count on, and you are an

8

excellent choice. Members of Congress think that France will play a pivotal role in our conflict. You have ties in France. You know the language and the minds of the people."

"You might overestimate my attributes. I am an untitled member of the nobility. I don't have the ear of the King or his administrators. How do you see this working?"

Christopher clicked his teeth with his tongue and sat on the edge of his large desk. "You are now one of the people, a merchant with ties, an educated, intelligent Frenchman. And you are now a South Carolinian. The ministers of France will trust you over British subjects like myself."

Louis laughed. "Perhaps."

Mid-morning was a little late to get to the store, but his uncle knew of his desire to spend time with his family. "Uncle Henry," Louis called into the storeroom. A lamp cast shadows on the walls. No answer. Only one place he could be—the basement.

The crate, usually covering the trap door blocking an outsider's view of the entrance to the stairs descending beneath the floor, was off to the side. Louis looked behind him before he joined his uncle below.

"Uncle Henry." Louis turned again adjusting to the dark quarters. A single lantern guided him to his uncle. "Here you are. What are you doing?"

"I'm going through the inventory again." Henry continued his counting, then placed his figures in his ledger. "When it comes time to disburse these items, we need to know preciously what we have and where it is." His uncle stretched his almost six-foot form and turned toward Louis with his honest gray eyes overburdened with bushy eyebrows.

"Why now?" Louis paced the familiar space amazed at the additional rows added in the past year.

"Precaution. The arrival of the delegates brings our situation to light. We must be ready. Anyway, once our shipment arrives from France, we need to have room to store it. Chaos and arms don't mix well."

"You're right. Do you need any help?"

"Not today, but later I want to go over with you the location of everything for when the time comes."

"If the time comes," Louis corrected. His uncle's words sounded too definite. The two of them differed on the certainty that arms would be needed against the British. A part of Louis held out for peace, but each day his hope diminished.

"If the time comes, we won't be scrambling for items. Why don't you help Jeannette with the customers while I finish here? I won't be half an hour."

Slowly Louis' belief wavered that the disagreement with the Tea Act and King George's strict adherent to the laws guarding the prosperity of the East India Tea company would wear off and peace would resume. He doubted Britain would give the colonies more independence to avoid further conflict. But the scrutinizing today of their secret stash of arms and ammunition confirmed his burgeoning conviction that the new battle would remain. He hoped for an answer tonight to seal his involvement.

His aunt had an abundant stream of customers, many not familiar to him due to the citizens attending the meeting. January eleventh, 1775 had been marked on agendas since the December nineteenth meeting. Planters, artisans, backcountry men, merchants plus their wives and families had seized the opportunity to come to Charles Town.

"Where do you need me, *Tante?*"

"Anywhere and everywhere. Tom is managing the floor. If you could be available as my extra pair of hands, I'd appreciate it. Can you believe the mass of people?"

Louis followed his aunt's finger and reached up to retrieve a box of nails from a shelf behind the counter. "Are they just looking?"

She smiled. "No. They're buying. We might not have any French or West Indies items left after this. Look at the bolts of material dwindling in only two days. Fortunately, your brother's cargo is due soon."

André supplied most of their extravagant items from France. Wilson's Mercantile no longer sold British items since the Tea Act of May 1774. Because Louis and his Uncle Henry had made the decision early last year, their revenue had increased. At first their self-imposed boycott lost them some customers, but others switched to their store because it contained local goods and non-British items.

"How are Elizabeth and Harriet? I hope they come by today, but I don't know if they can get through the door." Jeannette sighed as she smiled at a young woman trailed by two little children pulling on her skirt.

"There's always the side door from your house." He leaned in closer. "She was planning to come see you. She's a little miffed at me because I'm leaving her tonight for the meeting."

"Well, I might just spend the evening with her since Henry will be with you." She touched his sleeve. "She's not really upset. Just like me, she wants the truth and the details. And for some reason you men are determined to keep it veiled."

He laughed, covering his growing concern. "Have no fear. I can't get away with hiding things from her for very long." *Perhaps she is more upset with me now because she knows I'm not telling her everything.*

Jeannette patted his hand. "She's strong. She can bear the truth."

The truth as he would hear it or the truth as in reality? His truth or the committee's truth? "I wish I knew the truth."

Louis heard bits and pieces of conversation as he rambled around the building while stocking the shelves and carting off produce for customers. Tom Engle with his youthful enthusiasm and energy did most of the carrying of items, minimizing Louis' physical labor. Close to Louis' height now, in a few more years Tom would probably be stronger and taller than Louis.

Words floated down the aisles, although Louis tried not to eavesdrop. "Unfair." "War." "Arms." "Reconciliation." "Continental Congress." "Rebellious." "Boycotts." So many opinions.

"Where's the tea?" One woman stopped Louis with the common question.

"We don't have any. But we do have coffee." Was it a test? Louis noticed the quick grin the lady gave her companion. Wilson's had not carried British labeled tea in almost a year. Even their stock by way of the West Indies and France had disappeared. His brother promised a few chests in this next shipment.

"So, it's true," the woman said. "No one is selling the recent East India shipment. I had heard the rumors."

"That shipment of two hundred fifty-seven chests on the *London* was confiscated in December and stored away from merchants and citizens. Charles Town refused to accept it." Pride tinged his words.

"It wasn't dumped or turned away as in other ports?" She looked at other shelves.

"No, it wasn't." Unfortunately, even though the General Committee wanted it otherwise. The lady didn't need to know his opinion although he felt she would agree.

"Well, at least it's not sitting on the shelves drawing attention to the British tyranny." Louis had encountered a true South Carolinian who didn't control her liberal views. He grinned. Perhaps she should be a delegate.

The bell sounded, and a cheerful voice lifted over the shelves. "Good morning, Jeannette." He moved in closer to the front of the store to gaze at his wife.

"I was hoping you'd come by. Can you stay for lunch?" Jeannette asked.

Elizabeth rolled the carriage to the counter. "I think that's a lovely idea. It will be my only chance to see Louis again today." Jeannette, originally from France, was after twenty plus years more South Carolinian than Elizabeth. Her friend had only a few gray strands in her light brown hair. Her apron covered a home-spun dress. Arduous work in the mercantile beside her husband had kept her thin and shapely for her years.

Jeannette pulled the soft, warm quilt back to view her great-niece, sound asleep for the moment. "Let's see our little princess. Is this the first time you've taken her out alone?"

"Yes, though Mrs. Engle almost didn't let me leave. The nice warmer weather convinced her to let us out to stroll. It's not as if I'm going far, just around the corner."

"I know. But be glad you have her to be concerned about you. Her children are about grown. Isn't Amy now thirteen and Tom seventeen? Of course, Ellen enjoys fretting over a baby."

"She's truly a godsend, as well as her children. They've become like family. Amy is learning so much at her lessons. She'll be able to do anything she wants—sew, cook, care for children, maybe even be a governess."

"Slow down. Cherish each day because they go by so quickly."

Elizabeth couldn't imagine not having children of her own. She admired Jeannette's ability to extend her love willingly to others, especially to Louis and now to Harriet.

"Why the faraway look?" Jeannette asked.

Elizabeth ran her finger gently on her baby's cheek. "You are right about time. I'll try not to wish it away."

"By the way, would you like company tonight? I could join you."

Elizabeth loved the fact Jeannette seemed to recognize any low point in Elizabeth's life.

"I do. Why don't you come for supper? We'll eat something

light with Ellen and Amy. We can try to solve our country's woes."
A very big order for four women or even for a group of delegates.

Minutes later Louis found Elizabeth manning the counter while Jeannette cuddled the alert Harriet. "My three favorite girls." He gave each a kiss. "All in one place. What have you been planning?"

"Jeannette offered to spend the evening with me. We will contemplate the world's problems while you and Henry and the rest of the town debate the issues. We'll see who comes up with a better plan." She winked at Louis and found the prospect appealing. The battle of husbands and wives. Whose plans would win? He grinned but didn't look at her. What did he know that she didn't?

Her words were in jest, realizing the seriousness of the times. They all would rather there not be an entanglement with the British government. After all, most of the citizens of Charles Town were British, subjects to the king by birth. Louis, a citizen of France, was one of the exceptions, yet he had been willing at one point to pledge his loyalty to the king and Parliament. Not now, though.

He laughed, dropping his distant stare. "If you find a better solution, I promise to bend the ears of all the powerful men around here."

Elizabeth situated her baby back in the carriage and lifted her head to Louis and Jeannette. "Enough of politics. How about I see to lunch? I'll take Harriet and feed her and see if the cook needs any help. We'll see the rest of you in an hour."

Lunch from noon to one every day revived the men and Jeannette enough to face the afternoon shift. Elizabeth knew her friend relished the feminine company, unusual on a day-to-day basis.

Tom fit right into the hard-working family. After his father died over a year ago, the Wilsons gave him a job. Elizabeth couldn't do without his mother and sister's help. She glanced around the table at her family, all because she had fallen in love with Louis.

"Has anyone met the boy living at Reverend Turquand's house?" Tom asked.

"A boy? How old?" Jeannette passed the bread to Tom.

"About sixteen. He's an orphan from Orangeburg. His name is Raymond Girard. Mrs. Wilson, I thought you would know him since you speak French."

"No. Reverend Turquand hasn't mentioned him. I'll go over and speak with the minister this week."

"I think I know who you're talking about." Louis sat back, resting his head on the high-backed chair. "Does he work in the shipyards? There has been a new young man there for about a week. Hard worker. Quiet."

Tom smiled. "Maybe because he doesn't know much English."

"Could be. I'll go meet him tomorrow. Ask a few questions. Mr. Gadsden probably knows him. I'll try to ask him before the meeting." Louis twirled his glass by the stem and stared at the moving liquid. Elizabeth glanced from Louis to Henry, concerned about Louis' distraction.

"Are you concerned about this meeting, Henry?" Elizabeth asked, hoping to obtain more insight although not expecting a different response from Louis'.

"It could get heated, but the main business of approving the Continental Congress's proponents and electing delegates for the next Continental Congress should keep us focused. I have a feeling though that Gadsden will clash with someone, probably John Rutledge." Henry's words did little to convince Elizabeth.

"What do you mean probably? I hear it has already started." Tom seemed very interested and knowledgeable. "The paper states their views clearly. Mr. Gadsden is for the deletion of the rice exportation, and Mr. Rutledge wants to keep the rice exemption. I wish I could go. If Mother would let me, I would, but she says to let the educated and business owners make the decisions."

"I promise to let you know what is happening, Tom," Louis remarked as he grabbed an apple for later. "It is best to obey your mother. Anyway, I want you around tonight to look after the women."

Elizabeth followed Louis to the door. "Will we see you before the meeting?"

He wrapped his arms around her in the foyer. "With that look in your eyes, I think I can spare a few minutes around four. I'm meeting Christopher before the assembly." He took her face in his hands and kissed her gently. "Now, you be careful going home."

She rolled her eyes. "I'm not an invalid. I'm a mother."

She spent a peaceful afternoon in the drawing room with Harriet in her day cradle. Elizabeth was content to let the men handle the outside world. Her world slept in peace and contentment.

"Elizabeth, Mrs. Wilson is here." Ellen Engle and Elizabeth dropped all formality, except in public when others wouldn't understand. They were both more comfortable with their given names.

Elizabeth straightened her green wool pleated skirt. "Send her in."

"And, Mrs. Cochran is here," Ellen said, raising her eyebrows in question since Anne was unexpected.

"Anne? Well, that's a surprise." Not often did she leave eight-month-old Charlotte as well as nine-year-old Robert and seven-year-old John. Elizabeth bounced on her toes as Jeannette and Anne walked in at the same time. Elizabeth hoped after three children she'd look healthy and beautiful like her sister. Her touchable brown hair and rosy cheeks bellowed fulfillment. No wonder

Robert had eyes only for Anne in a crowd. Would Louis be enamored with Elizabeth after ten years?

"No reason to be relegated to the house with a bunch of children when I could be here with you. Do you mind?" Anne asked.

"Not at all. I'm thrilled. Ellen, be sure to set another place for supper."

Ellen left but returned very quickly with a note. "This just arrived, awaiting an answer."

"Let's see." Elizabeth perused the letter and laughed. "Add yet another place, please. Sarah is joining us too. This will be a regular party."

She scribbled a note back to Sarah Evans, her best friend, hoping she would join them soon.

"Ellen, I'm glad we made the lemon sponge cake and the apple fritters today." With a group of ladies, sweets satisfied lots of ailments including worry, fatigue, boredom, and anticipation.

"Where are the children, Anne?" Elizabeth asked.

"Mother has them." Anne relaxed in the overstuffed chair with her feet curled under her. "She was thrilled to keep them when I decided to get out of the house. Can you believe Father is going to the meeting? Last year he would not have darkened the door of a 'Liberty Boys' gathering. Now, he is one of them."

Elizabeth respected all involved in the development of policies and procedures to help South Carolina move forward. "Although a very conservative one. He's at the opposite pole of Mr. Gadsden. I'm glad Louis, Henry, and Samuel are somewhere in the middle. Maybe their names won't appear in the paper." She saw nothing wrong with a little debate. Variety was a good thing. Basically, everyone was meeting for one cause, to support the Continental Congress with the goal to heal the rift between the mother country and the colonies.

Ellen cleared her throat. "Mrs. Evans has arrived." She led a quiet woman into their midst. It always took Sarah a few minutes to warm up to the group. She'd come a long way in the past year, though. Tonight, she wore a rose-colored dress with a white petti-coat. Since her wedding, Sarah continued to emphasize her previ-ously covered up beauty. Along with her thick blond hair and brown eyes, a little lace and color hadn't hurt her at all.

This evening, Ellen and Amy joined the talkative women. The six formed an interesting association from ages thirteen to forty-one. Pleased with the event, Elizabeth wished she had included each guest from the beginning.

"All right everyone, Ellen, Amy, and I have prepared a supper of sandwiches, vegetable stew, potato bake, and desserts. I say we should eat and talk. And try to set aside formalities."

Elizabeth checked on Harriet, making sure she was warm and content for the moment. The table was close enough for her to hear even a slight cry or stirring.

Elizabeth turned to Ellen. "Did we leave some food for Tom in the kitchen?"

"Yes. He's in there now having his full share." Ellen talked more than she usually did to Elizabeth's friends. "He's still upset with me for telling him to stay home. I just don't think that meeting is the place for him. He would be lost in the mob." Ellen usually avoided military talk, especially having a son on the verge of manhood.

Diverting her gaze from her mother to her plate, Amy added, "All his friends at church talk about joining the South Carolina regiment, if there is to be one."

"Oh, such talk. What is happening to our colony?" Ellen fretted.

Jeannette reached for a biscuit. "Has Tom mentioned a boy named Raymond to you?"

"Yes," Ellen stated. "I even met him on my way to the market earlier this week. He was helping Mrs. Turquand with her purchases. Amy met him, too."

Amy jerked her head to the side, staring at their mother,

crossing her arms, and frowning. Raymond didn't seem to be someone she wanted to discuss.

Elizabeth smiled, wondering if perhaps Amy *did* in fact find the young man interesting. "Was he polite to you?"

Amy smiled. "Oh, yes ma'am. He talked with a different sort of sound, but I understood him."

"Like an accent. Sort of like Mr. Lestarjette?" Elizabeth asked.

"Yes, exactly. So, I guess that means he speaks French." Amy bit into her piece of sponge cake.

"I asked about Raymond because—well, because Henry and I would like to offer a home to him. We miss having someone to take care of ever since Louis left. So, what do you think?" Jeannette asked. Elizabeth beheld all the open mouths and surprised expressions and immediately sealed her own jaws.

"I say, you would be perfect." Without hesitation, Anne voiced her approval.

Jeannette beamed with the new possibility. "Then I'll talk to the Turquands tomorrow and see where it goes."

Savory desserts sealed the evening. At eight o'clock Harriet chimed in, longing to be fed. With baby in arms, Elizabeth said farewell to her dear friends. She sighed and swayed with Harriet's head on her shoulder. Why would anyone desire to disturb the world for this baby? Perhaps the more appropriate question, how could they *not* fight to protect her world?

Hours passed before Louis returned.

CHAPTER 3

*L*ouis had exited his tranquil home with a sincere wish that he could recline in front of the fire with his family. The only way that would become reality was when Charles Town had solved all its problems. He understood, and Elizabeth perceived, their existence hung on the verge of great change. How would they survive and keep their faith and love intact? Traveling with a heavy heart, yet a very committed one, he faced the task at hand.

"I'll be back as soon as I can, but don't wait up," Louis had promised.

Elizabeth had smiled. "That won't be a problem. If Harriet sleeps, I will too."

The eyes, ears, and hearts of Charles Town filled the Exchange Building. Their livelihoods, way of life, safety, and freedom depended in part on what transpired within the walls tonight. Louis, Samuel, and Henry managed to secure seats to the far left of the room behind those reserved for the delegates. Most of the delegates had claimed their seats, leaving about ten vacant—the absent delegates Louis assumed.

He searched the crowd. "I've heard this could last for days.

Now, I can see why. Getting one hundred eighty-four men to agree on issues might be beyond possible." He heard before he saw Christopher Gadsden who was already in a heated discussion with John Rutledge.

Samuel smiled and looked down. "Our friend has met his match. Those two were on opposite sides at the Continental Congress, and here they are again. I bet it's over rice."

Henry followed the men's stares. "My bet is that they each get some provisions and considerations in the voting. Each will win some and lose some."

Men stood around the walls, in the halls, on the balconies. Those not present would read detailed scripts of the debates in the *Gazette*. Louis could count on the editor to provide colorful description of the crowd, not leaving much to the imagination.

The General Provincial Committee came to order. The first piece of business—they declared the Committee to be the Provincial Congress. From that point on it acted as the independent government of the colony. The one hundred seventy-three men from all over the colony of South Carolina represented the city, the backcountry, the farmers, the planters, the merchants, and the artisans—citizens from all walks of life.

"How could a delegate be absent?" Henry remarked. "This is very important. It appears the British rule was just eliminated, at least in word." Louis wondered, too, at the absence of the eleven. Wasn't this important enough to drop everything? Would he have left everything if he didn't live in the city? *I shouldn't be so quick to criticize. I'm not a delegate. I'm here to listen as a citizen.*

Gadsden's continued role in leadership impressed Louis even though his friend's radical views astounded him. What if Christopher was right? What if the only way out of this mess was total independence? Cut all ties with Britain, not just import and export.

"One order of business for the Congress is to approve or disapprove of the actions taken by the Continental Congress. Is there any discussion?" The question pulled Louis away from desire to solve the separation issue.

Discussion, disputes, debates. Gadsden demanded the export of rice be included in the ban list. He was the spokesman for the small farms who produced no rice. John Rutledge argued that rice should be excluded from the non-exportation agreement because two-thirds of South Carolina rice went to British ports and the farmers needed the income

Louis' head volleyed as he followed the heated discussions. What more could be revealed? The Congress dissolved into an uproar, order dissipated. Finally, the gavel summoned the attention of the inhabitants of the hall. The delegates voted—eighty-seven to seventy-five. The resolutions of the Continental Congress were approved intact.

"Gadsden lost that round." Louis sensed the debate and conflict had crouched, subdued for the moment, ready for another day. Emerging from the building with the crowd, he dodged the men scrambling for lodging and a decent meal.

Home to Elizabeth. Could he shield her from the disputes? No, not with the paper and the town gossip. Truth from him was a better source. In the almost three years that he'd known her, she always found out what lurked behind his façade. Honesty won out every time. So tomorrow, he would tell her the facts. South Carolina would act as an independently governed colony. *And I will do my part. Yet, I'm not sure when I will divulge my secret involvement in the conflict.*

"So, it's not over?" Elizabeth quizzed Louis the next morning over coffee and warm porridge with cinnamon and apples.

"True. Now everything will be focused on the South Carolina government. I'll poke my head in every now and then, but I won't be staying for hours again. I'm interested in the question of debt to the British government, though."

She sighed and tilted her cup, staring at the brown liquid. "At least you and Henry aren't under any obligation to them."

"We've done everything we can to be independent. But so many others are in debt." At least they had done that one thing. Some lived on borrowed land, houses, stores, businesses. Thousands of individuals continued living on the fringes of the British Empire.

Enough government talk. "What are you doing today?" Louis cared more about his wife and child. A cold shiver gripped the nape of his neck. If not for them, he would have remained in France. He caught Elizabeth's blue gaze. The same soul-searching grip that captured his life and secured him to this piece of earth.

"You're not going to like it. You'll say it's too soon." Her eyes peeked through batting eyelashes pleading softly with him. It certainly wasn't the first time she used them to get her way. "I'm going to the school to see about starting individual piano lessons again. Before you say 'no,' Ellen has agreed to take very good care of Harriet for two hours."

He knew her love of music and her students couldn't be buried in the past. "How can I say 'no' when your face lights up just saying the words 'piano lessons'? I knew this day would come, but please limit yourself to two to three hours a day."

"I will." She ran her fingers down the front of his shirt. "Harriet needs me and so do you." He covered each of her hands with his. "And don't forget it. You still amaze me. Somehow God placed this beautiful, stubborn, smart, loving woman in my life." With her face between his callused hands, he smoothed her rosy cheekbones with his fingers. "I have been blessed."

"You should see my view of the situation. Somehow, I feel I acquired the better deal. Only God could imagine a wandering, lonely soul finding a home in Charles Town miles from all he knew. As you changed, you changed my life forever."

Louis grinned. Yes, he had been transformed from a non-believer to a God-fearing Christian man, from a rootless adventurer to a solid citizen, from a non-committed, hardened man to a faithful, loving husband. *Can I continue to live up to her expectations?*

She squeezed his hand, refocusing his meanderings. "By the way, would you keep an eye on Tom? He has some ideas and interest in regiment or military endeavors in South Carolina. Have you heard mention of something forming?"

Tom had whittled his way into Louis' heart. Visualizing him in battle caused unusual palpitations. "Rumors at this point with no organized group. Be assured, I will speak with him. Boys, or should I say, young men his age can get carried away."

As Elizabeth rose from the table, Louis followed. She draped her arms around his neck. "I know I can count on you to be wise and not hot-headed."

He returned her embrace, tempted to stay a little longer. But business couldn't wait. Already he had to take time from the store to meet with Christopher about the incoming shipment. Without indigo and other exports going to Britain, the outgoing cargo to France had to be organized carefully. Farmers and planters vied for space on their ship, *The Rose.*

Louis knocked twice. "Christopher?" He pushed the door open. The man sat with a stack of papers neatly arranged in front of him. "You're here early even after a late night." Louis noted the dark circles under the older man's eyes. For a fifty-year-old man, he had the stamina of a thirty-year-old.

"I couldn't sleep. The congress will go on for days. There's too much to get accomplished in just a few days. But I do always have to take care of business." Christopher shuffled papers around. "How are Elizabeth and Harriet?

"Well. As you know having a baby in the house is different, but I wouldn't trade it for all my bachelor days back again."

"I know. Just wait though, Harriet will be a young lady soon. Look at my brood." Christopher had been married twice and had five children from ages eight to seventeen. After the death of his last wife, Christopher lived with his children and managed with the help of an elderly governess. Louis admired him for carrying on so well.

"Either way, there are sleepless nights." Both men laughed.

Christopher secured the door. "Now, about the next shipment. I have a list of exports for you to approve. Then we need to think about the next order from France. Do you think we can increase our order of arms and basic supplies like ironworks, nails, shovels, and hammers?"

"I'll send a letter today asking André. The last I heard the French are still willing to supply us with the goods. I believe France will continue to support the independence of the colonies."

Christopher drummed his fingers on a stack of papers. "I hope so. They might play a vital role in our success. Do you plan on returning to France, Louis?"

He hesitated. "Not unless I am asked. Mr. Deane had mentioned involving France on a deeper level in the future. I know that Benjamin Franklin has contacted the French government. Things are hush, hush now at least from my end. I'll do what is needed." Even travel again to France away from his family during uncertain battle lines? *Yes, I will.*

"I know you will. But with a young family, I understand your hesitation. I'll know more at the next Continental Congress in May—if I am elected to return."

"Is that on the agenda today?" Louis didn't know if Christopher really doubted his election.

"No, not until the end. We still must discuss the secret

committee. Keep your ears open to that discussion. Your role might be tied to those men selected."

"I'll pay attention. You can count on me to be selective in my words and actions."

Louis pulled papers out of his jacket pocket. "On another subject. Here are the suppliers and the results." He handed them to Christopher. "The locals are ready to send their goods—pottery, furniture, crafts, as well as dried goods. Of course, we can ship indigo, rice, and other products. Since *The Rose* strictly deals with France, we're clear of the provision from Congress."

"I'll finish looking over this list this afternoon. Anything else?"

Louis wanted to commend him on his debating last night but didn't know if Christopher was content with the outcome. "Do you expect more debates at your meetings?"

"Yes. When Rutledge and Laurens are present, I'm their target." His tough, vocal personality seemed to thrive on tension.

Louis laughed. "Well, I'll check in occasionally and make sure you are surviving."

"Thank you."

As they exited toward the piers, Louis stopped and touched Christopher's jacket sleeve. "By the way, do you know a young boy by the name of Raymond Girard?"

Christopher dipped his head to the left. "I think he works at the wharf next to this one. In fact, he is right there. I can tell by his long, dark curly hair."

"Good. I want to meet him." Louis shook Christopher's hand and advanced in the boy's direction. It wouldn't hurt to interview him before Aunt Jeannette made a rash decision to take him in. When they gave Louis a home, it was a natural relationship. This would be a complete stranger. *I'm probably wasting my time. If Aunt Jeannette has her mind set on taking this boy home, she'll do it anyway.*

Raymond worked as hard as the grown men around him, toting crates and barrels off a ship. Many of the men used to seeing Louis on the docks nodded in greeting "Mr. Lestarjette" or "sir." The boy looked up from his chore.

"*Jeune homme, êtes-vous Raymond Girard?*" Louis ventured in French.

"*Oui, Monsieur.*" The boy straightened to his full height only an inch shorter than Louis. The lad had years of growth yet. He'd soon tower over many grown men including Louis.

Sticking his gloved hand out, Louis said, "*Je suis Louis Lestarjette, un ami des Turquand.* I've heard good things about you and wanted to see for myself." Louis continued in French, hoping to comfort the younger man.

"*Parlez-vous anglais,* Raymond?"

"*Un peu.* My mother and I lived far from the village, and I had little time to practice English." Raymond stood straight without nervously shifting from foot to foot. Louis didn't remember having such confidence at the youth's age.

"Are you willing to learn?"

"*Ah, oui, Monsieur.* I've already picked up a lot here on the docks."

Louis chuckled. "Well, be careful what you pick up here. Stick to learning from the Turquands and church. I hope to see you again, young man. *Au revoir.*" Louis tipped his hat.

The boy stood still, probably not sure what to do or say. "*Au revoir,*" was all he ventured.

At the store Louis surprised Aunt Jeannette with one of his bear hugs.

"Why, Louis, what was that for? You know sneaking up on an old woman is not a good thing."

He released her and leaned on the counter. "I just met Raymond Girard."

Her eyes twinkled as they expectantly waited for him to elaborate. "And?"

"And, he is a hard-working young man with a good grasp of French. His English needs work, though."

She clasped her hands under her chin. "Is he manageable and respectful?" Her eyes were wide as she held her breath.

He laughed. "A nice young man who is almost as tall as I am. If you house him, he will eat up your stock at home and here."

Jeannette's startled look faded. "I want to offer him a place where he knows he'll have three meals a day, a bed, and all the love he can stand. We're meeting him tomorrow at the Turquands." She leaned closer to him, making him look straight into her eyes. "On a personal level, do you approve?"

"I'm surprised you would ask," he teased. "But, yes, I do. He has the same hard-working spirit as Tom. He'd be a good addition to your home."

Anne paced with her hands on her hips in Elizabeth's bedroom. "I want you to come with me, Elizabeth. You know I don't like going to Mother's by myself, but it is the right thing to do. For us to do." Anne's persuasive tactics worked on her sister's guilt.

Elizabeth grimaced. "If only we could see Mother without Victoria. Perhaps she won't be there." She clapped her hands like a child wishing for ice cream. Victoria and their brother George had secretly and hurriedly married last September. Their baby was due in April. Elizabeth and Anne's mother had been gracious enough to give Victoria a place to live.

"You know she has nowhere else to go. George deposited her there, and so far, he hasn't wanted to set up his own household. You have to feel a little sorry for her."

"I would if she wasn't so rude, outspoken, arrogant, and annoying." Did Anne need more descriptions to dissuade her?

Elizabeth's relationship with the vocal Loyalist from Philadelphia went back to March of 1773 at Middleton Place. Since then she had endured slights against her family, Louis, Charles Town, the Sons of Liberty, and even George. Why couldn't she have a nice sister-in-law?

Looking in the glass, Elizabeth forced a ringlet under her cap and pasted on a fake smile. "All right. I'll go with you. Since you have Charlotte, I'll bring Harriet. The babies will be a good topic of conversation."

"And remember, this is for Mother's pleasure. She loves her granddaughters." Anne commented at times that she couldn't believe she had another child after so many years of waiting, her little miracle. Elizabeth knew she had been content with the boys, but Anne's daughter was a special, surprise gift from God.

Elizabeth smiled a fake toothy grin, cocking her head. "I'll do it and put on whatever face I need to show joy."

"You'll have to do better than that." Anne mimicked her with a lopsided grin.

As soon as they entered their mother's parlor, the hugs and kisses from her mother erased her chagrin. Mother picked up the wide-eyed Charlotte as Harriet slept. Elizabeth paused, wanting to remember her mother like this— the baby in her arms. Her mother had a spark in her hazel eyes, blush on her flawless cheeks. Her graying hair shone with the golden-brown streaks reminiscent of a younger woman. But it was her smile that made Elizabeth thankful. Last year the happy gesture, including the smile lines by her eyes, had been rare. But since her mother confessed her true feelings about her love for her family and her true loyalties to the colonies, she was free to be herself.

The peaceful situation continued for half an hour. No one mentioned Victoria. Elizabeth felt the woman was the invisible, unspeakable in the room. But Elizabeth could stand it no longer. "So, where's Victoria?"

Her mother nudged her head upward. "She's resting, as she does every afternoon. She'll be down soon for afternoon tea."

Elizabeth raised her brows and smacked her lips like a child contemplating a fruit drop. "You still have tea?"

"Yes. Victoria's mother sends it."

"Does her mother forgive her yet for her...discrepancy?" Anne asked.

Mother nuzzled Charlotte's cheek. "Forgiven, maybe, but she wants her to stay right here in Charles Town." Elizabeth admired her mother's playfulness with the baby while responding to a fretful question.

"Out of sight," Elizabeth whispered. *Why can't I accept this situation with forgiveness? I must try if Mother has accepted her charge.*

The subject changed many times before the aforementioned appeared, gracefully gliding into the room. For being six months along, she sure held herself in a stately manner. Why didn't she look or walk like an elephant or a cow? Even in pregnancy, Victoria rose above the ordinary, aloft in her demeanor.

Victoria paused as if waiting an introduction. "Good afternoon, sisters."

Elizabeth cringed at the hissing of "sisters" before nodding. She wanted something to like about Victoria. *God, show me something. It's been months.*

"How are you feeling, Victoria? You look very rested," Anne said.

"All I do is rest. I find it difficult to believe you did this three times, Anne. One is too many for me." Victoria glided to the window, avoiding the family circle.

They had all heard that before from her lips. All recalled what George felt about the baby and even Victoria—both burdens he easily discarded to the care of his family.

Although Elizabeth believed in the sanctity of marriage, 'til death do they part, Victoria would push the limits of the vow.

Perhaps this arrangement strained the marriage the least, separate quarters, individual lives.

Victoria's words against motherhood pulled at Elizabeth's heart. Instinctively Elizabeth reached for her baby, to cuddle Harriet, letting all know of her unending love. Harsh words from a cruel soul, or a hurting one, didn't change the love in the room for the children present.

Elizabeth's thoughts surprised her. Could Victoria be hurting and covering up with a spiteful attitude? "Surely a part of you wants the baby growing inside you?" Elizabeth gasped in unbelief as the words escaped her lips.

Victoria turned toward Elizabeth and smirked, a tiny growl. "Only if it is a boy. George will not accept anything else."

Mother shook her head. "He will. He loves his nieces and his sisters. Of course, he'll welcome his child no matter what." Mother drove her point in, and Elizabeth wanted to know it would stick. No woman or man rejected his own child because of gender, at least not in her family.

The disgruntled woman sat down. "We'll see."

Elizabeth chose not to respond. She knew she couldn't win this battle, not today.

Victoria raised her hand and snapped her fingers. "Where is Alice with the tea? I know I didn't sleep that long."

"It will be here shortly. It's not even four o'clock yet." Mother's patience with Victoria spilled from an inner strength Elizabeth wished she had when dealing with Victoria.

It is God that girdeth me with strength. She had memorized the verse for just such an occasion. Shutting her eyes for a second, Elizabeth prayed for God's strength.

"I'll go help with the tea. I think we could all use some." Elizabeth escaped on a positive note.

And when she returned, she offered a new sincere remedy to fill in some rifts. "Victoria, whenever you need help with the baby, I will be glad to help. It can be very time consuming."

"Me, too," Anne added.

"Well—" Victoria paused, staring at the sisters. "Thank you. But George has promised a live-in nurse and even our own lodgings. I want to trust him."

Elizabeth served the tea, recently placed on the table, complete with biscuits and small cakes. "Yes, of course. Anyway, the offer still remains." Her occupied hands relieved Elizabeth's involvement in further conversation.

Harriet helped also, ready to be fed. Some solitude in another room acted as an escape from the superficial prattle. Fashion, concerts, plays, rumors, local gossip. There was no discussion about the Congress since Victoria held firmly to her Loyalist beliefs.

Half an hour later, Elizabeth joined the ladies in the parlor with a content baby. Victoria had departed to rest, leaving the three to discuss relevant issues.

Her parents, Mary and Artemus Elliott, had switched to the liberty side months back. At times, the sisters had to confess their surprise by asking again and again, "Did our parents really become Partisans?" Since their conversion, the subject of politics was open for discussion in the Elliott house.

"From what I hear the meetings should end soon," Anne said. "Five days is a long time. I'm ready for the streets to empty a bit."

Elizabeth passed her sleeping baby to her mother. "The mercantile is feeling the effects. The shelves are emptying. Fortunately, a shipment is due soon."

"Robert should be arriving in a few weeks from his voyage to the West Indies. This boycott has helped the independent captains. If Robert worked for the British, he'd be out of a job with the new policies."

Elizabeth leaned back into the curve of the sofa, resting her head against the soft fabric. "Christopher and Louis can keep him busy going back and forth to France." Was it safe anymore for any travel, on land or sea?

Walking home later Elizabeth thanked Anne for persuading her to visit her mother. The outing produced a determination to help Victoria see the value in her role as a mother and her place in her new family. *I'll try, God. She's a big challenge, but I see her as one You've given to me.*

On Sunday afternoon, the Wilsons joined the Lestarjettes for a light supper of venison and vegetable stew. The news they brought added sunshine to a cold dreary day. Cold for Charles Town meant cloudy skies and a brisk breeze from the ocean. No chance of snow or ice, but they could see their breaths outdoors.

Elizabeth sat forward in her seat ready to take it all in. "So, what is the news?"

"Do you want me to tell them, Henry?" Jeannette asked.

He laughed, patting his wife's hand. "Yes. I don't think you would let me anyway without finishing it for me."

"As you know we ate dinner with the Turquands and met Raymond." Jeannette laced her fingers together. "The young man had no idea of why we were there. Just friends of the Reverend as far as he could tell. What a pleasant, well-mannered boy. We found out so much about him."

"All in French, mind you," Henry emphasized, rolling his eyes. Elizabeth knew how he felt, struggling with a language he didn't know very well. At least her lessons with Louis as her teacher had advanced her understanding of French.

Jeannette eyed her husband and smiled. "Mrs. Turquand translated for him. You understood most of the conversation. Anyway, he has a dream to be a ship owner or a captain. Anything to do with ships and water. For now, that is. Sixteen is still so young."

Louis chuckled. "I think I wanted to be a knight at that age."

His aunt's lips quivered. "After the meal, Henry and I talked in private and made our decision. We discussed our answer with the

Turquands. We spent a nervous fifteen minutes in their parlor. Then Raymond told us he would love to come live with us if he could keep working at the docks." Jeannette released her tears.

Henry continued the recitation. "Tomorrow Raymond Girard will become a part of our family and live with us as long as he wants."

Elizabeth rushed to Jeannette's side, embracing her and adding to her tears. "God did this for you and for this special boy. I'll enjoy watching His plans unfold. We'll have a party for him, here, on Friday night. I'll invite Anne and the boys, Tom and Amy, the Evans, and the Turquands."

"Whoa, this isn't a banquet hall." Louis tried to control his wife with his teasing.

"It won't be formal. We'll have food the young people like," Elizabeth promised.

Jeannette hadn't stopped smiling. "A party would be appreciated. Thank you for welcoming him. We have our job cut out for us. One of the first things is teaching him English." Elizabeth could imagine the lively dinner conversation with the English and French combination.

"I could help," Elizabeth offered. "I'm sure I could apply my piano teaching strategies to teaching English. At least the alphabet is the same. And I know enough French to understand his reference points. Would it be all right, Louis?"

Louis placed a light kiss on her cheek. "As long as it doesn't interfere with your piano students and Harriet."

"It must be in the evenings after his work." Jeannette remembered the promise she made to Raymond.

Elizabeth used her hands to count off all the ideas flying out of her mouth. "Maybe he could come two days a week around six o'clock. In no time, he will have progressed because Jeannette and Henry will be teaching him as well in everyday conversation."

"Sounds like a plan. Thank you, Elizabeth." Jeannette kissed her on the cheek.

At the lunch table on Tuesday, Henry voiced his concern about rumors circling the town. "You must be mistaken. How could they do that?"

Louis acknowledged his uncle's earlier prediction about Christopher. "You were right. Christopher gained his own concessions after he lost some."

"But to forgive all debts?"

"All debts owed to the Crown." Louis looked around the table at Jeannette and Elizabeth who hadn't said a word, yet. Elizabeth fidgeted with her fork. He could tell she wouldn't hold back her concerns.

She sat forward. "I don't understand. What does this mean?"

Louis placed his elbows on the table. "Here is the simple explanation. Congress forbade suit for debt in the local courts unless the full Congress approved. In other words, it ended the authority of the judicial branch of the royal government."

"You heard the debate?" Henry asked.

"No, it was in today's paper. Henry Laurens and John Rutledge soundly approved the action, saying the debts owed the Crown should be paid. But they were defeated. Christopher's pleas were accepted." He dropped his head. "To me, it moves us closer to inevitable independence."

"You're right. Now that the court's power is taken away, what next?" Henry questioned to no one in particular, probably not expecting an answer.

Louis hated to pass on the next part. Could he avoid the issue? He stared at Elizabeth and knew he couldn't let her down or put her in harm's way unprepared. "Congress recommended that the inhabitants of the province give diligent attention in learning the use of arms."

The ladies gasped, and Henry hit the table with his fist.

"So, it will come to that in the end." Henry looked at each person, all family members.

"Many think so, Uncle. It's still up to the British to compromise. Each action we take is a message for the king and parliament." Silence. Were they each picturing the women with arms with the possibility of wounding or killing someone?

The Congress concluded with the election of the same five men as before—John and Edward Rutledge, Henry Middleton, Thomas Lynch, and Christopher Gadsden—to serve at the Second Continental Congress in May. That information did not surprise Louis.

Louis read the last of the summary from a pamphlet. "The final business established February seventeenth as a day of fasting, humiliation, and prayer, before Almighty God, devoting to petition Him to inspire the king to avert the impending calamities of civil war."

Looking in Elizabeth's eyes, he felt the concern and the effect of the words "learn the use of arms." That shouldn't be the destiny of his small family, but it seemed a great possibility.

CHAPTER 4

"You're serious, aren't you?" Elizabeth asked the next morning over breakfast with Louis. Coffee cup brimming with the dark liquid reminded him that the times demanded he be serious.

Louis folded his napkin and put it on the table. "Yes, I am. I'm going to talk to Uncle Henry today about the pistols. I want you to write to your cousin Lucy and see if we can stay for a few days while we train." He took his role as protector seriously.

"You have thought it all out." How could she ever use a pistol on another human? Harming a human being wasn't in her constitution. He studied her using his furrowed brow as his "I'm serious" weapon. "I'm not taking a chance with your safety. You need to learn to use a pistol—you, Ellen, and Amy. No arguments."

"I'm not going to argue. I've always wanted to shoot a gun. It was never fair that George and Father would go off hunting and shooting while I had to needlepoint. I just don't like the circumstances."

"Me either." He reached for her hands, holding them firmly. "We'll try to make the outing as pleasant as possible." He'd have a tough time convincing anyone that carrying a pistol held a certain pleasure. No, this chore wrapped around safety and guarding precious lives.

Elizabeth shrugged her shoulders. "I haven't seen Lucy in over a year. It will be time well-spent gathering memories and binding us closer."

Louis had slept little the night before while formulating a plan to protect his family. "We'll plan to be gone for five days." He felt God telling him to take firm action. Yet, he didn't relish placing a pistol in Elizabeth's hand. Would she ever be forced to use it?

Hopefully, Elizabeth would never need to aim a pistol at a person. But Louis had an obligation to care for his family, especially when he wasn't present.

The taste of strong coffee accompanied him to the office. The bitterness of the black drink connected with the bitterness of the colony's dilemma. Would he ever wake up and crave coffee? Perhaps. But never would he desire the conflict lurking around the corner in any number of forms. The lack of tea was just one tangible outcome--a minor one.

Entering the storeroom Louis could not believe he had to secure arms from the secret basement stash. He shook his head. How did it come to this? Egos, stubbornness, pride, misplaced goals. England had lost her purpose and disregarded her number one commodity, her people.

So, Louis crept down steps to a secluded storeroom to secure a means of defense. Two years ago, he could not have imagined he would be uncovering one of the crates disguised with heavy burlap sacks with the intention of arming his family. Inside he saw many wooden boxes with ornate metal clasps. Each contained a pair of target or dueling pistols.

Made in France, these flintlock pistols lacked the gold and ornate engraving of many sets found in wealthy homes. These were commissioned for practical purposes, not to show societal status or affluence. A weapon of precision. Pocket pistols. Or in Elizabeth's case a petticoat pistol. He grinned. Another item to possibly hide in her unseen pockets.

His brain had a tough time procuring his purpose in the dark basement. A weapon to protect his family. A weapon of life or death. If Elizabeth had to use it, someone would die or be wounded. He shuddered. Either that or she would die.

Henry's body blocked the light from the stairs. "Louis, did you find them?"

"Yes, sir. I'm just having a problem accepting this new reality. I know I need to take these, but I don't like the reason for it."

Henry crouched at the top of the stairs. "I know. I moved a set into our house too."

"Now I must teach three women how to use them and how to make bullets." Louis put his cargo on an empty shelf. "And do it with the hope that they will never have to be used." He added a bullet mold and enough materials to replenish ammunition if needed.

"In God's strength, Son. Allow Him to bring you near enough that you can feel His strength. This is the only way."

Louis replaced the covering, put the case securely under his arm, and climbed the steps, heavy-hearted. This journey began over two years ago. He chose not to retreat then, and he wouldn't now.

When Louis reached the store floor, Tom handed him a message. "It's from Mr. Gadsden."

Louis read it quickly. "Just as I thought, the ship has arrived. Are you ready to bundle up and help unload, Tom?"

"Yes, sir. I love seeing all the new cargo, and we sure do need stuff to put on the shelves after Congress wiped us out."

"Let's tell Jeannette and Henry and be on our way. We'll get something done before lunch."

The Rose made Louis' heart pound. He found himself entrusted with half ownership of the beautiful vessel as well as partaker of the profits.

The captain sought him out personally. "Here you go, Mr. Lestarjette, the packet of correspondence from your brother's hands to yours." Louis missed Robert Cochran as the captain for this voyage. But Robert was on a ship to the West Indies gathering needed supplies for Christopher.

"Thank you. Any problem getting through?" Louis hoped blockades would not be a problem in the French ports.

"None, as long as we aren't carrying British goods."

Louis extended his hand and patted the man on the shoulder. "Good work."

The routine followed the same pattern as the shipments before. The crates divided among merchants and individuals. And as usual, some of the chests had false compartments for the arms and ammunition. The other items to be put in storage such as heavy material, iron pots, shovels, and hammers traveled in regular crates since they wouldn't bring suspicion.

Olive oil, wine, spices, china, fabric, silk, fruits, crystal, jewelry, and furniture were all distributed to their owners or merchants without question. It helped having Christopher on the General Committee. The members monitored the shipments. Since they had no British goods, they passed inspection without a search. The Committee knew Christopher's strong abhorrence of Britain at this point and trusted his word.

"The Committees of safety and observation will have their work cut out for them," Christopher stated. "I'm glad my office is right here. I can already imagine some angry citizens when we turn away their shipments."

"It's not so strict yet?" Louis watched the crates come ashore.

"No, the Committee of Observation is organizing. I expect in mid to late February continuous, systematic searching will occur. Their job is to enforce the non-importation, non-exportation agreement of the association."

"I'm certainly glad of your wisdom and foresight. Henry has been a tremendous help too." Louis recognized the gifts of his business associates. "Our shipments will always get through."

Christopher grinned. "Well, as long as the ports are controlled by us and not the British. This isn't over yet."

Such ominous words plagued all conversations recently. All their hopes and prayers for peace tugged against the unrest begging to be released. Then what do they pray for in the months to come? A short battle with little bloodshed? Personal safety? Wise tactics? Leaders?

"I'm not giving up yet on peace," Louis stated more to the air than to Christopher.

Elizabeth fingered the metal clasp on the walnut rectangular box placed on the dark mahogany table. "What a pretty wooden box. Is it for me? May I open it?"

"If you must. I wish it were full of shining napkin rings or pewter goblets."

She gently released the catch and pulled back the hinged lid. Two identical pistols. "Such a pretty box for weapons."

"Well generally, the wealthy who carry and own them can spend more on the container than the pistols."

"Oh." She stepped back. "Now what do we do?"

"We wait for a reply from your cousin and place these in a locked cabinet. And then we think about something else like…"

Elizabeth turned her back to the box. "Like Raymond's party. Nothing could be farther from the subject of weapons."

"How are the plans?" Louis moved the box to a table in the corner of the room.

"Everyone responded with 'yes.' We'll have a houseful." She had the uncanny ability to latch on to a positive subject. He wished he could do the same so quickly. The weapons and the conflict clattered against everything he encountered. "How is he doing anyway?"

"Fine. I've seen him at the noon meal a few times this week. We only speak English. At first, he was quiet, but now he is loosening up his tongue with broken English."

She clapped and spun around, dancing without music. "We start lessons next week. If you all can keep up the conversation, I'll concentrate on grammar, pronunciation, and vocabulary."

When Amy rang the dinner bell, Louis hid the box in the library, while Elizabeth checked on sleeping Harriet in the drawing room next to the dining room.

Ellen served poached fish and potatoes. "Ellen, what does Tom like to eat?" Elizabeth quizzed.

"Hmmm." Ellen straightened. "Meat pies, cheese puffs, fried chicken, anything smothered in gravy, and biscuits and sweets."

Elizabeth giggled. "So, nothing green or resembling vegetables."

"Right."

"Then that's what we are having Friday night minus the gravy covered items. We'll go to market tomorrow morning."

"Are you sure you don't want adult food, too?" Ellen asked.

"Not at all. The party is for a sixteen-year-old boy, remember."

After Raymond arrived Friday evening, a bit shy and intimidated by the attention, the guests stood or sat with plates of food in their hands or laps. Elizabeth realized they laughed and mingled more than any previous party at her house. Once she discarded the formal setting, the remaining elements of comfort and tasty items formed the foundation for the celebration.

"I'm tempted to hand Charlotte to someone and join the children in their games," Anne said, watching her young boys interact with Amy, Tom, and Raymond.

"You can, of course. I'm just enjoying seeing them all together. Amy is not as shy tonight even with a group of boys," Elizabeth commented. *Next time I need to find a few girls for Amy.*

"Do you think Raymond understands their games and conversations?" Jeannette asked.

Elizabeth perused the faces and rubbed her hands together in satisfaction. "Tom seems to have found an uncomplicated way of explaining things to him. Raymond understands more than you think." She winked at Jeannette who relaxed, knowing her ward had made some permanent friends.

Even at a festive occasion, the ever-present cloud of politics hovered. Louis gravitated to the men who rallied in the library to discuss the conflict. Grinning, he concluded they had no intention of avoiding what manifested as the heartbeat of Charles Town.

"So, you are going to teach the women to shoot, Louis?" Reverend Turquand, a pacifist at heart, questioned the action.

Louis pressed his palms on the desk for support handling a difficult subject. "You are a rational, practical man. You must understand the need for protection. The Safety Committee advised it, making it a strong suggestion without turning it into a law. If teaching the women to protect themselves is wrong, then I have made that decision anyway and will be held accountable."

The minister bowed his head. "I didn't say I disagree. I'm struggling with it personally. I'm leaning toward teaching my wife to shoot, too." Reverend Turquand rolled his eyes to the ceiling, revealing his shock that he had shared that information. The world really was changing if a Huguenot minister set aside his beliefs against violence.

"Don't worry, Reverend," Louis said. "Many other ministers in the town, like Reverend Smith at St. Philips, have admitted the same thing."

Samuel stuffed his hands in his pockets. "I don't know if I can teach Sarah to aim at anything and shoot it. I'm afraid her fear and tears would blur her vision." Louis tried to picture Samuel's demure, peaceful wife raising her voice much less a pistol.

Louis chuckled at the vision of Elizabeth, Ellen, and Amy aiming a weapon at a target on a tree. "Maybe they'll never have to harm anyone, but a least they would know how to protect themselves and others. I'll let you know how the lessons go in a few weeks." If only a tree would be the extent of their destruction. Having shot a deer, he'd never aimed at a man or shot one.

Sarah joined the men's circle. "Did I hear my name?"

Samuel took ownership of the subject. "I'll not lie. Yes, on the subject of pistols. Would you let me teach you to shoot for your safety?" He stared at Sarah.

"I don't know." She placed her hands on her hips. "Are you a good teacher?"

They all laughed at her lack of confidence in Samuel.

A huge outburst of laughter came from the parlor by the foyer from a pile of arms and legs. Louis raced to the mass of people. The children's game of hide and seek had come to an end in a heap of bodies. One by one a whole person emerged, each straightening his or her clothes. Flushed cheeks, messed up hair, and pure joy on faces displayed their contentment. Except for her attire, Amy was one of the boys. Louis knew that would change all too soon.

"Time to finish this food and get another drink," Elizabeth suggested. *Oh, to be so young again.* She and George had spent many hours in play as children, carefree and innocent. Let them enjoy it now. Hopefully, this group won't develop into enemies and strangers as she and George had.

"Raymond, what do you think of my rambunctious boys?" Anne asked as she hugged her son John for a second.

"*Rambunctious?*" Raymond raised his eyebrows.

"Wild and lively." Anne enlightened him.

"I like them fine. I always wanted a brother or a sister."

"Yes, well, you can borrow these two any time you want," Anne added.

Elizabeth noted how nicely he fit in to this extended family. It could be more than he bargained for when he signed on with the Wilsons. *I can't think of a better family to join. Hopefully, he feels the same way, perhaps like Louis does.*

Elizabeth watched Jeannette and Henry as they spent most of their time observing their new son. Only the Lestarjettes claimed blood kin to the Wilsons, but the others, the Evans, the Cochrans, the Engles, and the Turquands claimed Raymond too. *A child God gave for us, for me, to love and cherish.*

Jeannette inched her way to Elizabeth's side. "It was a success. Thank you for introducing Raymond with such a welcoming event."

"I'm so glad to see him smile and speak with everyone." Elizabeth wanted to remember the children as they fused together tonight in the middle of pure, youthful joy. "That reminds me about the English lessons. Let's finalize them for Monday and Wednesday afternoons from six to seven at my house, and I'll serve refreshments."

Jeannette took Elizabeth's hand and squeezed it. "Perfect. I'll tell him it's starting this Monday."

"I'll enjoy it. I miss all my teaching at the boarding school. This and a few piano lessons will settle my restlessness."

Jeannette looked at her with a crooked smile. "Harriet needs you more than anyone."

Elizabeth laughed. "I know, and she doesn't let me forget it." Not once but twice the baby had made her presence known this evening. Harriet's constant needs grounded Elizabeth's days in a present reality instead of in a cloud of future unknowns. *But what kind of world will be left for her if there is war?*

CHAPTER 5

*F*ebruary roared in with a cold snap leaving ice dangling from roofs and tree limbs. Ice with no snow meant just enough discomfort to hope for an early spring. George roared into Elizabeth's life like that icy wind, dumping his icicles of malice. He opened and slammed doors, shouting her name with Ellen in tow, the latter apologizing to Elizabeth for the disturbance.

"It's fine, Ellen. George doesn't always follow proper etiquette. You many leave, I'm sure I'll be fine."

Anger showed on his flushed cold cheeks. "Proper etiquette? Why should I, when your husband and his radical cronies make up their own outlandish laws and procedures, casting aside centuries of proper etiquette? You have to stop him, Elizabeth." She glanced toward the small drawing room where Harriet slept safely in her basinet.

George continued making huge circles on the floor in front of her. She remained seated on the sofa with her needlepoint in her lap. "I'm sure I have no idea what you are talking about. If you would take a seat, discard your coat and hat, then maybe I can help you."

He stopped and stared. "I won't sit and relax while Louis, Gadsden, and their friends are wrecking Charles Town with their ludicrous, far-fetched schemes. Do you not know what I'm talking about?"

She balled her hands into fists and sat on them, with a calmness she found hard to contain. "Not a clue. It could be anything." How did this calm courage cover her when she wanted to yell back at him?

"Well, your Provincial Congress and its committees just dumped the contents of the *Charming Martha* into the harbor." He paced in front of her. "Why? Because they were British goods."

"I hadn't heard. I don't see what I can do." Straight backed, hands now kneading the fabric under her, Elizabeth braced for the rest of his rampage.

"You can tell Louis he is crazy to support this riff-raff. The funny thing is most of the cargo belonged to wealthy, independent citizens, not the British government or merchants. But private citizens' furniture, trunks, and possessions are all at the bottom of the ocean."

"You have Lieutenant Governor Bull to report to the authorities, and as you see Louis isn't here. He's working like normal citizens in the town."

His balled fists swung in the air. "The citizens aren't normal anymore. Don't be fooled. Don't think you are safe and secure, sister. Parliament will respond with harshness. You are warned."

She glanced at the cabinet hiding the pistols. "Are you threatening me, George?" She grimaced for she could never use them on her brother. Could she shoot another man?

He paused, possibly checking his anger and words. For a minute, George her brother surfaced, peeling back deep wrinkles as his flushed face cooled. "Elizabeth, I'm not a monster. I would never hurt you or your family, but there are ones who could. I can't stand guard over your house."

Kneeling in front of her, he pleaded as a beloved brother. "This

48

must stop. I've made my choice. Louis and Robert have to come to their senses before action is taken; action I can't control."

She touched his sandy hair with affection and saw a glimpse of her childhood friend. "I'll pray for you every day. God is in control of this now. All we can do is follow the direction we believe He is giving. And you must do the same."

Although no more harsh words escaped his lips, the anger returned to his features darkening his eyes, puckering his lips, and flaring his nostrils. Neither the fiery outburst nor the heart-warming pleading swayed Elizabeth to his side of the widening divide.

"Well, that's it. I have done my duty. Tell Louis to be careful." George stormed out the front door, slamming it behind him.

Elizabeth wept. Tears for the sweet past, the turbulent present, and the confusing future. Tears for George, her family, and Harriet's innocent life. For a brief time, strength and reason deserted her. *What do I do now, Lord?*

Then a whisper reminded her of Psalm 32, "Thou art my hiding place; Thou shalt preserve me from trouble; Thou shalt compass me about with songs of deliverance." *Surround me now, Lord.*

Louis found her a few hours later, cheerful and composed, holding the baby, seeming to not have a care for the outside world. She held her veil in place about George until after dinner.

When Louis pulled out the *Gazette* to read her an article, she nodded, "I heard the news from George in a less eloquent manner. If only he had the power of words like Mr. Timothy." She relayed her encounter with her brother, importing her words calmly.

"So, he came to ask you to influence me to change the minds of the Provincial Congress. He has a lot of confidence in both of us to even think that is a possibility. Did he threaten you?"

"No, not personally. He advises you to be careful in general. The British authorities are ready for a conclusion to this drama." She hugged Harriet close, smelling her clean hair.

"Me too." Louis sat back in his chair. "But we're waiting for the king's response to the Constitutional Congress' proposals."

"Then until that time, more ships will be turned away and cargo destroyed?" The destruction bothered her, although she understood the situation and decree.

"Yes." Louis painted an honest picture for her. No reason to disguise the seriousness of Congress' actions. After all, she could read the news in the paper herself.

"I heard from Lucy today." Elizabeth grinned. "We can come for a visit anytime this month. Maybe after the museum event next Thursday?" She envisioned Lucy's children entertaining her with their antics in the endless front yard. Did she really care that their time would include target practice? Perhaps they'd be quick studies, leaving more time for visiting and playing.

Louis stood and joined her on the sofa. "We'll definitely want to wait until the ice clears."

She smiled. "You know our weather. Tomorrow will probably be clear, sunny, and warm." For the rest of the evening, they had each other and plans to make.

The third annual gala for the Charles Town Museum of History centered on the addition of many recently acquired items to the collections. A few family Bibles from the 1600's, military uniforms from the French Indian war, coinage from many nations—Germany, France, Italy, Switzerland, and China. Citizens valued the concept of preserving some of the past for the future eyes of society. Proud of her role in the opening of the first museum in the colonies two years ago, Elizabeth joined her mother and many others in the organization of the upcoming event.

Elizabeth helped Sarah set out cups next to the punch bowl in the foyer. "For a moment, I forgot about the museum's function."

Somehow, three hundred cups appeared from collections in various homes across the town.

"How could you after our mothers talk about it constantly?" Sarah made neat rows of cups around the bowl. "They are making it as big an event as the opening."

"Bigger. Remember we only planned for a hundred that first year and now maybe over three hundred guests. Anyway, the reason I was sidetracked was the recent dumping of the cargo in the harbor." Elizabeth admired some old paintings hanging by the entrance and trembled. "I try to put myself in the place of the owners of the merchandise. Some of it was family possessions from England—heirlooms and paintings. I know they were warned, but it seems harsh." She pointed to the art. "Look, these most likely came from England. Some just like these have been forever lost at the bottom of the sea."

"They were advised to turn the ships around. All of it could have been saved. But you are right—it is sad." Sarah shared Elizabeth's concern, yet no one could grieve except the ones involved.

Picking up today's *Gazette* from a side table, Elizabeth skimmed it to find the appropriate article. "Listen to this from Lieutenant Governor Bull: 'I hope that the men of property who suffered most from the association would ultimately be able to break the many-headed power of the People.' Is that what all Loyalists believe and hope?"

Sarah didn't answer. But that didn't stop Elizabeth. "The only way to break the advancement of the people would be for Parliament to listen and heed their wishes. Basically, if Britain gave equal representation to her colonists in the decision-making, the problem would be solved."

"I get so tired of hearing about the turmoil." Sarah waved her hand as if the conflict would go away. "I want to just make Samuel happy, teach the girls, and raise a family."

"A family? You're not expecting, are you?" Elizabeth squeezed Sarah's lower arm.

"No. Not yet. I hoped to be," she smiled. "But we've only been married a little over two months. That is demanding a lot right away."

"Enjoy your time with Samuel. In God's timing and will, you'll have a family."

"I know. But if I don't, I have the girls at the school and Harriet."

"You have years to work on your family." Elizabeth's bolt of excitement made her forget her job on hand. "Right now, I need help with the guest registration table. Blue or white for the table covering?" She held each out for examination.

Sarah chose white, perfect for any of the flowers chosen for the evening. They gazed at the foyer, their area of responsibility. "Will our mothers approve?"

Elizabeth looked around. "I think they will. With the flowers, candles, food and punch, and gorgeous dresses, it will be beautiful. I've asked Amy to help. You did ask a few girls to help serve that night?"

"Yes, we'll bring them personally an hour early. Don't worry so much. As usual, if something goes wrong, our mothers will work their magic to fix it."

On Thursday evening, their mothers expertly rearranged tables, repositioned trays of sandwiches and pastries, recovered a missing guest book, and replenished the punch. Elizabeth wore a shimmering gold-trimmed yellow dress with an overlay of sheer gauze. It matched Louis' yellow, gold trimmed jacket. Sarah stepped out in a rose-hued skirt and bodice with a petticoat of tiny roses on a cream silk.

But no preparation anticipated the riotous rally outside of the museum. Elizabeth pressed her face against the window, hoping to see around the corner toward the entrance to the museum. "What is happening?"

Mother, Sarah, and Mrs. Collins took different vantage points, but didn't answer her question. Earlier men and women, young and old, familiar and unfamiliar, congregated at the steps at times blocking the entrance of the attendees to the gala.

Upon entering, Elizabeth had read signs: "Disband the Committees," "Commerce for All," and "Safety and Observant Beware." A protest at an event that should have united the citizens who shared the same past didn't seem to be the place for rioting.

Elizabeth stepped back and surveyed the beautiful foyer. Instead of bringing the town together, the event divided the citizens. The ones inside, both Partisans and Loyalists had decided the past was a neutral ground, a place that succeeded in bringing many together.

Louis came to Elizabeth's side. "I know you don't understand. I think the outsiders must see the gala as a disregard of the present situation. To them as people feast and revel, the British lose more control."

"You mean these people outside are the ones who want the town under the British flag and rule?" Elizabeth did not have time to solve the large political scene. "What do we do? The guests have to push their way through that mob."

"Christopher has gone for the town safety officials. Ironically the British guards will be here soon to control the Loyalists."

Elizabeth laced her fingers with Louis' and stood on tiptoes and kissed him. "I suppose even they don't want any violence or hindrance to public events." She knew his strength. There was no canceling the event; therefore, she'd put on her most beguiling face and change her attitude to one of acceptance and service.

He brought her fingers to his lips, and then released her for the moment. "For now, Samuel and I will station ourselves at the door and discourage any advancement of the protesters."

Half an hour later, the people barring the steps and door

dispersed. But their message lingered. Division entered the chambers, whispers echoed in the alcoves, stares peeked from spread fans, and coded remarks escaped pursed lips. The seed of dissension worked its way into an otherwise normal social gathering.

Elizabeth smiled at Sarah, more to encourage than to present her true feelings. Their jobs increased with the pressure to cover any fear or disgust. They wanted to scream and hide. Instead, they endured their public roles—extending hands, answering questions, guiding, and serving refreshments. Louis, Christopher, and Samuel stood close by the foyer entrances as unofficial guards and keepers of the peace.

Was this a sign of the future when Loyalists and Partisans couldn't attend the same functions? What about concerts, plays, and church? Would events be boycotted like products?

"The day of prayer is not soon enough for me." Elizabeth grinned at Sarah beside her, slurring the words through her teeth.

"Will prayer make the problem disappear?" Sarah whispered as she nodded to guests passing by. It was time for the gala to end. The event itself was a success. No one complained about the exhibits, the presentation, or the displays. The remarks and comments stifled behind gloved hands dealt with the bigger issue of Congress and Parliament.

Elizabeth counted the number of guests remaining—close to twenty-five. "I'm ready to breathe normally again. I feel like my lips are frozen in this upturned false fashion."

"Let's wander through the rooms to see how many stragglers are here." Elizabeth linked arms with Sarah and gracefully sashayed through the corridors and galleries. Mannequins in uniforms, Indian attire, formal dresses and suits of the past times smiled at them as they journeyed from 1620 to the present. One hundred and fifty years captured behind glass.

"I wonder what will be said of us when someone records 1775." Sarah stopped in front of a display with fans, china, and jewelry and the model wearing a beaded silk gown in Elizabethan style.

"I wonder into what kind of world I have brought Harriet. Will she know the peace and prosperity I have known or only war and disputes?"

Sarah sighed. "This won't last forever. Some side will win."

Yes, Sarah voiced a truth I'm avoiding. I want to know the Patriots will win. I don't want to have given so much for freedom to be denied experiencing it.

Sarah's comment comforted and agitated Elizabeth. *Would I be able to live in a society ruled by Loyalists again?* Time would tell. One thing was certain; she would endure for Harriet's sake.

CHAPTER 6

*N*o ice or severe weather meant no opposition to leaving Charles Town. Lucy March expected the Lestarjettes on Saturday. A twelve-mile trip on messy roads developed into a bumpy ride. The carriage wobbled along, adjusting to the weight of two trunks and six passengers. Fortunately, the Engles and the Lestarjettes could share a house and a carriage with ease.

Louis placed the walnut box of pistols, the purpose of the voyage, under his seat. The weapons themselves held no value to Louis, but what they offered did. Protection.

Elizabeth adjusted Harriet in her arms. "I wish we could avoid an agenda this week."

"It won't be that hard, Mrs. Elizabeth," Tom said, misinterpreting her comment. "I learned to shoot when I was just nine years old. Easier than learning math."

She smiled. "I'm sure I can learn. I'd rather learn to hunt than to protect my life. Why can't life be peaceful? Should a woman have to be able to defend herself?"

"I'm with you. I'll follow Mr. Louis' instructions, but I don't like it," Ellen said. Amy sat still and silent, hiding her concern.

Louis gazed at each lady, stalling on Elizabeth. "A lesson a day. The rest of the time you can gossip, sew, walk, cook, or sleep. Just humor me in this," he begged.

Elizabeth sighed even as she laughed at the irony. "Hmm. Humor is a bit out of the question, my dear."

The journey ended at Lucy and Cliff March's sprawling two story house on three hundred and twenty acres. Lucy stationed herself on the front porch with her two daughters on either side and her almost three-year-old son on her hip.

"Lucy, it's so good to see you." Elizabeth hugged her older cousin firmly. "You are so gracious to have all of us."

"You are always welcome. Let me see my little cousin, Harriet."

Ellen stepped forward with the small bundle securely in her arms.

Lucy peeked at Harriet's face under the blanket while Elizabeth tried to look at little Cliff. "Do you remember when Clifford was a baby? You came to help me when the other two were sick. Now look at him."

"I don't even recognize him." The shy boy hid his face on his mother's shoulder. "Louis, this is Lucy." Elizabeth pulled her husband beside her, proud of his handsome looks, and even more so for his strength and stability.

Elizabeth continued with the numerous introductions. "And these two beautiful girls are Amelia, age ten, and Diana, age eight. You have changed too. Beautiful young ladies now."

As the Engles joined the new family, the girls immediately warmed to Amy, in awe of her advanced years, all of thirteen now. "Nice to meet you, Miss Amelia and Miss Diana." Amy added a small curtsy.

"None of that this week, Amy. You are here as a guest. My girls will keep you busy with their little adventures and antics," Lucy said. "And Ellen, I'm sure you and Elizabeth will have your hands full with the baby. I have plenty of help, so try to relax and enjoy your time here."

Elizabeth motioned to the young man standing close to Louis. "That leaves Tom. It appears the men are greatly outnumbered. I can imagine Tom remaining at the side of Louis and Cliff." She laughed. Already Tom's features relaxed, revealing his dimples as he smiled. Remembering this was his first experience outside of cobbled roads and crowded streets, Elizabeth surmised the country air and activity would give him a little taste of the way others lived.

"Where's Clifford?" Louis asked.

"He's checking out the fields making sure they are being prepared for the planting. You'll find him over there in the back-left corner." Lucy pointed. "Now, let's get you all settled in before supper. Ellen and Amy, I put you in a spare room upstairs next to the girls. Tom, you can take the small room at the far end of that floor. We always put any of our single guests there. Not very big but comfortable. And you and Louis will be in the big room at the opposite end of the hall."

"All right, Tom, let's deliver the trunks and start our exploring." Louis grabbed one end of a trunk. "We must find an appropriate spot for target practice. The estate will double as a petit military camp for a few days."

His last words startled Elizabeth. *This is not a child's game but a man's fight.*

Half an hour later, Elizabeth found Lucy in the dining room, putting the final touches to the table. "How do you do it, Lucy? Listen, barely any noise. You have a house full of people, and there is peace."

"For now. The girls are upstairs filling Amy in on all their treasures. Clifford is napping, and I assume Ellen is with a sleeping Harriet."

Elizabeth pulled her cousin to the settee beckoning Lucy to spill her secrets. "And no sign of the men. So, let's steal the minutes to talk."

"Do you remember the summer in Boston at Grandmamma's house? You and Anne would sneak off to the parlor and set up your own off-limits gossip sessions." Elizabeth stuck her lower lip out, pretending to pout.

Lucy giggled. "Yes, and you would hide behind the big over-stuffed chair with the covering all the way to the floor, so we couldn't see you. How long did that last?"

"Two summers. Until I told Grandmamma about what you said about the neighbor boy."

"That's right." Lucy nodded, her green-blue eyes twinkling. "Then we always looked behind the chair."

"I know. I missed all the gossip about you and Clifford. Anne finally told me that our older cousin was marrying someone from South Carolina who had no Boston family name. You really surprised all of Boston."

"But not Grandmamma. She knew that I loved Clifford March, not for his money or title. If it hadn't been for her, I would still be in Boston married to an old man in a big mansion."

"Well, you paved the way for Anne and me. A captain and a Frenchman." The cousins shared a deep belly laugh at the shock each one gave the old Burnham family.

"God knew what He was doing. All three of us are blessed with our men." Lucy's tone changed from joy to concern. "I need to know what has happened in Charles Town to make you come here for such an austere assignment."

Elizabeth explained as an educated citizen not an alarmist. Plantations outside the town didn't live the drama day-to-day. The daily tidbits in the *Gazette*, the words in the cafes and restaurants, the gossip in the stores and the sermons from the pulpits fed the people in the city doses of truth and lies from every angle. Lucy didn't hear that every day. Part of Elizabeth envied her. Would the Marches even be a part of the conflict?

"One of the recommendations of the new Provincial Congress was that the colonists learn the use of arms," Elizabeth said. "I'm afraid our friends and contacts strongly believe the threat from the British will increase the need to protect our homes and our families."

"Our neighbor was a delegate. When he returned, he expressed concern, too, but more about import and export than arms. You see out here we all know how to use weapons for snakes, wild hogs, and hunting."

But not for men.

Elizabeth grinned at an image of Lucy playing with dolls and animals. "Even you? Sweet little Lucy who collected every stray cat."

"A snake? Yes, in a second. The pistol stays in a handy place."

"What about shooting an intruder?"

"I don't think I could unless he threatened the children." Silence. Elizabeth understood the necessity of killing reptiles, harmful creatures, or animals for food. But a human?

Elizabeth looked out the parlor window and focused. The view was peaceful, a lawn ready for spring growth, a forest of trees housing birds and animals tending their families. It was hard to imagine a human enemy poised to harm or kill. Elizabeth shook the image out of her head, determined to leave it in God's hands.

"We can ask God to deal with our enemies," Lucy said. "But at the same time, He strengthens us to watch out for our own families. I guess we don't know what to expect out here so far from town. We never see British militia on these roads. I don't know if we will ever be bothered. Anyway, Clifford stays very close." Lucy shivered, but not from any draft that Elizabeth could feel.

"Well, now you know why Louis has brought this unlikely group to your doorstep."

"He can only train you a little each day, so the rest will be at our disposal."

Elizabeth followed her cousin back to the table to help prepare for their first meal together.

Louis respected the Lord's Day and the ladies' request to start the lessons on Monday. On Sunday, the Marches, Lestarjettes, and Engles walked a mile to a field at a crossroads where a small three-sided shelter with a slanted roof stood. The lean-to served as a stable at other times. Logs posed as pews. No pulpit existed. But, right on time other families arrived bundled in their coats and scarves ready to worship and hear a word from God.

Louis and his group were by far the most numerous of all the guests under one roof. Five other families completed the small congregation. A farmer stepped up, Bible in hand, as the spokesman for the Lord.

Although Louis never expected to participate in such a simple worship service, he never worshipped so purely and deeply. Young and old sang the hymns without hymnals or organ. He listened as the voices joined in praise. *"Let the Redeemer's name be sung, Thro' every land by every tongue."*

Could that be any more appropriate? Out in a field under blue skies? He didn't even know the words, but he sang them in his heart as the others voiced the cadence.

He heard Elizabeth sing as if the words touched her heart, too. And the others, their faces lifted in praise. God truly inhabited this place, a stable in a field.

Mr. Stafford read the Scripture. He had neither the education nor the polish of Reverend Smith of St. Philip's, but Louis knew the man spoke truth.

"The Gospel of John Chapter eight says 'and ye shall know the truth, and the truth shall make you free. If the Son therefore shall make you free, ye shall be free indeed.' We come here today from different backgrounds, different languages, different classes, but Christ has given us one truth and one hope, and that is what unites us all. With our belief that Christ is the answer to our freedom in this world, then we can face anything, absolutely anything. Do you believe that?"

"We believe it," rang through the crowd. The message was clear. The freedom people needed and received centered on God's love and peace, not the freedom from government or laws or acts. Peace and freedom belonged to God and His guidance.

Conversations ignited on the walk back about the sermon, the hymns, and the people. "Will you ever be asked to preach, Cliff?" Louis saw that possibility as daunting and humbling.

Cliff held Diana's small hand in his. "I have before but only once. It's a volunteer situation. Usually for the past six months or so, Mr. Stafford has led, but if difficulties arise another man will step up." The man shrugged as if the accepted role was as easy as plowing a field. Both of which would intimidate Louis.

Louis dropped his head and watched his feet kick up dirt on the path. "I don't think I could." Even after almost two years, Louis felt like such a newcomer to his faith.

Cliff leaned his head to the side as if that wasn't important. "We come together twice a month to hear a word from God and worship together. It's not who reads the Scripture, but what God says through His word. A man doesn't have to say anything. I know it seems simple, but it works out here. Perhaps, one day we'll have a proper church building and a minister."

Louis touched Cliff's sleeve and shook his head. "I don't know that you need that. You have more than enough right now." Louis honestly experienced God's presence in that barren field as much as in the stone walls with huge stained-glass in the city.

Though there was no shooting lesson that day, Louis and Tom

set up the "classroom" with targets and yard lines—ten, fifteen, and twenty yards. The target was an old piece of burlap wrapped around a hay bale secured between sturdy trees.

"We need to make sure we have enough musket balls." Louis chuckled picturing the upcoming fiasco. "These ladies will use a bundle before hitting the target." He had no qualms about this being the best thing to do with his family. But would the lessons be successful? He only had brothers, and he knew his mother had never lifted a pistol. Was the "talent" innately for men only? He would see soon enough.

Tom nodded his agreement. "Sir, I don't know if Mother or Amy will ever get near the target." Tom's lack of confidence amused Louis.

"You are going to be surprised. I bet you Amy will become as good as you are." Louis didn't believe his words, but he knew a lot about sibling rivalry at least between boys.

"Not possible," Tom determined.

"So, tomorrow morning we'll begin. Make sure we have twenty bullets for each person."

"That will be a start." Tom's sarcasm rang true in Louis opinion too.

Success was a needed outcome for Louis' peace of mind. "Then we have Tuesday and Wednesday mornings to perfect their skills." Louis knew Tom's faith in the ladies didn't include a picture of success. Louis hoped Tom was wrong. Between all the chuckles, a seriousness festered in the whole exercise.

In the kitchen, Louis and Tom spent a few hours making musket balls using the mold within the pistol box. They heated the lead over a fire and poured the hot substance into the mold. Later the men opened the molds and shook the balls out.

Louis motioned to Tom. "Run to the parlor and have the ladies come out here to have a quick lesson in bullet making."

"They won't be happy," Tom warned. "Bullets and a Sunday

afternoon won't quite mix in their minds." For such a young man, Tom understood women as well as Louis. Perhaps better.

"Do it anyway. It will save time tomorrow. And you can blame it all on me."

Minutes later the group appeared, open with their feelings about the lesson. Elizabeth rocked Harriet in her arms and stood wide-eyed close to the action. Ellen crossed her arms and hung her head. Would she ever warm to this idea of pistols and shooting? Amy stepped as close as she could and studied all the equipment. Perhaps Louis guessed correctly about Amy excelling in this area.

He eased the group into a semi-circle. "This is a precautionary lesson. If I'm not around, you'll need to know the procedure."

Elizabeth hovered a little closer, most likely sensing the serious need to know all she could. Now, Louis had two willing students.

"Maybe with the three of us we can remember how to do this," Elizabeth encouraged putting equal emphasis on each lady.

Louis had it all figured out, but he knew his three female charges had doubts. He showed them the process. "The mold and the instructions are in the box. The lead and powder will be in separate containers in the house in a cool area." He scanned the ladies' faces. "Any questions?"

"When do we learn to shoot?" Amy asked.

He expected questions on bullet making, at least another demonstration. "Tomorrow morning after breakfast," Louis suggested. He heard no objection and received a slight nod from Elizabeth. Amy stood tall and rigid, hands on her hips and her chin jutting upward. "Could I go first? I really want to do this." Her enthusiasm caused her mother to pale and her brother to roll his eyes.

"Why, Amy?" Tom asked.

"I know exactly why," Elizabeth laughed. "Probably, like me, she wants to know what her brother gets to learn at an early age just because he's a boy. I always wanted to go hunting with George and Father and the answer was always 'no.' Now we get our chance. Unfortunately, the circumstances are dire, and it is forced on us."

"Is that right, Amy?" Tom eyed his sister as she poured the next batch of musket balls.

"Perhaps I'll be just as good as you." Louis felt the punctuation of determination with each of Amy's words. He hoped a British soldier never ran into her. He wouldn't have a chance.

Elizabeth made certain her daughter was fed, dry, and sleeping before setting out for the field. "Lucy, are you sure you don't mind watching Harriet this morning?"

"Not at all. The girls will love having a baby to coddle. Anyway, I knew what your plans were this week. I'll work on a picnic lunch, and we can all go to the river after a while."

"Perfect." Elizabeth kissed her cousin before trotting off to the makeshift artillery camp. Who said women couldn't join the army? *The Lestarjette squad.* She giggled visualizing these women and men following Louis' command. *What could they accomplish? Or perhaps what couldn't they accomplish?*

Louis stood ramrod straight, feet close together, holding a pistol to his side. A regular soldier. "Welcome to your first target lesson. A couple of fast and firm rules. Never point a loaded gun at a person unless you intend to wound or kill him. Next, always put the weapons safely away out of reach of children. Know what your target is. Don't shoot randomly, for it could be a cat or dog or a neighbor. Use the pistol as a last resort."

"Yes, sir." The three women chimed in unison. Elizabeth wanted to salute but thought Louis would not appreciate the gesture under such serious circumstances.

The light-heartedness from yesterday had disappeared,

replaced by a solemn, serious teacher. Elizabeth understood the change. Louis desired for them to be protected and safe in the future.

Tom explained the target and yard lines. "From right here the target is twenty yards away. That is the farthest distance a pistol can reach with accuracy. But it works a lot better at a closer range. The next line is fifteen yards and the last one is ten yards." Elizabeth noted the logs designating the distances. "Any intruder in the house will be ten yards or less. At that distance, you are most likely to hit your target."

Ellen grimaced. "Easy for you to say, Son." Elizabeth couldn't remember the last time Ellen had smiled. Not since they had left Charles Town. The woman certainly didn't approve of weapons in the hands of females, especially her thirteen-year-old daughter. Yet, her presence here reinforced her trust in Louis, the "head" of her fatherless clan.

They all lined up on the ten-yard line.

"Amy is first. Watch Tom as he loads your pistol." Powder first, then bullet with the help of a rod.

Louis took the pistol from Tom and placed it in her hand. "I want you to feel the pistol in your hand, pointing it at the ground." He stood beside her with everyone else a safe distance behind her. "Slowly raise it up and find the target. This has a spring-loaded trigger that is light and easy to fire without disturbing your aim. When you are ready, pull the hammer back and aim."

Elizabeth noticed the weapon shook in her hand, but Amy's determination and purpose landed a good first shot, just to the right of the target.

"Try again, Amy," Louis coaxed. "Adjust your aim. Follow the barrel of the pistol to the target." This time the shot made the target although well below the bull's eye.

"One more." Louis' finger mocked the motion for her as she released it once again. The bullet flew to its target a half inch from the center. As Amy started to jump up and down, Louis reminded her to always remain still and composed with a weapon in hand.

Once the weapon was safely in Louis' hand, she ran to her mother for a congratulatory hug. "I'm proud of you, Amy." Ellen didn't smile, but her nod at least showed a renewed confidence in her brave daughter.

Elizabeth stepped up to the line. Her enthusiasm waxed and waned as she contemplated why she had to fear this. Her brother did this years ago. No longer was she jealous. No, now it was for protection in an uncertain time, not hunting with her father. *I understand that I must do this for my family and my countrymen.*

Louis took out the second pistol and guided her through the loading steps. "I promise to be a good student, Louis."

His eyebrows raised. "I'm confident that you can. Now, feet firmly planted. Cock the hammer. Raise your arm when you are ready. See the target and pull the trigger."

Her aim missed entirely as her arm jumped up, sending the bullet soaring over the target into the deep woods.

"Did you close your eyes, Elizabeth?" he accused, knowing that she did.

"Guilty. I feared the noise. And I thought my arm would stay down."

"Those are common reflexes. Now, you must concentrate more on these two areas. Open your eyes and steady your arm. Again."

This time she visualized the result and hit the target, although in the far-right corner. The third time brought her closer to the center.

Louis kissed the tip of her nose. "You'll improve. I'm proud of you." She'd take that special treatment from the instructor any day.

Ellen would be the main challenge. Just getting the gun in her hand was a feat. Elizabeth wondered what Louis expected from her.

"Steady, aim, fire." Ellen hit the bull's eye on the first shot. After the shock of her perfect contact, everyone clapped in astonishment.

"Hard to top that, Mother," Tom said.

But she did, not once but twice more. Three bull's eyes in a row. The perfect aim and control didn't change her solemn attitude toward the whole situation but seeing the pride in her children's eyes made her graciously accept their congratulations. Elizabeth clapped again. At least if they ever had an intruder, they knew who to trust for a good aim.

"One more round for everyone at the ten-yard line, then we'll step back five yards," Louis the drill sergeant commanded.

Fifteen yards posed a challenge for Amy's first shot, but two landed in the outer range of the bull's eye. Elizabeth hit the target all three times circling the center by five inches or so. Then the crowd silently watched Ellen land another three bull's eyes. Amy and Elizabeth improved, but neither surpassed Ellen.

Louis just shook his head. "It takes years to teach someone to do that, Ellen. I don't envy anyone who comes up on you."

She gladly relinquished the pistol into Louis' hand. "I don't ever want to have to use this pistol, but at least I know I can. You were right, Mr. Louis, I needed this piece of confidence."

"The session's over for today. More of the same tomorrow." Louis dismissed his troops.

"Time for the picnic that Lucy has prepared." Elizabeth invited them all to hurry to the house.

"I'll go find Cliff and be in shortly." Louis started walking to the back field.

Elizabeth yelled and waved to her husband as the distance expanded. "Don't expect us to wait too long. We've worked up an appetite."

The cook had put together a feast of cold chicken, ham, bread, apples, potato crisps, and small blueberry cakes, sprinkled with sugar. Blankets and jars of lemon water rounded off the load.

Every hand was full as the party trekked the quarter mile to the stream, a tributary of the Cooper River.

"This is one thing I love about South Carolina," Louis remarked. "It is February and it feels like spring. Boston and Philadelphia could be covered in snow, but not here. We are picnicking outside with no coats."

Clifford laughed. "Wait a week or even a few days and the weather will change. Lucy, you remember the snowstorm in March a few years back?"

Lucy adjusted Cliff in her lap. "Yes, we woke up ready to plant the vegetables and instead made a snowman. But honestly, that is a rarity."

"I'm glad we can enjoy this one breezy, warm day," Elizabeth said.

Clifford sat back against a tree. "Count your blessings. This is one of them."

Elizabeth started counting them, all out in front of her. The healthy children running along the stream, Harriet sleeping and growing daily, her husband holding her hand, family and friends sharing the moments, the weather allowing them access to the outdoors, and God's internal peace directing them. Blessings indeed.

Wednesday morning came too soon. The last lesson over, all three students passed the course at the ten and fifteen-yard targets. Except for Ellen, the twenty-yard line had a fifty percent success rate.

Louis helped the men load the trunks in the rack of the carriage. Elizabeth and the women prolonged their goodbyes on the front porch. Though he understood their reluctance to leave, he missed the access to daily news and anticipated the return to Charles Town.

Elizabeth received one more hug from her cousin. "Thank you, Lucy, for your hospitality. You're welcome at our home any time."

"Amelia and Diana would love that. They have a new friend in Amy," Lucy said.

"Maybe they can come stay for a week this spring or summer. We have plenty of room. Perhaps you can all visit in May for Charlotte's first birthday. The rest of the family would love to see you."

Louis inched closer trying to hasten the departure. As his arm draped behind Elizabeth's back, her arm instinctively did the same to him. Lucy looked from one to the other.

"We'll keep that in mind. Now, you take care of your little family." Lucy gave Elizabeth one more quick hug. "And Louis, you are the best thing that could have happened to Elizabeth."

Louis accepted Lucy's kiss on his cheek. "You have a wonderful life here. Be careful."

Arm in arm, Louis guided Elizabeth to her place with her family in the carriage. Back to Charles Town with a passel of pistol-savvy ladies. What would the petticoat brigade think now?

As he pulled the door shut, he prayed. *Please, Lord, shelter them from the use of a weapon against another child of yours.*

CHAPTER 7

$\mathcal{T}$he talk during the ride home reflected the animation of the past few days. Louis' face, if not his words, shouted "success."

Elizabeth poked him in the ribs. "I know what you are thinking, Mr. Lestarjette."

"Really?" Could she feel the pride of accomplishment? Or the fear that accompanied the pride?

"Yes. You're proud of your ability to teach three weak innocent women the art of dueling."

He faced her. "Your choice of words suggests I didn't have much to work with. *Au contraire,* you three aren't weak by any means. I would acquiesce at any command you gave with or without a weapon." He laughed. "And...I didn't teach you how to duel. That would be another lesson or two. I just used dueling pistols as the weapon of choice."

"I stand corrected. Still, you must admit you are proud of us."

"Yes, as if I haven't said it enough. I'm just glad that is behind us. I can put this box away safely and hopefully indefinitely." He lifted the seat and placed the box firmly in the corner out of sight and reach of curious hands. "Now, to change the austere subject to a more appealing one. Does anyone know what day tomorrow is?"

"February sixteenth, Thursday, I think," Tom said.

"And?" Louis fished for the more important answer.

"And Elizabeth's birthday." Ellen beamed with the recollection.

Louis snapped his fingers and pointed to Ellen. "Exactly." He grinned at Elizabeth. "I think twenty-one years deserves a bit of a celebration. So, I planned a little *fête* at the house at three o'clock. Tante Jeannette and Mrs. Elliott have it all prepared."

Elizabeth's hands covered her mouth. The effect Louis wanted, surprise mixed with joy. Hopefully, he didn't see concern as her eyes crinkled. He knew her well, and she'd be overwhelmed with the prospect of baking and cleaning after days away. Louis winked at her unnecessary anxiety.

"Thank you, Louis. You've made our return so special." Her hand patted him on his leg, but her smile and slight blush topped her words.

"I had help." He grinned. She didn't need to know everything.

The day dawned as any other except Louis pampered Elizabeth from the start. "Breakfast in bed? Will you join me?" Elizabeth asked while stretching among the pillows.

He crawled back in bed. "Just this once, since there's enough here for two."

"And there's tea." She held a bone china teacup, hand painted with tiny butterflies in blue and purple.

"Sent from your mother's stash."

"You mean Victoria's stash."

"Well, yes. It's still tea." He brought his cup to his lips and inhaled the rich aroma.

"I'll savor it." Today it didn't matter about boycotts or

rationing. The amber liquid eased its way to her toes. Coffee would never truly replace tea in Elizabeth's palate.

The only thing the household allowed Elizabeth to do pertained to feeding Harriet and entertaining herself, like playing the piano or walking in the garden and picking early daffodils.

Cake and refreshments arrived in the arms of party guests a little before three. Jeannette carted a triple layer coconut spice cake from a local bakery. Anne and Sarah bore gifts and sweets from their homes. Anne surprised Elizabeth when Robert accompanied her with the two boys in tow.

Elizabeth reached high to give Robert's neck a firm embrace. "You're back. I'm so glad."

"As of Tuesday. The good weather permitted an easy sail into harbor."

Anne deposited Charlotte in a high chair. "Happy birthday. Twenty-one is so very young, dear sister. Look what you have to look forward to in ten years, three children instead of one."

Louis welcomed the women and Robert. Samuel, Father, and Henry all remained at work. Someone had to run the town. A party in the middle of the afternoon on a weekday was a luxury. Mother arrived later with more food items, sandwiches, and meat pies.

"I feel a bit guilty with this consumption and celebration the day before the Day of Prayer and Fasting," Elizabeth said. Tomorrow was time enough to be serious with petitions and reverence.

"Today is the celebration of life," Louis said. "Tomorrow is an appeal for peace. We want to be able to continue to enjoy the gift of life in a peaceful colony, an existence far removed from turmoil, don't we? Now on to the feasting."

All ignored the formal table and chairs. Comfort won out with plates of food set in laps. Fingers replaced forks. Conversation switched gaily as many talked at once. Gifts appeared out of festive wrapping--scarf, book, combs, sheet music. And then

Louis' gift. She sought his eyes longing for this moment to carry her through the days ahead. Wasn't he gift enough? *Yes, but honestly, I'll never tire of his gifts,*

The package was awkward in her lap. She ran her hand over the rectangular thick form taking up most of the small settee. "It is rather large and heavy. I can't guess what it is or where you found it."

"Well, stop guessing and open it." Louis squeezed her hand, encouraging her to discard the wrapping.

String cut and paper flew. She unfolded a tapestry of the finest material and artistry. A countryside scene with a castle in the background. And a party of picnickers enjoying an outing. Blues, reds, browns, and yellows. *Brilliant colors and exquisite needlework. How is he able to always surprise me?*

"Louis, it is wonderful. Where did you find such a treasure?" Her fingers continued to caress the fabric and trace the pattern.

"From an old chateau in France at an estate sale. I had André ship it on the last run. I'm glad it made it here in time."

"Me, too. Thank you." She pulled him in closer by his chin, close enough to plant a lingering kiss. The room exploded in clapping and laughter. Later, out of the crowd's view, she would have to find a better way of thanking him.

The *Gazette* printed the Congress' recommendation again. Informal gatherings took place at various churches under the direction of members and not the clergy. Elizabeth supported the cause for prayer vehemently yet questioned her reason for attending. "February seventeenth. This is a day of fasting, humiliation, and prayer before Almighty God, devoting to entreat him to inspire the king to avert the impending calamities of civil war." *Please, Lord, let me be here for the right reason, not for curiosity or*

gossip. Whether her plea changed her attitude or not, she'd have to see.

Looking at a printed bulletin from the table in the foyer of St. Philip's, Elizabeth observed that Reverend Smith's work and words covered the sheet although his name was absent, as was his role as leader today.

"How will this service proceed without Reverend Smith?" Elizabeth whispered.

Louis leaned close to her. "I'm sure he has given the men some suggestions on procedures, but I would assume the body as a whole wants God to lead. This is no ordinary occasion."

"I know. Attending this service will label the citizens even more as part of the Sons of Liberty." Elizabeth held her gaze forward to the altar, avoiding seeking who sat in the pews for now.

"But more than that, it imprints our desire to prepare to do God's will whatever that might be."

Louis followed her through the door. Elizabeth stopped suddenly as she surveyed the sanctuary, every pew filling with citizens of Charles Town, Christians willing to bring petitions to God. Louis nudged her to continue her advancement to an available seat.

The light push reminded her of her purpose, not to gawk, but to pray. Men, ordinary men, stepped forward to read Scripture and pray. In humility, they presented themselves as willing mouthpieces for God. Scriptures from the bulletin were read as well as others from individual wells of faith.

As the hour progressed Elizabeth found her shock and surprise turned to praise and worship of Holy God who chose to use humble men to spread His Word.

"Acts 13:3: And when they had fasted and prayed, and laid their hands on them, they sent them away."

Elizabeth could apply this to her life. Would God ask her to do something uncomfortable or difficult? He could. She wanted to be obedient, but under pressure would she stand strong?

"James 5:13: Is any among you afflicted? Let him pray. Is any merry? Let him sing psalms."

More, Lord? Affliction bore down on her in many forms. Presently in the form of the king. The prayers Elizabeth and others offered didn't even mention the king in specific words, but in general, Elizabeth saw all on both sides experiencing hardships.

She glanced at Louis, his head bowed, hands clasped, brow knitted. Her strong man shared the burden of every other person in the room and across the town. The burden to make wise decisions and the burden to carry out God's ultimate plan. She placed her gloved hand over his, lacing her fingers over his firm ones.

At the conclusion, a lovely voice filled the spacious sanctuary. "Oh, God our help in ages past." A solo for a few words only. Then the voices of God's people joined like a heavenly choir. "Our hope for years to come."

People filed out in utter silence. The awesome reverence of the hour braced them to renew dedication to prayer in the months to come.

"Never have I experienced such a deep, heart-felt service." Elizabeth's speech returned as she inhaled the fresh cool air outside.

Louis took Elizabeth's hand and squeezed it. "God showed us that He is still working. He's still in control, and He has a plan. I'll be there with you all the way."

Her tummy rumbled on the walk home. How many times would God call them to fast before the conflict ended?

"Think about the sound you want to pierce the air. Aim for that sound. Now start again on the third stanza." Elizabeth engrossed herself in these lessons a few hours a week. The slightest advancement of a student carried her from week to week.

Sarah stepped in to the small rehearsal room at the boarding school. Elizabeth tiptoed to the door keeping one ear on her young student. "What brings you here?"

"A break before my next class." Sarah nodded toward the piano bench. "Rachel has improved."

"Yes, slowly. My ears don't hurt as much anymore. Her confidence will take over one day. For now, it is baby steps."

"Baby steps." Sarah dipped her chin. "Speaking of babies…"

Sarah had her full attention then. "Are you?"

"I don't think so." Sarah's eyes glistened. "But I do hope it happens soon. I see you and Harriet and Anne and Charlotte and my heart just pounds for one. I just have to believe it will happen one day."

"Of course, it will. Be patient and enjoy your new married life." How did she tell Sarah that once a baby entered the whole household turned inside out?

Sarah wrung her hands. "I can't help being jealous of Victoria. She didn't even want a baby, and she'll have one soon." Elizabeth knew the result of jealousy would taint Sarah's life as she waited.

"Please don't be envious." Elizabeth took Sarah's hands, feeling the clammy palms. "The baby isn't entering into the best situation with neither parent wanting him."

"But he will have loving aunts and uncles. I think he'll find his life surrounded by love anyway."

"You have so much love to give. God knows that. Remember He will provide what you need." Elizabeth believed in his complete control, but what if Sarah never had a baby? Like Jeannette. Would Sarah be content? *Would I have been content without Harriet?* Elizabeth prayed quietly and quickly for her friend as the last notes of a Handel piece concluded the lessons.

At other times Sarah's level of confidence was like this ten-year-old girl sitting straight backed on the piano bench, still developing and growing. Other things developed and grew at a rapid pace, such as the political arena. Elizabeth wished for stagnation in all the talk and threats. Somehow, she didn't think babies and war fit together in God's perfect plan.

❀

At breakfast the next morning, Elizabeth tried to gain some truth. She didn't think it would settle her anxiety, but her mind could find a foundation in truth. "I'm tired of the rumors, Louis. Do you know anything?"

He shrugged. "I can't tell you anything. If the harbor could speak, maybe the answer would roll in on the tide. We just have to wait until ships try to unload their cargo."

She bit into a roll spread with juicy fig preserves as the taste of summer lingered on her lips. "It doesn't seem fair that items could be destroyed or confiscated."

He leaned on his elbows, giving Elizabeth that all too familiar plea with his raised brows. "No. But it is a law passed by the congress." His glance meant, "Stay put. Don't get involved." But knowing she desired to see for herself, how could he protect her from secrets and decisions if she wanted to be in the middle of it?

"Perhaps the wharves will give me some answers. Harriet and I will head that way."

Louis bent to kiss her, adding his buttery sweet taste. "Just be careful. Lots of citizens have the same idea."

The late February morning offered a mild breeze. Elizabeth steered the carriage toward the open sea and the Cooper River. Louis was right. It seemed half the town did have the same idea.

There was rapid movement toward the docks. Crew members and dock workers sprinted to an impressive ship. "What's the occasion?" she asked a woman beside her.

"The *Charming Sally* just arrived from Bristol," the lady said.

"And our reliable Committee of Observation will not let her unload."

"Why? What is she carrying?"

The lady shrugged. "It really doesn't matter. She's from Britain and that prevents the off-loading."

"Oh." The rumors floating across town from day to day were true. The Provincial Congress applied its rules meticulously. Louis most likely knew the outcome. Why wouldn't he stand here with the rest of the town?

She moved closer. All the work hands had no role now. Their muscles and strong backs turned away like the cargo.

Elizabeth called to her young friend on the wharf. "Raymond. Raymond, over here." The strapping youth veered toward her, concern etched on his face.

He tipped his woven hat. "Madame, what are you doing here?"

"Curiosity. Do you know anything about this?" She gestured to the pier with her free hand, leaving one attached to the carriage containing a sleeping Harriet.

"I was told to leave the dock along with the other hands. It's another ship full of British goods. This one has salt, tiles and coal, all consigned to local merchants," he said. "They won't be getting their merchandise today."

The noise level intensified, bringing a pounding in her head. Citizens yelled at the committee, and more citizens returned the barrage. This was the part Elizabeth didn't like. Citizen against citizen. Neighbors arguing with each other.

"Who are these people on the docks?" She pointed to a group of men circling another group of men close to the ship.

Raymond's attention followed her pointing fingers. "The men in the middle are the committee members, including Mr. Gadsden. I've seen this before. My guess is he is telling the others that the *Charming Sally* is not welcome." She was glad Louis wasn't in the group, trying to enforce the law.

"And the other men are?"

"The merchants. Word got out quickly it seems." They walked in silence as the ship soon drifted out to sea.

Elizabeth searched Raymond's face. "Now what?"

He frowned and nodded to the ship. "The goods will be dumped."

"Dumped? What a waste." Surely, there was another way. But it appeared the committee took its police role seriously.

"Thank you, Raymond, for explaining." The gestures and roars from the crowd voiced her thoughts. Reality prevailed. The goods would perish.

"Well, I'll be off now. There is other work, legal work unloading a few docks down. I'll see you later for my lessons." He tipped his hat and joined other workers congregating on other docks.

"Until then." Slowly it dawned on her that Raymond had spoken the entire conversation in coherent English with barely a pause for a missing word. At least there was some positive growth in the town. One youth advancing in his studies.

Turning back toward the bustling city, she caught Christopher's eyes. In a few strides, he joined her on the walkway near his office.

"Elizabeth and Miss Harriet, what a pleasure. I assume you witnessed the latest episode of our progress in holding back the British." He seemed so proud, as usual. Could he not see the incident with a little sadness?

"Yes, I did. I had to see if the rumors were true. What happens to the cargo?"

He smiled. "The goods will be dumped into Hog Island Creek and the ship will return empty to Bristol." His reputation oozed out of the corners of his mouth. Such pride in the act.

"Our new policies at work." She lowered her gaze, hiding her regret that the policies had to be enforced. "I'm glad you and Louis deal with other cargo. This must hurt the merchants and suppliers."

"Yes, but they were warned. You're not having doubts about our cause?" Christopher bent to peer under the brim of her hat. She lifted her head.

Was she? His probing disturbed her sense of loyalty. The cause was a big entity, yet citizens were individuals, real people with families. "I support the views of the Sons of Liberty and of the Provincial Congress. I'm just sad that so many citizens are feeling the effects. Many wanted a different outcome."

He rubbed his hands together, emphasizing his victory, South Carolina's goal of independence. "But that is behind us now." Harriet cooed at Christopher demanding attention and movement. He smiled. "I heard you followed our advice and learned to use a pistol."

Elizabeth giggled even with the seriousness of the topic. "After many attempts, I finally mastered the use to a certain degree. I won't guarantee my accuracy in an actual situation."

"It shouldn't come to that."

"I hope not." A wiggling Harriet interrupted the morning outing. "Well, Christopher, I need to get this little one home. Tell your family hello for me."

Straight backed and confident, the man entered his domain overlooking the harbor. Elizabeth wondered how many men stood their ground against him. He had enough on his side to confront the British head-on, including Elizabeth and Louis.

Preoccupied with crates in the stockroom of Wilson's, Louis missed the action on the wharves, but only physically. Word of it permeated the walls of the building from customers and friends. He didn't have to feel left out at all. It was probably better that he accomplished something instead.

"You wouldn't believe the people on the docks," Tom said,

brimming with the news. "I was able to deliver your note to Mr. Raley before the activity commenced."

"Slow down and tell me. What activity?"

Tom panted and sweated as if he had run a mile. "The *Charming Sally* and her cargo were turned away to be dumped elsewhere."

"Really?" Louis knew it was a possibility but how dreadful for the passengers and what a waste of goods. *Elizabeth. She had headed that way.* She probably saw more than she desired. Why wouldn't she stay away?

Tom's grin reached his eyes. He appeared to enjoy the drama. "Yep. And your friend, Mr. Gadsden was right smack in the middle of it. He sure knows how to command attention."

That put it mildly. When Christopher spoke, things got done. The dismissal of the ship didn't surprise Louis. One of many to come. Just another instance to make him thankful about their prior decision to deal with all non-British products. If they hadn't, their profit could be resting at the bottom of the ocean.

Henry entered, shaking his head, which brought Louis out of his thoughts about solving the world's problems. Louis guessed his uncle had heard the latest.

"What do you think, Uncle?"

"That it will only get worse. The British aren't listening. They won't cease or change their minds." He walked to the crate by the secret door and stomped his feet. "And this," indicating the basement below, "will be needed and used soon, if the tide does not turn."

"How will we know when it comes to that?" Louis certainly dreaded distributing or using the store of arms beneath his feet. Each weapon placed in a man's hand meant death to someone else.

"Parliament will say or do something that triggers a reaction, a violent reaction. And then the need to protect loved ones and possessions will emerge and change lives forever."

Louis studied the man beside him. A strong, godly man jostled but not broken. Could it be that conflict made him stronger? If men in his life faced impending change with vigor and strength, so could he.

"I hate to bother you, Louis." Aunt Jeannette poked her head in the storeroom. "But, George Elliott is here to see you."

Never a good situation. "George in the middle of the afternoon. It must be important." Louis cocked his head toward his uncle. "Any ideas?"

"Either the dumping of the goods or his wife? Good luck." Uncle Henry offered no advice, and his forced grin gave little confidence to Louis.

"You're not alone, Son. I'll be praying." There was the confidence boost Louis needed.

George stood straight-legged, as posed for inspection, by the front door of the store. He hadn't ventured very far into the Wilson domain. Didn't he ever relax? Or smile? His brother-in-law's stare made Louis want to do just the opposite. Possibly even laugh.

Louis ambled closer with a huge smile plastered on his face, covering his uneasiness. He extended his hand. "George, what brings you by?"

The younger man bowed in salute, rejecting Louis' hand. "Could we talk outside, maybe a walk around the block?"

"Well, let me tell Jeannette." A private conversation with George delivered a new opportunity to peel away a layer of his complex character. Though success was not a guarantee.

They exited the mercantile to the right toward Queen Street.

"Thank you for leaving without notice. I know we don't see eye-to-eye on many things, but as a husband and father, I need your advice or at least your ear."

George bending his ear for domestic issues warmed Louis' perception of the uncommon encounter. "I'll help as I can."

"As you know, Victoria's baby, that is our baby, is due soon.

She has been threatening to leave me and the baby in due course. My relationship with her has never been solid. Yet, I do want this child. Is it wrong to hold out for the possibility that the child will bring us together?" George never once looked at Louis. His eyes fixed on a distant object.

"I think the baby could bring you closer, but Victoria would have to have a change of heart. I do believe God can do anything, including mending your relationship."

"Leave God out of this. I have no need for religion. I need just plain, solid advice. Do I need to try to keep my family together?"

No room for God? A life without a Savior? Louis had lived that way for twenty-six years and never felt peace until he gave up that selfish lifestyle.

"You can try to do it on your own. I did for many years. But nothing ever quite made sense." He paused. "From a purely human position as a man, I feel you should do all you can to care for Victoria and the baby. I know Elizabeth and I will help where we can. Don't give up on your wife."

George halted, turned to Louis, and touched his shoulder. The pinched skin around his eyes and mouth warned Louis of the strain George experienced. "I will try for a while. Thank you for listening." Determination laced his words, yet Louis saw a layer of fear shadow his eyes.

Human determination was frail at best. Louis would pray for George and Victoria. Without God in their lives, determination would falter in time. Then what would happen to the innocent baby?

Elizabeth cherished the days she had at home with no plans, nowhere to go. A clear schedule to concentrate on Harriet. The precious two-month-old captured her heart. In her sleeping hours, Elizabeth meandered in her garden. The daffodils danced in the breeze sending their sweet potent aroma ahead of her steps.

Ellen interrupted Elizabeth's perusal of her handiwork. "Elizabeth, you have a visitor." She stooped to pick a yellow and white face peering up at her.

She turned to Ellen and found her mouthing the name "Victoria."

Victoria? Really, what could be the reason for her visit? At least Ellen knew her well enough to give her a head's up on her surprise guest. She straightened her skirt, patted her hair in place, and planted a smile as a reminder to be cordial and guard her mouth. If only she could just stand like a doll without using her voice. Her sister-in-law didn't bring out any compassionate attributes.

"You look fine. I'll be praying for you," Ellen added at the back steps.

"Do I look as afraid as I feel inside?" Her confidence in the presence of Victoria wavered on the best of days.

"Maybe she is just making a brief social call."

"Well, we'll see. Please bring me Harriet if she awakes, and how about coffee and tea cakes in half an hour if Victoria remains?" Elizabeth still grimaced at the dark beverage. This partisan household succumbed bit by bit, unlike Victoria who somehow managed to procure tea.

Elizabeth squeezed Ellen's hand and fortified her steps. "The smell of coffee might send her running."

Victoria reposed as best she could in the overstuffed chair. The woman hadn't accepted the inconveniences of her condition with grace, but rather with disgust.

"Good afternoon, Victoria. How well you look. Are you feeling all right?"

"Do I look like I feel fine? I have yet to understand why women do this over and over."

Elizabeth had heard it all before, so there was no reason to try to convince her of the joys of motherhood and the merits of siblings. Elizabeth chose the settee opposite Victoria with the view of the sunroom. A slight tilt of her head gave her a sunlit diversion. "What brings you out today?"

"Your mother's house was closing in on me. Someone is always hovering over me; therefore, I end up in my room by myself."

"You picked a beautiful day for a stroll." *Smile. Don't give in to her cloudiness.*

"I didn't walk here. The carriage is waiting outside. I might go to a dress shop or two and admire the fashions that I can't wear."

"It won't be long until you are once again laced up in your finest." The superficial subject covered over the real issue. The baby contributed to some of Victoria's woes, but outside of that, the woman's doubts about George, Charles Town, and married life shadowed her perspective.

Victoria moved quicker than seemed possible. "I don't want this baby." Anger poisoned her words. Elizabeth could almost touch them hanging in the air. "I told George I would leave after the birth. There is nothing here for me. No one wants me here." She glanced at Elizabeth. "What do you think of that idea? Maybe I will leave the child with you. You seem to love the family life so much." Sarcasm and mirth oozed with each word.

Elizabeth's heart skipped some beats as it pounded unevenly. "Surely, you are not serious. You've been promised a nanny and extra help. George will buy you a house. You must make this work." Elizabeth didn't know of anyone who left her child, although the orphanage rang of proof that it happened.

Elizabeth presented another option. "Let me help you. I'll talk to George, to Mother. And you can talk to Reverend Smith too."

Victoria spun around. "I will not talk to a minister. I don't want to hear how this baby is a child of God. No, this child is of a man whom I do not love." She spat her harsh words toward Elizabeth. "I've shocked you. Well, good. Now you won't be surprised when it happens."

Tears pooled in the corners of Elizabeth's eyes, threatening to overflow. *I must be strong and not be a sniffling fool. Victoria might define that weakness as the worst sort.* "I know you will think differently when you hold your baby. You will feel those motherly instincts and change your mind. God has a plan for you and your baby."

"Do you really believe that?" Victoria whispered, calmed for a moment.

"I do. Each of us has a unique purpose. One of which is to love God first. He wants to bring you near. Let Him love you and show you how to live."

A calm quiet permeated the room, adding warmth to Elizabeth's being. *Let her hear You, Lord. Mend her broken and distorted life. Protect the innocent baby. Show her Your purpose and Your will.*

"Thank you for listening. However, you have not changed my mind. Let's talk of something else." Victoria's calmness had been a ruse, a façade. The warmth morphed to a chill that Elizabeth recognized as rejection. Yet, Elizabeth's prayer remained heavenbound.

The coffee tray arrived as if on cue. Awkward conversation ensued between tiny bites.

Victoria flicked invisible crumbs off her skirt. "Every time you and your husband attend a Liberty meeting or boycott British products, you are stepping closer to treason."

Elizabeth's cup tipped, spilling dark liquid on the saucer. Gently, she set it down, preferring to clasp her jittery hands in her lap. Surely the woman could have brought up a more congenial subject. *I won't be baited. She can have this conversation with George.*

Victoria sipped her coffee, grimaced, and replaced her cup. "You should come by the house for a proper cup of tea. My supply is dwindling thanks to your efforts to refuse the shipments."

"I'm willing to sacrifice tea and a few other items to secure freedom, to live a life of equality."

Ellen chose that moment to bring in a bright-eyed Harriet. The squirming baby settled into the crook of Elizabeth's arm.

"That is my cue to leave." Victoria pulled herself up and headed to the front door, leaving Elizabeth no time to follow. "It's been an entertaining hour."

"Remember what I said, Victoria. God has a plan." She bounced her baby on her lap.

"I've already forgotten."

From the window, Elizabeth watched the sad, mixed-up woman enter the enclosed carriage. She sighed, held Harriet closer, and turned from the outside world.

Louis came home at five o'clock, sharing his encounter with George. "It doesn't make any sense," Elizabeth ventured at dinner.

Louis drummed his fingers on the table. "It sounds like Victoria is warning every one of her plans. She has George worried, and it appears you have reason to believe she'll abandon her baby. I can't imagine her following through with it."

"She won't. She couldn't. A mother can't do that to a child just out of spite." Or could she? Would she abandon a baby?

"Let's keep an eye on them. Both seem to be on edge."

"If it did happen, and she left the baby, would you let me care for him or at least help Mother?"

"You know I wouldn't turn a child away, but you have your hands full with Harriet and who knows when another will enter our lives." He reached for her hand and kissed her fingers.

"That's why I don't understand Victoria. I will welcome any children God gives us, and she is willing to reject hers."

Louis sighed, closed his eyes, and rubbed his temples. "Let's just pray that they will be open to God working a miracle in their lives." He sat up straighter and reached for Harriet. "Now tell me about Harriet's antics of the day."

Elizabeth felt selfish because she spent so much time with the wee one. "She smiled and kicked her feet and waved her arms."

He rubbed his fingers across her soft cheeks. "So, no talking or running or thinking too hard about problems."

"Small steps, Louis." Elizabeth giggled. "Your job is to solve our problems. She'll be working on 'Mama' and 'Papa' soon enough. Let's try to make her life peaceful and prosperous."

CHAPTER 8

*E*lizabeth poured coffee early one morning in March. "Do you remember this time last year?"

Louis sat close to the sitting room window. "How could I forget? We were departing for our belated wedding trip to Boston."

"Yes. So much has happened since then. I'm glad we took the trip when we did. I worry about Grandmama. Should she remain in Boston?" Could they even travel safely to Boston now?

"More are staying put in Boston than leaving. Knowing your grandmother, it will have to get a lot worse before she leaves."

Elizabeth shook her head. How would anyone reach her if she refused to leave soon?

"By the way, what have you heard from Mr. Deane lately?" She knew Louis received correspondence from Silas and assumed he glossed over the details except for the general political situation in the colonies.

"I'm glad you mentioned him. I need to answer his most recent correspondence."

"Is he still involved with John and Samuel Adams?" The influential cousins impressed Elizabeth with their grasp of the colonists' agenda. Abigail Adams, John's wife, befriended her last year while acclimating her to the political world through shopping and constant chattering. Elizabeth missed her, but not the friction in the volatile arena. How could Grandmama stand it?

"He does see them occasionally. They'll all be at the upcoming Continental Congress meeting. There's talk of how to involve the French in negotiations. Silas is involved in ongoing correspondence between the parties."

This was more information than he usually discussed. Louis stared into his coffee. Fear and surprise sent heat to Elizabeth's neck and ears. "And he wants your involvement, too, I guess?" She surmised at the direction of Silas' request. Her palms sweated as her pulse raced. "How involved does he want you to be?" She fidgeted with the tablecloth. What had she missed over the past months? What was now surfacing? Could Louis have kept secrets from her? Big secrets? Why?

"That depends on the mission." He looked up, catching her hand before she destroyed the lace. "It could involve a simple act of interpretation of letters or being an official interpreter in France. I don't know yet how I will respond. Without a clear direction of the colonies, I won't commit myself to travel." She pulled her hand from his.

What was he saying? Secret missions? Possible travel? And who was behind this? Probably Christopher and Silas.

He stood and stared out the window, hands stuffed in his pockets, shoulders slumped.

What weight did he carry that caused his faraway look? Could he really be called away to perform dangerous deeds? Dampness seeped from her eyes. If there was a war, would Louis be part of the secret correspondence and be drawn into webs of intrigue?

Of course, he had kept this from her, not because he didn't trust her, but in order to protect her. How could she be angry when he acted in love? She walked to his side, placed her hand on his arm, and sought his eyes, bringing him back to face her. To face the truth.

"Why are you so concerned? Tell me the truth."

He turned and took both of her hands. His furrowed brow and release of pent up breath expressed his concern and his relief. Relief that he had now involved her fully? "Because this conflict might take me away from you for a time. And anything like that makes me hesitate and consider the sacrifice."

"Louis, I know you will do all you can to take care of us. I trust your decisions. Please don't leave me out of this. You know we do have someone else to turn to beyond the government and men."

He kissed her and held her tightly. "I know. Let's leave it in God's hands." For now, she had his presence and his protection. She breathed him in and didn't want to let the essence of him out, not now or ever. She'd rather share in his work and mission than live a life of secrets. She realized he couldn't tell her everything, but she could pray for an additional amount of protection over Louis.

He placed his hands on her shoulders and pressed his forehead against hers. "I'll answer Silas's letter now and go to work."

"And I will prepare for Raymond's lesson." She spun out of his arms, spurred on by his kiss and commitment.

Louis walked to the library and turned around toward Elizabeth. "Thank you for understanding my hesitation in involving you."

She sighed. Hints of scrimmages on the horizon took a distant position as she faced her day.

"Did you hear the news, Mrs. Elizabeth?" Raymond asked, fifteen minutes late for his English lesson.

"No. Hear what?" Curiosity coursed through her. His rapid

French was a sign that the news held excitement or at least something out of the ordinary.

"I'll tell you in French, if you don't mind. I won't be able to control my English." That posed a problem, for Elizabeth had to flip in her mind to French.

"Go ahead. I'll try to stay up."

"I was down at the docks waiting to unload a ship. A family from South Carolina returning from England requested to land their furniture and horses. Supposedly, all the items were personally owned by the man."

"I can see where this is going," she interjected. Elbows on the table, chin poised on her hands, she waited for the conclusion.

"At first the Committee of Safety decided after hours of debate to allow him to bring the goods ashore. But then, today," he paused and took a deep breath, "a mob appeared. Can you guess, Mrs. Elizabeth, who was leading the group?"

No idea, but she made circles with her hands and encouraged him to continue.

"Mr. Gadsden appeared at dockside. I had no idea what he would do. But he was the spokesperson. He threatened to shoot the horses if they were landed."

"Are you serious?" She believed Christopher was bold, but to shoot innocent horses? How far would he go?

"Yes. So now the Committee is meeting to make a decision. Nothing is being unloaded."

Told from the eyewitness account of an excited youth added elements of drama callous adults ignored. Raymond calmed down. She imagined the scene playing out on the docks and in the town. Louis would probably know more, perhaps a different perspective. Now, how was she to get Raymond in the mood to speak English. She sighed and buckled down for the task.

An hour later, after a mini lesson in English, Elizabeth followed Raymond out of their make-shift classroom and met Tom in the foyer.

"How long have you been here?" Elizabeth noted the time on the mantle clock. "You're home early."

"Yes, ma'am. Mr. Louis let me off early, and I figured Raymond and I could check out the progress on the docks."

"I'll have to check with Mrs. Jeannette first," Raymond stated.

"And you have told your mother, Tom?" He nodded. Elizabeth crossed her arms, raised her brows while enjoying the enthusiasm of the boys' plans. Did they see beyond the drama of the day's event as one of many scenes in a bigger play? Probably not. It was instant entertainment, free for the viewing.

"Be sure to stay on the sidelines, out of trouble." Mother of neither, she hoped her words carried a little weight.

"We will. Goodbye." She smiled at their rapid departure. She imagined the youth running to the docks, taking all the shortcuts.

A quarter of an hour passed. Elizabeth checked on Harriet, sleeping in her bassinet in the parlor, and then she sat at the piano. A soft bright melody trickled from her fingertips. Soothing to the baby, she hoped, and a balm to her own weary spirit. A minute of a minuet to cover her concern about Victoria, another for the family coming home with the possibility of losing their possessions, another for Raymond and Tom, and one for Christopher.

Before long, her melody was a prayer, a reminder of a Higher Power.

"Excuse me, Elizabeth? A messenger just left this note from Mr. Louis." Ellen placed the missive on the piano bench.

"Thank you." Elizabeth's hand shook a bit.

Ellen waited. "I hope all is fine."

"Well, he won't be home for dinner. The Committee of Safety is holding an open forum at the Exchange Building. He apologizes and asks that you leave him a plate on the warmer." She folded the letter and turned to Ellen.

The woman accepted the information yet voiced her fear. "Do

you suppose everything will be fine? I worry about my Tom. He's so young and impressionable."

They'd had this conversation before with Louis present. Since Tom's father died, Ellen feared the lack of a father would hinder Tom from making wise decisions. She had asked Louis to lend as much advice as possible, to fill the gap even a little bit.

"I would love to guarantee that a peaceful outcome is ahead. But I can't." Elizabeth took Ellen's shaky hand. "But I do believe this little incident tonight is not a danger for Tom or Raymond. They are curious and letting them go takes the edge off of wanting to do something more aggressive one day. I'm glad that Tom is honest enough to ask permission. And now, it sounds like Louis is right there with him." Tapping her lips with a finger, Elizabeth envied Tom and Raymond. Why couldn't she be in the midst of all the talk?

Right in the middle of a heated debate, Louis listened from the center of the crowded hall. Samuel stood on his left and Henry to his right. Focused on the debate, they exchanged no words.

Louis saw Raymond and Tom against the right-side wall among other youth. He smiled. Why shouldn't they be here? Each decision made by their elders molded their innocent future.

The General Committee members present posed a question. "Why do you think the South Carolina family should not have permission to unload their possessions that they had transported to England and now back again?"

"I'll answer that one," Christopher provided. The confidence exhibited by his friend continued to enthrall Louis. "The general population is too poor to own horses and furniture to transport back and forth between Charles Town and England. How can we allow this family as the exception to the established rule of no unloading of items from England, even if they were previously purchased from our colony? We must be firm and stand on our policy." He slammed his fist on the podium.

Silence ensued, then heads leaned together across the table of board members. Whispers in the audience created a suspenseful air. Louis gave in to the pressure and shared in the contagious ramble.

Henry, Samuel, and Louis formed a circle, one of many think pots. "He has a point," Henry ventured first. "If our committee's stand is no cargo from Britain, then this should apply in this case."

"But how long will it last?" Samuel asked.

Louis glanced around at the similar conferences all over the floor. "As long as Parliament proceeds with its unfair demands. From a practical side, I hate to see good furniture and fine horses sent away. I do feel remorse for the family, too. It's a lesson to all of us. When Lieutenant Governor Bull hears of this, he will have more harsh words to pass on," Louis said.

His wandering eyes meandered to the space where Raymond and Tom had been earlier. No longer one group of youth, but two distinct ones. Had they drawn battle lines?

He recognized the stance of defensive boys—hands on hips, piercing stares, words spoken with tight shut lips. In reality, they followed the example of the citizens in the hall. Divided by the upcoming decision, to allow the unloading or to reverse the decision, factions formed complete with finger pointing and raised voices.

"They better come to a decision soon before a riot breaks out," Louis voiced.

A gavel caught the attention of the crowd. A vote had been taken. Gadsden's motion carried thirty-five to thirty-four. "Neither the furniture nor the horses will be allowed reentry."

Henry edged his way to the backdoor. "The *Gazette* will have news for days about this. It might even make the Philadelphia and Boston news in time."

"If Mr. Timothy has his way, Gadsden will be sung as a hero of high degree." Past reports proved to Louis that Timothy was a follower of the radical man. It made for spirited reading. The editor never failed to offer the other views as well. But the Sons of Liberty always emerged victorious. And tonight, they were.

Although the adults exited in peace, the youth rallied behind the Exchange, just out of sight but not out of hearing. Louis turned his ears toward the heated words. The dividing line between the young men was not Loyalists and Partisans. Louis noticed a new distinction, wealthy and poor. The vote tonight seemed to ignite the wealthy class since they were the ones denied their future purchases and possessions.

Louis elbowed Henry when he spotted the two. "Let's get our boys and go home. The law can handle the possible riot."

In a few brief strides, Louis grabbed Tom, and Henry secured Raymond. "You'll thank us later," Louis explained. He didn't release his hold until Tradd Street. Henry did the same.

Both boys shook their arms and shrugged their shoulders at their freedom from their captors.

"We weren't going to do anything, Mr. Louis, I promise," Tom said.

"Maybe not, but your friends, yes some were your friends, had other ideas. I recognized the signs." Louis sought support from his uncle. "The last thing we want is to have to explain your beaten bodies and bloody noses to your mother and Aunt Jeannette."

The boys hung their heads. It always worked, putting the fear of the women in the formula.

"I'm sorry, Mr. Henry. I guess I wasn't thinking about the outcome," Raymond stated.

Henry placed his big fatherly hand on his ward's shoulder. "No harm done, Son. Just one of many lessons you have to learn."

"I'm sorry too." Tom scuffed his boots on the gravel. "I should have seen the potential danger. After all, I am older."

Louis accepted the humility of the two as a positive step. "If only age were the key to good decisions. As mature men, we can't anticipate all the consequences of our actions. But we do try to avoid the bad ones that we can."

Drama diverted, all four pledged not to mention the last event behind the Exchange to the women. They would be entertained enough with the rest of the evening's details.

Louis and Tom ate their leftover dinner in record time, and only then did they enlighten Elizabeth and Ellen.

Tom spurted out his rendition with unbridled enthusiasm. "You should have heard Mr. Gadsden. He made his point so clearly. He was able to reverse the previous vote. It was exciting."

Louis wiped his hands on his cloth and reached for Elizabeth's hand on the table. "Exciting to some. But not to the family who just lost a lot of their possessions."

Elizabeth looked off, not meeting his eyes. "I'm glad to see you have some sympathy left for the people involved." She brought the incidents to a human level.

If he wasn't already deeply involved with the congress, Louis could concentrate more on the individual. "And that's the hard part of any of this. The votes and decisions will affect each of us in some way." Louis just hoped he ended up on the side of justice, and that God would show him what to do. So far nothing was as clear cut as he desired.

The next morning confirmed the reality of the night's ultimatum. Even through the heaviness of the news relayed hours earlier, Elizabeth slept in the peace of her husband's arms.

She glided into the morning room, stood behind Louis, and draped her arms around his neck. He set his coffee down but not the morning *Gazette*. She glanced at the headlines. "Riot Averted Decision Reversed."

"Mr. Timothy wasted no time." She kissed the top of his head and took her usual place at the small table, room enough for two, a pot of coffee, and a platter of eggs, rolls, and sausage.

Plate filled and steamy coffee poured, Elizabeth settled into digesting the printed words. "Give it to me, word for word, Louis." Elizabeth squirmed, anticipating the entertaining views the editor always printed.

Louis shook the paper to relieve the creases. "All right. Here is the rendition according to our Timothy: 'Gadsden and his followers rendered another victory indicating increasing power. This man and many other Charles Town citizens are not embarrassed to be thorns in the sides of the royal officials.'" Louis looked up. "I can imagine Christopher thinking of that as a compliment. If he causes enough discomfort, Britain will change."

"I'm sincerely glad he is on our side."

"Me too." Louis folded the paper and continued. "Lieutenant Governor Bull responded that 'authority and reason unsupported by real Power are too weak to stop the torrent of popular prejudices. I hope that the men of property who suffered the most from the association will ultimately be able to break the many-headed power of the people, who have discovered their own strength and importance.'"

Elizabeth traced the intricate pattern on the white lace tablecloth with her index finger, circling the vivid words in her mind. "I like that description 'many-headed power of the people.' The Lieutenant Governor sounds worried." Worried about the strength of the people in support of a righteous cause? *He should be.*

Louis folded the paper in half, placed it behind the coffee pot, and focused on Elizabeth. "I've heard more emphasis from radical Sons of Liberty and royal officers to look to their arms. It makes me wonder if Loyalists know of our arms or is it just a threat for the colonists to behave and obey? If they really knew, the words 'strength' and 'importance' would be a true interpretation of our power."

"Do you think any Loyalist would be scared of me now?" Elizabeth tried to lighten the subject.

He laughed. "You with a pistol is a real threat."

"I don't know how to take that." She smirked. "I would give the enemy an element of suspense. He wouldn't know to protect his heart or his leg."

"Unlike Ellen, who would not miss." Both chuckled at the image.

Ellen entered the room. "I heard that. Hopefully, I'll never be in that position." She grimaced at them and cleared the table.

"That would be the best scenario," Louis said. "By the way, you are becoming a professional at making coffee."

"Thank you, Mr. Louis. I still don't like the taste."

"It's not so bad with sugar and cream," Louis confirmed.

He relaxed, turned his body in the chair toward Elizabeth, and propped his chin on his hand. "What are your plans today?"

"I thought I would go to see Victoria." She glanced at his one raised brow. "Does that surprise you?"

"A bit. It would seem her demeanor would be getting worse as her time approaches. Will you take Harriet?"

Harriet would love being the center of attention. That was her job, wasn't it? "Of course. I can use her as my escape. Anyway, Mother always enjoys any surprise visits with the baby."

Louis half-smiled as if he didn't really hear her. His wrinkled forehead confirmed her doubts. "I have been praying for Victoria and George. Their marriage just isn't what it should be."

"Hmmm. It never had the foundation of ours. Don't stop your praying. The difficult times have not even begun."

Thank you, Father, for my faithful husband. What if they did not have that firm commitment?

He squinted his eyes and drew in a deep breath. "I'm curious. Would you have married me if I hadn't become a Christian?"

She hesitated and placed her elbows on the table. "I don't know. I'm glad that decision was taken away from me. So much about you captivated me. I was probably doomed from the beginning."

"Doomed?"

She paused and giggled. "Yes, doomed to a life of drowning in your love and protection."

He laced his fingers with hers. "Now you're being silly."

With tilted head, she brought them full circle. "Back to the original subject. Anything on your agenda today?" His day never failed to intrigue her with the random people he served in business and the politics discussed.

"I must talk to Christopher. He leaves in a month or so for Philadelphia. The Congress might keep him for months. I'll need to know what to do from here about shipments over the summer."

Ellen presented a squirming, fussy Harriet in the middle of the dialogue. "Well, it looks like I have my first obligation right here." Elizabeth raised her hands for her bundle. The whimpering transformed into a fit of glee.

"I agree with her. If only I could spend my day with you." Of course, he wouldn't include visiting Victoria as part of the agreement.

Louis kissed each on the cheeks and added a final one to Elizabeth's lips.

"Well, then we might just have to drop by the store later. I will probably need another one of your kisses."

CHAPTER 9

*S*eated by Samuel in Christopher's office, Louis observed Christopher pacing while ranting about the latest news. "All I'm saying is that we need to be extra careful with the protection of the stores of goods we have."

Louis received the advice with surprise. "What has happened?" Louis looked from one friend to the other. "Both of you know something I don't. Out with it, please."

Christopher stopped and crossed his arms. "Here is the basic concern. William Drayton and other citizens have brought to the forefront the possibility that the government is storing greater than normal amounts of powder and guns in magazines in all the colonies. Word from other leaders suggests that colonists should take control of the stocks to keep it out of the king's men's control." The man staged the drama, adding a sweep of his finger across his brow finally landing under his nose across his lips.

Louis remained seated, intrigued by the news.

"And to what extent would the colonies go to control the stores?" As usual, Samuel's participation alternated from agreeing to restating the information in layman's terms.

"Seizure of arms." Christopher's suggestion hung in the air, heavy with truth.

Louis dropped his stare and stood. "While others seize the magazine, what do we do? I can't believe you are suggesting that Samuel and I steal from the governor." He braced himself on his arms on the desk and digested his friend's explanation.

Christopher put his hands in his pockets and joined Louis on the other side of the desk. "Not exactly. But perhaps in some way. Right now, you need to protect your own stores. I'm just warning you about a possible scenario."

Samuel moved to the door and confirmed his desire to change the direction of the morning. "Let's put the subject aside and go to the café for now."

"Good idea." Louis paused. "Thank you, Christopher, for including me in the plans." Although Louis calculated there were missing elements.

They secured a table in the back of a crowded room. Christopher disappeared into a web of local well-doers exhibiting an interest in the leaders' take on various subjects. Louis and Samuel used the time to order, sit back, and avoid the locals that came out.

Samuel leaned on his elbows placed on the table. "I need to ask a personal question if you don't mind, Louis."

"I'll answer if I can. What is it?" Louis conjured up a possible subject—either Sarah or work, maybe religion.

"It's Sarah. She seems so preoccupied about one thing."

Louis smiled at the perplexed new husband. "I think I know what that is."

Samuel's tall torso turned toward Louis. "How could you?"

"I am married too. Let me guess, Sarah wants a baby."

"Yes." Was he shocked that he wasn't the only husband possessed of a longing mother-to-be?

"How long has it been? Four months?" Louis shook his head in remembrance of the first months of his marriage. Some couples go years without a sign of a baby.

"You're not going to tell me to relax, are you? I want to make her happy and I think she is, with me. But she wants more. I could be content just to have her alone with me forever."

Louis remembered saying and believing the same. "I thought that too. But once you hold that baby, your heart will expand for the new life."

"So, what is your advice, Mr. Experienced Husband and Father?"

"Be patient. If it is supposed to happen, it will. And pray. God has a plan for the two of you."

"Thank you." Samuel gulped his water. "I think she has discussed this with Elizabeth already."

"I know she has. They talk a lot. And Sarah loves Harriet. She'll make a wonderful mother one day. And you a good father, faithful and loyal."

At times Louis fretted over his role. Was he all he needed to be for his family? Hopefully, he had a few years to perfect his qualities. If war didn't relieve him of years on earth, he'd continue to strive to improve. But what if war took away all his finances? Would he be able to find self-worth in poverty? He had an inkling that he'd experience a portion of life with meager means soon, unless the tide veered to another route.

Sarah burst through the kitchen door. "Elizabeth? Where are you?" Elizabeth and Ellen both stopped kneading their dough. Dusted with flour and hands sticky and gooey, Elizabeth dropped her jaw.

"You found me. What is the problem? You'll wake the baby with any more bouncing and jumping."

Sarah flushed from jostling up and down, halted before colliding with the flour-laden table. "I couldn't wait or send a message."

Lifting her skirt and billowing it out a bit released a screen of flour. "Do you have time for me to clean up or change?"

"No. I'll tell you and Ellen right here, right now." Sarah swayed and twisted her body as if to music.

The two shrugged at the same time, hands free from the mass of dough resting on the table.

"Should we sit, Mrs. Sarah?" Ellen ventured.

"You might want to." Ellen took her cue, while Elizabeth advanced toward her friend. She couldn't shake Sarah's shoulders to induce a quick response with floured hands, so she wiped her hands on her apron and waited.

Sarah posed as if on stage, controlled for a moment, then let loose a high-pitched squeal. "I'm going to have a baby."

Elizabeth reached for her. They twirled around and opened their circle to Ellen.

"A baby. I told you it would happen." The dance slowed, and a few tears flowed.

"I know, you did."

"Does Samuel know?"

"Not yet. Mother and I are just putting the pieces together. I had to tell someone. I'm planning a big dinner tonight to tell him."

"And you will slow down at school? Those girls can be a handful without adding your condition." Ellen asked a question that concentrated on the practical not the romantic.

"Yes. If I feel I can't do it, I'll talk to Mrs. Reynolds."

"Good." The older woman commenced with the bread-making, taking over Elizabeth's share of the chore.

Apron discarded, hands cleaned, Elizabeth pushed the baby carriage into the house and followed Sarah to the parlor.

"I need some advice, Elizabeth. I think I might have been a little, no maybe a lot, of a nuisance about this with Samuel. I talked all the time about a baby. I don't want him to think I am unhappy. I'm not."

Elizabeth checked on Harriet who was still sleeping, oblivious to her surroundings. "I think he knows you love him. But now you must show him even more. Nothing can replace your relationship with your husband. Louis and I work at finding a good balance between our life as a couple and as a family. You'll find that."

Sarah pasted a frown on her face then giggled. "Sam's so shy when it comes to talking about all of this. It took him a while to adjust to the thought of marriage, then to marriage itself, and now a baby. Poor Samuel."

Elizabeth remembered the same feelings about Louis. So many years as a single man. "Samuel had thirty years alone. Now he must share his life with you. He'll need time to grow into his role."

Sarah picked a daisy from the vase and placed it in her hair. She smiled and posed, a picture of happiness. At that moment, Elizabeth's prayer changed for her best friend. *Thank you, Father. Now, help Sarah have a healthy baby.*

"Do you want to stay for tea?" Elizabeth tried to coax Sarah to sit and remain in one place, possibly containing her energy and bouncing.

"No, I have to go and help prepare the evening meal. I want everything to be perfect."

"Remember that Samuel won't care about it being perfect. He cares about you."

Sarah stooped down and placed a kiss on Elizabeth's cheek. "You are such a dear friend. You always make me feel like I can just be myself. And you are right, he does like me, faults and all."

"Not many of those." Elizabeth spoke the truth about the quiet, angelic lady in front of her.

Dinner at the Lestarjettes centered on the good news of the Evans. "After my conversation and advice to Samuel today, I'm relieved to know he doesn't have to worry about that anymore."

"I do have one question. If I could not have had children, would you have been happy with me, Louis?"

"You have always been enough. What a gift it would be to face endless days with only you. God just chose to give us Harriet, but in a few years, she will be gone, and I'll still have you."

Her heart fluttered with the freedom to love Louis and Harriet for however many years God gave her. "I'm so glad. I feel the same way. So, if we have only little Harriet, you will be content?"

Louis bent over the table to kiss her. "Yes, my dear. You, Harriet, and I would be fine. Now, let's just enjoy our meal with the two of us, alone."

Anne dropped by once a week usually on Thursday morning. "Please bring the boys when you can?" Elizabeth had encouraged each time.

"They have their tutor most mornings, so it is a perfect get-away for Charlotte and me." Elizabeth understood. The four girls, old and young, had shared tea and stories for uninterrupted two-hour periods.

Adding fresh flowers to a vase in the foyer, Elizabeth called to Amy in the breakfast room. "Send Anne to the sunroom when she arrives please, Amy. The morning sun will cheer us all."

Amy peeped around the door facing. "Yes, ma'am."

Moments later with babe in arms, Anne joined the lady Lestarjettes.

"Good morning, Anne." Elizabeth hugged her and took the eleven-month-old in her arms. "How do you carry her? Compared to Harriet, she weighs a lot."

"You get used to it. She'll be walking soon and won't like to be toted around. Then, our visits won't be so calm and peaceful."

Elizabeth bounced her niece on her knees, then tilted her over to view the sleeping baby. "She'll wake up in a minute, Charlotte, then you can play with her."

Charlotte reached her chubby hand out to grab the edge of the bassinet. "Not so fast, little one. Let's play with the blocks instead."

Plopped down in the middle of the rug, Charlotte had access to multiple diversions.

Anne basked in the sunlight like Elizabeth intended for her. "Have you had word from Robert?"

"Yes." Her chin angled toward the ceiling, eyes closed. "All is fine. He reached the first port in Jamaica last week. He won't turn around for home until the end of April."

"Will he make it in time for Charlotte's first birthday?"

Anne looked at Charlotte who was talking to the stuffed animals surrounding her. "That's the plan, but I don't know. He always tries for the boys' birthdays too. It's hard to judge the length of his voyage."

"Well, we will have a nice party anyway, and he will be the bonus." *Wouldn't it be hard if Louis had to travel often? Would that be a part of their future?* "Have you seen Victoria lately?" Anne asked.

Elizabeth shook her head. "Have you?"

Anne opened her eyes and adjusted her body toward Charlotte. "No. She won't let anyone see her but Mother."

At least Anne received the same treatment as Elizabeth. *Though I don't enjoy Victoria's company, I don't want her to avoid me.* "Mother says she stays in her room. A few weeks ago, she looked ready to explode."

"I think it's any day now."

Pushing herself up from the wicker chair, Elizabeth walked to the window, viewing the birds splashing in the fountain. "I'm not worried about her delivery, but what she will do afterwards?"

Anne wrinkled her brow. "What do you mean? Surely she is not still saying crazy things about taking the baby away."

"I just don't trust her, neither does George. He's trying to help her, yet I'm afraid she continues to reject his efforts. It might be too late for his pleasant talk."

Ellen delivered the tea tray, and Amy raced in with a letter. "A messenger from Mrs. Elliott's just arrived, and he's waiting your answer." The young girl placed it on the table.

"It's very unlike Mother to want a response," Anne said.

Elizabeth unfolded the note and read out loud.

Elizabeth,

Come as soon as you can. Victoria is in labor. I've sent for the doctor. I need your help.

Yours,

Mother

Elizabeth remembered how panicky their mother became about births. *Now we have to add Victoria to the drama.* "Oh, my. That sounds like an unpleasant place to be. But I guess we must go." Anne nodded. There was no way out of this family gathering.

Elizabeth stood and peeped at Harriet twitching in her sleep. "Ellen, could you and Amy look after the girls for a few hours? We'll go see what's needed and return later." Elizabeth didn't know what help they could be, but if her mother needed her, she would go.

Ellen winked at her daughter. "Amy and I would love to take care of the babies. Amy enjoys every chance she gets, right?"

"Yes, ma'am." The young girl sat down on the floor with Charlotte and rocked the cradle with one hand.

The sisters walked at a brisk pace toward the ominous happenings at the Elliott house. For a brief second, they stared at the knocker. "Breathe and stay calm." Elizabeth hoped to encourage them both.

The butler took their shawls and gloves, covered his ears at a piercing scream, and disappeared into a back room.

"I don't blame him," Anne whispered.

"Do we dare go upstairs?" Elizabeth inched her way to the bannister and looked up. "If only Mother would meet us down here."

Anne mounted the stairs. "Oh, come on. We've both been a

patient before. It's not as if Victoria can jump out of bed and attack us."

Elizabeth wasn't so sure. She raced to catch up.

Mother poked her head out the door as they rounded the landing. "I'm so glad you are here." She embraced her daughters.

"What can we do?" Both asked at once.

Mother wiped her brow. "Talk her out of the silly notion to give the baby away. It's all nonsense."

"I'll try," Elizabeth said. "But if she wouldn't listen before, she's not going to in the middle of this pain."

Her mother rambled on, directing people in her wake. "Please do what you can. Anne, come help me get the items needed for the baby. I wish George were here. I sent word."

Elizabeth stiffened at Victoria's door and breathed a prayer. "Father give me the words to say and the right spirit to deliver them. Protect Victoria and this baby. Amen."

Fortified, she opened the door.

The normal, composed woman didn't exist in the four-poster bed. Her replacement raged with fear and anger.

Victoria gritted her teeth. "I know why you are here, Elizabeth. You want to see me at my worst. And then you want to coerce me into loving my baby like a proper mother." A pain gripped her sputtering words.

Elizabeth hesitated to say anything, but she wanted to try to ease some of Victoria's misgivings. The contraction died, and Elizabeth's conviction to speak returned.

"You are going to be fine. The doctor said before that everything is normal. I hope when you see your baby, you will want to keep him. Please give him and us a chance to make you happy. I still believe God has a purpose for this new life."

Victoria stared at Elizabeth or perhaps through her. For mere seconds, she appeared to concentrate on the words.

In minutes, the doctor and midwife motioned Elizabeth aside. All was in place to receive the new life.

Elizabeth backed out of the room, not convinced that Victoria had truly understood her plea. *I am a witness for Him and for this new baby, my own flesh and blood. This is in Your hands.*

꙰

Typical for early April, Louis' day began and ended with cataloging new inventory, leaving the majority of the manual labor for Tom.

Louis leaned against the wall, admiring Tom's strength. "I don't know what we'd do without you. Between this store and the shipyard, I couldn't face all the unloading and carting." The lad seemed to grow right before his eyes. Wasn't he a straggly boy just yesterday?

"I'm glad I can help. I don't know if I ever thanked you for giving me this job and giving my family a home." Tom was now eighteen, tall and strong. If he grew into his height, this young man would be a solid tower of muscle and power.

Louis patted Tom's shoulder, wanting to encourage the man to feel a part of the business and future of the store. "God knew what we needed, and he sent you to us. I thank you for staying around." Would Tom stay close and live in Charles Town? He was hitting the age when young men wanted to seek adventure and wander a bit.

Tom shuffled from foot to foot. "Mr. Louis, I do have something to discuss, and I hope it won't make you think less of me."

Louis sat on a barrel of apples and crossed his arms. "I'm sure it won't. Go ahead." At these moments, Louis never felt worthy to be the father figure for Tom. But he would do his best.

"I don't know if you've heard or not, but there is a military unit being organized here in Charles Town that supports the cause of the partisans." Louis nodded. Tom stopped his fidgeting and continued with renewed confidence expressed in his rigid stance. "Well, sir, on my afternoons off I've been participating, unofficially, of course."

Louis' curiosity rose. "What do you mean by participating?" How did he miss Tom's involvement?

The youth stood straight almost at attention. "I go through the marching drills and the preparation of arms. Captain Shanks is in charge of us."

Louis corralled his tone, avoiding any condemning words. "I have lots of questions. How many men are training? And where does this take place?" His list of questions grew, but Louis waited for a few details to fill in the blanks. *Patience.*

"Right now, it is only about thirty of us. I go once a week, but others go more often. We meet about a quarter of a mile outside of town in an open field owned by Captain Shanks."

"Is this the same man who fought in the French Indian War and received medals of bravery?" Louis pieced the trails of tidbits. He knew from former Sons of Liberty meetings that something like this was afoot. He didn't expect it in his household at present.

Tom laughed. "The same. He tells colorful stories about that experience." How could he laugh about war stories? Did he not see past the glamor of fighting to the seriousness of the result?

"Does your mother know about this?" Louis knew the answer, realizing Tom's first step had been with him, right now.

"No. It only involves about two hours of my time a week. It's not serious yet." He stressed the last word. Louis considered the fact that Shanks had a bunch of green youth, playacting as soldiers. He imagined the game changing in the future. Toy soldiers replaced by real ones. And Tom would be one of them.

"Yet? And when do you expect it to get serious, Tom?"

"When the Sons of Liberty hear the news from Parliament about accepting or rejecting the Continental Congress proposals." Tom had more of a plan than Louis.

There was a meeting scheduled for next week at Christopher's house. Everything Tom said held the ring of Gadsden behind it.

Leave it to him to form troops ahead of time. Where would Louis fit into the man's plans? A soldier? A runner?

"And if Parliament rejects the terms?" Louis couldn't believe he was having this discussion with an eighteen-year-old.

Tom squared his shoulders and smiled. "Then we double our efforts and prepare to fight. Captain Shanks says there are many others, older men about your age…"

Louis half-smiled at the reference. "Thanks for the emphasis."

"You're not old, just older than I am. Anyway, other men like you have committed to fight."

"And if it comes to that, I will too." Louis relinquished his seat and stood before Tom. "I'm proud of you, Son. Of your sincere love for this colony and for a better way of life. But be careful and don't be too eager."

Tom lifted a bag of potatoes to carry to the front. "Believe me I'm not ready to leave this job or my family, but I would. It's the right thing to do."

"Keep me posted, please. I'll keep quiet around your mother and Elizabeth, for now. I'm sure you will tell them when the time is right." Secrets appeared to be piling up. He still had his correspondence with Silas Deane and his commitment to the safety committee to share with Elizabeth. The farther he let the secrets go, the harder it would be to explain.

"Thank you, sir."

Tom's revelation posed some complications for the future for the mercantile and the house chores. But more than that, it sounded like young men all over town were willing to join a regiment with little encouragement.

Aunt Jeannette poked her head in the storeroom. "Elizabeth sent a message. Victoria is in labor. She'll be home when she can." Jeannette rolled her eyes. He felt the same, for even Victoria's name brought tension. He'd rather unload three ships than be in that house right now.

At the noon meal, Louis faced an empty table. The house

wasn't quiet though. Amy entertained Charlotte and Harriet upstairs, laughter and singing seeping through the floorboards. The children made his heart sing, even following Tom's news. And Victoria was bringing another infant into their lives. If only that situation could be solved along with the looming political battle.

Ellen entered. "A message, Mr. Louis."

"Thank you, Ellen."

"Is it good news, sir?" She waited by his side.

"Let's see." He glanced before reading the message out loud. "To the household: Victoria is fine and has a healthy crying girl named Christine. I'll be home soon. Elizabeth."

Ellen clapped her hands. "Another girl. We'll have to keep the boys away in a few years."

Louis chuckled. "Now that's a contemplation worse than war." He placed the note on the table. Now the colony had to be protected in order for there to be any boys around.

A Sunday afternoon stroll with Louis and Harriet buoyed Elizabeth's resolve and confidence for the next week. A bit of sanity to her life.

Louis patted her hand looped through his arm. "Is Victoria any better today?"

"No, not according to Mother. She won't even hold the baby." She shuddered at the image of a heartless mother. "I'm afraid she is holding firm to her earlier premise."

"And George?"

"He's been over to the house only once to see them. Victoria's open hostility sends him running." Elizabeth pulled on his sleeve and halted. "What will happen, Louis?"

"For one thing, the child will be loved by her grandmother and aunts as well as her male relatives. I'm still praying that Victoria will come around to caring for Christine."

Elizabeth resumed her steps, turned to the ocean, and let the breeze sweep through her. A nagging fear hovered close. What if Victoria did something foolish? Run away with the baby? Harm herself or, heaven forbid, her child? The wind tried to carry her thoughts out to sea, but Elizabeth held on to them. Until they were resolved, the sea couldn't have them.

She rolled her shoulders back refusing defeat. "I can't change Victoria, so I will have to wait patiently for an answer. God can work a miracle and bring Victoria near to Him. Everything I have tried doesn't work."

Louis draped his arm around her shoulders. "And knowing that God is in control should give you comfort. You're a wonderful friend, mother, and wife. Now you are called to be an encouraging sister-in-law and aunt. Big roles to fill." Her tottering confidence needed Louis' boost.

They followed the path through the park. People rushed past them to a grove of oak trees. Elizabeth peered through the trees at a gathering of citizens around a speaker standing on a barrel.

Mr. Timothy stood beside the turned over barrel and held out a large parchment to Christopher. The newspaper editor seemed impatient to pass on the written news.

"Over here, out of the way and in the shade." Louis directed. The carriage settled, Elizabeth noticed Harriet's blue eyes had caught the rustle of the trees, entertaining her.

"Ladies and gentlemen," Christopher began. "I have some very important news discussed with me by Mr. Timothy half an hour ago. We have finally heard from Parliament." The crowd murmured and focused on the message. Elizabeth sought Louis' intent gaze. He squeezed her hand before he turned back to the platform.

Christopher cleared his throat. "In October of last year, 1774, we, the Continental Congress, sent a petition to Parliament requesting a reversal of the Tea Act. Six months later we receive this response: Parliament has ignored the petition and granted the King's request for additional troops to enforce the laws of the empire in America."

Gasps of disbelief and proclamations of disgust mingled with "Huzzah for the king" as Partisans and Loyalists inhaled the news in different ways.

Negative words wouldn't stop Christopher. Elizabeth could see that they inspired him. "In my opinion, citizens of South Carolina, we are approaching a state of war. Under the direction of the Provincial Congress of South Carolina troops will be organized and drilled in preparation of defense if needed." Christopher Gadsden stepped down into the protective care of loyal Sons of Liberty.

Elizabeth wanted Louis to reject or explain away that notion. "A state of war. That sounds so official. Is he saying, there will be war?" He bowed his head and closed his eyes. "War is inevitable, I think. We'll know more after the next Continental Congress meeting convening next month." Matter of fact. Little emotion. Acceptance. She surmised Louis knew more than he shared, possibly more than he wanted to know.

"Oh." Elizabeth lifted a squirming baby out of her carriage and held her close to her heart. War meant death and uncertainty, upheaval and broken dreams.

The Daughters of Liberty had prepared her for the possibility. Louis had instructed her in defense. And God had surrounded her with love and hope. Now, it was up to her to follow His direction as independence pressed her desire to the forefront. No longer a vague idea, but a prominent reality. Louis' protective wall had to let her in, if she were to contribute to the cause in an educated manner.

CHAPTER 10

*D*uring April, Elizabeth helped Sarah at the boarding school with a few of her classes in the mornings. "I don't mind." She reiterated to her friend. "Harriet takes a long nap, and Ellen can help."

"I just don't know when I will feel sick. Samuel wants me to quit, but I couldn't do that to the girls. You can't even tell I'm going to have a baby."

"The girls know, although they won't say anything. Don't you see them giggling down the hall?" Elizabeth peeked around her friend, capturing a few heads in close whispers.

"I know. By summer it will be obvious."

"What do you need me to do today? I'll be your arms and legs. You can just sit here and teach from your desk." Elizabeth guided her friend to her throne for the morning. Their roles had reversed since last summer when Elizabeth had the same tiredness and lack of energy.

Sarah shuffled through some papers. "What do you think of the new troops in town?"

Not quite an uplifting subject. "According to George, the

barracks are almost full. He might have to be stationed in Philadelphia."

"How can he leave his wife and new baby?" Sarah stared at her lap. Elizabeth had asked the same question over and over, but only once to George. He told her to let him handle his own life. That seemed to be the problem. He fought to remain the one in charge, not God. And George continued to make a mess of it. At twenty years old, he carried a heavy weight that he wasn't managing properly.

"He blames it on his occupation. Anyway, he knows Mother will take care of Victoria and Christine."

Sarah placed her hand on her belly, not yet evidence of a new life. "I look forward to seeing how Samuel reacts to our baby."

"You don't have to worry about him. I've learned from personal experience that a long-time bachelor makes a good father and husband."

Ten girls entered the room with the usual fanfare, whispers of gossip, and giggles behind cupped hands. Elizabeth passed out the books and notebooks. She knew all the girls from her theory and music classes.

Sarah gained control of the class from her stationary position. "Turn to page one hundred and fifty where we'll begin reading 'Twelfth Night' by William Shakespeare."

Elizabeth's meek and docile friend had morphed into a qualified and respected woman in society and the classroom. With a little coaxing, she'd blossomed into a confident person. If only Elizabeth could influence Victoria, though it would be a daunting task. The thoughts of the rejection of Christine haunted Elizabeth. Would Sarah, or any woman she knew, deliberately turn from her own child?

Elizabeth leaned forward and gave Harriet tiny kisses on her face.

"Louis, I want to have a dinner party, nothing fancy, just a few guests."

Louis reposed on his side of the bed and looked at Elizabeth cross-legged beside him. Harriet giggled in between them content with the attention she received. He wouldn't mind being showered with kisses and lavished with hugs and gentle caresses throughout the day. Lately, he had to steal a few minutes from Elizabeth's care of Harriet and her other duties.

He laughed to himself. "Just tell me when. I'll clear my calendar for you." He answered too easily, but her request didn't really need his approval. Since it would make her happy, the answer would most of the time be "yes."

She peeked from behind her lashes. "A week from this Friday."

Turning on to his back, he brought Harriet to his chest. "Is that enough time?"

"Should be. Remember I have lots of help. Actually, Ellen could whip up the whole event all by herself." He knew Elizabeth would never ask that of Ellen. His wife enjoyed the planning too much to let Ellen do it all.

He couldn't resist teasing her. "And the guests? You said a few." A few was never five or six.

She used her fingers to count. "Let's see. The Evans, Anne, the Laurens, Christopher, Dr. Ramsey, the Turquands, the Smiths, the Singletons, the Wilsons, and maybe a few more sprinkled in."

"I thought as much. So, twenty would be a safe number."

She scrunched her nose and shrugged. "Maybe."

He captured her toes peeking out from her skirt. His other hand held his daughter. "I can't deny you anything, you know."

She leaned towards him offering her lips. "My charm has not vanished after a year?" Her soft hand caressed his cheek.

"Not at all." Two years ago, he would have denied needing a wife and family. Now they made his life complete. He would do anything to keep scenes like this safe and secure.

Anything? Would he fight? Leave his family for battle? He

already stored arms and corresponded with rebel leaders. Would he leave the fighting to the young like Tom? He couldn't put his personal gain over everyone else's, especially if God told him to go.

The questions invaded the tranquility of the evening. He shook his head to send the thoughts to a dark corner. He needed to concentrate on the light in Elizabeth's face and the peace in Harriet's breathing.

"To bed for all of us."

After he put the baby in her cradle, he wrapped Elizabeth in his arms, forming a wall of protection around her. A symbol of his determination to shield her from the web of uncertainty ahead.

Jeannette hugged Elizabeth upon her entrance to the mercantile Friday morning. "Jeannette, I desperately need material for a new dress. I have only a week to get it finished."

"Do I hear panic in your voice?" Jeannette stepped back.

"Not panic, only excitement. I see this party as a spark to relight my enthusiasm. I felt my life was shrinking, as if I were closing myself up in my comfortable, little world."

"Well, let's see what I have."

Elizabeth rummaged through the selection with Jeannette close at hand. "I think I want a light green fabric with cream or blue accent."

"Does Ellen have time to help you?"

"We're using a simple pattern. So between Ellen, Amy and me, Harriet, the dress, and the dinner plans will be accomplished."

Elizabeth glanced at a shimmering green satin with tiny threads of cream crisscrossing the soft material. "This is it." She pulled the roll out and placed a delicate strip of lace on top of it.

"Perfect. You have a good eye. You won't be upset or embarrassed if I wear an old dress for the dinner?"

"Oh, Jeannette, I certainly don't care. As long as you are there with me." Elizabeth faced her friend, grabbed her hand, and confirmed her sincere desire to have her near. Her own new dress was only a way to boost her spirits. "You are a blessing to me with or without a tiara."

She chuckled all the way to the counter. The special purchase and her close friend already worked their magic. Bouncing on the tip of her toes like an excited child, Elizabeth watched the liquid green disappear into the wrapping, tied with a string, and dropped in her bag.

Jeannette straightened the button containers on the counter. "Raymond is learning so much from you. His English and his confidence have improved."

"Does he talk to you in English around the house?" Elizabeth wondered if he practiced like she asked him or if French, or even silence, prevailed.

"Yes. Henry asks him to since he and the cook don't speak a word of French. But I'll confess, we do steal moments, just the two of us to practice my French."

"That's a good idea. Louis and I do that often, too." Elizabeth paused. Her heart skipped a beat as she pondered broaching the next question. "Is Raymond asking questions about the political scene? I know that Tom is very interested. I just wondered since Raymond is only sixteen. There just seems to be a spark in the young men and a keen interest in war."

"Raymond hears a lot on the docks. Henry has tried to warn him about getting too involved with the gossip and rumors around town. I think Henry knows more than he's telling me about issues."

Elizabeth drummed her fingers on the counter. "I feel the same with Louis. But he says he doesn't know things as facts, just rumors. Monday night is the next Sons of Liberty meeting. They'll know more and hopefully share a little with us." Could the rumors Louis placated really be facts he was covering?

She peered around Jeannette anticipating a glimpse of Louis.

Jeannette smiled. "He's not here, dear. Samuel sent a message for him about an hour ago."

"Was I that obvious? I don't need him, I just like seeing him. Is that so strange after being married over a year?"

"Not at all. I watch Henry sometimes without saying a word." Jeannette winked.

"Thank you for your help with the dress and for listening to my prattle." Elizabeth kissed her friend's cheek and spun toward the door.

Louis questioned Reverend Smith's recent scripture reference, "My righteousness is near." How could God be near with such turmoil so near? Louis knew God didn't promise an existence without conflict, but He did promise to remain near to His followers. Lately, it seemed "near" had moved a few miles further away.

On Sunday afternoons, Elizabeth always joined him for two hours in the parlor alone with a pot of coffee and biscuits. He disliked bringing up politics, but it prevailed in every area of their lives. Today was no exception. "I'm going to the meeting tomorrow to find out how serious the colonists are taking the new stand from Parliament."

"I'm glad." She paused. "Look at me, Louis. I need you to promise to include me. Give me pieces of information. I don't need to know everything, just include me in conversations. I won't break. Our household includes more than just the three of us. The Engles deserve to know what to expect."

What did she guess? Had she learned something about Tom or Raymond? He needed to confide in her, but when and what? Why should he dump any more conflict in her lap? Yet, she just asked him to include her in the good and the bad.

He ran his hands up and down her arms. "I will make you a promise." Her gaze, glued to his now attentive eyes, revealed her trust. He couldn't put her faith in him on the line to protect her feelings or delicacies. "I promise to give you the details on my return tomorrow evening. And," the part that concerned her, the question he figured burned at her nerves, "I will fill you in on our Tom's actions."

"Oh? So, I was right."

He placed a finger on her lips. "After the meeting. I want rumors to be explained and facts to surface first before I involve you."

"But—"

"But you must wait. It's not as if it's Christmas morning, and I'm keeping a gift from you." More of a grave bundle of debris, rather than a gift to cherish.

"All right. I'll stop pestering. But, note that I won't forget your promise."

Christopher's house teemed with dedicated partisans. Mentally, Louis checked off each man as a true Son of Liberty, no spies in the midst. He then surmised that his promise carried many more aspects than he realized. Elizabeth would get an earful later.

The fire in Christopher's voice ignited a flame in Louis' interpretation of the news. "A state of war already exists in South Carolina. In accordance with the directions of the Provincial Congress, troops are being organized and drilled."

And Tom was one of the first. Drilled for what, exactly? To fight the increasing number of British troops in Charles Town? Would every other colony be expressing the same premonitions?

How did he tell Elizabeth without excess drama, and only the bare essential details? A promise he wouldn't break. As the Sons of Liberty sought to protect the colony, he strived to shelter Elizabeth. The only problem was she knew him too well.

His feet dragged as he rehearsed his words. He could be blunt or delicate. No, there was no way to be delicate.

Although the hour was advancing on eleven, Elizabeth sat up in bed with a book propped on her stomach.

"Why are you awake?" He knew the answer. Waiting. He released his cravat and the confining buttons of his stiff shirt.

"I waited for you, of course." She sat upright and bounced on her hands, her book discarded. "You promised."

"Yes, I did. Are you ready for a late night?"

"I napped with Harriet this afternoon."

He crawled into the mahogany bed and settled in for the inevitable discussion. At least, he'd be comfortable.

Louis sighed. "The outlook isn't good, as you most likely expected. We're in a state of war now. Troops are being organized, preparing for retaliation or preservation." Brief, but lacking the fire in Christopher's words.

Her cheeks tensed. "It has come to that?"

Silence. He let her digest the big scenario first. The shock had steeped in his mind for weeks. She needed time. Had he been fair leaving her out of the daily advancements toward this?

Head bowed, hands clasped, Elizabeth said. "And Tom? What of him?"

The real-life application. "He has been training with the new troops already. I don't know what that will mean yet. But if the troops are called out, I assume he will go."

Her hands went to her face. "And what about you? Oh, Louis, would you have to go?"

Why didn't he see that coming? Of course, she'd put him as an able-bodied young man. Somehow, he hadn't envisioned himself on the frontline, at least not in a full-blown battle. Would he?

"Well, if it comes to that I would do whatever I needed to protect you and Harriet and Charles Town."

"If it comes to that." She leaned her cheek into his palm as he cupped her face. "You seem to think it won't."

"For now, *mon amour*, there are plenty of men who have military experience, who are soldiers at least. They will be the first to fill the role. Remember we don't know if troops will even be needed." *"If it comes to that" is slowly leaving my vocabulary. It has come to that, if not in Charles Town, then in some places.*

"Will Tom tell his mother?"

"I've asked him to. He's waiting for the right moment. And that is probably soon before things start appearing in the paper."

Elizabeth wiped a tear away. "I'll be strong for her. We knew this could happen."

Louis took in the transformation as Elizabeth shed her remorse and put on bravado. "Now, let's go to sleep. We have time to make plans. We won't be at war tomorrow."

"Maybe not physically, but we are at war."

Louis spent the next few hours listening to Elizabeth breathe and the fire crackle. *We are at war.* He breathed a prayer. *Heaven help us.*

A party in the making eclipsed the raising of an army in Elizabeth's mind. Her preoccupation with the details relieved a bit of the tension.

Ellen spoke often of Tom. Pride prevailed instead of fear. "He has found an honorable place among some fine men."

"Yes, he has. Louis has met with Captain Shanks and witnessed a training session. He's impressed. I really don't think we have much to fear right now."

"So, let's just make this the best party ever." Although Ellen's smile didn't meet her eyes, her leaning to the side of cheer buoyed Elizabeth.

"Thank you for finishing my dress and making all this food." A mixture of spices escaped from covered dishes on a side table. Elizabeth walked around a table with a variety of desserts including some of her favorite lemon tarts. "Do you have enough help tonight?"

"Yes, once Mrs. Jeannette sends her cook and butler over, all will be perfect."

"I'll leave it to you, then." The spicy aroma drifted into the parlor, giving the house an ambiance of festivity. At five o'clock Amy released the last ringlet framing Elizabeth's face. "Have a look Mrs. Elizabeth." The hand glass reflected her rosy cheeks and baby's breath laced through cords of her shiny brown hair.

Elizabeth spun around exposing satin slippers. "Perfect. Do you like the green fabric?"

Amy clapped her hands. "Always a complement for your coloring, ma'am."

Louis appeared from his dressing room as Elizabeth finished another twirl. "Are you ready?" He stopped a few feet in front of her and reached for her hand. "You are beautiful."

She was glad she had the foresight to have Ellen make him a vest out of the remnants of the green material. "Actually, I think you'll outshine me tonight." She straightened his collar and cravat.

"Enough." He lightly pushed her hand away. "May I escort you downstairs?"

"*Oui, monsieur. Je suis prête.*"

Each guest ushered in wisps of an April breeze. Stylish skirts and jacket tails billowed as they caught the air from the front entrance. Elizabeth breathed in the freshness as a gift from her loved ones.

Louis leaned toward Elizabeth during a lapse of greeting. "You were right. This came at just the right time. Have you noticed the lack of worry lines and grimaces? It's as if a layer was shed from each person before entering."

She sighed. "Well then, our friends complied with my wishes."

"Which were?" He leaned toward her while maintaining his smile and nodding to their guests. She looked up at him. "No unpleasantness for one evening." Then she turned and welcomed Christopher, the last to arrive.

Elizabeth looped her arm through Louis' and followed the laughter and noise into the drawing room. She pulled his sleeve and pleaded with batting lashes. "You wouldn't be able to promise me no talk of politics tonight?"

"With Christopher in the midst? Not likely. Anyway, we are among friends who view things as we do. No surprises or disagreements should surface."

"Good. Now, we must separate and mingle." She stretched on tiptoe and placed a light kiss on his cheek. "We'll make the rounds and rejoin before dinner."

The ladies and men gathered in small circles. Elizabeth popped her head into each group, checking on drinks and eavesdropping a bit.

Sarah glowed, sheltered in Samuel's protective arm. "Are you feeling well tonight?" Elizabeth whispered, not intending to draw attention to Sarah's condition.

"Oh, yes." Sarah beamed and said for Elizabeth's ears only, "Samuel took the news of the baby with excitement. It seems he has forgotten how badly I behaved." Sarah giggled.

She left Sarah and found the Turquands and Jeannette reminiscing about France, leaving Henry to fend for himself. He joined Dr. Ramsey and the Laurens close to the table of appetizers. Although the tingling scent of spices hovered around the table, Elizabeth avoided the temptation.

The only people left, the Smiths, the Singletons, and Anne, discussed the church picnic at the end of the month. Elizabeth clapped silently. Success. Her favorite people together and, by outward appearance, happy and satisfied.

She ducked into the hallway to check on Ellen and the status of dinner. With a bounce and a twist, Elizabeth returned to Louis. "It's time."

He grabbed his walking cane from the canister and hit it on the floor a few times. "Dinner is served. But before we partake, I would like to return thanks to our Heavenly Father, the Provider of this food."

Elizabeth spied a few holding hands, a spontaneous gesture between spouses and friends. She reached for Louis. *Thank you, Lord, for this group of friends and family.*

Heads bowed. A second of pure silence. Then Louis' strong voice thanked God for those gathered, for wisdom and peace, and for the food.

Peace in the commencing storm. Would there be peace in the middle too? With God and friends like these, she believed He would prevail.

Steam misted over each plate of veal, vegetables, and creamed potatoes. The aroma was almost enough to take away hunger pains. Elizabeth peered through the thin air at each person around the two tables, noticing the quiet hum of conversation.

Quiet until Christopher's words resonated all over the room. "It's a fact that the magazine is receiving excess arms and ammunition almost daily. And we know why."

Mr. Laurens boomed across the table. "Not everyone sees war on the horizon, my friend."

"Maybe not war, but there is a conflict present that won't disappear overnight, especially with more militia in our streets and arms in public storage." Christopher barely paused to stab and inhale his veal.

"Do you have a plan? Maybe a provincial decree you'd like to share?" Mr. Laurens returned between bites.

Christopher laughed. "None that I will share." Elizabeth

wanted someone to draw the attention away from the looming canopy of war. For one evening. One hour. Was that too much to ask? Maybe Christopher's laughter succeeded in calming the rumbles.

Dessert was served in the library for the men and the parlor for the ladies. Elizabeth stomped her foot to suppress an urge to join the men. So unfair. Though she desired peaceful subjects, she hated being a room away from the seeds of controversy. Why should she have to float among ballads of silk and dances and romance? She couldn't have it both ways—delicate words and harsh commentary. She had to remember history was not made over casual ladies' after dinner gossip.

Or was it?

Mrs. Singleton hurried them along the path of active participation. Instead of frilly gowns, they discussed woolen trousers. "The young men need shirts and warm pants plus gloves and scarfs for the winter. I think we could help through the Daughters of Liberty." Elizabeth gasped at the change.

"That is a good idea." Jeannette sat at the edge of her chair as if to gain more information. "Raymond is wanting to join the troops, but he is so young, only sixteen. We think he should wait until he's seventeen in the fall. It hurts my heart to think of him practicing maneuvers and going to battle. The warm clothes for any young man would ease my conscience."

Mrs. Turquand patted Jeannette's hand. "Remember it might not come to a battle, my dear. We all need to continue to pray. Our God can turn this around. Perhaps it won't even happen here."

"I do believe in prayer," Mrs. Smith said. Elizabeth hoped that was true since the woman was the Reverend's wife. "But we spent the last five years in prayer for peace. Peace and the British government don't seem to be possible partners. Yet, I won't let that stop me from praying."

Elizabeth sought Anne's eyes, but her head was bent. Was she worried about Robert and his safety? Or was she praying? With a smooth transition of a few feet, Elizabeth placed herself in Anne's vicinity. She folded her hand over Anne's two hands that caressed a pleat in her skirt.

"What is it?" Elizabeth knew her sister well. Her strength crumbled at times when she and Robert were apart.

"I want Robert to be here, listening to all the plans, protecting us, and determining his place in all of this. I feel so alone." No tears escaped, although there was a catch in her words.

"Soon, you will all be together." Elizabeth couldn't possibly know what sorrow or pain her sister felt at the moment. But the strength that Elizabeth admired in her stalwart sister returned. Anne pulled in a deep cleansing breath and smiled.

The men burst into the room not bothering to silence their roaring. Elizabeth wondered who instigated the laughter and light spirits. Christopher or James Laurens? She spotted Louis right in the middle of the pack.

He strode across the room, reaching her as she stood accepting his secure arm around her back. He shook with lingering laughter. "I can't wait to hear what caused the outburst," she whispered.

Louis winked. "Nothing more than Christopher's rendition of the king's jovial rejection of the compromise of Congress. In Christopher's mind, King George is more a silly jester than a tyrant."

A bit like the cartoons Elizabeth viewed in the paper. Satire in place of serious rhetoric. Laughter instead of tears.

He recovered from his bout of amusement, sighing to control his speech. "There was one interesting request. These men and other locals want to learn French in order to communicate with future French sympathizers, whether soldiers or merchants."

"And who better to teach them than you?" Elizabeth guessed. From the trouble in his eyes and the lopsided grin, she predicted his answer was "yes."

"I'll share that job with Reverend Turquand."

"Well, I'm glad to hear that since your schedule is full enough," she teased. The times were presenting odd requests and activities of people, and somewhere in it all she realized they would have to guard their family time too.

Ellen appeared at the back entrance of the parlor. She waved a note in the air. What could be so important at this late hour? Ellen seemed anxious almost, motioning Elizabeth out of the room.

"Mrs. Elizabeth, this just came from Mr. George. He asked me to read it before delivering it to you. It's very important."

"Let me see." Elizabeth placed a hand on Ellen's shoulder and the woman stopped her prancing.

Elizabeth,

In brief, Victoria has left town. The baby is with Mother. I'm at her house considering the options.

George

Considering the options? This wasn't a military drill. This was the life of a child. His child. Precious baby Christine. What instructions could she give? Or was he even asking her? As a soldier, he wanted someone to tell him what to do next.

Her shoulders drooped, and her hands shook. The note crumbled in her grasp. Destroyed, as Victoria had done to her child, only to be thrown away, forgotten, and abandoned.

"I'll get Mr. Louis." Ellen wove her way through the guests and returned with him.

She had a house full of friends, most who did not know about George and Victoria and their problems. Did Elizabeth's distress show? She didn't want to alarm her guests. Louis appeared from the crowd and reached for her. She fell into his embrace. He pulled her out of the way of curious eyes and listened to the saga.

"What do we do now?" Her moist eyes pleaded with Louis to give her a solution, an answer.

He paused and lifted Elizabeth's chin to meet his eyes. "Christine is safe, and she is loved. Your mother has the nurse and staff to keep her for tonight."

His compassion reached her from the depths of his blue eyes.

"And now, we let the party finish and see our guests on their way. Then, we decide on the next step. I'll write a note to be sent to your mother. Tomorrow, we'll be there to help."

He kissed her forehead as if she were a child in need of courage. He turned her toward the parlor and pushed her forward into a sea of unsuspecting observers. She smiled, laughed, and nodded when appropriate.

Her acting abilities fooled everyone but Anne.

"I'll tell you in a few minutes." After all, Anne was as involved as she. Their flesh and blood, a child, practically left on a doorstep. At least it was at a house of loving relatives ready to tackle the inevitable.

CHAPTER 11

$\mathcal{E}$lizabeth chose pacing over sitting in her mother's parlor. She wrung her hands, then wiped them against her navy skirt. "Louis and George have been in there with Father for over an hour. What could they be discussing that hasn't already been said?"

While Anne rocked Christine, a child who knew nothing about her upside-down world, Elizabeth knelt in front of her mother. "You must be exhausted. Don't you want to go rest? I'm sure we can handle things for a while."

"No, my dear, I want to be here when your father comes out. I need to know how things stand." Since their arrival, her mother had shed all her tears, leaving puffy rings around her eyes.

Elizabeth stood and let out a deep breath, frustrated by everyone's denial. "You know how they stand, even if you won't admit it, Mother."

"Elizabeth." Anne's reprimand sliced the tense air.

"Well, she does. We all do. Victoria is gone. George is away all the time. And Christine is here without her parents. The only question is who brings up Christine-- Mother, you, or me?"

"Or all of us." Her sister whispered.

She was right. Gentle Anne saw the practical side of the issue. Of course, Christine would join her girl cousins in her upbringing under the wings of the Elliott household. Charlotte, Harriet, and Christine—a trio of hope. Bound by blood, plunged into a world of change in a sphere of potential.

Elizabeth no longer quivered or ranted. "Mother, is that what you think?" She listened and basked in the stillness in the room.

Silence. The creaking of the rocker emphasized the bundle surrounding their dilemma.

The emotionally broken woman, slumped against the cushions, straightened as the rocker ceased its soothing motion. "Yes. I will take Christine and bring her up as a proper Elliott. And I will depend on you both to help me. She will never lack for love and care." The creases in her brow disappeared and the wrinkles by her eyes crinkled as she smiled. Elizabeth witnessed the moment her mother accepted the gift of caring for Christine.

Silence. What could anyone say to a truly selfless proposal? The men entered. Elizabeth rose to join Louis as her father crossed to stand behind her mother.

George glanced at Christine who was oblivious to the scene around her. He cleared his throat and shuffled his feet. This was a side of George unknown to her. A humble man? Elizabeth experienced the sensation as of watching a play. What was her role? A member of the audience? A major player? George's head bowed, practically hidden within his red jacket. "Due to Victoria's departure and my inability to care for my daughter, I come before you to ask for your help as a family. I…" he faltered. Then he fixed his eyes on a distant object, perhaps a portrait on the wall. "I apologize for my past actions and selfish deeds. It is obvious to me, although too late, that my desires have affected many lives. Now, I place Christine in your care, if you will have her."

His gaze traveled to Mother, to Anne, and then to Elizabeth. As if rehearsed each said, "I will," in unison.

A serious commitment, but the right one. At first, Elizabeth swiped at tears, but then gave in to the flow. Louis' handkerchief helped absorb the downpour.

She reached to rescue Christine from Anne's grip when sobs wreaked her sister's body. As she looked at the sleeping baby, Elizabeth remembered Harriet about four months earlier. The pure joy her own daughter brought was why she couldn't understand Victoria. What a gift from God. The woman had thrown it back in God's face so frivolously.

It's not for you to understand, Elizabeth. Just do as I command.

Yes, Lord, I will.

Mother took the lead. She stood and faced everyone. Elizabeth's jaw dropped. Her mother, the spokesperson for the family?

"The deed is done, and we all have agreed to step up. You, George, have relinquished your control." Her firm, steady voice permeated the room as George seemed to fade into the corner. "We hope there is a change in your life. Whenever you like, you will be allowed to visit your daughter. You are still our son and are welcome here anytime as long as you don't bring trouble with you."

Trouble in the form of fights with partisans, outspoken women, rowdy friends, and condescending words. Elizabeth willed her mouth shut.

"Actually," her mother continued. "Christine is the only good thing you have produced in years. She will be cherished here. In time, you might remember your heritage, the love of your family and of the Almighty. That is my prayer, at least." Elizabeth didn't remember the last time her mother had voiced her opinion with a tone of deep conviction.

As if she had enough, her mother stalked out of the room. In the past, Mother would have seen this situation with George and other events surrounding the pulse of the volatile city as blotches on her reputation. Now, it appeared the community's opinion of her family was the last thing on her mind. She had put Christine first.

Father exited next, followed by George. A collective sigh escaped the three remaining witnesses. Elizabeth leaned back on the sofa. Louis sprawled out in the chair, head resting on the back, eyes to the ceiling. Anne collapsed on the sofa by Elizabeth and placed her hand on Elizabeth's arm next to Christine's tiny feet.

A giggle pushed its way up Elizabeth's throat. Once exposed, a full vocal laugh followed. A release of tension. Contagious in nature, Louis joined with a deep throaty sound. Anne, the last to let go, uttered a most unrehearsed noise. The room reverberated with the sweet, healing, wordless melody. Christine joined the chorus with a few gurgles, perhaps they would have been of glee if the wee one knew what had happened for her sake. This child would know love unconditionally. Too many relatives had their hands in the upbringing of this precious one.

"Who would have thought Mother would have George cowering in the corner and Father speechless? I feel like I walked into a play, something no one had read or rehearsed." Elizabeth shook with leftover energy.

"A tragic comedy." Louis remarked, sitting up a little straighter from his slouched position.

Anne bent forward, toward Elizabeth. "A bit of Grandmamma surfaced today in Mother. The new general of the Elliott house. I think Christine will be just fine." Anne played with her niece's little toes. "Just fine."

Louis didn't understand why George chose him of all people. Foes from the beginning, initiated by his brother-in-law, George tended to avoid Louis. So why was he here in the mercantile office on a Monday morning?

They met behind the closed storage room door. George refused to sit. Instead he stood with his hat in hand twirling it by the rim. Louis leaned against the desk with arms crossed. He let the younger man commence the conversation. After all, George had sought Louis out.

"I need to tell someone in the family this information. And well, Father would dismiss me, Mother would cry, and Anne and Elizabeth would beg me to change things."

Louis stood up straight and looked at the hurting young man. "That leaves me."

"Yes, and you might choose to throw me out anyway." George peered at Louis without raising his chin. His brow shadowed his eyes.

"Go ahead, speak your mind." It couldn't be worse than what they already knew or experienced.

"I have been reassigned to a New York regiment." His shoulders shot back, his stance strengthened, and his position froze at attention. "I will leave later this week."

Louis almost admired George's respect for his role in the military. Almost.

"And my job is to what?" Of course, Louis knew where this would end.

"I'd like you to share this information with the rest of the family."

"I'm to inform them that you have left Charles Town, and your daughter, for New York for an indefinite period." Louis did try to hold back sarcasm, but the nerve of George to walk even farther away from his responsibility sparked a raw nerve with Louis. "And maybe, a goodbye, so long, I'll write?"

George no longer looked at Louis but at a picture on the wall. "I don't expect you to understand."

"Good, because I don't." Louis walked around the desk and stood in front of George. He could have been a brother, a friend.

"I've done a lot of listening to you and your excuses and nothing makes sense. I've stopped trying to figure you out. I will share this with you, though. I tried running away from life and purpose for a few years. Nothing changes until you find what God wants you to do and be."

"That might be never. If I have to depend on God, I'd rather stay as I am." George put his hand on the doorknob and turned one last time. "Thank you for relaying my message and for sharing yours." He left.

Go with God, young man.

There was nothing else Louis could do to help George, except pray. Elizabeth would not be surprised at George's absence. It wasn't as if the man came by to see Christine. The nursemaid, Mrs. Elliott, Anne, and Elizabeth handled everything that involved the baby. What more did the child need? Except perhaps two loving parents.

At the noon meal, Louis received welcome kisses from Elizabeth and smiles from Harriet, Amy, and Ellen. And the guest for the day rested in Amy's arms, baby Christine. A house full of women.

"Where is Tom when I need him? I'm surrounded by fair maidens." He didn't mind. Anyway, the bulk of his afternoon promised to be filled with just the opposite—Christopher, Samuel, Henry, and a few others.

"I heard from George today." Louis began his news.

Elizabeth dropped her fork on the table. "What?" She rescued her utensil, but her unblinking eyes expressed surprise as she latched her gaze to his.

"I know. He was the last person I expected to see. I don't think you could guess what he has added to this drama." Louis stared at the baby wrapped in Amy's loving arms.

"With George, nothing would surprise me," Elizabeth said. "He doesn't want Christine back, does he?"

"Far from it. He's leaving Charles Town indefinitely, reassigned to New York."

Elizabeth's gaze dropped. She folded her hands in front of her on the table. Louis wondered what else the family would face because of one man's selfish actions.

Her head leaned from side to side. "Louis, as a man and a father, do you understand any of this?"

"Honestly, no. I would like to think that at his age, I would not have been so selfish. In a way, I was, but I didn't have a wife and child. We must remember that God has a purpose for this child and for George."

He gave Elizabeth all he could. His embrace conveyed his love and commitment to her and his daughter. "I will not ever let you or Harriet slip from my life. I love you."

Over the mealtime, everyone held the babies, laughed at their antics, and expressed words of love over the children.

God protect these women in my care.

At two o'clock, he headed toward the river. For once, he allowed himself enough time to study his environs. The gardens, behind ornate iron gates, beside mansions, bloomed with color. A few gardeners with their wide-brimmed straw hats stooped in their plots picking weeds, pruning, or planting. It reminded him of Elizabeth. She could easily be one of those bent over a bed of vegetables.

He sighed in admittance. No matter how many servants or gardeners Louis had, she would continue to enjoy the dirt and the process. Nurturing new life out of the ground was like a spiritual discipline to her. A unique prayer life.

And where did he find that relief? Certainly, not at meetings such as the one ahead of him. No, probably when he slowed down, right now, and really looked at life around him. Just the hums of existence from the nature teeming from the plants, to children playing or the ocean ringing.

The past thirty minutes of peace encircled his being. Hand ready to knock, Louis inhaled and exhaled. He doubted a spiritual realm existed beyond the door.

Christopher ushered him into his office. The others sat around a large oval mahogany table. Samuel, Henry, Mr. Timothy, and Mr. Drayton completed the group.

The addition of the editor and another prominent partisan intrigued him. They all acknowledged each other with handshakes and nods. Were they assessing Louis the way he contemplated them? What was the role of each, the common thread? Louis put aside guessing, knowing Christopher had a plan.

"Gentlemen," Christopher began. "You are the only handful of citizens who will know this information. You are to guard it as highly confidential. I have the authority of the Provincial Congress to relay this to you."

Louis scrutinized each man. Henry, Samuel, and Mr. Timothy all had the same puzzled expressions. Mr. Drayton was the only one not squirming, fidgeting, or adjusting his posture. Louis surmised Drayton knew the scheme, possibly a co-author of the plan.

Christopher placed his hands on the table. "Your job will be to share information with me after the incident takes place." His bent position gave him direct eye contact with the seated guests.

"I think you know you can count on us, or you would not have called us here," Samuel said. Louis nodded as did the others.

"True. In a few days, Mr. Drayton is going to lead other Provincial Congress members on a raid of the magazine." Christopher paused and smiled. He must have received the response he wanted. The others appeared as Louis, shocked with eyebrows raised and sudden jerks forward as if on a leash.

"Raids? Did I hear you correctly?" Henry asked.

"Yes. And also, on the State House," Christopher added.

"That is indeed a bold move," Louis said. "And where will the arms be stored for now?" And how much? And what if they were caught?

"Right here at my wharf." Christopher spread out his arms swinging them in all directions. Right under the nose of the government.

Really that was no different than what Louis and Henry had under their store. The difference was these men were stealing from a public supply, owned by the British.

Christopher peered at each Patriot, as if gaining access to each thought. "It's all for the cause, men. I have word that other cities and towns are doing the same thing. This is not an original idea of mine. Do you have anything to add, Mr. Drayton?"

"Only that it will happen soon. Every detail has been laid out."

Louis marveled at the turnaround of this new convert to resistance. When Mr. Drayton changed his allegiance, he set the example of giving one hundred percent to his new loyalty. Louis regarded men like Mr. Drayton as fuel for a successful defeat of the British tyranny.

"Are you all on board?" Christopher used his over six-foot height to bark his bold question.

"Yes." Unanimous around the table.

Louis' "yes" resounded with a healthy anticipation. Pulling off this feat would inspire and escalate the colony's refusal to accept Parliament's proposals now or in the future.

"Now, we await the event." How was Christopher able to change subjects so quickly? Louis needed time to absorb information, but with his friend, it was always on to the next item.

"Louis, how about starting these French lessons soon?"

Louis' head swiveled toward his friend. "I've cleared it with Elizabeth. Tuesday evenings would be best. At eight o'clock?"

Christopher nodded, thumped a piece of paper with his finger, and glanced at Louis. "Good, we'll leave it to you. Next Tuesday evening? Expect about ten of us."

"Fine." Ten to learn a language to help them communicate with a possible ally in a time of war. Louis could do it for the cause. The joy escaped his usual willingness to teach. The sensual words of love and poetry would be replaced with terms of business and trade, weapons and strategies. None of the men would read litera-ture of the French or philosophies of the sages. Louis sighed. *War instead of love.*

CHAPTER 12

$\mathcal{U}$nder the ruse of a Sons of Liberty meeting Thursday night, Louis left the house and quickly made his way to Christopher's wharf and warehouse.

Be ready to accept produce. CG

A lantern put off a weak light in the huge half-full warehouse floor. Louis entered through the front door slightly ajar. From the first landing leading to the upper storage rooms, Louis saw Henry leaning on the rail with a lantern at his feet.

Louis joined him. Did Henry know the mission or the purpose of the meeting? "Any ideas, Henry?"

"My only guess is possibly a special shipment, the one Christopher promised in his office."

A side door creaked open, letting in the light from a lamp on the wharf. In its wake was a tall silhouette followed by men and crates.

"Come on, that's Christopher." Louis and Henry retraced their steps to the ground floor.

Louis shuddered as he realized his presence collided in a semi-dark warehouse late at night with men and suspicious crates.

He quieted his footsteps, although it didn't appear silence was the top priority

Christopher wasn't whispering commands, but rather barking them.

Louis stood next to Christopher and watched seven or eight men carting boxes and crates up the stairs to the landing. "What do you need me to do?"

"I need you to help with the crates. They are on a wagon in the alley. Then we need to secure them in the upper room, hidden among other crates." Christopher guided the men by pointing his lantern toward the steps.

Louis discarded his coat and rolled up his sleeves. He obtained warmth from his overactive nerves, considerably more than a jacket could provide. The faces of the men were familiar, including Mr. Drayton. This had to be the heist on the magazines. It took less than twenty minutes to store the items. Henry had experience in disguising the arms and ammunition in the crates since his mercantile storeroom doubled as an armory.

"Good work, men." Christopher replaced his coat and retrieved his cane and lantern. "Now let's scatter. Remember, no one is to say a word. I know the news will spread by morning. We don't need our names attached."

Louis entered his house feeling like he had personally stolen the goods. He was an accomplice and guilty by association. He determined not to draw Elizabeth into his stealthy deeds. After closing the door to his night's foray, he joined his family upstairs within the protective walls of home.

Elizabeth hastened the baby carriage around the corner of Tradd Street to the mercantile on Friday morning, April twenty-first, in record time. The news, passed from Tom to Ellen to Elizabeth, burned in her ears. Louis would know the truth.

Would he share his part in it? Looking back, it seemed suspicious that he was at a meeting when the events of the evening took place. What were the details about a major theft? Surely, Tom got the story wrong, an exaggeration circulated by overenthused youth.

She opened the door to the store, backed the carriage inside, and headed straight to Jeannette. Elizabeth read the nod of Jeannette's head and slight smile as a sign she'd heard the message too.

Elizabeth leaned toward her friend and whispered between gritted teeth. "Is it true? Were weapons stolen from the magazine last night?"

"You heard the same thing? Raymond told us this morning. I don't know how these young men find out before the older men." Jeannette paused and shook her head. Why did she stop? Elizabeth needed to know now.

She wanted to shake Jeannette to hear the news sooner. "So, is it true?"

Jeannette looked in all directions, then she whispered. "Yes, the men have all the details. I don't think Raymond exaggerated at all. You should see the pure excitement in his eyes. To him, this action was a good thing with no sign of trouble attached to it."

Elizabeth could imagine, for she had seen the same excitement in Tom's expressions, a sense of recklessness. What were these antics teaching the boys? Were they actions the young men would continue to emulate after the conflict was over? "Is Louis here?"

Jeannette motioned to the back. "Let me look after Harriet." The baby focused on her aunt. "We'll have a good old time."

Elizabeth kissed Jeannette on the cheek. "Thank you."

She knocked on the storeroom door. "Come in," Henry said.

Both men sat casually on two crates. Louis sprang up and embraced her. "Is everything all right? Harriet?"

Elizabeth laughed, releasing a bit of pent up tension. "Yes, fine. Everything at home, at least. But I hear that something happened last night in town. Do you know anything about it?"

Had she caught them in a secret *tête à tête?* They sheepishly glanced at each other, heads drooped, and arms crossed.

Louis was the first to peer up at her with a lopsided grin. "I'm to understand that Tom let out the news early."

She nodded. "Did you expect differently? Now, I want to know the real story. Why are you two smiling? A major theft and you just laugh. I think I'll sit for this." She chose a half barrel as her perch.

"All right. The short version." Louis looked at Henry and received a nod. "Last night five of the Secret Committee members took the public supply of gunpowder and arms from the Hobcaw and Charles Town Neck magazines and the State House." Louis did all the talking. Henry nodded in agreement, not bothering to hide his smirk.

Was this a game to them? "And this is not serious?" Leaving her seat on the barrel, Elizabeth eased her way to stand directly in front of Louis. She knew his eyes couldn't hide the truth from her.

"Of course, it is. But they did this without disguises, without confrontation, as if the items were handed over to them. It was amazing. No struggle at all."

"What was taken, and where did they put it? I hope not here." He didn't have to add the "why." She knew why. This was the resistance's reaction to Britain's renewed vow not to listen to the colonies.

"Let's see." Louis rolled his eyes to the ceiling. "Sixteen hundred pounds of powder, eight hundred guns, two hundred cutlasses and other weapons." Louis turned to Henry. "Anything else?"

"That's about it. A major feat indeed." She could almost see the pride gush out of Henry's mouth.

"I would say so. Is any of it stored here?" She imagined the government raiding the basement. Shivers commenced at the danger element.

"No. Christopher has taken care of that," Louis said.

"Oh." She shook the chill off. "How do you know so much? And why are you so happy, almost giddy?"

"You don't need to know the details," Louis stated. "We were careful. This is a defeat for the British. One that is being repeated over and over in other colonies. It could be a way to get their attention and a compromise for peace."

Henry's smile disappeared. "Or it could be a precursor for battle."

"Exactly. Please be careful." What was he hiding? Part of the work of the Secret Committee? He was here, not hurt, and laughing. She laced her fingers behind Louis' neck and kissed his cheek. "I want you to do your part, Louis, as I will, but remain out of harm's way." She poked his chest, emphasizing each word. How could she say that and believe it, when beneath them was their own storehouse of arms?

She had to believe that God was continuing to bring them nearer to Him. He was working out the details. If she thought her life was directed by men, she'd resist more. In reality, she believed these members of the Sons of Liberty did surrender to a higher command.

Saturday night, Louis and Elizabeth entertained Christopher at their house. "You don't mind it being so impromptu?" Louis put his coat on for the evening event.

"Not at all. He's a friend, and he's leaving in a few weeks. You need the time together. He'll just have to eat what Ellen was preparing for us anyway." Elizabeth brushed imaginary specks off Louis' shoulders.

He hadn't been concerned. Elizabeth had the knack of being the best of hostesses, no matter what. He did feel a twinge of guilt, though. They used to enjoy quiet weekends every now and then. When was the last one? The months had slipped by. How could he let the upside-down events around them take away that time? Tomorrow, he would set aside the whole afternoon just for his family.

It was a bit odd having Christopher alone without an entourage of followers. After two years, Louis could count on his fingers on one hand the time they had socialized casually. Louis thrived in the challenges presented by Christopher, and he didn't expect any less tonight.

In the library, Christopher gravitated to Louis' desk. "I see you have the latest report from Lieutenant Governor Bull." Louis had spread the paper out on the table earlier, meaning to put it aside. Did he subconsciously leave it there? Elizabeth would reprimand him if she saw it.

Too late. She glided into the room, raised her eyebrows at Louis, and greeted Christopher. "Good evening. I see that Louis has laid out the evening's conversation in plain view." She laughed, which put Louis at ease. "Don't mind me. I want to hear every tidbit of information, including rumors and gossip. Maybe you'll fill me in on my husband's escapades."

Louis shook his head and grinned. "As you can see, Elizabeth knows as much as I do when it comes to the maneuvers of the town."

"Not everything." She pointed a finger at Louis. "Perhaps, Mr. Gadsden can shed some light on the situation and let my mind rest from guessing Louis' contribution."

Elizabeth was no stranger to Louis' friend and business partner. Would Christopher take her interest and insinuations as permission to brooch the subject on everyone's mind?

Christopher took her bait. "Well, let me read the latest from the *Gazette*." Elizabeth handed him the paper already folded to the front-page story.

While Christopher read, Elizabeth passed around a cool raspberry punch. Louis was the last to sit. He chose to share the sofa with Elizabeth, close enough to touch her hand or shoulder. She added a fresh outlook on a tedious or monotonous subject.

The reading continued: "Bull commented that 'the theft of the King's stores was an act which constituted high treason. He has asked the Commons House of Assembly to investigate.'" Christopher burst out in laughter. "That should be interesting."

"Why?" Elizabeth glanced from one man to the other.

Louis patted her hand. "Because some of the prominent members of the House participated in the seizure of weapons."

"Oh, I see." She smiled and shifted her gaze to Louis. Her raised eyebrows asked for an answer. Could he tell her? It was obvious she suspected him. Would Christopher understand his need to share with his wife especially since the deed was done?

"He says, he will report soon on the culprits." Christopher set the paper down on the tea table.

"I do hope I don't see your name there."

Louis met her accusation with closed lips. "Let me put your mind to rest, Elizabeth. I did not steal anything." He received a nod from Christopher to proceed. Louis let out a heavy sigh. "I did help store the items immediately after the raid."

She gripped his arm and shook him. "I knew it. You don't have to keep your late-night ramblings from me. And you also don't have to tell me all the details. From now on, tell me you are going on a mission, and at least I can pray."

Louis stared. How did he end up with such an understanding wife? No, not just understanding, but determined to be a part of the solution or the changes. He shuddered. She could end up a petticoat version of himself.

Her firm grip loosened on Louis' arm. "See what you are missing, Christopher? A wife who supports you, no matter what."

She leaned forward with her hands gripping the seat. Louis knew she was not ready to discard the subject. Since she had Christopher's attention, she continued. "When you go to Philadelphia in May, do you expect some of the same scenarios?"

"I do. All the others received Britain's call to more arms at the same time. If we have reacted, they will have also. I can't wait to hear." Christopher sipped his punch and motioned to the paper. "I can guarantee every major port will have similar stories."

Louis set his cup on the side table. "Silas has written hints of plans, much to do with arms and ammunition. I don't think anything will surprise me." Louis no longer questioned the seriousness of any of their actions. Wasn't each event one step closer to the call for independence?

Elizabeth stood and set the goblets on the serving tray. "Have you heard from Robert? I'm just wondering if you have more information than Anne does about his return."

Christopher sat forward in his chair. "The runner said the ship should arrive the end of this month, right before I set sail for Congress."

"I'm so glad. That means he'll be home for Charlotte's birthday. Anne will be thrilled."

Louis glanced from Elizabeth to Christopher. With his finger tapping his temple, he notably preferred his life with family and moments with Elizabeth over the world of arms and danger.

By Tuesday afternoon, the House responded to Lieutenant Governor Bull that its investigation had failed to produce the culprits of the weapon heist. Louis grinned. *We won this round.*

He read on in the *Gazette*. "But it had reason to suppose that some of the inhabitants of this colony may have been induced to take so extraordinary and uncommon step in consequence of the late alarming accounts from Britain."

Louis set the paper aside and commented to the four walls of his study. "At least Bull knows only that the items were taken and nothing more."

A knock on the door preceded Elizabeth. She peered in the

room. "This is your classroom for the evening?" She folded her arms and clicked her tongue. "It will do just fine. I don't suppose you will be studying poetry or literature?"

In mere seconds, she crossed the room and positioned herself directly in front of him, her stance begging for an embrace. He locked her in his arms and whispered, "I only discuss poetry with you, *mon amour*." He fingered a ringlet, wrapping it around his finger. "These men will use French as a means to discuss war tactics, not how to make love."

"So, what you will teach them wouldn't interest me. I'll stick to the love part."

She left his protective arms, ran her hands over his open books, and captured his attention with her bright playful eyes. With ease, she sat on his desk and adjusted his cravat, making it hard for him to concentrate.

"I'm glad you asked Raymond and Paul to assist you. Although Raymond is progressing well in English, he still loves using his French at every opportunity."

Louis refrained from kissing her lips poised close to his. If he started, he didn't trust himself to stop. He enclosed her hands in his against his chest and joined in the chatter. "If he remains focused on the cause and the French do come to our aid, he will be an asset to any number of officers."

"Just be careful before you plant glorious pictures in his head. He's young and anxious to break loose right now. We both know he needs some time to mature."

"I agree. But with Tom already practicing with the troops, Raymond is ready to go. Uncle Henry is standing his ground and is asking him to wait a few more months." Louis helped Elizabeth off the desk and glanced around the room. He straightened a chair and opened the door for his guests.

"Well, I will leave you to your empty classroom. Tom will see the students in, and I'll retire upstairs with Harriet." She giggled and reached for his chin. He met her halfway with a kiss.

"What's so funny?"

"Your students. A bunch of old men." She departed out the door swishing her skirt. Was she trying to entice him away from his male students?

Old men? Tom was only eighteen. The rest were older than Louis, but some only by a year or so. When did he get to be an old man? He admitted he felt older than his years. The carefreeness of youth dissipated with the seriousness of rebellion.

Louis was proud of Tom playing the part of butler, friend, and host. With that part taken over, Louis could freely maneuver the men into the study. Due to the late hour, they needed to start on time and accomplish as much as possible.

"*Bonsoir, messieurs. Bienvenue chez moi. Commençons avec les introductions.*" He focused on the big round eyes of the men. Fear? Concern? Louis smiled remembering learning English as a child. It could be intimidating and much worse for an adult. Who was more anxious? Christopher, Samuel, Henry, Tom, Mr. Elliott, Mr. Laurens, Mr. Singleton, Mr. Collins, or Reverend Smith? Well, it had to be better than teaching a room full of eighteen-year-old young men. No silly comments or fidgeting bodies. These men had one goal: to learn enough French to communicate with an ally in a desperate time.

"*Ici*, here. *La-bas*, over there.

Venez-ici, come here. *Suivez-moi*, follow me.

Où est? Where is? *J'ai besoin*, I need."

Vocabulary followed commands. It was a shame that their first words would be for guns, knives, powder. A typical lesson would introduce greetings, feelings, and menus. The closest he'd get to food would be "Where's the flour? The sugar? The apples?"

After an hour, Louis placed the men in three groups of three. "Raymond, Reverend Turquand, and I are each going to lead a group. The object is to carry on a conversation in French. The mission is to lead a newly arrived Frenchman from the docks to the commander's headquarters. Point out different places, people, and plans. Pointing and hand gestures are acceptable. *Allons-y.* Let's go."

When all finished their assignment and departed, Mr. Elliott held back. "Good job, Son. I never thought I would be a part of a group planning to dupe the British by learning French."

"A lot has changed, sir. I guess you see that every day, even in your home."

Mr. Elliott pushed his hat in place. "I assume you mean with the baby?"

"Yes, sir."

The older man laughed. "Who would have thought a man my age would have a crying baby in the house." He stopped by the front door. "I stayed to ask about Elizabeth. Is all going well with Harriet and all Elizabeth's projects?"

Louis knew Elizabeth's father cared for her, but why the concern now when he saw her an hour before? "She's fine. She wants to know all the news so none of the gossip will be a surprise. She's accepted her role and time with Christine. So yes, she's as strong as ever."

Mr. Elliott peered over Louis' shoulder, then into the drawing room. "Good. I need to tell you something. You know how close Elizabeth is to her grandmother in Boston who has been ill during the winter?"

Louis nodded. "Yes." What of this stalwart woman? The last report had been one of progress.

"Well, she's well enough to come for the summer. I've convinced her to stay an extended period. I feel she can recoup better with family around her. We have the room, and I think I can count on Elizabeth's help. The doctor I correspond with wants to see more progress toward complete recovery." He tapped Louis arm. "Can I count on you to pass that on to Elizabeth?"

"Of course. We'll be praying for her safe journey and recovery." Was his father-in-law covering a few facts? Was there another reason for her extended stay? Louis could understand why someone would want to leave Boston and the hotbed of conflict. But was it any different from Charles Town?

Louis snuffed out all the candles and placed his feet quietly on the stairs, parting the silence with the barest scrape against the planks. Was he as tired as his heavy feet felt? He had to relegate the various pieces of information into categories of his mind, demanding respite for solutions until the morning.

Soon he joined the sleeping angels in his room, oblivious to the whispers of the house as it settled.

CHAPTER 13

*C*harlotte entertained Elizabeth, Harriet, and Christine on a huge blanket in the sunroom at Anne's house. May first turned into a play day for the girl cousins. Christine slept through Charlotte's antics of picking up and placing every toy she had in boxes and baskets. Harriet laughed at the continuous meandering of the almost one-year-old.

For a moment, Elizabeth managed to capture Charlotte in her lap for a story. Just when the knight was fighting the dragon, Anne screamed. Charlotte jumped up and clung to Elizabeth's neck. Anne's scream turned to laughter.

"It's all right, Charlotte." Elizabeth patted her niece's back. "I think your Mama is happy."

And she should be. She was wrapped in Robert's arms. Charlotte hid behind Elizabeth, shy in her father's presence.

"Well, how's my little girl?" He opened his arms to her, bent his knees, and let her fly into his embrace.

Anne rubbed tears from her cheeks. "She does remember you. She just needed a second." She exited and called up the stairs for the boys.

"And who is this?" Robert peered into the bassinet at the tiny four-week-old.

Elizabeth brought her feet from under her to a standing position. "This is your newest niece, Christine Elliott." She realized there was no way Robert would know the circumstances of the youngest family member.

He adjusted Charlotte in his arms, allowing her to take his hat into her tiny hands. His eyebrows rose. "Babysitting for the day?"

"You could say that." Elizabeth paused. "A lot has happened since you left. April was a busy and dramatic month. Christine was born, and two weeks later Victoria left. Since then, George has been transferred to New York. Now, Christine is in the care of Mother, Anne, and me."

Robert laughed. "I was only gone for two months or so. Charles Town has been busy." He shook his head, his untrimmed hair falling over his eyes.

"More than you know. But I'll leave those details to Louis." Harriet reached for Elizabeth. "And this is Harriet. Hasn't she changed?" Elizabeth stooped to retrieve the active bundle.

"Almost five months old now." She felt Robert's concern. When he was gone, the children continued to grow, and the government continued to change. It was a promise that things would not stop in someone's absence. Not for a moment. Time could be an enemy or a friend.

"Papa!" Robert and John collided into Robert's sides. Charlotte's free hand reached down and pulled at little Robert's hair. He seemed not to notice. Anne stood in the doorway, hands clasped.

"My, you two have grown, too." Robert's voice wavered, until he cleared his throat.

Anne joined them to complete the family group. She rubbed Robert's upper arm. "I'm so glad you arrived in time for Charlotte's birthday party."

"I told you I would do everything possible, but I had more

reasons than that to get home." He pushed Charlotte up on his hip and touched Anne's cheek, then kissed her.

Elizabeth occupied herself with the babies, picked up Charlotte's toys, and prepared to leave the lovebirds alone. Well, as alone as they could be with three children.

"I'll take Christine back to Mother's and leave you to your reunion." Elizabeth noted Anne's aloofness to her comments and suggestions. Her sister was already basking in her husband's return.

Robert responded. "Thank you, Elizabeth. We'll call on you soon. I'm anxious to hear everything from Louis' point of view."

"Yes, make it soon. Things seem to change daily." The two babies fit snuggly in the carriage and within mere minutes, Elizabeth was out the door.

She knew her sister well. Right now, she had an agenda— Robert. Elizabeth smiled all the way to the Elliott's'. Of course, she would be the same way if Louis returned from a long journey. So far, all of Louis' business had been handled via correspondence with his brother. She didn't know how long he could keep up his end. Both Silas and André mentioned a voyage in the future. How would Elizabeth handle that? Would she adjust like Anne or complain every minute? Would he be safer fighting in a possible battle here or across the ocean in troubled waters? Shaking her head, she realized the waters here were dangerous too.

Elizabeth entered through the garden gate and pushed the carriage toward a magnolia tree, full of sweet-smelling blossoms. "Mother?" She advanced to the back door, hoping someone would hear her. "Mother, we are back from Anne's. We're in the garden."

Mother waved from the sunroom window. "I'll join you momentarily. I'll request a light meal."

"Good. I'm famished."

The nursemaid took a hungry Christine, and Elizabeth fed Harriet who demanded attention too. By the time her mother and the meal arrived, the babies were content. Elizabeth held Harriet and munched on a sandwich while watching her mother resting on a bench with her feet crossed, relaxing in the afternoon sun.

Adjusting Harriet to a secure nook in her arm, Elizabeth mimicked her mother's repose. "Robert is home. You should have seen how excited the boys were and of course, Anne. Charlotte was shy at first but warmed quickly in his arms."

"I'm so glad. Children need their father." How her mother struggled with the absence of George and Victoria in Christine's life. It hurt Elizabeth to watch the raw pain her mother experienced, evident by the dark circles under her eyes and the pale skin wrapped over her cheeks. There was nothing Elizabeth could do except participate in the rearing.

She reached for her mother's hand. "You are doing all you can do, and she definitely isn't suffering from lack of attention."

"You're right. I take one day at a time. And now with your grandmother coming, this house will be so full of activity."

Elizabeth clapped her hands over Harriet's and sang, "Grandmamma is coming to town. Huzzah for Grandmamma!"

Never could Elizabeth hide her joy when it came to the special woman. Louis had shared her father's news this morning. Was Grandmamma up to the trip? How was her health, really? Always so hearty, her grandmother never showed any signs of weakness or illness. But whatever her condition, Elizabeth wanted her here in her life and in Harriet's.

"It's still a few weeks away. I'd rather her safely here than far away in Boston. She's bringing her maid with her."

"Oh, Martha is coming. I'm so glad." Her mother's house was indeed almost full. She did hope Mother and Grandmamma put all differences aside and existed in peace. "Now, you know Martha isn't any more a maid than you are. She's a member of the family, especially since her husband passed away."

"All right. Her companion and nursemaid, her friend. She's a lot like your Ellen."

"That's the way it should be. I accept her as family." Elizabeth spoke in Harriet's ear. "What would we do without her? And Amy. All three of the little girls love her like an aunt."

Elizabeth headed home within the hour. Sarah expected her at the school to complete the recital plans. Harriet had enough for the day, so Elizabeth left her in Amy's care.

At three o'clock, Sarah exited her classroom and bumped into Elizabeth. "I'm so sorry. I seem not to be able to concentrate at this time of year. So much going on."

"That's why I'm here. To relieve some of that pressure." They reentered the classroom, now minus the students. "You sit while I take notes and be your feet. By the way, how are you feeling?"

"Tired. A little sick in the morning. I'm ready for that energy spurt you say is coming."

"It hit me at about four months." Soon Sarah would be able to rest. No classes in the summer. The heat and stuffiness promised in the months to come weren't a friend to Elizabeth last year during her pregnancy. She remembered days of melting away in a chair with a fan for a slight breeze. Miserable in a normal state, but for an expectant mother, double the inconvenience and misery.

But she wouldn't share that with Sarah just yet. "You have days to look forward to with nothing more pressing than a cool lemon water in hand."

Sarah laughed, her hand on her stomach. "I imagine Samuel will think I'm lazy."

"Louis will set him straight and tell him exactly how to act. Now, let me see the recital schedule." Elizabeth took the list and perused the schedule of performers and pieces. "I still miss Martha Laurens. She wrote about life in England. She'd much rather be here with her father. Her new acquaintances are nice on the surface, but the whispers about the colonists have a way of floating to her. She doesn't acknowledge them."

Sarah closed her eyes. "Do you think she will come back soon?"

"No. Not as long as things are heating up here. It might be years. I just think her father could have protected her here." Elizabeth set the list on the desk. "I see no mistakes, and I like the arrangements. At least my students are ready. When you get final approval, I'll take it to the printer. So, what next?"

"The reception. I've turned that over to Miss Miles. She has connections through her aunt."

Elizabeth tried to conjure an image of the lady. "Is she the mathematics teacher?"

"Yes, she came to us from Williamsburg. She's worked out splendidly."

Elizabeth retrieved her mental notes from last year. "And that leaves the invitations and the flowers."

With slow motions, Sarah opened her eyes and pushed stray strands of hair behind her ears. "Mrs. Reynolds is overseeing the invitations. And Mother took over the flower arrangements. She's calling on the same flower shop that she used for my wedding." She hit her palm against her desk. "And that's it. Can you think of anything else?"

"Not at all. I think you deserve a trip to the tea house before going home." Elizabeth guided her tired friend to the door and shut it behind them. Enough work for now.

Sarah giggled. "You mean the coffee house, don't you?"

"It's still a tea house to me even though they don't serve tea." If she couldn't have the soothing drink, she could say the word and hope for a day of tea to return.

Louis kissed the top of Harriet's head. She squirmed and reached for him. "Not now, little one. Papa has to go to work." He covered the baby with the light blanket, then he embraced Elizabeth. His hand twirled a ringlet of her long hair, making him wish he could stay. It was still early on Wednesday morning, but May third was Christopher's departure date.

"It is awfully early. Why does the ship have to leave almost before dawn?" She insisted on preparing coffee for him, though still in her dressing gown.

He sipped his second cup of coffee. "One of those navigation details. I'll be back at noon. I need to get my final instructions from Christopher. He'll be gone quite a while, perhaps even two months."

One more kiss, and then he had to leave or crawl back in bed with Elizabeth. He shook that thought out of his head.

She leaned against the drawing room doorframe. "I understand. We love you. I think we will rock ourselves back to sleep for an hour or so."

He turned and exited to the street, picturing his daughter curled up in Elizabeth's arms. He was very thankful he wasn't leaving for months at a time. A few hours were enough.

Picking up his pace, he chose the shortcut weaving in and out of narrow streets and alleys. As the minutes ticked by, the morning fog hovered low over the river, sending off a light mist. Within half an hour, the ship would begin its journey on the barely visible gray sea.

Louis found Christopher with his son on the wharf. Once again, the young man would accompany his father. Was he being groomed to enter the world of politics or was the goal more exposure to life lessons? The Second Continental Congress in Philadelphia anticipated major votes and recommendations. Louis knew Christopher's role would be as vital as before and having a family member present could help ease the burden.

Christopher broke from his son and advanced toward Louis. "You will write me about any news? I'm counting on you and

Samuel to be my eyes and ears. And, I'll send most of my information to you and Mr. Timothy at the *Gazette*. I expect action on a dramatic scale." Of course, his friend seemed to thrive on large-scale drama.

"Hopefully, things will remain calm here, but I will let you know." Why should he expect the town to suddenly avoid conflict? If the recent past held any clue about the future, in the days to come he would have news to share with Christopher. "I have everything under control for the next shipment in July. You try to enjoy Philadelphia. Please say hello to Mr. Deane and the Adams for me."

Louis waved farewell when they boarded. The other South Carolina delegates would depart later. This time there was no fanfare, no canon salute. Only a few men going on a journey, doing a job for their colony.

Hands in his pockets, he continued along Broad Street to the park. The vast expanse of ocean, clear of fog and mist, loomed for miles until the water became the blue sky and eventually met with England and France. An ocean apart and a lifetime. How quickly Charles Town had become home. But anywhere Elizabeth existed would be his home.

Five days later, the streets erupted with news of enormous proportions. Louis didn't have to walk far from his house. On the street corner, a few feet from his front door, a youth shouted, "Shots heard around the world. Read all about it." The paper waved in his extended hand.

"What's all the commotion?" Louis asked, exchanging coin for a paper.

"It's all there, sir. It looks like we're going to war." The youth ushered the word "war" as if it was the sweetest candy. The event and a smile should not be connected in an ideal world.

Louis considered turning back with his paper and reading it in private with Elizabeth. But before he overreacted, he needed to get the facts first.

On every corner, the alarm sounded. It rang as a chorus echoing off the buildings around Louis. How had Mr. Timothy found so many boys so early in the morning, especially on a Monday morning?

The bell above the shop door announced Louis' arrival. Aunt Jeannette stood reading over Uncle Henry's shoulder behind the counter.

"Have you heard?" Henry's eyes lifted once, perhaps to check who approached, though customers never came at this early hour.

Paper in hand, Louis joined them and sat on a stool facing the couple. "Only two sentences. The words 'shots' and 'war' stood out."

"Well, prepare for a shock. Our escapade here in April was mild compared to up north." Henry folded the paper and continued with the second half.

The front page shared great detail. Louis skimmed the first paragraphs to acclimate himself to the severity of the story. Between his uncle's grunts and his aunt's sighs, Louis soaked up the words silently. "On April eighteenth and nineteenth, General Gage and his army attempted to seize rebel arms and ammunition stored at Concord in Massachusetts. Colonial scouts, namely Paul Revere, rode ahead to warn partisan leaders and local farmers of the advancement of the militia. Local armed colonists exchanged shots, first at Lexington and then at Concord. No one knows who fired the first shots."

"All of that for a few supplies." Louis shook his head.

Henry glanced up from the paper and clicked his tongue against his teeth. "Read on, Son."

How could it get any worse? Local farmers against the British troops smelled of disaster. "During the British army's march back to Boston, partisan militia repeatedly attacked. By the end of the day, two hundred seventy-three redcoats and ninety-five partisans had been killed or wounded."

Louis set the paper down and laid his chin on his hands. "So, it has begun."

Images of young men with arms defending their homes and towns scattered across the colonies rose to meet Louis' fears. Another picture of Elizabeth, Ellen, and Amy poised with pistols in the air at a makeshift target startled him. Tom and Raymond embracing the fight. And Louis? Would he join them? The target now was a true enemy, maybe a single man or perhaps an army.

"If you continue, some doubts among the British authorities have been raised. They don't think plain police action can quell the rebellion," Uncle Henry said.

Jeannette left the dismal men to fiddle with items on the shelves, then wiped a tear and found another chore. If his aunt shed tears, he knew many more were released around the city. What would Elizabeth think? He knew he had to tell her and Ellen, if Tom hadn't already.

"Is Tom around?" He usually came in early about the same time as Henry.

His uncle motioned his head behind him. "Yes, he's in the back."

"Do you think he knows?"

Henry stored the paper under the counter and shuffled toward the office. "I don't think so. He didn't appear excited about anything." Knowing Tom, if he had heard he would have been out the door, finding his comrades.

"Good. I'll go tell the women at home, and we can deal with Tom later. I don't want him to exchange his apron for a gun just yet."

His sprint home energized his mission. How to break the news? Did he expect a room full of distraught women? Instead, a serene scene greeted him. Elizabeth and Ellen sat in the breakfast room over coffee, planning the day ahead. He smiled. The care

Elizabeth took with the Engles sealed their friendship and loyalty. And that made what he had to share more important.

Hat in hand, he cleared his throat. "Ladies, good morning. Do you think I could interrupt your morning routine?"

Elizabeth jumped up, rattling the table in the process. Fortunately, Ellen grabbed a tea cup before it toppled. "This is a surprise. Would you like some coffee?" she managed to ask between depositing kisses on his cheeks. He'd only been gone a little over an hour.

"No, I need to get back, but," he hesitated and took a seat next to Elizabeth. "I do need to share something with you."

Amy sitting in the corner rose to leave. He realized a thirteen-year-old wasn't usually invited to sit in on an adult conversation, but he motioned for her to remain. "Please stay, Amy. You need to hear this too."

The smile he received from her thanked him for including her this time. If she only knew how hard it was for him to impose conflict on her young life.

"The news, Louis?" Elizabeth raised her eyebrow. If she knew what he had to share, she might want him to delay as long as possible.

"The news reached Charles Town today of combat between British troops and Massachusetts militia. The first shots were fired on April nineteenth and continued all day until almost 400 were killed or wounded, most of those British soldiers." He paused.

Ellen grabbed Amy's hand, and Elizabeth covered her mouth before releasing a plea of "no." Her unbelief progressed to understanding in seconds. "War has finally started."

"Yes." He had readied himself for tears or any form of hysteria, not quiet acceptance. "Rebellion has now resulted in death and open attacks. I don't know what the plans are for South Carolina. I can only guess."

Ellen interjected in a whisper. "What about Tom? What will become of him?"

Louis' head dropped. How did he look a mother in the eyes with the truth? Suddenly, it got very personal. Tom would leave for battle. The fact shocked him as fear etched into wrinkles on Ellen's face.

Hands clasped in front of him on the table, he raised his head and performed his duty as head of the household, as a friend. "Tom will have to make his own decision. He has been training with a regiment and has strong partisan commitments. This rebellion is as much his as any man's in the colony. I'm sorry, Ellen, but he will be confronted with decisions soon."

The tears he expected didn't happen. Ellen's shoulders straightened, her hands steadied, and words formed. "I understand. I'm proud of my son. Although I want to keep him safe and protected, he's eighteen now and on his way to making mature choices in life. What better one than to fight for our rights and freedom? I won't stop him."

Her strength buoyed Louis for the task he faced. "I'm going now to talk to Tom. Would it be all right if I shared your sentiments?"

Moisture glistened in her eyes yet did not escape. Not yet. "Yes. And add that his father would be proud of him too."

Louis bowed his head to her in respect to the memory of Tom's father. "Yes, ma'am. I surely will."

He left the house in the hands of tenderhearted, yet strong women. Elizabeth could handle Amy, and it seemed Ellen would pull through better than he imagined.

Ultimately, God was in control of his household, and in His timing, all would make sense. Louis searched his mind for strength and assurance. He rattled off Psalm 145:18 "The Lord is nigh unto all them that call upon Him, to all that call upon Him, in truth." Truth and the Lord, a combination he needed now more than ever.

Louis counted on God's nearness, especially in his words to Tom. In fact, he prayed God would enter the equation mightily and bring Tom very near to Him.

In the past hour, Tom had stayed busy in the storeroom and no one had ventured in to stir up the breaking news. A slight miracle. Broom in hand, the youth tackled the four corners of the room.

"Tom, I need a word with you." Actually, Louis needed a book of words, a handout of what to say. *Courage, he's a smart young man. He won't overreact if I don't.*

"Yes, sir." Tom wiped the sweat from his neck and face with his handkerchief.

Louis leaned against a stack of crates. "Have a seat in front of me."

Tom adjusted a crate to make sure it held his weight.

Louis couldn't remain standing casually with his arms crossed. He used the floor in front of Tom as a stage, pacing back and forth. "We've received news from Boston today about scrimmages between British and rebel militia. Shots were fired, and many were killed or wounded. The British see it as rebellion. We don't know yet what will happen here." Tom stared and hung on every word. "I want you to be cautious around any plans of unorganized riots or demonstrations. You have to confront this as a man, not a boy. Do you understand?"

"Yes, sir. You want me to wait on word from my regiment," Tom said.

Louis halted inches in front of Tom. "And follow the commands of your captain, not of random men on the street. There will be lots of talk and hundreds of opinions. Please listen to men in charge." He wanted to take his shoulders, embrace him, and tell him to go home, to not think about war. Yet at this moment, he treated Tom as a responsible young man who had the right to follow his purpose.

Tom nodded. He did not break contact with Louis' eyes.

"And one other thing. Your mother is proud of you, and she

said your father would be too." Louis patted Tom on the shoulder. "Any questions?"

Tom shook his head. "No, not right now." Louis sometimes wondered if his own father would have been proud of him. Perhaps. His father stood up for rights to worship freely with the Huguenots, and Louis now fought for freedom of a nation. He had lived the consequences of his father's beliefs. Now he would have to accept the challenges and inevitable consequences of his own choices in seeking freedom.

hile Charles Town brewed with damaging rumors, Elizabeth concentrated on family, mainly Charlotte's birthday celebration.

Anne planned the affair as a family dinner at her home. All the better for Elizabeth. She gravitated toward familiar, controlled environments. Too much changed daily around her outside of the walls of home. It wasn't that she feared the increased number of redcoats in the town, but more of what it signified. They existed under the scrutiny of the crown.

She adjusted her straw hat and buttoned her gloves. The early morning breeze helped to organize the latest infiltration of ramblings. This morning the paper stated: "The British are planning to incite Indian attacks and slave rebellions across South Carolina."

Rumor? Was there any support to that fact? Perhaps an interception of a letter? No source was listed. Was Mr. Timothy just adding fuel to the fire?

"The rumors are causing the boiling of much blood," the paper continued. At least they were recognized as possibly false. If she believed everything she read, she'd see an enemy in every slave or Indian she met on the street.

She rounded the corner of Queen Street, Anne's house in view. Still she mused over a vision of Charles Town citizens storming the barracks and destroying the British troops there. That piece of gossip came from a royal official in the city.

Well, the only storming I'm going to do today involves tackling little boys and corralling stray toys. The British are safe from me.

As expected, Anne had the party progress well in hand. "Did you leave anything for me to do?" Elizabeth surveyed the front rooms. Nothing amiss. She followed Anne to the back of the house.

Anne laughed. "Voilà. Here is our project. The boys have turned this area into a fort." A fort of grand proportions.

"Is it safe?" Elizabeth got on her knees to peer through the makeshift door. Sheets and blankets draped over furniture concealed the boys and their essential gear.

"Well, hello. Am I allowed to enter?" Four eyes wrinkled with glee.

"Aunt Elizabeth. Come in," Robert said.

John cleared an area of toys and pointed for her to sit. "It's not made for big people, but you can fit right here."

"What are you playing?" With a bit of finagling, she coerced her skirt through the lifted sheet and wrapped the lengthy material around her. She noted the soldiers and horses in neat rows, the redcoats and the bluecoats facing each other. How much did her nephews know about the colony's situation? In the past, red depicted the good side. But now? What did red symbolize in their little minds? Did Robert talk to his sons about the possibility of war?

"It's a battle between the bad troop and the good troop," Robert said, holding up a blue bad soldier and a red good one. While he had it wrong, it was not her role to impose politics on the young boys.

"Continue on, troops." She saluted. After ten minutes fighting an imaginary battle, Elizabeth ungracefully gathered her skirts ready to crawl out of the cramped space. "I'm going to help your mother. And remember, later the fort must be cleared."

"Do we have to?" both whined.

"I think so, but I'll talk to the general in charge."

Their mother had laid down the law. "Then we have to."

At her full height again, Elizabeth found Anne, shaking her head a few feet from her. "Did they convince you to keep the fort up?"

"They tried, but I said I answer to a higher command." The fort took up a fourth of the sunroom, a major hindrance to movement of guests.

"I hate to destroy their work and their fun."

"What if I help them move it upstairs? We can build the same fort out of the way." Elizabeth had a basket ready to begin the process.

"Would you? That would keep the boys occupied and give us more mingling room."

"Consider it done." Having found her mission, Elizabeth gained the title of commander and quickly ordered her soldiers to methodically disassemble the fort. It was a game of orderly destruction. Toys in the basket, blankets and sheets folded, and troops marched upstairs. Elizabeth turned for a last look. Only the disarranged furniture showed signs of previous occupation.

Elizabeth and the boys fought imaginary battles until early afternoon. A break for the noon meal relieved her of duty. The living quarters, transformed into their former glory, gave weary soldiers a respite.

"Now all we need are the guests," Anne said, remaining immobile so that Charlotte could walk around her skirt.

Elizabeth worked a clean cloth over the silver before placing it in a basket lined with a linen napkin. "It's a shame Lucy couldn't come. She wasn't comfortable leaving her home. She wrote that families in the country are concerned with activity, including gathering supplies and even housing relatives from the cities. The events in Massachusetts have the backcountry worried."

Anne stopped folding a dishcloth. "I wouldn't want to leave mine either. Do you ever think maybe we'll have to?"

"Not yet. And not today." Elizabeth stood, glancing around the room, approving of their progress. She kissed her sister, nephews, and niece goodbye. "I'll be back with my portion of the family around four o'clock."

Anne waved Charlotte's little hand. "Thanks for your help with the boys."

Missing her small bundle of energy, Elizabeth walked home with a skip in her step. She had a little over two hours to ready herself and Harriet.

Amy presented Elizabeth with a giggling baby when she stepped into the parlor. Arms extended for the transfer, Elizabeth received the nicest welcome of the day. Legs pumping and hands ready, Harriet squirmed in her arms.

"You and I need to change clothes and go to Cousin Charlotte's party." Upstairs Elizabeth enjoyed the menial task of picking out clothes and dressing them both up for the occasion.

"Yellow for you and blue for me." Both outfits trimmed with ribbon and lace beckoned a celebration. Elizabeth bent to fasten tiny laced booties on kicking feet.

Louis silently slipped up behind Elizabeth and deposited a kiss on her ear. "I've found my two adorable girls." One hand on the baby, Elizabeth turned sideways to get a proper greeting. Louis never passed up a kiss and some attention.

"You smell good." Louis tucked a loose tendril behind her ear.

"I should. I had to get all the dust and grime off me after playing with the boys."

He smiled and ran his fingers across her cheek. "You've managed to clean up perfectly."

She laid Harriet in the middle of the bed and turned to Louis. "Are you nearly ready?"

"Give me a moment to change my shirt. I don't think anyone wants me to wear the shirt I've worked in all day."

The party consisted of the Elliotts with Christine, the Evans, and the Wilsons. Laughter, gifts of toys and trinkets, food and singing equaled a success. Somehow the five families mutually excluded the subject of war. Pleasing to Elizabeth, the celebration of life overrode anything else.

Yet, she knew behind the curtain of celebration and joy was a backdrop of anticipation, no longer "if" but "when."

Louis sat next to Elizabeth on the sofa, sharing a piece of sponge cake with strawberries. She leaned her head on his shoulder. "Look at the children. I want to remember them like this." At peace before the war, making memories to sustain them through the decades.

"The girls are beautiful. It looks like Charlotte enjoys the role of queen with her little princesses. She'll be in for a shock when Harriet and Christine challenge her reign." Elizabeth giggled at the image. "I want them to be the best of friends. Promise me we'll keep them safe, and we'll be around to watch them grow."

He set the plate on the table and took her hand. "I promise that I will do everything I can to make that happen."

CHAPTER 15

*T*wo weeks later, three letters arrived--two addressed to Louis and one to Elizabeth. Louis noted the familiar handwriting of Christopher and Silas Deane. The other appeared to be from Elizabeth's grandmother.

He gripped the envelopes and clapped them against his palm. A part of him wanted to know every detail of the congressional meeting in Philadelphia, but the hesitant half liked the cocooned world of normalcy. His curious and practical side won. A fantastical world could be shattered at any moment.

"I have a letter for you, *ma chérie.*" He placed the missive by Elizabeth's teacup.

"Thank you." Her fingers caressed the envelope, and she pulled it to her heart. "I'm scared to open letters from Grandmamma since she's been ill. I want my grandmother of the past who was healthy and vivacious like last spring. Do you remember the time we had with her roaming all over Boston?"

"I do. She might not be able to do that now, but she is the same inside." He wanted to hear news of the lady's imminent arrival. At the same time, his letters burned a hole in his hand.

With no further ceremony, she pulled open the sealed envelope and peered inside. One single sheet of blue paper unfolded at her touch.

Louis waited for a sign or a word of hope and answered prayers.

"Her ship should be here one week from today, on Thursday morning." The signs he needed shone through, a huge smile, and a bounce on her seat. He breathed a sigh of relief. With her grand-mother under her watchful eye, Elizabeth could experience some usefulness in helping her grandmother heal. Perhaps she could put aside her role of watchman, waiting for the battle to hit Charles Town.

She smiled and put her letter in her desk in the corner of the drawing room. "We'll be there to greet her, all three of us, as I'm sure the rest of the family will too."

Louis kissed her forehead. "I'm glad. Now you can relax since you know when she'll be here."

"Oh, there will be no relaxing until she is safely in Mother's house. There is so much to do. I'm going to make my list right now." She sat at her desk, pulled out a piece of paper, and began her project.

Without any fanfare, Louis released the wax of Christopher's letter. It was only a note of five sentences. So far, the debate of the congress centered on establishing a continental army and who would command the troops.

He read silently: "The session has convened for only a week now. Opposition to war still exists. The difficulty of thirteen colonies agreeing as one overpowers us." It seemed the Congress could conceivably meet for months. The details involved in raising an army against the established rule posed thousands of details.

Louis set the paper aside and opened Silas' note. Scrutinizing his scribble proved a chore. Either he had been in a hurry or his handwriting had deteriorated, for Louis had to concentrate more than usual on the marks.

Silas emphasized the task of procuring a commitment from the French. From Louis' point of view, that was possible. The Congress would set up a secret committee to investigate their options.

"I would anticipate a problem on my end since I don't know the language. When the time comes, I will call on you for guidance in correspondence and a possible stay in France."

The two pages filled in blanks where Christopher lacked details. The division over each colony's participation in the war resurfaced daily. Silas commented that each man would have a different take on the structure if asked.

Although he would like to listen in on the conversations, or debates, of those learned and prestigious men, Louis knew his place in the day-to-day flow of supplies in Charles Town needed a vast amount of time doing ordinary things for the citizens.

He stood and reached around Elizabeth's seated form and secured her chin. "I'll be home around four."

She turned her head for his kiss. "Perhaps we can steal away for coffee in the garden."

"*Oui. À bientôt.*"

Grandmamma's temporary room materialized with Elizabeth's mother's tender care. Christine kept Elizabeth occupied. How would her mother manage a seventy-one-year-old and a one-month-old under one roof?

With my daily help. I promise, Lord, to do everything I can to bring comfort to my family.

And one way involved organizing Christine's schedule: wet nurse, nursemaid, Anne, Mother, and herself. Each with a part. Every day continued to run smoother than the last. "There," Mother said. "The room is finished."

Elizabeth ran her hand over the lilac counterpane and the lace-trimmed pillows. "Perfect."

The small drawing room on the first floor converted easily into a bedroom. The sturdy door gave privacy and easy access to other parts of the house, minus any stairs. *Grandmamma will feel at home in her own little room.*

"All we need now is Grandmamma." Elizabeth rose up and down on her toes.

"True." Her mother's hands fidgeted with a pillow. "In a few hours, the real test will begin."

"Test, Mother?"

"Will she approve of her accommodations?" Mother moved across the room and ran her finger across the mantel checking once again for a speck of dust.

Elizabeth laughed. Grandmamma wasn't the picky perfectionist like Mother. She could make do in an attic room, if necessary.

Mother crossed her arms and stared at her. Elizabeth tried to control her giggles and wayward thoughts. In one stride, she embraced her mother. "She'll love it."

"Perhaps she will." Mother smiled, although it never reached her eyes.

Elizabeth stepped back, resting her hands on her hips. "I'll see you at the dock in two hours, around twelve. Harriet and Louis will be there too. Do you need anything else?"

Her mother reached for Elizabeth's hand. "Thank you. I feel I have depended on you for much lately. Remember, I appreciate you even if I forget to tell you." For her mother to admit her need for Elizabeth and her appreciation of her presence crossed the boundary her mother had fashioned years ago. Was this one of the reasons Christine and Grandmamma surfaced in her mother's life now?

They surveyed the room for anything out of place or missing, stepped into the hall, and slid the door closed, leaving the fresh lavender to permeate the room.

The vivid, green world, clear blue skies, and circling breeze from the ocean didn't erase the fear of the unknown. Would her grandmother regain her strength? Was the voyage too much for her?

"What if she's worse? What if?" Elizabeth voiced her jumbled fears.

Louis stopped the baby carriage and turned to face her. "Your grandmother wants to be here, with you, no matter what her condition. All your questions will be answered in time. The answers may not be to your liking, but they are God's answers anyway."

"But." He placed a finger on her lips.

As her stiff shoulders relaxed, her features softened. His words anchored her to the task at hand. She smiled at his gentle way of refocusing her doubts into hope. "Let's go see Grandmamma."

A passerby would think a dignitary had arrived. Eleven individuals with three carriages lined the wharf—all greeting Elizabeth Burnham and her companion, Martha Johns.

A pale woman on the arm of a stout matronly woman emerged from the deck. Although she had lost weight and her healthy glow, Grandmamma still wore a smile. Elizabeth focused on that and not the slow dragging steps of a fragile woman.

Elizabeth was the first to kiss her grandmother's cheeks. "Oh, Grandmamma. I'm so glad you are finally here." She backed up a step to make way for the carriage. "I want you to meet Harriet."

The alert baby beamed at her great-grandmother and waved her fist. Grandmamma caught it in her hand and kissed the tiny fingers.

"Just like I imagined." Grandmamma looked around and sighed with her fingers on her lips. "And look at all the baby girls.

We will have fun getting to know each other." She greeted everyone in turn. Elizabeth noticed the flush and sweat on the woman's cheeks and forehead. *This is too much for her. How could one year make so much difference?*

Elizabeth supported her grandmother on one side and Martha held her permanent grip on the other. Once in the Elliott's closed carriage, the Lestarjettes and Cochrans said goodbye until the family get-together tomorrow night. Leaving Grandmamma in the care of Elizabeth's mother made Elizabeth uneasy. On the best day, they barely got along. If only Elizabeth could trade places with her mother.

Louis slipped his arm around Elizabeth's shoulders and turned her toward home.

I must have strength for Mother and Grandmamma. She allowed her gaze to linger on Louis. Although he couldn't feel the depth she did for her grandmother, she detected he understood her pain.

"She'll be all right now that she is here, won't she?" Her wobbly words slipped out in a whisper.

Louis nodded, took her hand, and pushed the baby carriage with the other. "She'll be fine." If he had doubts, she didn't see or hear them. Determination flowed through her veins on the walk home. Sheer will helped her face the "what ifs" of tomorrow.

Elizabeth's prior commitments kept her bouncing from place to place. Between visits to her grandmother and jaunts to help Sarah with the recital, she grabbed every second she could to stop and breathe deeply.

Monday morning, Elizabeth met Sarah at the boarding house. "How is your grandmother, today?" Sarah asked. The large parlor morphed bit by bit, changing into an elaborate recital platform complete with the centerpiece, the pianoforte, and rows of chairs.

Elizabeth spruced up the flower arrangement and collected wayward leaves and debris. "Yesterday was the first time she got out of bed since arriving. The trip was strenuous on her. As far as I can tell, her body is weak and won't allow her to do the things she used to do. Dr. Ramsey said her heart has to work overtime. She needs bedrest and stress-free days." That meant the babies had limited time with her. Elizabeth would have kept Harriet away, but Grandmamma insisted on her company for a few minutes each day.

"I could use a day of rest." Sarah wiped her brow with her handkerchief from her sleeve.

"Here, you sit down. There is nothing else you need to do." Elizabeth pulled a stuffed chair from the corner, placed Sarah in it, and then found an ottoman for her feet.

"For this once, I won't refuse."

Was Sarah not telling Elizabeth something important? Her friend's hands rested on her belly. She wasn't in pain. Maybe she was only tired. After the recital Thursday afternoon, Elizabeth wanted Sarah to take the needed rest, to disappear for a few days where the only responsibility would be her health.

While Elizabeth shuffled chairs around, leaving a center aisle, Sarah laid her head back and napped. Elizabeth smiled. Pregnancies were not the same for everyone. Sarah's energy would return after this, but a prayer wouldn't hurt.

Please protect my friend and her precious baby. Give her Your strength. Amen.

Morning with the young and afternoon with the old. Both needed Elizabeth's care, her presence. She had no knowledge to offer medical relief but love and time she could give. Grandmamma advanced to the back sunroom in the afternoon to a comfortable chair. On her knees beside her grandmother, Elizabeth stroked the gnarled joints of the woman's hands.

"Look at you, basking in the sun. Are you getting enough of a breeze?" Elizabeth tried to rise to check the windows, but her grandmother's grip held her in place.

"I'm fine. I want you to relax and stay a while by my side. Talk and perhaps read a little, but don't fidget over me. I miss all of your stories." Grandmamma comforted Elizabeth even in her sickness. The woman's touch soothed where medicine couldn't.

"All right." Elizabeth grabbed a nearby stool and presided next to the chaise lounge. "I'll talk, if you promise to give me your wise advice as before."

"I'll probably be doing that until the day I die." That smile that gathered lines at the edges of her eyes was the one Elizabeth craved. It hinted at the past, the time when Grandmamma flitted all over Boston.

"Is there anything you want to know?" Neither woman thrived on gossip or rumors. Instead, they filled their time on accounts of people they knew or loved.

"Yes. Explain your brother George to me." She would pick the one thing Elizabeth couldn't decipher. Elizabeth puckered her lips. If she could have figured out the strange new George, she could have possibly changed his destiny.

"Well, now, he's a puzzle." Elizabeth held her head in her hands braced on her knees. "I think all of us have tried in our own unique ways to reach him. But he has put up a wall without any opening."

"And his wife? She's left the city?" The rest of her body might be weak, but her eyes sparkled in the sunlight, vibrant with points of gold.

"Not a word in over a month. The one good thing they did was leave us Christine." Elizabeth smiled, focusing on the gift left behind.

"It breaks my heart when I see that baby." Tears trickled down Grandmamma's cheek.

"Don't let it." Elizabeth handed her a handkerchief from her sleeve. "She is a true joy. It tore me apart at first, but now I see that God has her exactly where He wants her."

Grandmamma crinkled her brow. "And if George shows up and wants her back, or even Victoria, would you give her up?" The family had discussed that before, and Mother had some strict stipulations if either parent requested to take their daughter.

"That is one thing I discuss with God often, and I pray that we all will know exactly what He wants us to do." If it were up to Elizabeth, then Christine would never leave their family. Selfish, perhaps. She struggled with banishing bitterness from her motives.

"Good girl. I can give you no advice. I am proud of your mother for accepting this child."

For Grandmamma to utter these words about her daughter was a major feat. Their personalities leaned toward opposites. Like her grandmother, Elizabeth tended to respond in love and emotion; whereas, her mother performed duties with legality and practicality. Taking in an abandoned grandchild labeled her life imperfect and lifted it into the realms of scrutiny.

But Elizabeth's mother had mellowed and had thrown off a bit of her stuffiness last year, beginning with her partisan leanings, support of Louis, and now, baby Christine. Her humble state smoothed over some rough, cold edges. Grandmamma had gathered that fact quickly.

Elizabeth reached for *Robinson Crusoe* on the table. "Since I can't fix George, let me read to you. We'll escape into a novel."

She read, "Page 26. 'This was Game indeed to us, but this was no Food, and I was very sorry to lose three Charges of Powder and Shot upon a Creature that was good for nothing to us. However, Xury said he would have some of him; so, he comes on board, and ask'd me to give him the Hatchet; for what, Xury, said I? Me cut off his Head, said he. However, Xury could not cut off his Head, but he cut off a Foot and brought it with him, and it was a monstrous great one.'"

Elizabeth shivered. In comparison, her life at the moment shone bright and hopeful. She monitored Grandmamma's response and found her dozing.

She had managed to put two dear people to sleep, three if she counted Harriet.

Louis pulled Elizabeth to his lap before she found another chore to tackle. "I'm ready for you to stay home again." He pushed the few stray ringlets caressing her cheeks behind her ear. How easily he could be coerced to remain at home.

"Are you jealous? Or feeling neglected?" She wiggled in his arms until she settled snuggly against his chest.

"Let's see, I share you with Harriet, Sarah, Christine, and now Grandmamma." He counted on his fingers. "And I could add Raymond's English lessons and your students' piano lessons."

She pushed his fingers into a fist. "I see your point. And who or what should I give up? My students and Raymond's lessons have ended for the summer."

He smiled. "Good." A few more hours for him, not that he would be home more often, but knowing that Elizabeth had fewer outside engagements thrilled him.

She raised an eyebrow. "And the recital is tomorrow afternoon. That still leaves you, Harriet, Sarah, Christine, and Grandmamma." Clever to include him. Did he stand a chance against that lot?

He threw his head back and laughed. "You should see how red your face is. I'm not asking you to give up anything. And as for neglect, I think you take care of me just fine."

Still trapped in his arms, Elizabeth's face was half an inch from his. He claimed her lips for a long kiss. His hold had loosened, enabling her arms to wrap around his neck.

"If you would do that more often, I'll never complain again," he said.

"I will always have time for you." As if on cue to test her promise, Harriet's crying in the background and Ellen's hurried footsteps in the hall concluded their intimate encounter, but only for the moment.

At the recital, Louis and Samuel took their usual places, as they had the year before, against the back wall of the converted parlor. Sarah and Elizabeth fluttered in and out of their view.

"When this is over, I'm making Sarah take a long-overdue rest. I might not let her out of the house," Samuel said.

"Good luck with that. I would like the same thing for Elizabeth, but there's no chance. At least you can say it's because of her condition."

"Maybe Sarah will concede because of that. She really wants this baby."

Louis knew a percentage of babies were lost in miscarriage. Elizabeth had been blessed with an easy delivery. But anything could happen. He patted Samuel on the shoulder trying to allay his concern.

The fear was normal; at least Louis had experienced it. But Elizabeth hadn't been overly dramatic or paranoid. Not like Sarah. Samuel had his hands full.

A silence descended over the babbling crowd as Sarah took to the center stage, enveloped by the piano and plants. Louis knew center of attention for her was an uncomfortable place. Her rosy cheeks, either from heat or nerves, accompanied her throughout the introduction.

Louis didn't notice Samuel breathing during her whole welcome speech, but he did sigh, almost a whistle, when she finished. Applause erupted for Sarah and for the upcoming performers. Beginners to advanced students paraded their talent, playing pieces from Bach to Mozart, hymns and sonatas and a few lively pieces like "Yes, I'm in Love" and "*Le Coucou.*" The only reason Louis knew them had to do with Elizabeth's playing and planning the program.

He looked around the room at each chair filled with a parent or grandparent or friend. Charles Town was lucky to have a group of women who wanted to spread music into so many homes and lives. Perhaps the homes would still resonate with harmony throughout the dishevelment of war. Would Elizabeth play in the months ahead with the intent of easing fears and uncertainties?

The last piece, Sarabande in G Minor by Bach, performed by one of Elizabeth's older students, brought the audience to their feet. Applause resonated from the exuberant crowd.

Elizabeth and Sarah curtsied and smiled. Did Louis read relief in Elizabeth's countenance? Their eyes locked, and he raised his hands higher, clapping with the rest. He nodded his head in approval and blew her a kiss. She acknowledged him with a bow. Joy at the success was evident as her eyes glistened with tears.

"Now to endure the reception and get these women home," Louis said.

Samuel laughed. "After you. I could use a cup of punch. I think I was anxious as much as the performers. Does that mean I've the emotions of a little girl?" He followed Louis into the drawing room along with the stream of well-wishers.

Samuel rescued Sarah from a crowd of parents, found her a seat, and delivered her a cool drink. Louis and Elizabeth hovered close by. Louis whispered in Elizabeth's ear, "Are you glad that's over?" Her eyes twinkled in the lamp light. If nothing else, she was happy.

"It's strange." She turned to him. "All that work and stress and then in an hour it's over. I want to let it all soak in before I relinquish the event. Does that make sense?"

"In other words, you enjoyed the process, and now you want to revel in the conclusion of a successful season." Would she be able to find fulfillment in her time at home?

"Yes."

"I'm proud of you. Look at all those faces, of the girls and parents. They are definitely happy." He wondered if the feeling was akin to how he felt after a completed venture or task following months of planning. Although the merchant world was not an art form, maybe it was a talent in a way. The fulfillment of a job well-done spurred him on to continue, like it did these girls.

Elizabeth burst into her parents' house Saturday morning full of news of the recital. "Where's Grandmamma?"

"She's had a little setback. Dr. Ramsey saw her yesterday," Mother said.

"And?" Elizabeth lifted Harriet out of the carriage and handed her to her mother. Then, she removed her straw hat and gloves.

"She's weak, very weak. She's asked for you."

Elizabeth reached for Harriet, but her mother sent her in alone. "I'll watch this little one. You take your time with Grandmamma."

Like a child, Elizabeth followed the instructions. She peeked around the door and crept into the temporary bedroom. The petite form, covered in blankets even on a hot morning, stirred and whispered, "Come in."

Elizabeth glided to the bed, not wanting to disturb her grandmother's rest. "How are you feeling today?" She stroked the pale, chilly hand laying outside the covers.

"Tired with no energy. But you've changed that. Where's Harriet? Surely you brought her."

"Mother has her for now."

"So, she is making decisions for me now. Who I can see or not see? I'm glad she let you in." The frail woman grinned, witty even in weak health.

"I don't think she could have kept me out. You know how I am when I'm determined."

"A lot like your old grandmother. You'll need that streak of stubbornness and determination to conquer life's challenges."

Elizabeth straightened the pillows, tucked in the covers, and brushed back a piece of her grandmother's hair. What did Grandmamma know about her illness? Was there hope of renewed strength and recovery?

Hope? Always. God's will of restored health? That might be a different story. Elizabeth prayed her grandmother had many years left, but looking at her diminishing body, she realized God possibly had other plans.

"I came to tell you how wonderful the recital was Thursday. You would have loved the performances. Almost like the concerts we heard in Boston." Elizabeth giggled. Comparing her girls to professional famous musicians conjured up the image of how proud she was of them.

"I always thought of you that way when you played for me. Remember the mini concerts you held for Grandpoppy and me and your dolls? And cats?"

"I know—anyone or anything that would listen." This was one of the reasons Elizabeth continued with piano forte lessons and teaching. If not for Grandmamma's encouragement of a mediocre music student, Elizabeth would have pursued another art form.

Grandmamma grabbed Elizabeth's arm with the strength of a woman half her age. "Promise me, you will teach the girls, all three of them, to play the piano forte. Please don't forget Christine. She will need you. I wish I would be around to help. But you and your sister will see her properly reared along with my Mary."

Rarely did Elizabeth hear her mother referred to as Mary and never "my Mary." Such an endearment had to come from a deep well of love for a little girl of the past, but one vivid in her grandmother's memory. Her daughter. She loved her still, as strongly as Elizabeth loved Harriet.

"I promise." Elizabeth took the outstretched hand. "But you need to stay around to help. You're the only one who understands me."

"Don't be silly. You have Louis and Anne and from what I have seen, your mother. She is changing, perhaps a little more accepting."

"But none of them are you, Grandmamma." Elizabeth wiped away a tear. Grandmamma had always been her trumpeter, her supporter, a kindred spirit.

"When the time comes, you will have all these years of memories to draw on. I won't be far away." Grandmamma's eyes drooped, and her grip lessened. "I'm sleepy now. Next time bring little Harriet to me no matter what your mother says."

Elizabeth kissed her cheek and placed her grandmother's hand under the covers. "Sleep well. I love you."

She slipped out of the room. How many more times would she get to say that to her dear grandmother?

In contrast to the fragile sleeping form a few doors away, Harriet sprang to life and activity. It appeared Father instigated the rambunctious noise. Cradled in one of her father's arms, the baby rocked to and fro, reverberating with high pitched giggles of glee. Father's deep bursts of laughter vibrated from the depth of his being and lunged out at Harriet's antics.

"Papa, you have created a scene I can't duplicate. You are spoiling her. She'll want to shout all the time." Elizabeth shut the sliding doors to the parlor. Maybe the walls would absorb the hollering.

"No, I'm not. I'm just rocking her and tickling her feet. She's the one carrying on so loudly. Your mother planned on putting her to sleep, but Harriet said, 'No, I want Granpapa.'"

He winked at Mother, tatting a placemat. Poor man didn't have a hope of getting his way with daughters, granddaughters, and his wife in his life. The stern man of yesteryears mellowed in the past year as the tide of change swept into the colony. Elizabeth never thought she'd see such a staunch, legalistic Royalist turn his commitment to the colonists. Was he still happy in his stand? She didn't dare interrupt his playtime with such a solemn discussion.

The spacious room offered a view of her father and the baby from a comfortable chair next to her mother. Elizabeth leaned over toward her mother, inspected the elegant flower design, and let out a sigh.

"Why did Grandmamma travel all this way in her condition?" Elizabeth really didn't expect an answer, yet her mother set her work down and folded her hands on top of it.

In a whisper, a smooth, soothing, comforting cadence, Mother said, "She came here to die."

"Oh." Elizabeth sucked in the word and covered her mouth with her hands. "How do you know?"

"Because she was so determined to get here at this time, even against doctor's orders. She knows wherever she is the outcome will be the same. God gave her a slight recovery in order to make the journey. Now, she is at peace, surrounded by her family." Her mother wiped away a tear and smiled.

Elizabeth could count on her fingers the number of times she'd seen her mother cry or witnessed a sniffle. The sound punctuated the revelation of her grandmother's decision. She tried to make sense of a tear and a smile at the exact same moment. The closest she could get was the pain of childbirth at the same moment as a baby's first cry.

"I'm glad she's here. Although, this will be the hardest thing I've ever done. I love her so much."

Mother secured Elizabeth's hand in hers and ran her thumb over the top. "You know that you are her favorite, and you are the most like her." Elizabeth vaguely remembered her mother holding her hand as a child but not in recent years. The touch erased years of doubt about her mother's acceptance of their differences.

Mother held tight. "I was jealous for years at the ease you had with her. She and I would argue and fight, whereas, the two of you would laugh and share."

This gentle supportive, honest mother surprised Elizabeth. "What changed?"

"I did. As I tried to understand you more, it opened my connection to my mother. Your free spirit, vocal opinions, and love of life guided me to an open window to understand your grandmother."

Elizabeth sprung from her chair and hugged her mother like a child hugging a big sheep dog. Hugs and kisses, a freedom she didn't normally experience with her mother.

A deep voice boomed. "Careful, you're going to knock your mother out of the chair. You talk about me being rambunctious. Humph." Elizabeth had completely forgotten about her father in the room.

Laughter filled every crevasse of the closed-in room. Harriet ceased her giggles and stared from face to face. The child lost her single focal point and reached for Elizabeth.

"Well, we've enjoyed our stay. And if it's all right with you, I'll come again tomorrow and the next day. And if there is any change for the worse, please send word right away."

"Yes, dear. I'm glad you accept the prognosis and your grand-mother's motive," Mother said. "It's pure love for all of us."

"I know that now."

How could Elizabeth have a spring in her step and a tune in her heart with the news of the day?

Remember, Elizabeth, I am in charge, and I choose joy for you even in the valley.

With a tear and a smile, she lifted her face to the sun and jour-neyed home.

CHAPTER 16

*J*une buzzed in with mosquitos and a called Provincial Congress meeting. Louis expected the insects and preferred them to the hum and sting of war.

"While you visit the sick and poor in spirit, I'll join the ones not faint of heart," Louis teased, sending Elizabeth out the door on Thursday morning.

"The first day of June and not one, but two sick. The heat will not help Grandmamma or Sarah."

"But you can." He peeked in her basket and tried to steal a blueberry biscuit.

She moved the basket out of his reach. "Oh, no you don't. You had plenty at breakfast." She winked. "What time will you be home?"

She fastened her bonnet strings and slipped on her gloves before Louis finished recapping his agenda for the day. "Anything could happen and then change the next day. I miss the predictability of routine."

"It sounds like Robert will be as involved as you are this time."

"Actually, we are both requested to be present. It should be interesting. What do they need with a sea captain and a French merchant?"

She wrapped an arm around his neck pulling him in for a kiss. "Unfortunately, a lot, *mon amour*. Both occupations are useful in a war. The combination is an asset."

He wanted to make light of the occasion, but not Elizabeth. She hit the nail on the head. A war, a merchant, and a captain were more of a fit at a second glance. He chose not to miss the meeting and fanfare, if he could help it.

Elizabeth left to tend to Sarah, now confined to bed for rest and observation, and to visit with her bedridden grandmother. Ellen had Harriet for the morning as Amy collected Christine. Louis exited his house of joyful baby activity for a gathering of yelling, debating, and rioting men. He laughed, for the noise level at his home and the Exchange could be the same. Although the needs of babies could be met easily with food and sleep, meeting the needs of the colony could prove impossible.

Yet, he chose that course of action instead of passivity. He'd rather be on the inside of the decisions for his life than the outside with no say and no warning. He began to understand Elizabeth's desire to know his involvement. These decisions affected her life, also.

Robert and Louis arrived together. Henry Laurens motioned for them to proceed close to the front row of seats. "I want you in a position to hear everything and to ascertain all you can. Mr. Gadsden requested you to receive firsthand information for your own use. You'll know what to do when the time comes." Mr. Laurens' words held no comfort, even though coated with compliments.

Louis immediately missed the back wall of his previous visits. Feeling slightly guilty for taking a front row seat, Louis looked around at the gathering crowd and leaned closer to Robert. "Well, the town has come as well as representation from the whole colony. This Provincial Congress won't be speaking of peace, I'm sure." Louis finished his perusal and focused on the podium.

"I don't think we really know what this Congress will do," Robert said. "I've a feeling it's the accumulation of what we've campaigned for over the years. Remember, we joined the Sons of Liberty freely. Now, our commitment will be challenged."

"It's the next step. I just hope we don't skip any vital steps in between. If I know this group, we're in for a long jump. They're tired of crawling."

The gavel pounded on the podium, the echo embedded in Louis' head as if a drum announcing a warning. "The Provincial Congress of South Carolina is called to order on this the first day of June 1775." Colonel Charles Pinckney commenced the meeting with the consideration of his rank.

With no opposition, the body elected Henry Laurens as president of the Congress. No surprise to Louis. Along with Christopher's fervency, this man supported the cause in his dealings at home and abroad. The only thing Louis didn't understand was why he had sent his daughter away to England, the enemy. The man feared for her safety beyond normal anxiety. Louis wanted his family close to him under his protection to deal with everyday problems together. Was that selfish? Did Mr. Laurens have the right idea?

Louis learned quickly about the seriousness of the circumstances. Congress ordered the raising of three regiments, authorizing funds for the defense of the colony, and installing a thirteen-member Council of Safety.

The people and the Congress members set out to draft a document for citizens to sign, declaring loyalty to South Carolina.

"What if someone doesn't sign it?" A man stood up in the back and belted his question over the heads of hundreds.

Mr. Laurens said, "His name will be noted and in time, hopefully, he will be persuaded to sign."

"He should be tarred and feathered. Shown as an example," another said.

"Not so fast. We don't want to start a lynching campaign," Mr. Laurens responded.

Louis gauged the spirit of the crowd. The radicals versus the moderates. He leaned toward the moderate side. Each man should have the right to sign or not sign.

Personally, he wanted to hear what the document stated. Most likely, he'd agree and sign. He had invested his career in this cause and his life in this colony. He even taught his wife how to protect herself. There was no turning back for him.

"What does the document state?" A man from the middle of the room asked. Louis didn't turn to investigate the owner. The anonymous man voiced Louis' question. At this rate, Louis could remain seated and silent, out of the center.

"The document is called the 'Association'," Mr. Laurens began. "It states that the representatives, those who sign, should be prepared to go forth and sacrifice their lives and fortunes against every foe in defense of liberty." He paused and stared out over the crowd. Why didn't he make eye contact with anyone? The speaker seemed to have a focus beyond the group. Surely, he didn't expect to get opposition from the crowd. It took great willpower for Louis to remain focused on the speaker instead of the crowd behind him.

"Furthermore, although not stated in the document, citizens who refuse to sign the 'Association' are to be treated as enemies."

Louis understood why he paused. The clincher. Wouldn't a refusal drive everyone towards independence?

All around the room whoops and hollers from radicals drowned out the solemnity of the moderates. Was anyone picturing friends and neighbors who were Loyalists, and what this would do to them, equal until this document?

"Tar and feather. Tar and feather," burst from different sections.

The gavel descended. "Please don't turn this into a violent tar and feather mentality. The purpose of this document is to see who has joined and supported our ranks. We don't want to provoke riots."

Louis shook his head and leaned forward, elbows on his knees. He turned back to Robert and whispered, "Would some people do that? Tar and feather a person?"

"Unbelievable, but yes. It's been done in the past over disagreements, and I could see it happening again," Robert said.

Once, twice, and a third time the gavel sounded, booming attention. Order restored for the vote. The Congressional members unanimously passed the resolution for the "Association" document.

"The Council of Safety will secure the signatures over the next three months. The document is available to be signed today when the Congress recesses," Mr. Laurens said.

Louis and Robert signed the document placed on a center table for all to see, manned by Mr. Laurens. With no qualms or misgivings, Louis knew he had to commit once again.

The crowd dispersed for the noon meal. Across the street from the Exchange, Louis and Robert entered a tavern for a savory, steamy fish pie.

They took their food and drink to a small table crammed in a corner. "This will have to do. The people and the noise aren't conducive to a quiet, peaceful meal," Robert said.

Louis set his items down and pulled his chair to the table. "At least our conversation will go unnoticed and unheard."

A few bites later, Louis settled back in his seat and looked over the room. Men in their groups of comrades paid attention to their own conversations much the same as Louis and Robert.

"Did you ever contemplate removing Anne and your children from Charles Town?" Louis twirled his moist glass, watching the clear liquid splash to and fro.

"I'll admit I did pose the question a few years ago. I decided that here with her family in a familiar place is the best protection I could give her. And I still believe that. Why do you ask?"

"Seeing Mr. Laurens this morning made me wonder why he sent his children away when so many others didn't." Louis wanted the best for Elizabeth. "Like you, this is the best place for my family. My only other option is France." He sighed. "But the state of politics there is unstable as well."

"Sometimes we have to face obstacles head on. Anne and Elizabeth know that. They are strong and intelligent and know what the situation is, although none of us knows what will happen."

"True. I did offer to send Elizabeth away to her cousin's, but she would not budge on the issue. Here she has family and support. This is all new to me, having two people who depend solely on me. Make that five, if I include the Engles. I'm glad to know someone who has been at this marriage thing longer than I have. It's a huge responsibility."

Robert laughed and scooted his plate away. "Just wait until you have more children."

"Perhaps that will happen after the war." Louis still hoped concessions would be made and bloodshed avoided. Any duration of war was too long. What would this one be—a year, two years, five years? Could the colonies hold out that long?

A messenger from Congress delivered messages to them at their table in the obscure, dark corner.

"How did you find us?" Robert took the letters and handed Louis his.

"Mr. Laurens said to check the taverns, and this one was the closest. Anyway, the owner knows you."

"Thank you, young man." Robert placed a coin in the messenger's palm.

"You're welcome, sir."

Louis opened the seal. "Please return to the Exchange at five this afternoon for a briefing. Henry Laurens."

"Mine is exactly the same. That gives me time to go home and see my family."

"Me, too. I never know who will be there—Christine, Charlotte, Anne?" Louis shrugged. "At least at your house you are guaranteed two boys."

Robert patted Louis on the back. "Just you wait, if you don't have sons, you will have boys courting at your house in a few years."

Louis laughed. "Quite a few years, I hope." Harriet and visions of courtship danced in his head, followed by scenes of Louis scowling in the young men's presence.

"I'll meet you at the Exchange a bit before five." Robert donned his hat and exited to the right, Louis to the left and Church Street by way of Tradd Street. He needed to fill Uncle Henry and Aunt Jeannette in on the details.

"You signed, of course," Aunt Jeannette said.

"Number fifty-five on the list." Even in the front row the line to sign had queued up quickly.

"I don't know when, but I'm sure the list will make it to you, Uncle Henry."

"This has Christopher Gadsden written all over it. He must have commissioned it before he left," Henry said.

Louis leaned on the counter facing them. "I agree. Overall it is well-supported by the citizens at the meeting but at various levels of agreement."

"Let me guess. Some want the signatures, others want whole lives." Jeannette hit the concerns exactly. Louis cocked his head toward her. How did she do that?

"Right. The problem will be for the ones who don't sign," Louis added.

"Let's just hope lynching and dueling don't start back up," she said. "There was a time when that was how people handled diversity or division. We'll see." She shook her head and stepped aside to help a customer.

Uncle Henry rammed his fist on the counter. "But unfortunately, if war comes, citizens will be killed for their beliefs. That is part of taking a side."

It jarred Louis out of his casual position. Nothing like sharp vibrations to move an object. He stood straight. "Yes. And we have chosen ours. Now, I need to share with Elizabeth."

A few minutes later he found himself on the front steps of his home grasping the iron rail. It seemed like he brought home intense news all the time. What happened to days of planning an outing or anticipating a shipment or a wedding? Could he even use anticipation with a war scenario? Maybe dread or anxiety.

I'm in charge here, Louis. Follow me. A still, quiet reminder. No matter the inconsistency of man and his opinions, God would remain in control.

His life certainly hadn't become easier since he placed God in the number one position. He had to trust and continue to obey. Things were too big for Louis, but not for God Almighty.

One foot in front of the other. The harmonic sounds from the piano reached him before the domestic scene emerged. Elizabeth sat on the bench with Amy by her side. He paused, not willing to disturb the girl enthralled in the notes.

He knew Elizabeth took a few hours a week to advance Amy's skill. In a little over a year, the girl had changed into a cultured, educated young woman. All due to Elizabeth's care. Although a housemaid, Amy had benefited from their openness in bringing her up in society. Louis chuckled. One day this sprite of a girl would attract many young suitors. He was glad Ellen would have that task. His day would come with Harriet.

The ladies turned around. Did he laugh out loud? He meant to take a few more minutes, observing the domestic simplicity. Serenity in the middle of a mixed-up world.

"Louis." Elizabeth scooted off the bench and flew into his arms.

"What did I do to deserve that?"

"Nothing at all." She accepted his kiss and pulled him aside into the parlor. "Why are you home already?" The middle of the afternoon wasn't his normal, although he wouldn't mind this sort of respite more often.

"The meeting ended at noon. After lunch, Robert and I received a request to meet again at five with the committee. So, I have a few hours to spare. And there's no better place than here."

"And you are going to share all and not hold any tidbit back." Not a question. She looked at him from her lashes. She had proven in the past that she could handle troublesome news.

"Are you sure?" His protective instincts desired to withhold pieces of the puzzle, maybe just give her the edges or the corners. Leave the middle to fill in later.

"I'm sure. Have a seat and tell me all, the good and the bad." She patted the cushioned place next to her. Music continued in the background as Amy practiced as if oblivious to any disturbance.

"The good is easy—there's not any." He decided to avoid any fluff. No sun peeking through the dark clouds.

"Oh." She frowned but seemed to fortify her resistance to run or turn away.

He shared what he recalled. Repeating the words stirred the pot of reality. This wasn't make-believe. The consequences, only looming before, coursed toward possibility. Now, they pursued a path of vital certainty.

He paused, not sure where he stopped.

"And you signed?" Her question jarred him to the present.

"The 'Association' document? Yes, I signed."

"Although I'm fearful, I'm proud of you." She placed her hand in his. It shook until he clasped it tighter.

Part of the consequence of loving someone involved making decisions, possibly ones that could bring pain. The last thing he wanted to do to his family was to make the wrong decision and cause unneeded pain and remorse. "I want to do what is right.

And for now, I'm processing my role in the biggest event in my life so far. I'm listening to all options and finding my place. Maybe the answer will come this afternoon." Or would more be demanded of him?

"That's for later. Right now, you have an engagement date in the garden with Harriet and me. I'll go get her. You grab a blanket and meet us under the shade tree."

He loved the part of Elizabeth willing to accept the conflict and then sprinkle it with pleasure. Perhaps that was why he chose to spend the remaining hours with her instead of returning to work. They captured an idyllic hour, reposing on the ground shaded by huge magnolia limbs and leaves. Buoyed by Harriet's giggles and antics, including playing with Cleo's tail, Elizabeth laid on her back, ankles crossed, reciting nursery rhymes. Louis entertained the baby with a finger and toe game.

The bells of St. Michael's rang the four o'clock hour. "I must prepare for the meeting. I don't know if Mr. Laurens would appreciate the grass and dirt and possible baby drool."

Elizabeth laughed. "We're going to stay out here as long as she is happy. I'll get a little weeding done."

He kissed the top of Elizabeth's head. "I might be late. Have Ellen leave something on the warmer for me, please." Again. How many more times will he miss a meal with Elizabeth?

At a quarter before the hour, Louis met Robert outside of the Exchange. Two was better than one any time, not that Louis dreaded spending time with Mr. Laurens. The prospect of a talk with Robert by his side was always easier to stomach.

Louis knocked on the big double doors at the end of the second-floor hall.

"Come in," resounded from the chamber.

Only a portion of the Congress members assembled at the

huge oak table. Fifteen of the men huddled over papers and documents. Only Mr. Laurens rose and extended his hand.

"We've been working on the particulars of our new resolution. We'll break and confer with the matter involving you." Louis and Robert followed the man's lead to two seats close to Mr. Laurens. Nothing in his request suggested the committee would be involved.

Introductions were brief. Louis knew all except a few from the backcountry and lowlands south of Charles Town.

"We asked you to come in for special assignments as arms of the South Carolina Provincial Congress. You both are highly recommended by members of the Continental Congress too."

Louis looked at Robert and shrugged his shoulders. Robert raised his eyebrow. He didn't have a clue either. It rang of something Christopher would suggest.

"Mr. Lestarjette, the Congress needs your service as an interpreter for any documents or personnel that come our way in Charles Town. Later, the Congress of the thirteen colonies might need access to your expertise."

An interpreter. He knew that was a possibility. The only question was the element of danger.

"And," Mr. Laurens left no room for Louis' comments or questions, "we need you to coordinate French merchants and shipments in the future."

Riskier, for sure. It would not be much different from what he did now except on a grander scale and with an element of secrecy.

"Does this interest you?" Mr. Laurens posed.

Did Louis have a choice? Could he say "no"? It didn't matter. He had an ability that he could share. "Yes. I'll do it." If he could make an impact on the colonies' success, he would.

Mr. Laurens crossed his arms on the table, pushing aside some papers. "Fine. We don't expect any action for a few months."

The pace of the meeting amazed Louis. After a few comments shared among different men, the president changed direction and highlighted Robert's purpose. Louis relaxed. He receded to the background with pleasure. He let out pent up breaths, leaned further against the back of his chair, and rested his elbow on the arm.

"Now, Captain Cochran, we also have business with you. Your name has come up many times here and in Philadelphia. The Continental Congress and our local congress have need of good solid sea captains. You fit the profile."

Mr. Laurens took a sip of water. Louis didn't understand how the man kept talking all day. Did he even break for a meal?

"The Continental Congress will probably form a Navy, and we'd like you to consider giving your expertise as needed. In the near future, ships will need to be outfitted for battle. We are awaiting word on when and how many. Most likely, you will have to go to the ships and perhaps Rhode Island, for a time."

All eyes on Robert. If he didn't have questions, Louis sure did.

"Sir, what about my commissions with merchants? I plan to leave on one to France in July." More specifically, on the *Rose* for Louis and Christopher.

"I'm certain that one will be fine. But in the future, decisions and choices will have to be made. Your cargo might change as well as your boss."

For some reason, chuckles broke out around the table. Louis figured the mention of a new employer applied to everyone—merchants, planters, artisans. All would be called on to adjust time, contribute funds, and maybe even fight.

"So, do you accept this challenge?" Mr. Laurens gained control of the room with his booming voice.

"I will, gladly," Robert said. Louis assumed Robert had the same urge to propel his action toward the success of the cause. At this point, there was no need to hold back, for the sooner the exchange of power took place, the sooner life could return to normal. How long could the upheaval last? Two months? A year? Longer? It had barely begun.

The fresh air and light breeze outside the Exchange Building pushed air back into Louis' lungs. *Almost as I thought, except on a much larger platform. It certainly won't be anything near normal.*

Louis' new normal would be as French interpreter and merchant for the South Carolina and Continental Congresses. He didn't count on this when he landed in Charles Town almost three years earlier.

CHAPTER 17

The social season came to a halt in the heat of summer. Elizabeth and the rest of the citizens moved at a snail's pace through the days. Her ventures started early in the mornings, to avoid the extreme humidity and heat of the day.

Ellen wiped her hands on her apron. "Elizabeth, if you don't slow down in this horrible, sweltering heat, you won't be fit to help anyone."

Beads of perspiration glistened on Elizabeth's neck slipping into her bodice. "But I have to check on Sarah and Grandmamma and pick up Christine."

"And what if you get sick? Who will help you?"

"What is your suggestion?" Elizabeth hoped she didn't sound annoyed. She didn't feel like she had the luxury to stay home. Anyway, she couldn't wile away the hours with a cold drink in hand. Activity was the best remedy for summer doldrums. To pacify Ellen, she plopped in a chair and waited for the magical solution. As hard as she tried, she couldn't think of one.

"For today, let Amy and me take care of Harriet and Christine. You concentrate on yourself and the two invalids." Ellen paused and glanced at the ceiling before finishing her plan. "Then you go to lunch, preferably by yourself, perhaps to the Grand Hotel, and take as long as you like."

Elizabeth's mouth hung open as unladylike as her posture in the big chair. "You make it sound like I'm a woman of leisure making my calls and lingering over a casual meal."

"Well, you could disguise it that way. Do a little dreaming."

When did Ellen get to dream? Over a biscuit in the kitchen? Elizabeth couldn't shake the feeling of slothfulness.

Ellen's concoction won. Elizabeth's last glimpse before departing captured Amy on the floor with Harriet kicking her feet, and Ellen in a chair with a cooing Christine.

The click of the door and her release from the house for a few hours presented a slightly altered reality. She still had two sick loved ones. The hope of a quiet meal was the fairytale. She didn't see how that would happen.

First stop was Sarah's. Mrs. Collins showed Elizabeth to the upstairs room. "The doctor says she needs to stay calm and in bed until the cramping stops."

Sarah's mother squeezed Elizabeth's hand and whispered, "I don't know what she will do if she loses this baby. I lost my first two and remember not wanting to live." Tears glistened, and Mrs. Collins wiped them away.

"Sarah's strong physically and spiritually. Surely, her faith will see her through no matter what." *Would my faith have held if Harriet had been taken away?*

"I know." Mrs. Collins pumped Elizabeth's hand one more time before releasing her. "Anyway, you always do her a world of good."

Sarah's mother peeked around the door to her daughter's room. "You have a visitor, my dear. Just who you asked for earlier. I'll leave you two alone for a few minutes. Don't tire yourself."

Propped up on three pillows, Sarah, pale and weary looking, had her hair cascading in front of her shoulders, pretty and clean.

At least it radiated health. If only the shine would spill over into her friend's eyes and cheeks.

"Good morning. How are you?" Elizabeth hugged Sarah's delicate body, straightened the bedcovers, and perched on the side of the bed.

"Much the same. I'm so tired of this bed. But it is the answer. To keep this baby, I'll remain here another five months." Sarah's forced smile produced familiar dimples. If only rosy cheeks and sparkling eyes would follow?

"That's the spirit. You aren't the first young woman put to bed for similar situations. And many have healthy children just because they followed doctor's orders."

"But, what if…"

"Please, don't think the worst." What could Elizabeth say to convince her friend all would be all right? Would it?

"Maybe I did something to make God punish me. Some sin that He hasn't forgiven."

Elizabeth shook her head, surprised at Sarah's thought pattern. "You know better than that. God doesn't work that way. Bad things happen every day, but not because God makes them happen. He loves you and your baby. That fact remains true no matter what happens. Keep your strong faith, Sarah."

"It's so hard to pray without being angry."

"Then I'll pray for you. God understands when words don't come easily."

Could positive words and positive thoughts heal Sarah and Grandmamma? God could do it if He willed it. She'd voice Sarah's wordless prayers in her presence and throughout every day beginning right now.

"Father, Sarah needs You in this very room at this moment. You know Your purpose for her and this baby. Show her Your will. Bring Sarah so near to You that she feels Your arms around her." Elizabeth felt it flow from her heart to God's.

"Thank you." A true smile procured a place on Sarah's face, giving a twinge of sparkle to her eyes.

"What news do you want to hear? You know the social scene is rather dull in the summer, but I can fill in a few details." Somehow, Elizabeth found the positive bits and pieces of news and gossip. The emerging war or talk of war remained as background and not the center of their words. Church, current fashion, courtships, music, and the plans for the school dissuaded all negativity.

Did Sarah want to hear about the babies? *I can't hide that part of my life from her. How would I take it if I desperately wanted a child of my own?*

Elizabeth inhaled and exhaled. "Right now, Harriet and Christine are probably competing for Amy's attention. I'm sure Ellen had to escape to the kitchen either out of need or a chance to think without the constant baby talk."

"I'm glad you mentioned the babies." Sarah glanced at Elizabeth. Her smile had become more prominent. "I noticed your hesitation. No matter what, your Harriet will always be a part of my life, as you are. Don't cover up her life in order to spare mine. You promise?"

"I promise." Elizabeth spoke through tears while Sarah remained calm. Instead of being the comforter, Elizabeth was comforted.

Too soon, Mrs. Collins stepped into the room. "It's time for Sarah to rest." She adjusted her daughter's pillows and felt Sarah's forehead with her hand. Pregnancy was not a fever, but the gesture reminded Elizabeth of being a mother, a reflex.

"Tell your grandmother 'hello' from me," Sarah said.

"I certainly will. I'm off right now. I'll see myself out." Sarah was in good hands, the best.

The sunshine, and even the warm breeze, gave a jolt to Elizabeth as it bronzed her skin. Today would have been a good day for her straw hat. *Sarah will regain her strength, right, Lord? And Grand-mamma too?*

Elizabeth came to the Elliott house with the same expectation each time. Grandmamma would be better. And each time she left with the diagnosis of no recovery. Elizabeth never gave up hope, but each time she resigned herself to the fact that the seventy-one-year-old woman would not get better.

She entered the garden through the side gate into her old garden sanctuary. Someone kept the bushes trimmed and flowers weeded and watered. Was it so long ago when she had sat here and dreamed of the future? Of Louis?

Running her hand across the back of the bench triggered memories of a handsome foreigner teaching her French and in time, the art of love. In truth, she couldn't separate the French lessons from the wooing of courtship, a love affair out of a novel.

A giggle escaped. Love certainly reigned in the end. *My little childhood world of flowers and foreign words transformed into one of abundant color. A book still being written in many languages.*

The respite in the garden momentarily sheltered her from the harsh reality of Grandmamma's room. Elizabeth picked a fresh bouquet of zinnias, honeysuckle, and daylilies, and raised them to her face. The scent and intricate colorful details would brighten the bedside table.

She lightly knocked on the back door to the house and turned the handle at the same time. Even though it wasn't her home anymore, she enjoyed the familiarity of it.

"Hello, Mother?" Elizabeth slipped into the bright sunroom.

"Ah, Elizabeth. You caught me resting." Mother started to rise. It was only eleven in the morning, but Elizabeth knew her mother's days were full of worry about Christine and Grand-mamma. She had lots of help, but even the noise of a baby was tiresome. And constant anxiety over an invalid required rest. The last thing any of them needed was for her mother to become ill.

"Don't get up. I'm going to check on Grandmamma. You rest a bit longer."

Elizabeth's fatigue from earlier disappeared as she compared her daily life to her mother's, thirty years older. What did Elizabeth have to complain about when her mother lived each moment with a dying loved one in one room and a motherless baby in another?

The drapes rested secure in their sashes letting sunlight stream across the peach-colored covers and onto her grandmother's shallow, drawn cheeks. Elizabeth advanced to her bedside, looking for a sign of wakefulness.

"Those smell nice," Grandmamma whispered. Elizabeth had forgotten about the bouquet and the soothing aroma of honeysuckle.

"How are you this morning?" Elizabeth placed the colorful arrangement in an empty vase on the bedside table and poured a bit of water from the pitcher to soak the stems.

"I'm glad to see you, dear. Sit right by me, as close as you can," Grandmamma said, her voice raspy and faint. "Tell me all about the outside world--especially your little family."

The pattern was always the same. Elizabeth talked, shared, told stories, read, and Grandmamma listened. In the past, their roles had been reversed. Elizabeth had always sat at Grandmamma's feet to gain knowledge and comfort and to hear stories of the past.

Elizabeth heard her own voice in the room, but what was she saying? Her concentration vanished and slowly her words ceased.

"What's bothering you little one? You're far away." Grandmamma pushed up on her elbows and gave Elizabeth her full attention as Elizabeth was accustomed to from her. But did she know her feeble thoughts? Her negative inklings?

Elizabeth didn't know any other way to be in her grandmother's presence than with truth and honestly. Hadn't she taught Elizabeth as a child to come to her with anything?

"What if Sarah doesn't have a healthy baby? What if she loses the fight for the baby's life?" Elizabeth paused and caressed the smooth, soft cotton coverlet between her fingers. "Then, what if?" Her eyes widened, and her mouth formed an "o" with no words. Was she really going to finish the most dreadful question?

"And what if I die? Is that your question?" The hoarse whisper carried through the silence. "I will leave you soon, Elizabeth, and if Sarah's baby does, too, then rest assured I will be rocking him in heaven. You have nothing to fear on my behalf."

"But I need you. I have so many questions, so much to learn."

"You are surrounded by people who can help you with answers. Louis, for one. And the wisdom of your sister and Jeannette and Ellen. I've passed on all my worldly knowledge over the last twenty-one years to you. You'll be fine." Her gnarly hand rested on Elizabeth's. Her grandmother's voice gained strength as she filled Elizabeth with reassurance.

Still, Elizabeth shook her head, not ready to take the next step without Grandmamma. "But I don't have answers about this war or what to do if Louis leaves to help. Or what about the safety of Tom and Raymond or Robert and George? What do I know of true physical pain or death? I don't want to do this without you."

Grandmamma turned her face to the side and coughed. Her words lowered and softened. "Poor child. I didn't know either with the last wars. Remember you have a Heavenly Father who has all the answers. Depend on Him, not on me. I'm just an old lady, and I'm ready for home."

"I don't want you to go." Elizabeth bit her lower lip and tried to control the tears. No luck, though she did manage to prevent sobs. The slow trickle evidenced her sorrow.

Elizabeth scooted off the bed and knelt on the floor, her face only inches from her grandmother's. "I'm going to pray for you. And my prayer will be a selfish one."

"God understands those kinds too. Yet, why don't you ask God to show you His will. And then accept it."

Elizabeth nodded, and the remaining glistening tears dampened her grandmother's pillow. Another good piece of advice. With her grandmother's hand clasped between hers, Elizabeth prayed. "Father, I praise you for Grandmamma's life. It seems I am constantly asking You for healing. In my selfish desire, I request a miracle in the lives of Grandmamma and of Sarah. You have blessed me so much; now bless them and heal them. Now, I add in Your will. You have a plan and I can't imagine it without Grandmamma. Amen."

"Amen." Grandmamma's eyes closed, and her words fluttered on the lightest of air.

"Rest, now. I will sit here a few more minutes."

Elizabeth gently pried her hands from her grandmother's, pulled a rocker close to the bed and shut her eyes, too. Utter peace surrounded her. So calm, Elizabeth couldn't even think of a misfortune or negative ordeal from her present.

When she awoke a quarter hour later, her renewed spirit coaxed her to give thanks for having known Grandmamma in an intimate way. She kissed the dozing woman's forehead and backed out of the room.

The clock on the mantel in the parlor chimed half past twelve. She still had time for a light noon meal. Ellen's gift of a few hours would have been worth it even if Elizabeth had only had the nap. Now, a quiet luncheon, too. Even better.

"Mother, Grandmamma is sleeping, and I'm leaving now." Mother had embroidery in her lap. Her chair faced the back garden.

"Don't you want to stay to eat?"

"Not today." *I have other plans. Ones that include only me.* She couldn't tell her mother in those words. They sounded so self-serving.

By one o'clock the Grand restaurant contained a few guests, but most had returned to work or home. Elizabeth chose a round table for two in a far corner. She could watch the strollers on the boulevard and the guests inside without drawing attention to herself.

She ordered a plate of finger foods--cucumber on bread, spinach filled pie, cheese biscuits, and ham and cheese puffs. Each bite was delicious and savory, perhaps because there were no crying babies in the background or household questions to answer or the interaction with Louis. She held her biscuit in midair. Louis would be a perfect addition to her meal, even if he talked non-stop. Solitude served a purpose at times, but by the end of her repast, Elizabeth wanted the noise of her life to return. The sooner the better.

She settled her fees and walked out the door into the sunlight and a fast-paced trip home.

Louis hadn't made it home all day. Samuel found Louis in the storage room at Wilson's, bringing news of the British boarding ships and forcing them to leave the coastal harbors.

"All ships?" Louis took off his apron and laid it on top of a grain barrel.

Samuel paced and turned at the wall and strode back again. "No. All the British ships are allowed to enter. We must think of a way to make sure our ships can unload. The next shipment is due in a week. I spoke with Robert. He agreed to scout out a place to dock further south. I know of a few from an earlier conversation with Christopher. It's as if he seemed to know something like this would happen."

Louis crossed his arms and lifted his chin, deciding to focus on Samuel's face and not his ever-moving shoes. He half-smiled. "We could expect nothing less. He left his business in capable hands. Yours."

"Well, I'm fine behind a desk with a pile of papers and some figures, but espionage is out of my jurisdiction."

"Right. You have Robert," Louis suggested.

"And you. I need you to decide how to transport the goods to Charles Town. Obviously, it will have to be overland."

"I think we can trust some of our inland carriers, but I'll clear it with Henry first. Anything else?"

"Not right now. The foremost issue is safe delivery of the crew and cargo."

And keeping the road open for future deliveries. Secrecy played a major key in success. Louis' confidence had increased over the past two years. He had a small group of men he could trust, and so far, his name had not surfaced in the papers or propaganda. Discretion reigned at the top of his list.

After seeing Samuel to the door, Louis joined Henry in the office. Perhaps, a second opinion would make more sense of a solution.

"I know of three merchants from Orangeburg who will help," Henry said. "I'll contact them and have them ready when Robert returns."

"Good. Christopher's plantation outside of Orangeburg can house the bulk of the goods until we can cart them to town." Henry didn't pace like Samuel, but he didn't stay still for long either. He jumped from his stool when the discussion ceased. Louis surmised Henry had letters written in his head ready to begin the smuggling process.

Smuggling? It hadn't come to that, or had it? Louis shook his head, dislodging the negative connotation of "espionage" and "smuggling." Sins in any other situation, except war? At least, Louis hoped he'd be forgiven his dabbling in secrecy. After all, God had sent out spies in the past.

Louis' and Elizabeth's day merged around six o'clock most days. He tried to shield her from a collision course, but today left him perplexed. She had enough to muddle through without his additional ruts in the road. But they had promised to share at least some of what went on throughout the hours apart.

She rushed into his arms before he placed his hat on the entrance table. How did she do that? He doubted she waited at the door. *Instinct, I suppose.*

He fingered her cheeks and lifted her face to his, pressing the tiny wrinkles by her eyes, imagining he wiped away the stress. "How was your day?" She squeezed him tighter around his middle. Affection but no words. "Speechless?"

"It can wait." She released him and helped him out of his light jacket. He loosened his cravat. "How was yours?"

"Another repercussion of challenging the British. The boycott of non-British goods is in full-force. They are turning away ships."

"And how are you involved?" She held his hand and he followed her to the dining room. Harriet dozed in her carrier at the edge of the table, situated beside Elizabeth's seat.

"I have to help Robert figure out how to transport cargo inland from a southern port. Messengers have been sent and Robert is making plans. He'll have to be gone a few days."

"Without danger?"

He jerked his head in her direction. "We didn't discuss that. But, honestly, there is a possibility of a confrontation, if a British ship is trailing them."

Elizabeth stepped in the hall and motioned for Ellen to serve.

"Don't worry about Robert. He will be very careful." Louis pulled out Elizabeth's chair and gently set it right under the table.

"I'm concerned for Anne." Elizabeth adjusted her linen napkin in her lap. "But we both know your involvement is risky. I'm praying that you won't be pulled away from me any time soon."

He caressed her hair and rested his thumb at the base of her ear. "It's all in God's timing. For now, let's enjoy our meal."

Ellen entered, as if on cue, with a hearty vegetable soup. "Fresh from the garden—carrots, potatoes, snap beans, and onions. Tom says it's the best he's tasted."

"Thank you, Ellen." Louis picked up his spoon and hesitated. "I think we need to pray."

Louis led the prayer. "Thank you, Father, for this meal. We pray for Robert's safety and for the health of Grandmamma and Sarah. Guide us to do Your will. Amen."

"Amen."

He retrieved his spoon and consumed the steamy soup. He noticed the slow advance of Elizabeth's spoon to her mouth. She had listened patiently to him and hadn't mentioned a word about her day. That was his fault for bursting out with his poignant news.

Louis stopped and set his spoon down. "Tell me about your visits this morning."

"The same as before. Sarah, then Grandmamma. Sarah is ready to change scenery and feel normal. I just don't know when that will happen." She set her bowl aside. Ellen cleared the dishes and replaced them with plates filled with ham, creamed corn, and biscuits. "I'm afraid Grandmamma has only a little time left. I confessed to her today that I don't know what I'll do without her."

"And I'm sure she had wise words for you." He responded to her surprising smile.

"She did. She said she'd taught me all I needed. And now I have you and Harriet to take care of, and she is ready to go. Ready for heaven." Her shoulders drooped, but her smile remained. "She's happy, so how can I be sad? I'm not ready, but she is."

"Hmm. Sounds like God has prepared her, and she is preparing you."

"Yes. That's true."

Louis didn't remember his grandparents, but he had lost his father, which had been difficult. But now, as a Christian, death didn't hold the same grip. He knew Elizabeth's grandmother was close to God's side, and He was bringing her nearer every day.

That night on June twelfth, a servant from the Elliotts' house, delivered the message. Grandmamma died at eight in the evening.

Louis held Elizabeth as she sobbed. He saw her tears as a witness of her dedication to a unique, loving woman. Was Elizabeth prepared? Perhaps. The older woman gave her a gift of her last days. Louis was grateful. He rubbed Elizabeth's back. Slowly, the tears subsided as she slept in his arms.

CHAPTER 18

"*I* don't think I'll ever be used to viewing her body or anyone else's. It's been three days, and still people come by Mother's house." Elizabeth fiddled with her black satin fan, opening and closing it with her sweating fingers in black satin gloves.

Anne sat by her on the sofa in the back sunroom away from the casket and guests. "I remember grandfather's funeral in Boston. Streams of people and poor Grandmamma, greeting each one just like Mother is doing now."

"I don't see how she does it. Don't they know Grandmamma is not there? She left this world three days ago and is now peacefully with Jesus in heaven." Elizabeth wiped away a fresh tear. She hated the black hat with the veil flowing down her back. Black everywhere. Grandmamma would have wanted yellow and white and lavender.

"It's out of respect. All these people have no other way to show their love and concern for the family than this." Anne's hand over hers stopped Elizabeth's fidgeting.

"I wish Louis were here."

"He will be in a few minutes. The crowd will leave, and we'll prepare for the processional. At least the walk isn't far to the graveyard."

"True. Do you think the children are all right?"

Anne giggled. "With the nursemaids and the Engles, those little girls have a perfect situation. The boys wish they could stay and play, but Robert and I agree that the funeral is a part of life. They're old enough to experience this with us."

Elizabeth felt the unfamiliar bulk within her gloved right hand. She took the delicate covering off to gaze again at the silver band on her finger. The wedding band of her grandparents. She touched it, wanting the life back who wore it for fifty years. Grandmamma had set it aside in a box with a note for Elizabeth. "May this band of earthly silver remind you of heavenly rewards awaiting you."

Moments later, Louis caught her sniffling lightly. "Here." He knelt in front of her, handed her his handkerchief and remained patiently. "Wipe your tears. We need to gather in the parlor for prayer and instructions."

"I'm glad you're here." She dried her face and smiled for him and for Grandmamma. Louis' deep blue eyes beckoned her to obey. It wasn't the first time he used his sheer good looks and passionate eyes to draw her close. While lost in them, she felt protected and enveloped in love. She placed her glove back over her ring and allowed Louis to escort her to the family.

Only family assembled in the presence of the draped casket, closed now for the procession and service. Gone were the seemingly endless throngs of people. Reverend Smith gathered them around in a circle. Anne laced her fingers through Elizabeth's on the right and Louis held Elizabeth's hand on the left. Through glistening eyelashes, she studied each member for a split second. Anne, Mother, Father, Robert, little Robert, John, and Louis. Not many, and one was missing. George. Grandmamma loved him so much. One of her last requests was to not give up on him and to love his daughter. *I will, Grandmamma, I will.*

They followed the stark black velvet-draped casket, carried by six pallbearers, to the entrance of St. Philip's Church cemetery. The minister, followed by the casket and the family, filed in before the remaining guests filtered around the site. Elizabeth clung to Louis' arm. The seriousness attacked her senses. The profuse aroma of diverse flowers enshrouded her, weighing heavy as if hovering over the casket. The words of the minister droned with the beat of her heart. Her fingers ached to run one more time over Grandmamma's wrinkled cheek.

This was the end of her grandmother's life, surrounded by loved ones in a holy place. Actually, she knew it to be the beginning of a joyous life for her grandmother. The somber service became a celebration for Elizabeth looking through the eyes of her dear grandmother. The eulogy and prayers contributed to her smile and renewed commitment to rejoice.

When the last prayer was said, and the dirt began to fill in the hole, Elizabeth squeezed Louis' hand in hope and recognition of the resurrection into a new life in heaven.

He raised his eyebrows to her. Did she look different? His expression denoted a question. She would fill in the blanks for him later.

"You handled that very well indeed." Louis and Elizabeth walked slower than the rest back toward the Elliotts'.

"Yes, well, I had help from God and Grandmamma. I started viewing the whole ceremony as a celebration of her life, and the certainty that she is in heaven. How can I be unhappy for her? I will just have to live with the fact that I will join her in eternity one day."

"I wish I had felt that peace at my father's funeral. I was so bitter and selfish. I blamed the church and the government and even my father for his death. I know he has forgiven me since I now understand his beliefs. It does make me look at death, at least death of a believer, differently."

"Yes, it's comforting."

Silence covered them for a moment. They rounded the corner onto Queen Street and almost careened into a crowd of revelers.

The cries were jumbled. Elizabeth stopped, not understanding the words at first. "What are they saying?" She looked at the men and women and even a few children.

"Let's stop by this gate and let them pass." Louis pulled her to an iron railing.

"Send Campbell home. Send Campbell home." The words rang clear once Elizabeth stood still. An effigy of a man in black robes with a crown on his brow rose on a pole high above the crowd. The people followed a banner emblazoned in red "Down with the Crown."

"Lord William Campbell," Louis said, "the new royal governor of South Carolina, must have arrived. That's all I can think."

The group of forty or so filed by, and Elizabeth tried to figure out the purpose of the march and the items they carried. "Look, half the people have buckets, and some have bags. I hope that's not what I think it is."

Louis crossed his arms and nodded his head. "Buckets of tar and bags of feathers. I would say it's only symbolic, but last week a man was tarred and feathered for not signing the 'Association.'"

"They can't do that to the governor." Surely, Charles Town was more civilized than that. Signs, marches, and chants Elizabeth accepted as a mode of protest, but physical damage to a body was another thing all together. She couldn't see the streets of her town as a battlefield.

"Some participants at the Provincial meetings threatened these acts, but the Congress didn't condone their actions. I thought that would be an end to it." Louis craned his head.

The last reveler rounded the corner. Elizabeth shook out her tense arms and shivered. What would Grandmamma say to such a display? At least Elizabeth didn't recognize anyone in the crowd.

"Governor Campbell will have a rough time here. I don't think his power will reach to the level of the Provincial Congress. I'd say he'll last less than six months." Louis clicked his tongue and emphasized his prediction.

"Then what?" She linked her arm in his for the final stretch to her parents' house.

"I think the loyalists will lose the fight and give the colonies their freedom." *I pray that is the end result. If not, we are all on the losing side with the quest for freedom gone forever.*

She stared at him. "In six months?"

"No. In time."

Louis had a tough time digesting the fact that he had just come from a burial and faced a band of rebels. And harder still was the fact that he was labeled a rebel. He would never want to be associated with the lowness of tar and feathers, but in the end, they were on the same side.

Since compromise didn't work, perhaps the threat of war would jolt action from the British. Wasn't that what Christopher and the Continental Congress were hashing out day to day?

Louis placed his hat and jacket in the butler's hands and followed Elizabeth into the parlor. The only reminders he saw of the visitation were the vases of flowers accompanied by their rich fragrance. The chairs and sofas had been returned to their parlor-like places.

Robert motioned for Louis to join him in a tight circle with Mr. Elliott. "I suppose you saw the protest."

"We stopped until they passed." Louis released his cravat a bit. The heat of the day and tension of the walk tried to suffocate him.

"This doesn't bode well for Lord Campbell. I have many

colleagues with the college and business associates who won't be happy with the crude tactics of the townspeople. This isn't encouraged by the Sons of Liberty?" Mr. Elliott raised one brow in question.

"No, sir. As far as I could see, they were part of an independent group." Louis defended the organization; the one Mr. Elliott had joined.

"Good. You know where I stand on independence, but I don't want to be labeled with this level of demonstration."

"Neither do I," Louis said, and Robert nodded.

The three men dispersed. Louis satisfied his thirst first before mingling with the guests. He knew most of them. Almost three years in Charles Town rendered the faces familiar. Church, business, college, and all their connections with Elizabeth helped increase his acquaintances.

He watched his wife take some of the burden from her mother. She and Anne were as two stone pillars, supporting the roof over their mother's head. Just how long their strength would last, Louis dared not speculate. He hoped the whole event would end soon. If he could have Elizabeth home in their own room, he could shelter her better, reinforce his vow to protect her.

For the moment, he prayed. *Father bring her near to You and protect her where I cannot.*

Louis walked straight to Elizabeth. Even in mourning black, her trim figure attracted a second glance. His arm around her back made her pillar of rock a little stronger. He wanted her to pass on some of her anxiety to him.

She whispered, "I want Harriet. It seems like longer than a few hours. And to think she is right upstairs."

"I'll go get her in a few minutes, if the crowd doesn't dwindle before then."

"Thank you."

He marveled at the way she glued an interested, appreciative half smile in place for the remaining guests. He didn't have to rescue Harriet after all. As if on cue, the nursemaids and Amy brought the three girls into the parlor. Was it predetermined, orchestrated by Mrs. Elliott? Or even Ellen?

What a transformation on the three women's faces. Sorrow to joy in an instant. It was almost comical how the three pairs of arms reached at the same moment for their babies. A laugh escaped him in his mesmerized stare. The baby girls provided a medicine to Elizabeth, Anne, and Mrs. Elliott.

Little Robert and John joined in the arena, completing the scene. "This is when my wife is her happiest," Mr. Elliott said. "Surrounded by her daughters and grandchildren."

Louis stood with the men and viewed the tableau of mother-hood. On the outside, except for the somber clothing, no one would suspect the sadness of an abandoned child, a loss of a loved one, and a revolution brewing. If Louis could capture it forever, he would. For now, he smiled and soaked in the natural beauty of his family, each one of them.

Days later, Elizabeth hummed a hymn. Surprisingly, it helped her concentrate on the in and out of her needle. She wanted the stitches to be as even and professional as possible.

The words separated in her brain and mentally aided the humming. *"You fearful saints, fresh courage take, The clouds you so much dread, Are big with mercy, and shall break in blessings on your head."*

She almost giggled. Here she was making shirts for soldiers and singing of God's mercy and blessings. Strangely enough, she felt the words to be true.

"Judge not the Lord by feeble sense, But trust Him for His grace; Behind a frowning providence He hides a smiling face."

Hum, in and out, hum, in and out. A constant rhythm.

"Elizabeth," Ellen interrupted. Elizabeth lost her thread. "Miss Sarah is here to see you."

"Thank you. Show her in, please." Elizabeth discarded the shirt and rushed to her friend's side.

"Should you be out? Did Samuel bring you? Here, take my seat. Do you need anything?"

"Stop, Elizabeth. I wouldn't be allowed out of the house if it wasn't all right. I will sit, though."

Elizabeth grabbed the material she'd placed on the sofa and arranged the cushions for Sarah.

"There. All comfortable." Elizabeth took the wicker chair directly in front of Sarah. With elbows on her knees, Elizabeth stared. After over a month, Sarah had been released to move about in small doses around the city. She appeared pale, with a slight twinge of color on her cheeks, and a little wobbly and weak. But her round belly delighted Elizabeth. So far, the baby was fine and growing.

"What are you making?" Sarah pointed to the wrinkled wad of plain flannel material.

"My first shirt for the South Carolina regiment. The ladies asked what they could do for the new army and shirts were needed. Lots of plain, long shirts."

"Let's see."

Elizabeth held up the plain shirt. "This was from a rectangular piece of fabric. It pulls over the head with one single button at the collar." She placed it against her and stood up. It swallowed her petite feminine form, landing below her knees, almost to the floor.

"I could fit in that." Sarah laughed.

"We both could. Anyway, it must be full and wide for maximum comfort. Shirts are the first thing to wear out in active military duty."

"How many are you going to make?"

"As many as I can. Louis will supply me with the fabric." Elizabeth tilted her head and raised a quizzical brow. "Sarah, you could help too. It might take your mind off your confinement and the hot afternoons."

"I agree. It could relieve the long boring hours of inertia. I become weary of sitting with my feet up and reading the same pages over and over. So, show me how this incredibly huge shirt is put together."

Their mid-summer project continued over the week and coincided with news of George Washington's command of the Continental Army and the call for volunteers. Elizabeth couldn't help but think her hands created a shirt for someone she knew. Maybe someone like Tom or Raymond or, she hated to think it, Louis or Robert.

Shirt number five entered the basket. Louis would be proud of her progress. She stretched and closed her eyes while the open windows in her sunroom let in the barest of breezes.

Her lips parted at the faint pressure of Louis' familiar kiss. Slowly her eyes opened.

"Hello, my dear." He bent down in front of her, caressing each of her wrists with his thumbs.

"What time is it?"

"Early. Only four. I had some news I wanted to share, but upon finding you so peaceful and enticing, I might hold off on it." Elizabeth still loved the way he teased her senses into response.

"Maybe the news can wait. And I'll just go back to my dream of light kisses and caresses."

He moved her to his lap on the sofa in one swift action. She had no time to refuse, not even if she wanted to escape. She snuggled into his arms and let her head drift back on his shoulder. "Are you sure your news can wait?"

"Oh, I'm sure." He smiled, the same smile which captivated her two years ago.

The semi-seclusion of the sofa with its back facing the door sheltered them from unwanted eyes. Any minute Harriet or Ellen could interrupt, but at least she had one moment to relax in Louis' embrace.

He could stall no longer, or the time he set aside for a quiet discussion would overflow into supper and attention to Harriet. Gently, he settled Elizabeth next to him, draped one arm on the top of the sofa, and reached in his pocket for the letters, surprised they hadn't burned a hole.

"You've turned serious on me now." She straightened her skirt and folded her hands in her lap. He smiled at her attempt to render herself prim and proper all of a sudden. Humorous, since she was in her own house with him, hardly anyone to impress.

"I'm ready to listen," she said.

He pulled in a deep fortifying breath and let it out with his words. "I received three letters today—two from Christopher dated July first and July eighth and one from Silas Deane from the eighth. I won't bore you with all the minute details, but I think there are things you need to hear and understand." He unfolded the first missive, three pages long. Where was the vital information in this one? He ran his finger down to the paragraph he needed.

"Christopher writes: 'I have been appointed by the Congress President, John Hancock, to serve on a committee to put the militia in a proper state for the defense of the colonies. We are appealing to each colony to send ammunition and supplies to the Continental Congress.'" Louis looked above the page to Elizabeth. She focused on an object out of his vision, not moving a muscle.

He continued, assuming she had no question. "Edward Rutledge, Thomas Lynch, and I have each signed eighty-four fifty-pound certificates to be collected from South Carolina for the colony's share in the war effort. The Secret Committee is collecting the items. Please cooperate in handing over the items stored at my warehouse and your mercantile."

Still Elizabeth didn't speak or move. Did she know what was coming? Knowing her, she saw through the commentary to the real request lurking in the paragraphs to follow.

He cleared his throat and shuffled to the second page. "I always wondered what we'd do with our stash. Now I know. Let's see. He wants to use *The Rose* and suggests ways to hide the items. We're used to that. Most likely Georgia will send ammunition to ship with ours." Louis stalled with one important item left.

Elizabeth focused on him, her fists now balled up ready to, what? She used them to accelerate off the cushions. "You are avoiding telling me what Christopher really wants." Hands on hips she continued. "Let me guess, my darling." Sarcasm floated in the air. "He wants you, and most likely Robert, to escort the cargo to Philadelphia. And while there become embedded deeper in the workings of this." She waved her hands over the letter. "What is this? Oh, yes, the revolution."

He knew she was smart, but this bordered on mind reading. "How did you do that?"

"Oh, Louis, tell me it's not true." Her anger dissipated into sweet, loving words. He had to shake out the image of her anger and replace it with the present one.

His shoulders dropped in relief. "Well, yes, that is exactly what he requests. Robert to captain the ship and me to oversee the loading and transporting of the items." The worst spilled out and only the consequences left to endure.

"How long?"

"Christopher would like us to remain in Philadelphia for a month. With travel, about six weeks."

Her raspy, quick breaths whistled in and out. Was she getting enough air? He walked toward her, arms outstretched, and let her fold into them. Her breathing calmed with his touch.

He put his hands on each side of her face, making her look

only at him. "What's this all about? I've been gone before, remember, for a longer time."

"But that was before we were married. Now, it's different. It's dangerous and, well, I've gotten used to having you around. I just don't want you too far away." She pushed away, her hand covering her mouth, as a slight giggle escaped.

She was soon laughing. He would never understand her. "Now what?"

"I seem so silly and so very selfish. I do apologize, Louis. I see myself as a prissy old woman, always wanting her way. But I'm not that way yet. I'm just a young wife, loving and supporting her husband."

The transformed woman before him obviously knew her mission and mind, once she passed the "woe is me" stage.

"Of course, you have to go. We knew it would happen." But did he really believe it ever would? The future was always unpredictable. Now, it breathed down his back.

"You are a constant surprise." He held her closer. "Do you think Anne will be as understanding?"

"She's accustomed to Robert being away, just not on military business. We'll have each other. Now, what about the other letters? Are they as bad?"

"No. Assuming, I am going to Philadelphia, Christopher instructed me on some happenings, and Silas gave me things to think about and present to the Secret Committee."

She crossed arms and raised her eyebrows. "Read them to me and let me judge for myself."

Louis returned the first letter to his coat pocket and retrieved the second shorter one from the table.

"Dated July eighth from Christopher. 'I joined forty-five others in signing a document entitled the Olive Branch Petition. It's addressed to the king in a last, desperate request for autonomy within the empire. It is good propaganda to prove to people here and abroad that we are doing our share to halt hostilities.' Then he continues and says he looks forward to news from Charles Town soon."

"An olive branch was a nice idea. Do you think King George will even consider it?"

"Not at this point." Louis had already concluded last month that reconciliation was near impossible. But God could intervene and change the mind of any of His people. Louis tired of questioning why God allowed this conflict to continue. He changed his question to what? *What am I to be doing for God in all of this?*

Amy knocked on the door and entered with Harriet in her arms.

"Come here, my girl." Seven-month-old Harriet reached for Elizabeth at the sound of her voice. "It looks like the last letter will have to wait, unless you can win the place of center of attention from this little angel."

"I wouldn't even try. She wins without a fight." Harriet turned to his deep voice and bounced in Elizabeth's arms. His vantage from the sofa displayed his greatest treasures, his baby-talking wife and his cooing daughter.

As he expected, the conversation never turned back to the letter. No matter. The pertinent information he needed to share with Elizabeth was out. After dinner, he put the letters in his desk. A proper night's sleep would better lead to a comprehensive reply. He didn't mind delaying his commitment for another eight hours.

Louis sparked Elizabeth's curiosity. Surely it wouldn't hurt doing a little of her own unraveling of events. She almost called it snooping but stopped. What better source than someone who confronted the news from the ships every day? She realized the sixteen-year-old might not be the most valuable or reliable source. Who would share secret information with him?

With her student as a captive audience, Elizabeth tried her

questioning skills. "Raymond, what do you hear at the docks about the threat of war?"

"You mean about the war, not the threat. It's definitely started."

"All right, the war." Elizabeth encouraged her student's opinions, as long as he used his English skills. Their weekly lessons brought him closer to an advanced knowledge and usage of the language. But according to Louis, Raymond's French would be a commodity praised and sought by the Continental Congress.

"Of course, it depends on which ship the crew arrives. I just listen. The British crews laugh and carry on about the disorganized Continental forces, mostly their lack of trained men, ammunition, and weapons. Today one group made jokes about the uniforms. Is the American army brown or blue? One said our forces are wearing their best dinner jackets." Raymond wasn't laughing.

Elizabeth placed her elbows on the table between them, moving the grammar textbook aside. "Uniforms? If they aren't red coats, the army will be distinguished just fine. I'm sure the Congress has more to worry about than the color or cut of the jacket." She shook her head. They sounded like a bunch of women discussing the attire for the next ball. Sometimes she didn't understand men.

Raymond nodded. "True. Then the crews coming off the American ships talk of joining the forces and fighting. Some even have some battle plans. How to protect their hometowns and property. Miss Elizabeth, it's downright frightening at times to hear the conflicting views. Do you still think I'm too young to fight?"

"Yes, Raymond. You're not even seventeen yet."

"I will be in a few months. Do you think the Wilsons will let me go then?"

"Wait and see. All this might be over by then." She didn't want to dwell on Raymond and Tom entering the frays of war.

She grabbed a book from the pile. "Let's read a little about

William the Conqueror. His battle stories ended in triumph." Well, victory for one side. There was always a winner and a loser. Quickly she prayed for America's success.

❀

The next morning Ellen met Elizabeth in the foyer, pacing. That was unusual for the hardworking woman. Elizabeth gleaned from the dried tears and splotchy cheeks, Ellen wasn't concerned over a fallen cake or burned toast.

"Ellen, what happened?" Elizabeth took her hands.

"He's leaving tomorrow. My Tom is joining the town regiment full-time." Ellen wrung her hands loose from Elizabeth's grasp and resumed her to and fro path in the hallway. "Oh, what will I do?" Where was the courageous, proud woman? She was replaced with a mother, who loved her son.

Elizabeth led her to the parlor but didn't force her to sit. "I'm so sorry. I'm afraid we knew this was coming, maybe just not so soon." Elizabeth tried to fit herself into a mother's role with a grown son but couldn't quite imagine the desperation.

Ellen sucked in her breath filling her lungs for continued speech. "I know. At least he told me. So many others have left without notice. Not my Tom. I taught him better than that. I won't stop him. No, I won't. But how does a mother go on with a son in battle?"

Elizabeth certainly didn't know, except for one idea. "Prayer. You pray every day. And I'll join you in that promise. I'll pray for Tom's safety every day until he comes home again."

"Yes, I can do that." Ellen pulled a handkerchief from her sleeve and wiped her eyes and nose. "And I'll add all the other men who are risking their lives too. Thank you, Elizabeth. I think I can get back to work now."

Reaching out, Elizabeth hugged her before Ellen scurried away to duties Elizabeth saw as unimportant, considering the moment.

Yet, mundane chores brought simplicity and importance to an otherwise chaotic existence. Her duties like today's care of Harriet, and later Christine.

The evening meal turned into a farewell affair for Tom. The Engles joined the Lestarjettes for dinner. Elizabeth suggested the meal be self-serve from the side board, giving Ellen an opportunity to enjoy her son. Elizabeth wanted it to be relaxing for Ellen as well but doubted emotions could be subdued enough.

"So, you will be stationed south of Charles Town in the low country, I hear," Louis said.

"Yes, sir. I don't know exactly where. I'm sure we'll move often. Captain Shanks keeps the details secret for good reason." Tom devoured the roast and potatoes between sentences. Elizabeth guessed he knew camp food would not equal his mother's.

"We expect you to write to your mother when you can." Louis winked at Tom and nodded in Ellen's direction.

"I will for sure. And I'll throw in words for Amy, Mrs. Elizabeth and you, sir."

Ellen dabbed her eyes with her napkin. "And I'll be able to respond?"

Louis put his glass down. Elizabeth was thankful he knew so many answers to things she hadn't thought about. "Yes, the courier will know how to deliver your letters. Also, I have connections with the local regiment recruiting department. It will be taken care of somehow."

"I wish I could go." Out of midair Amy's words pierced the air. Elizabeth noted sharp twists of all heads.

"Really, Amy, what would you do?" Ellen was the first to gain a semblance of normalcy.

"I would tend to the sick or cook the food, make the beds, and

I can shoot, remember?" Amy sat taller, adding an inch to her fourteen-year-old frame. They all laughed.

"I will admit," Tom said, grinning widely, "you are better than half of my regiment. You would not be good for their morale. A girl better than a man. Unbelievable, if I hadn't seen it myself."

Amy smiled. Elizabeth remembered the sibling playfulness she once had with George. Hopefully, Tom wouldn't change toward his sister.

"I'm not ready for you to leave, yet, Amy. What would Harriet and Christine do without you?" Elizabeth turned to Harriet in her highchair. "And don't forget your friends at the school and your mother. I think Charles Town is the place for you right now." Leave the fighting to the men, Elizabeth wanted to conclude, but why draw the conversation back to unpleasantness?

"Time for dessert. Tom's favorite, pecan pie." Ellen used her palms to raise herself from the table.

"No, I'll serve it, Ellen," Elizabeth offered.

"If you don't mind, I want to serve Tom one last time, for no telling how long he'll be gone."

Elizabeth couldn't argue with that. She watched as the loving mother presented her son with a generous portion of pie covered with cream.

Louis' eyes grew big. "Give me only half that much. I don't know where he will put it."

The next morning Elizabeth stood with Louis, Ellen, and Amy and watched young Tom join others on Church Street marching to meet their regiment.

"God bless you, Son." Elizabeth repeated Ellen's whispered prayers.

Louis opened the storage room at the mercantile and stepped

inside. Faint whistling floated from the far corner. He peered around the shelves.

"Good morning, Raymond. You are here very early."

"Mr. Henry wanted me to clear away a few of these crates and barrels cluttering the middle passage. I had an hour this morning to help."

"What were you whistling? I've heard the tune before."

"It's called 'Free America' with a few new words. You want to hear it?"

Louis wouldn't spoil the young man's enthusiasm with a "no."

"Please." Louis perched on a barrel and folded his arms, curious about the message on the streets.

"*Torn from a world of tyrants beneath this western sky, We formed a new domain, a land of liberty. The world shall own we're masters here, then hasten on the day. Huzzah, huzzah, huzzah, huzzah, for free America!*"

Louis realized the catchy tune and rebellious words would rally young men. "So, that is what you hear on the docks. I need to mingle more on the wharves and pick up the local jargon."

Raymond smiled. "There are new words to 'Yankee Doodle', too, about George Washington. I don't know those yet. They seem to change daily."

"As long as you get your work done, I'm sure your boss doesn't mind." Louis left Raymond who continued singing and working.

Aunt Jeannette stepped through the front door. "Good day, Louis." She kissed Louis' cheeks. "It seems everyone beat your uncle here. The late nights make him slow in the mornings."

"It will be over soon. Once everything is loaded, his job is done."

"Until the next shipment, and the next." She dusted the counter and clicked her tongue against her teeth. "When will it end?"

"It's only just beginning." Louis turned to the back of the store. "I think I hear him now. I'll talk to you later."

His uncle emerged from the storeroom, covering a yawn with his hand. "How are you, Louis? It seems everyone is full of energy today. I just can't seem to get to bed early enough." Henry fastened his apron.

Louis pulled Henry back into the storeroom. "Tonight we will finish loading all the supplies." Henry seemed unaffected. His years of planning had resulted in this. "I'm meeting with Robert and Samuel and a member of the Secret Committee at Christopher's office today. All the details will be discussed, I hope."

"Good. It's time to set sail with this before somehow it is discovered."

Louis tried to discard doubts about secrecy. Surely with the weeks of planning on all sides, Robert and Louis could deliver the goods in one undisturbed voyage.

He briskly walked to the docks, exchanging the busy boulevard for the alleys. Usually punctual, Louis disliked walking in late to any function. He entered as the group of four men took their seats. At least he wasn't in charge of the proceedings. His role was one of messenger and carrier. Did any of these men know of his other role, the one that Silas mentioned in his letter?

"Louis, come in, we were just getting started," Henry Laurens said. The man represented the Sons of Liberty as a trusted old friend of Christopher. Even when their views differed, Louis noticed Christopher and Mr. Laurens had remained steadfast friends.

"Sir. Sorry I'm late. A customer's order delayed me."

"You haven't missed a thing. Now, gentlemen, we've received the five thousand pounds of gunpowder from Georgia and combined with weapons and our ammunition, the ship is ready to be loaded. The bags of rice are already on board to act as cover along with other items. I've lined the Secret Committee up to help with the loading tonight. We have three additional warehouses with goods plus yours, Louis. Help will arrive at each location at nine to cart the crates to the ship."

"And when is departure?" Robert voiced.

"On July twentieth? Is that agreeable?" Mr. Laurens looked at Robert then Louis. Ultimately, Robert would be the one to ready the ship for sailing.

"That gives me four days. Yes, that is fine. Louis and I will plan on leaving early that morning, per your instructions."

Four days? Louis was glad to have a concrete date. But only four days? He anticipated Elizabeth helping him pack, with an occasional frown or tear. Could he do anything differently to relieve her anxiety? Deep down inside him, he believed her inner strength would buoy her for the hard reality.

CHAPTER 19

*E*lizabeth settled on the sofa next to Anne at her sister's house. "Louis has his last French lesson tonight with his faithful students." They shared the same woes and fate. Everything emphasized his departure.

Charlotte ran around the sofa chasing their new kitten. "Meow, meow."

Anne captured her daughter in a playful embrace. "Leave the kitty alone for a while." Anne added playful Charlotte to her lap.

"I'm glad you dropped by. I hope I'll see a lot of you while Louis and Robert are gone."

"You can count on it because I know you'll understand." Elizabeth tried to pinpoint why she thought the trip was different for Louis than Robert. "What has Robert told you about this mission? Any secrets I need to know?" Elizabeth leaned over as if to listen to a whisper. Only Anne laughed instead.

"You think I would know more than you? I don't even ask questions anymore. I take what he tells me, knowing he will share what's important."

"But don't you wonder? What will they really be doing?"

"Oh, really, Elizabeth. Are you concerned Louis is hiding

something from you? Personally, I think all they know is what was in those letters from Christopher and Mr. Deane. Didn't Louis read them to you?"

"Yes. Well, he paraphrased the boring bits. I know why they want Robert, to captain the ship of goods. But Louis? Silas says he wants Louis to partake in the discussions about France. It seems Silas is a vital piece in that area, a secret committee member of sorts. What can Louis add?"

"You aren't that naïve. Besides knowing French and having business connections? He is an important link," Anne concluded.

Elizabeth accepted Charlotte onto her lap. "But Louis is not the only French-speaking patriot in the nation. Surely there are others willing to help?" The child's little legs wrapped around Elizabeth's middle, making it easy for her to play with the shiny buttons on Elizabeth's bodice.

"Who's to say there aren't fifty other Frenchmen invited to Congress? But more than that, Louis is a friend and business partner with Christopher Gadsden. The paper expounds on the man's important role on numerous committees." Anne stopped and enclosed Elizabeth's free hand in hers. Elizabeth glanced up from her niece to Anne's probing eyes.

"What is it?" Elizabeth asked.

"Aren't you proud of Louis?"

"Of course I am." Did all her questions and complaints mean the contrary? "Yes. And I trust him with all his decisions."

"Then let him figure this out and share with you when he can. I don't know if he even knows what else to tell you."

Anne's ten additional years of wisdom in marriage and life pierced Elizabeth's conscience. *I must stop the pity game and give Louis my love and support.*

"You are so right. It seems I have some things to get straight with my dear husband." On impulse Elizabeth turned toward Anne with Charlotte sandwiched in the middle, clinging with laughter, and gave her sister a fierce hug.

Anne returned the hug. "I don't know who enjoyed that more, Charlotte or me?"

"Or me? Now, I can go face my job at home with a lighter heart. I'll be back whenever I need pointing in the right direction."

Elizabeth deposited Charlotte in Anne's arms and scurried to the door. She was thankful the sun didn't set until almost nine each evening. The two blocks home seemed like seconds. Too bad Louis wouldn't be home yet. She determined to keep her mood cheery and attitude supportive. Somehow, she would let Louis know she was so proud of him.

The front door opened and closed as did Elizabeth's book. Not that she had read much over the past hour. Her candle, illuminating her curled body in the big overstuffed chair, was intended to lead Louis to his office. It worked. She viewed his head peering around the door.

"Well, I never thought I would see you here in your chair this late at night."

"How late is it? I lost track of time."

"Around midnight." He motioned for her to join him on the settee. She uncurled her form, discarded her book, and cozied up next to him.

"I expect then that all the details have been hashed out." Elizabeth suspected the French lesson turned into a business meeting. She loosened his cravat and a few buttons on his shirt.

He leaned his head back and closed his eyes. She followed his lead and relaxed against his shoulder. "Nothing more to discuss. I have tomorrow set aside entirely for you and Harriet."

"I'm glad. Since it already is tomorrow, let's start it out in bed." She coaxed him off the couch and grabbed the candleholder. A few hours in his arms would need to last her about six weeks.

Louis glanced in the carriage at his wide-eyed daughter. "Harriet, are you ready for an outing?" She kicked her feet at this question. He hadn't been away from her since her birth for more than a few hours. Would she even remember him after six weeks? "I'll make it up to you when I return. I expect you," he tickled her belly, "to keep your Mama happy." Her giggle encouraged him to continue his tickling rampage on her toes and chubby legs.

"Are you two coming with me?" Elizabeth adjusted her bonnet and pulled the hood of the carriage down as far as it would go.

"Perhaps we can avoid the extreme heat by making a direct path to the park where there are lots of trees." Louis admired Elizabeth's light-yellow muslin dress. His shirt was of light cotton. The lack of layers would surely help keep the breeze flowing freely.

"Just let me get the hamper. We'll need a little nourishment," Elizabeth said.

He took his position at the helm of the carriage and pushed the door out as Elizabeth held it open. Once she closed it, she attached herself to his arm. His two girls. He smiled at the pleasure they gave him. Others had been so right—family brought depth and meaning to life.

The big oak trees beckoned Louis to stroll under their branches. As long as the limbs and leaves were waving, then Louis suspected a breeze would follow. He lifted his face to the cloudless blue sky, peeking between the branches. He would miss Charles Town, even in the summer. But his true love was wrapped in the person of Elizabeth. Why couldn't he take her to Philadelphia? Anywhere with her would be home.

Reason rang through. Moving around in wartime posed safety problems. He even questioned his family remaining in Charles Town. After he delved into the mechanics and politics of the Congress, he planned to revisit the issue of safety. Perhaps it would be time to move away from the port town.

Elizabeth coerced him back to the present with a tug on his sleeve. "Let's stop here. Remember this tree?"

He glanced around. "Yes, I do. I declared my love to you here and devoured a few picnic meals. This is perfect."

Louis retrieved Harriet from the carriage and twirled her around. Held up high, her baby laughter and sprawled arms and legs reiterated the trust she had in him. If only he could bottle it and spread it over the decisions he made for all of them.

Harriet collapsed in his arms and rubbed her face on his shoulder. Pure trust. Elizabeth motioned to the blanket under a shady, grassy spot.

He placed the baby in the middle of the blanket and extended a rag doll to her. "Do you trust me, Elizabeth? I mean, really trust me like Harriet does? She lets me throw her in the air and spin her around without a fear in her little body."

"Hmmm. I do, although I don't want to be thrown or tossed." She laughed. "The day I gave my heart to you, I also gave my life to your protection. As long as you abide in Christ, I will feel honored and provided for."

"But all the decisions that I face."

"We face," she interrupted.

"That we face. Suppose I make the wrong choice? What if I put you in danger?" He paused. The sun through the branches displayed dancing shadows on Elizabeth's face. She seemed to light up. She didn't appear fearful at all.

She stopped her preparations and gazed at him, as if he were the only person in existence. "I've been meaning to tell you for days how proud I am of you. Yes, even proud of your decision to go to Philadelphia to face more decisions about your time and commitments. Why? Because I trust God to use you for His purpose."

She closed her eyes. "The Lord shall preserve thy going out and thy coming in from this time forth, and even for evermore."

Louis had memorized that verse when he sought God's love two years ago. "Psalm 121:8. I remember."

"Yes, and I believe it," she said. "Yet, I'm not naïve. I will fight this war both mentally and physically, if I have to. But I fear I will spend most of my time in a spiritual position of prayer. So, don't you worry about making mistakes. You follow God, and I will do my best to obey and trust you as we obey and trust God together."

"Well, I can't argue with a word you have said. I'm a little relieved." And hungry. He reached into the hamper and pulled out bread and a chunk of cheese. Harriet bounced at the sight of food.

"And some apples, grapes, and meat pies." Elizabeth laid out the rest of the light meal.

Louis sprawled out on the blanket, cushioned by the summer grass. He was a breath away from slumber when Elizabeth whispered, "Don't be alarmed, but there is a woman staring at us. She's behind a tree to your right. Just be casual when you look."

Elizabeth didn't usually let her imagination spill over into unwarranted suspicion. Therefore, he took her seriously. He rose on his elbow and glanced to his right. Odd. There was a figure clad in a full cloak with a hood. He wouldn't have guessed female except for the dark green skirt peeking out the front. The hood covered all facial features.

"Curious. How long has she been there?"

"Half an hour. Since I put the food away. What could she want? Some food?"

"Perhaps. Do you want to motion her to come over here?" Louis thought her harmless, and if all she wanted was food, they could meet that need.

"I'll walk toward her. You stay with Harriet." Before he could protest, Elizabeth was on her way. The figure stepped behind the tree.

"Please come out. If you need something, we'd like to help." Elizabeth's voice carried the few yards.

After a ten second pause, the woman moved forward. Elizabeth gasped, hands to her lips. "Victoria. Is that you?"

"Yes." The woman inched forward, removing her hood. Still as becoming as ever, although her eyes no longer sparkled, and her skin appeared sallow.

"Come join us," Elizabeth said.

How could his wife return hospitality to Victoria who abandoned her child and husband a few months ago? Would he ever understand Elizabeth's deep forgiving attitude?

"I only have a few minutes." Victoria whispered and moved closer to the blanket.

"Why are you here?" Louis didn't want them to side-step the purpose for the sneaky meeting. Victoria was cunning enough still to have a purpose of questionable motives.

The woman smiled or grimaced? Was she in pain? Louis' heart pitied her for a moment.

She cleared her throat. "I wanted to see for myself that Christine was all right. I know she has to be, but I want to see her for myself."

"She's fine. Mother has given her all she needs—food, attention, and love. The only thing she lacks is her real mother." Elizabeth remained calm. She stated the truth. Louis saw Victoria's baby a few times a week. She acted no different than other babies. The outside world would not guess the history of the parentless child.

"I know you think I am horrible." Victoria's shoulders straightened, and her chin rose. Her arrogant gesture escaped her humble façade. "I just can't do it, probably not ever."

Tears fell silently from Elizabeth, not Victoria. From the aunt, not the mother. Louis would never figure out the inner workings of this cold woman. Elizabeth felt more emotion and love for the baby than the child's mother and father together. In fact, Louis believed Elizabeth's love for Christine equaled hers for Harriet, if that were possible.

"What do you want from us?" Elizabeth bent down to pick up Harriet.

"I want to see Christine, just for a minute. But I don't want to go to your mother's house. I don't even want her to know I am here." Victoria wrung her hands, then reached for Elizabeth's arm. "Please."

"You want me to deceive my mother?"

"You can tell her after I am gone."

Elizabeth implored Louis with her eyes for help. His heart battled confusion. The woman abandoned her child but wanted to see her now. He nodded to Elizabeth, and she nodded back.

"Christine will be at our house this afternoon for two hours. You may see her then."

Victoria shook and this time a real tear drizzled down her cheek. Perhaps there was hope. Louis kept his verdict open.

Home now, Elizabeth had time to rethink her afternoon. "What do you suppose she really wants, Louis?"

"I can't begin to guess."

Her last afternoon with Louis had suddenly filled with a surprise visit from an unusual guest. How did someone entertain an unwelcome visitor? Elizabeth decided entertainment was not on the agenda. More of a presentation. A most valuable one, mother to child.

Amy took the message to the Elliotts' and waited to collect Christine. Elizabeth disliked the pretense, but at least this way she didn't have to confront her mother. And since looking after Christine was a normal occurrence, perhaps questions would remain at bay, for a little while at least.

"I'm glad you will be here. It's not that I'm scared of Victoria, but just in case she decides to do something crazy, like…"

"Kidnap her own baby?" Louis finished.

"Exactly. It would seem like that. Just like a crime, but legal." Elizabeth fidgeted with pillows on the sofa and books on the table, straightening the drapes and polishing the floor with her slippers.

And Louis poised in a chair, looking as carefree as a toddler. "Stop worrying. You'll wear a hole in your stockings. Sit down right here." He patted the chair closest to him.

She sat on her hands and rocked. The front door opened and closed with a creak. Amy stepped into the parlor with her bundle in the basket.

"Thank you, Amy. Is she fed and happy?"

"Yes, ma'am. She will last a few hours. The nursemaid will be here at three. And she says thank you for a few hours' rest." Amy giggled and exited through the sunroom.

Elizabeth unwrapped Christine like a Christmas gift. Bright blue eyes twinkled at her, so much like George. Her yellow gown matched her yellow curls.

"Hello, baby girl. Have we a surprise for you." Would a three-month-old know her real mother? Elizabeth didn't think so. But Christine knew Elizabeth's voice and her arms and came to her happily.

Ten minutes later, Ellen led Victoria into the parlor. How did she enter without Elizabeth or Louis hearing or seeing her in the foyer? Ellen cleared the puzzle. "Mrs. Elliott came in through the garden. May I take your cloak?" Ellen draped the long-hooded coat over her arms and left with a frown on her face directed at Elizabeth. Even Ellen knew something was out of place.

At least the dress underneath the hat and heavy cloak, although drab, was lightweight and suitable for the southern summer.

"Come in and have a seat." Louis offered his chair, which put her inches from Elizabeth and Christine.

Now what? Elizabeth's words didn't flow, couldn't exit her confused being. Her eyes volleyed back and forth between Louis and Victoria. He gave a crooked nod, but Elizabeth couldn't fathom what he meant. And the woman sitting so close could only stare at the baby.

Let Me give you strength and the words to say, Elizabeth.

She closed her eyes. The seconds refreshed her resolve. *I can do this.*

"Would you like to hold her?" Elizabeth turned Christine to face her mother.

Victoria shrugged and tilted her head in indecision. "I don't know. Would that be all right with you?"

"Of course. Here." Elizabeth gave a weak rendition of a smile and passed the squirming baby to Victoria. Christine's arms and legs pumped the air. Elizabeth caught a baby grin as mother and child locked eyes. Perhaps Christine did know.

Elizabeth fought the image of herself as an intruder. She rose quietly and joined Louis by the mantel. He placed his arm around her back, securing her to his side.

"Grandmamma would have enjoyed this," she whispered. "Although it's not perfect, it is a start." Louis squeezed her waist in concurrence.

"Perhaps forgiveness and healing can begin now." His words ruffled her hair sending shivers down her spine. Guilty. She hadn't forgotten, or forgiven, Victoria or George. Grandmamma had wanted her to complete the process, but Elizabeth held on to the one thing she could control.

George and Victoria were the sinners. Christine was innocent. Therefore, Elizabeth had a right to judge and harbor her resentment. Didn't she? But was she guiltless while she held so tightly to her grudges?

She focused on the scene before her, a woman her age, who made some bad choices, and a baby, who had no say in the outcome. And the scene changed to face herself, another young woman, standing confidently in a circle of love, passing judgment on another.

Do not judge lest you be judged. But? *Forgive others seventy times seven.*

Elizabeth sucked in her breath and let her tears flow. "Oh, I've been so wrong."

She escaped Louis' hold and knelt in front of Victoria, her sister-in-law, but more than that, a child loved by God.

"Victoria, I am so sorry. Please forgive me. I've not been the person God wants me to be." The words and the tears ran together, forming a puddle on Victoria's skirt. "I want to be loving and forgiving."

Her eye contact at first was with baby Christine who turned her head to the chatter and sobs. Then Elizabeth raised her gaze to Victoria's. The woman's eyes glistened with tears.

"Elizabeth, I don't deserve to be forgiven, but I do ask it of you. You have every right to despise me. I do thank you deeply for caring for Christine. I know now I did the right thing. She's in good hands. I don't deserve your family's forgiveness or love." Her eyelids dropped as if in defeat.

"But God forgives you if you ask Him, and He commands us to forgive, also. You don't have to accept it, but it's given just the same."

"I don't believe that. Because I am about to do the same thing again. I'm leaving. Deserting my child again. I can't live a life like you and Louis, and Anne and your mother."

"But you don't…" Elizabeth shook her head in disbelief.

"The best thing I can do for Christine is to have her reared by family who love her."

"Don't you love her?" Elizabeth no longer clutched Victoria's skirt or hands. She rose and towered over Victoria.

"I do, and that's why I want her here with you. Can't you see I can't give her all of this?" She gestured around the room.

Elizabeth looked around. "This is only stuff. She doesn't need all of this."

"Not the furniture. You and Louis. A family. I have no one. It's me in a two-room cottage."

"You could live here, couldn't she, Louis?" Where did that come from? But he nodded.

"No, I won't." Victoria handed Christine to Elizabeth and walked toward the foyer, retrieved her cloak, and turned. "I don't know when I will be back or if I will. Take care of her please." She pulled her hood tight obscuring her face.

"We will. And, remember God will forgive you, as I do."

Victoria disappeared out the back door, leaving Elizabeth clutching Christine and Louis' hand. "She's gone."

"Yes." He kissed the top of her head. "You are remarkable."

The guilt dispersed with her forgiveness of a woman who didn't ask for it or accept it. Relief mingled with sadness as love abounded for the precious gift in her arms.

CHAPTER 20

*J*uly twentieth. Would Louis ever forget the date? Raymond arrived for Louis' trunks at five in the morning.

"I wish I were going with you, sir," Raymond said. "Or with Tom to battle."

Louis patted Raymond's arm. "I need you to stay with the Wilsons. It's not your time yet." Already the youth stood three inches taller than Louis. He was glad his aunt and uncle had Raymond around for company and an addition to their home.

The previous day, Louis had given a brief goodbye to Aunt Jeannette and Uncle Henry, and they promised to check on Elizabeth and Harriet often.

"Don't you worry, Son. I have lots of plans for us." Aunt Jeannette had given him assurance.

Closing the door behind Raymond, Louis observed Elizabeth gliding down the stairs still in her night dress. *Perhaps that will be how I picture her each night.*

She touched his arm. "Are you hungry, Louis?"

"I shouldn't be after the lavish meal last night. But I know I need to eat something before I'm limited to ship food." He laughed remembering the numerous meals he and Robert had shared on their voyage to France. At least, a one-week voyage promised better fare.

"I doubt you will starve, especially once you get to Philadelphia. I've heard the food is incredible." Elizabeth walked with him to the breakfast table.

Ellen was up early to see to his meal. "Good morning, Mr. Louis."

"You didn't have to do this so early on my account." He opened the lids of steamy portions of eggs and sausage and took a huge whiff. "But I'm glad you did. Would you like to join us?"

"Oh, no sir. It's a bit early for me. I do want to wish you a safe journey and a productive one. You don't worry about anything here."

"Thank you, Ellen." He nodded and turned to the food, the aroma making his mouth water. After filling his plate, he smacked his lips and turned to Elizabeth. "And I suppose you won't eat with me either?"

"Perhaps part of a biscuit." Elizabeth chose the smallest one and added apricot jam.

His plate contained two spoonsful of egg, two sausage links, and two biscuits heaped with preserves to which he added a strong cup of coffee.

"You and Harriet will be at the dock by half eight? We need to pull off at nine."

"Yes, possibly before." She leaned in and wiped strawberry preserves off his chin. "I want every minute with you that I can get."

He chuckled and ran his napkin over his chin again. "What will I do without you?"

"Walk around with food on your face as all the other men without their wives."

Leave it to Elizabeth to somehow rescue them from a potentially depressing morning by dousing it with laughter. She made him second guess his decision. A happy, normal August in Charles Town on Church Street with Elizabeth, or a rowdy, controversial month with a few hundred rebel men? Was he crazy?

An hour later, Louis joined Robert inspecting the cargo. It continued to befuddle him how easy it was to disguise crates and barrels of contraband. Ammunition and arms masqueraded as merely rice, apples, and flour. Would they succeed this time?

There would be no British inspection here in Charles Town. The Provincial Congress ruled the harbor, keeping Governor Campbell and his men sequestered in their offices and houses. Not quite house arrest, but close to it.

Philadelphia could be a different story. Christopher and his committee would handle those details. Still, Louis wanted the cargo out of his hands as soon as possible. One difference in this trip than the previous ones rested in his own personal baggage, including the addition of his pistol that he refused to carry it in his jacket. He could get to it easily, if need arose.

Louis knew immediately when his family arrived. Elizabeth and Harriet in bonnets and colorful garb followed on the tail of Robert and John running down the wharf with Anne and Charlotte close behind. One day his family, or at least Harriet, would run to him. Robert was a blessed man.

Elizabeth greeted Louis with a kiss, a rather long kiss. He didn't care. There were no little old ladies to interfere, only a wiggly baby.

"I think she wants to say goodbye." Louis placed Harriet on his hip, tweaked Harriet's nose, then placed his forehead against hers. "It should be just a few minutes. Everything checks out. It should be smooth sailing under these skies." At least the weather in August was predictable, hot and clear on most days. Although hurricanes and tropical storms could arise, no bad weather was predicted. He'd prefer that to a run in with a British warship.

Elizabeth remained arm in arm with him. "I'm going to learn from my sister how to let you go gracefully."

"So, I don't get even one little tear?" He touched the corner of her eye.

"Not one." She sniffed. "Well, I think even Anne lets one or two out."

"That's better." He shifted Harriet to his other side. "September isn't too far away. If you get bored, go to your cousin's house. And remember you have Sarah and your family."

"I know. And Christine, and Raymond's English lessons, and piano starting soon. I'll be fine." Whether she really believed that or not, Louis couldn't tell with her strong suit of armor in place. Would he rather her this way or a weeping mess of sobs?

"I love you, Elizabeth. I'm doing this for us, for our country, and for Harriet's future."

"And I love you, too. You don't need to explain. Remember, I support you."

Little Robert rang the bell, signaling a five-minute departure time.

"I'll see you in six weeks." Louis kissed her one more time, squishing the baby between them. He handed Harriet to Elizabeth and walked the plank, separating them physically for a time, but not spiritually. He carried her with him as he did once before across the ocean.

CHAPTER 21

Six days later, surviving one rough day at sea, Robert steered the *Rose* into the Philadelphia harbor. Louis gazed through the morning mist at the sprawling city. Charles Town, Boston, and now Philadelphia. Slowly he added personal knowledge of ports in America to his memory. Would his role in this city prove to be a positive step toward freedom for his new nation?

Standing on deck, Louis scanned the dock for a familiar face. Christopher would probably have a runner ready to give him a moment's notice of the ship's arrival. Although Louis didn't think his friend waited solely for Louis and Robert, but he would be there for the prized cargo.

Christopher surprised Louis on the ship deck, not giving him an opportunity to disembark. "Welcome to Philadelphia, Louis." They shook hands. "It's good to be here." At least he assumed it was. Louis still wasn't clear on his role.

"Congress appreciates you bringing the cargo safely to port. We have men in place to distribute the items. I want to take you and Robert to your rooms before we start work. Let's go and find him."

Now the cargo was officially out of Louis' hands. They found Robert logging in the last of the trip's information.

Robert waved at them and concentrated on his figures. "Be with you in a few more minutes."

Louis followed Christopher to the dock. Solid ground. It always revived him. He stretched his arms over his head and behind his back, secured his hat, and straightened his coat. A bath and a quick shave topped Louis' agenda before he explored the city.

While Christopher turned toward the ship, Louis turned his head to take in all the commotion. "I didn't expect so much activity. Does the port handle more business than Charles Town?"

"Many shipments come into Philadelphia, but it does not handle much export like Charles Town. Much of our rice and cotton come through these waters."

Louis spied a coffee house and his mouth puckered up for a fresh cup and a hot breakfast. Did he lick his lips or allow his stomach to give him away?

"Clark's Coffee House is one of the best in town. Why don't you head there, and I'll wait for Robert? We'll join you soon."

Louis nodded, inspired by a hearty meal. "Would you like a full meal too?"

"Only coffee for me. I had an early rendition of breakfast around six."

Louis dodged the carriages and horses. He wasn't used to the constant traffic on foot or otherwise. He'd have to monitor his new surroundings to avoid an accident.

The busy restaurant offered a full plate of eggs, bacon, and biscuits. Immediately, it reminded him of his last meal at home. Memories popped up all the time. What would Elizabeth be doing? Had Harriet done anything new? Several times every day his heart tugged for their presence.

By the time the others joined Louis, the waiter had set the food in front of them. Robert pulled out his chair by a full plate, leaving the third seat for Christopher.

"What's on the schedule for today?" Louis took another bite of scrambled eggs. He'd find a way to listen, ask questions, and eat. Although if he had to order them by preference, the hot meal would come first. The way Robert attacked his food showed he shared Louis' appetite.

Christopher leaned back in his chair with his cup in hand. "Boarding house first. Then I will come for you at eleven for lunch at a tavern where Congress meets. The afternoon session begins at two at the Pennsylvania State House. I don't see any reason to delay exposing you to procedures."

Robert pushed his empty plate to the side and settled back with his coffee. "Any idea what's on the list?"

How did he finish so quickly? Louis decided to forgo the rest of his food. Relaxing won as his attention turned to Christopher.

"With all the ammunition and supplies arriving, discussion continues about distribution and storage, making sure General Washington has access to necessary weapons." Christopher managed to speak of war with an upbeat, springy cadence. As he twirled his coffee in his cup, he wove a dialogue of constant drama. "Every day committees meet as time allows. This day might seem like a whirlwind. You'll get used to the pace, though."

For four weeks, Louis could endure the constant motion of the political heads drawing up the roadmap for the Patriots. Perhaps, he could make his mark.

Mrs. Tate's boarding house was on a side street perpendicular to Chestnut Street, a few blocks from the State building.

"It wasn't easy securing rooms, but this fine lady," Christopher said, nodding toward Mrs. Tate, "graciously gave up her last two rooms."

"How could I refuse such a well-thought-of man? Why Mrs. Sutton has nothing but good things to say about Mr. Gadsden here." Her jovial laugh gave Louis assurance of a pleasurable stay.

"I just hope Mrs. Sutton doesn't get tired of me. I'm in and out at all hours."

"But ever so quietly, she says." The portly woman turned to Louis and Robert. "Breakfast is served from seven until nine and supper at seven in the evening. Just tell me each day if you won't be attending supper. Now, I'll show you your rooms. You will find the baths ready that Mr. Gadsden requested. This way, please."

Louis shook his friend's hand. "Thanks, Christopher. We'll see you at eleven in the parlor." He followed Robert and Mrs. Tate to the second floor. Two rooms at the end of the hall faced the garden. Christopher had remarked the traffic on this thorough-fare would be slight.

The delivery of his trunks half an hour earlier offered Louis a clean set of clothes. Refreshed from a basin of water and a needed shave, Louis had a few minutes before facing a hundred patriots. Uncovering his writing box, Louis set it on the desk, opened the ink bottle, and retrieved his quill pen and a sheet of paper. As he had promised to write often, he penned a letter to Elizabeth. Soon she would know he was safe.

My dear Elizabeth,

We arrived this morning after an uneventful voyage except for a brief two-hour storm days ago. Christopher met us and took us to our abode. Mrs. Tate appears to be a friendly matron, ready to care for two misplaced persons.

I feel each day will be crammed with meetings and discussions, and I know I will long for the peace of our house and life. Give Harriet a special kiss from her Papa. And for you, I'm sending my steadfast over-flowing love, Louis

Short, for now. He placed it on the tray in the foyer to be delivered post-haste. He used his spare minutes to walk around the dining room, study, and parlor. An elegantly set table for ten revealed the number of boarders or family members. The books in the study emphasized there was indeed a Mr. Tate, present or past, for the collection spanned agriculture to history to transportation. The parlor's prize possessions included portraits of Mrs. Tate's family, ancestors and descendants. He was sure he'd know the details before long. A proud grandmother wouldn't remain silent.

Robert entered, adjusting his cravat. "Louis? There you are. I was hoping I wasn't too late." This was the man Louis saw in Charles Town, clean, well-dressed, and relaxed. *Hopefully, I look and smell better, too.* On board ship, it was business first then his attire.

"I had to write Anne a note." Robert reached in his pocket for the envelope.

Louis smiled. "Put it on the table in the foyer right on top of mine."

"Between the two of us they will know what's happening." Robert stepped out and entered again with Christopher in tow.

"Ready?" Christopher asked. "Did you find the facilities to your liking?"

"Perfect," Louis stated.

"Fine for me too," Robert replied.

"Then let's go. I have a table reserved at Fox's Tavern for six of us. No reason to waste two hours when discussions and debates can continue." Christopher was always working on a schedule or agenda. Louis certainly couldn't argue with him. After all, this wasn't a pleasure trip.

By the time they claimed their table, the rooms were almost full. Were most of the clients part of Congress? Through the tavern's window Louis spied the State Building with its clock in the spire. Probably men just like him, a tiny part of a whole, preparing to fit into the big wheel.

"Silas." Louis stood and held out his hand to his acquaintance.

"It's nice to meet again in person, though your letters have kept me up to date. Congratulations on your daughter. How is Elizabeth?"

"Fine. She sends her regards."

Before they sat, Thomas, Christopher's son, joined them. "Mr. Lestarjette, Mr. Cochran, Mr. Deane." Thomas was not yet an imposing figure like his father, but Louis noticed the signs of his training taking shape. The young man's confidence at nineteen exposed his tutelage.

"Mr. Langley sends his regrets. He had to return to a meeting," Thomas added.

"Then let's order." Christopher controlled the minute details, as well as the cumbersome ones. From the reports in the paper and letters from friends, Louis perceived the man had a reputation to uphold. Everyone expected to hear a radical word or two daily from Christopher's lips. And rarely were they disappointed.

"I'll have the beef and onion pie." Robert had no qualms about ordering first.

"Fish pasty for me." Louis followed suit. He had recently eaten a big breakfast, yet it seemed food was to be a big part of the agenda, especially if the gatherings doubled as a committee meeting.

"I'm glad you are here, Louis," Silas said. "It appears I will be sent to France at some point. I know about enough French to order a meal. I'll need some pointers."

"What Silas means to say is we need to know about contacts, supplies, the heart of the people, a way to garner their support." Christopher stole the direction of the conversation, but Silas laughed, not seeming to mind. Contracts and contacts were far removed from menus.

"And knowing French will help." *Touché.* Louis grasped the nuances of humor mixed with serious deeds. These men faced life changing decisions every day. Lacing a little sarcasm in the debates would be healthy.

"Robert, this afternoon we meet with the committee on export and import. I'm pulling for a fleet of American vessels to be commissioned for our use. But I must say Congress is far from that notion."

The food arrived. Steaming pies and pasties vied for attention, but even Robert put aside the temptation for a moment.

"I'm honored to be asked to attend. I don't know what I can add to your discussion." Robert took his mission seriously. Louis admired his dedication to the possibility of a navy.

"This is all preliminary." Christopher ate little of his stew. Louis wondered if Christopher ever finished a meal. "I promise no decision will be made soon."

As Louis ate his food, he let the idea of an American navy sink in. His mind couldn't envision any fleet capable of defense against the British navy. There had to be a piece he had not considered.

Suddenly, fork in mid-air, Louis saw the connection. He placed his fork on his plate and cleared his throat. "I'm gathering you might have the vision of using French ships to aid the Americans."

"Exactly." Christopher raised an eyebrow and his glass. Louis wondered if his friend would start clapping. It appeared Louis had what Christopher or Silas didn't, a knowledge of a people and a language necessary to beat the British. Robert, Louis, captain, navy, commerce, French contacts. Louis connected all the relevancies. His racing heartbeat and rapid mind wanderings transferred him across the ocean. *Are the colonists ready for this grand scale of action? I might not be prepared but the adventure begins here and now.*

The massive Pennsylvania State Building on Chestnut Street dominated the center of the city. The red brick building had two wings on either side of the central tower. Louis and Robert followed Christopher through the front entrance. Before the official afternoon meeting at two, men gathered in the roomy hall connecting two large rooms. Tables, chairs, and podiums filled the spaces and left a lot of standing room.

Familiar faces and voices filtered toward Louis. He watched the activity and tried to put the people with the sounds before venturing reintroduction. What would it be like day in and day out, month after month working and living with these men? Did the ones involved even know, or care, what the papers and the rest of the world said about their every move? The way Christopher talked, there was no time for worrying about reputations and casual comments. After all, they were forming a nation, not a commemorative gala.

"I'd like you to meet Mr. John Jay of New York and Mr. John Hancock of Massachusetts. Gentlemen, Mr. Louis Lestarjette and Captain Robert Cochran." Christopher led them to the middle of many unfamiliar faces.

Mr. Hancock began the circle of handshakes. "A pleasure. We've heard a lot about you. You're in good hands with Mr. Gadsden showing you around."

"Thank you, sir." Louis nodded to Mr. Jay and shook his hand too. The president of the Congress, Mr. Hancock, mingled with the others as easily as if it were Sunday church. No doubt he remembered names as well. The new acquaintances moved on to the room to the left.

Christopher leaned closer to Louis, covered his mouth with his hand and commented, "I was hoping to introduce you to Mr. Franklin, but he has already taken his seat. I need to find mine before the gavel falls. Will you two be all right here in the hall? I think you can hear everything."

"Of course," Robert said. "And it doesn't look as if we will be alone."

Louis smiled. He wouldn't consider a crowd of seventy-five to a hundred being sparse or lonely.

"Let's step over to this open panel to see the proceedings." Louis led them to a viewing point.

A window into history opened right before his eyes. The images framed in Louis' mind depicted men with diverse backgrounds, dreams, and wealth. They put aside, for a time, their differences and concentrated on a higher matter. A new, independent nation.

Mr. Hancock began. "The safe arrival of gunpowder and arms will enable the Patriots to continue the siege of Boston. Mr. Gadsden, do you have a current report from your committee?"

Christopher stood, towering over the seated men. "We have raised a company of artillery men in Philadelphia who are on their way to Boston now to assist General Washington."

"Thank you. And the trade committee?" Mr. Hancock looked from Christopher to Mr. Franklin and Silas then back to Christopher.

"No solution, yet. We are meeting again this evening." Christopher's voice, although still audible, had lost its boldness. From Louis' vantage point, he saw men clutch their fists and heard them mumble to fellow members of congress.

The same old problems, Louis assessed. How to keep products flowing. The new twist? How to transport them through blockades during wartime.

The volleying began. Ideas and accusations, insults and rebuttals. "Free trade." "Open the ports." "Close the ports." "Export to Britain." "We'll starve." "Export everywhere but Britain." "Trade with France instead."

The gavel came down and Mr. Hancock rose to his feet. His scowl possessed the qualities of fire, ready to consume the bickering group. "We've appointed a committee. In time, they will give us their ideas. Next item of business."

Louis and Robert stepped back through the pulsing crowd to get some air and to let others in on viewing the action.

"And that's what we have to look forward to tonight." Louis guided them to the stairway. The voices echoed up the passageway to the second floor. Fresh air circled from open windows.

"The difference will be five to ten men not a hundred." Robert leaned on the banister.

Louis stared at the high ceiling. "If you remember, our meeting at the Exchange held four hundred men and was a lot less organized. At least there is eventual control in the hall downstairs. These men were elected to make decisions for all of us. At some point the debates will end." His eyes shut, he let the remaining conversations from the room below filter into his brain, finding a place to rest and make sense.

The debates weren't held only in the rooms of the state building. Louis witnessed ongoing churning of words and ideas later in the lobby of the Philadelphia Grand Hotel.

After an hour, Louis could have exited. The conflict between the states, represented by Christopher, John Jay, Silas Deane, and Richard Henry Lee and of course, Benjamin Franklin, stretched Louis' imagination.

Christopher wanted to change the patterns of trade. But Louis knew there was no way to do that without declaring independence formally and permanently from Britain. What was Louis getting into by being here? Christopher banged his fist on the table. "No one colony will have any preferential treatment. Let the point be whether we shall shut up all our ports and be all on the same footing."

Silas sat back, crossing his arms. "So, you don't think South Carolina, your home, should have special privileges to export rice to Great Britain?" Was he challenging Christopher's word?

Louis stuffed his hands in his pockets. *Interesting.* His own colony and ships and business poised on the line. Christopher paused, but Louis doubted it was for consideration. His friend just wanted the drama of the moment.

No longer yelling, Christopher said, "One colony will envy

another." He paused. Louis leaned forward, drawn by the intensity of Christopher's words as if each word was a paragraph. "All American ports should be closed to all trade with Great Britain."

On impulse Louis stood and clapped. All eyes on him for half a second before other hands joined in the applause.

"Now to convince the rest of Congress and your fellow South Carolinians," Mr. Jay added with a grin while nodding his approval.

CHAPTER 22

*E*llen's voice traveled up the stairway. "Miss Elizabeth, a letter just arrived from Mr. Louis." Elizabeth shook her head and shoulders as she sat on the edge of the bed. Could she trust her legs yet?

"Coming." Her light headedness and queasy stomach begged for slow motion. After a week of the same routine every morning, Elizabeth had to smile. Her suppressed giggle escaped despite her rumbling stomach.

One step. Two. Her precaution paid off. Wouldn't Louis be surprised? A baby, another baby. If her calculations were correct, the spring would welcome a new little one.

For now, she had to make it downstairs to breakfast and her letter. Perhaps she should tell Ellen no more eggs and sauces for a while, at least not so early in the morning. Toast and oatmeal were all she could handle.

Elizabeth held the envelope from Philadelphia close to her heart, then she placed it on her cheek delighting in the smell. *Louis. If only you were here in person. What news I would share.*

She found her favorite chair in the parlor. It faced the window with the morning light bouncing through the trees and off the sidewalk. Her legs dangled over the arm of the overstuffed chair.

The three pages fell in her lap. His words blurred at first. She wiped the dampness away and saw his handwriting clearly.

Dearest Elizabeth,

It's only been two weeks apart from you. I keep my sanity by picturing you in all my favorite places. Perhaps right now you are sitting in your comfortable chair with the summer sun reflecting off your hair. I cherish the pictures I have in my mind of you.

Nothing here rivals my commitment to you. Meeting after meeting pulls us closer to declaring independence. King George has officially rejected the Olive Branch Petition. Therefore, Britain won't give any concessions or thoughts to granting our petitions. There's only one way out of this. And Congress is getting ready.

Elizabeth sighed. Without lots of details, he shared a few of the struggles and a typical day surrounded by powerful men.

Be sure to hug and kiss Harriet for me. Hopefully the next four weeks will pass quickly.

Your loving husband, Louis

She sprawled her fingers over her flat belly. *Oh Louis, I have so much to tell you.* But never could she divulge that in a letter.

Elizabeth folded the sheets carefully, kissed the envelope, and walked to her desk in the corner of the room. In a fluid motion, she tied the letter on top of the other two letters. There were more to come, she had no doubt.

Her slippered feet shuffled her to the breakfast room. Ellen set a plate of toast and a bowl of hot cereal at Elizabeth's place. She stared at the food and then at Ellen. "How did you know?"

Ellen smiled. "You haven't touched your normal breakfast in the last three days. I'm not dense, you know."

"Oh, Ellen. I'm so happy." The older woman hugged Elizabeth's shoulders. "If only Louis were here."

"Let's keep you healthy and by the time he returns you will be feeling more like yourself." Ellen's suggestion spurred Elizabeth's attack on the dry toast and creamy, but bland, cereal.

Amy brought Harriet to Elizabeth. Her chubby arms wrapped around her neck. Nose to nose, Harriet cooed and then Elizabeth stood her up on her lap. "What do you think about a little sister or brother?"

"What? A baby?" Amy squealed out the questions. Elizabeth had forgotten about the young girl's presence and lack of information.

"Yes. Harriet will be a big sister in a few months."

Elizabeth heard Amy's skirt bustling behind her chair. Amy's hands clapped as words spilled out. "Now, what do I need to do? We need another bed and sheets, and then I need to get Harriet's newborn clothes from the trunk. And what about...?"

"Wait." Elizabeth halted the rambling and laughed. "Dear girl, we have months to prepare. There is no hurry at all."

Amy hung her head and stood still. Her blue eyes peeked through her lashes. "I'm sorry. I forgot how long it takes. Why, Harriet will be walking and talking by then, and Mr. Louis and Tom will be home, and the war will be over."

Oh, to be so young and to believe all things will work out in a good way. Elizabeth was not going to be the one to refute anything Amy said. In fact, Elizabeth would dream the same dream. A peaceful world for her children.

A few days later, Elizabeth was ready to share her special news as long as others kept it quiet for another month. No letting it slip in a letter to Louis.

Elizabeth moved her shirt sewing time to Sarah's. The heat kept Sarah indoors, at least that was what she said. But for this day, Elizabeth wondered if Sarah's health was not improving as hoped. Samuel met Elizabeth at the door. Why was he home at ten in the morning?

"Good morning, Elizabeth. I was just headed out. Sarah will be glad to see you." He twirled his hat around and slowly looked up.

"What aren't you telling me?"

"She just doesn't have any strength. She puts on a show for you and her mother, but most of the time she is in bed. The doctor says she needs rest, but he also told me her body is fighting the pregnancy."

Elizabeth placed her hand on his arm. "You know I will do whatever I can." Which was what exactly? *March in and tell her I'm expecting another baby? Hardly.* Her plans had changed.

Samuel paused. "She needs this baby. And I need her." Elizabeth searched Samuel's face and found furrows probably created by doubt and worry. Samuel knew Sarah's life was in danger and that weight covered every thought. How could a new, young husband function with that heaviness of heart? How could she?

Elizabeth searched for words, but none quite fit the tense situation. "I'll go to her now."

Samuel squeezed her hand and left.

Deep breath. Elizabeth determined not to drag her feet. Poised like a soldier, she entered the drawing room, more marching than walking all the way to Sarah's reclined figure on the daybed.

"Elizabeth, come in, sit right here close to me." The ottoman at her friend's shoulder begged for a guest.

"How are you this morning?" Elizabeth's smile reached her eyes, genuine enough. She was happy to see Sarah; therefore, her features didn't lie.

Poking her lower lip out, Sarah said, "I'm tired of putting my feet up, lounging around all day. I miss the market, promenades, parties, and church."

"Stick your lip back in place. You have visitors, and you have me right now. What do you want to do this morning, a game of backgammon or finish another shirt?"

"I finished one yesterday. It's in my basket. You can add it to your collection."

"That's wonderful. Your confinement isn't all bad. Just think of the men who will wear these one day. They will be warm and comfortable."

"I don't want to think too hard. They might be wounded and cold too."

"So, backgammon it is." Elizabeth retrieved the velvet lined case from the corner cabinet. The ivory disks with velvet bottoms glimmered in the morning rays. Half contained black inlaid dots. After setting them up, Elizabeth gave Sarah the lead move with the solid off-white ones. Would the game distract Sarah for even a moment?

"Have you heard from Louis?"

Elizabeth nodded, watching Sarah move her first piece three spaces.

"I have three more long weeks." Elizabeth made her first move on the board. Her competitive edge had diminished with Sarah's failing health.

"You have lots to keep you busy. I hate it that I'm on your list to visit. For a while there was your grandmother and," Sarah paused. "I'm so sorry. I know it's still so hard to talk about her."

"Grandmamma wants me to talk about her and life. I'm selfish when I lock away her memory. Anyway, don't you worry about me visiting you. I'll do what I want to do."

Sarah winced and covered her lower belly with her hand.

"What is it?" Elizabeth sprung up to assist.

"It's nothing. I get sharp pains all the time. See, it's gone now."

Elizabeth sat back down with a plop. "You scared me."

"I don't mean to. But I can't help my reaction. Didn't you feel that kind of pain during your time?"

Elizabeth wanted to say "Yes, it's normal" but couldn't outright lie. "I did toward the end." She straightened Sarah's pillows, propped her feet up again, and returned to the game in progress. Concentration had all but disappeared.

Scenarios of new life and death, battles and reunions, flitted in separate frames. In the midst of daydreaming, Elizabeth moved her pieces around the board capturing some of Sarah's disks and trapping others. Like life. Good moves, bad moves, and some unavoidable moves.

"Now, you have to tell me what is really on your mind." Sarah laid her head on the pillow and stared at Elizabeth, not the board.

I can't, not yet. Elizabeth had no doubt Sarah could see under the façade. What were the tell-tale signs? Slow reactions, pauses in speech, smirks, and nervous hands? Whatever they were, Elizabeth had to gain control.

"It's only Louis. I miss him." True. "I don't want him to miss too much of Harriet's life. I know six weeks won't really matter, but she changes so much so quickly."

"Surely, you tell him in your letters about her antics."

"I do, but I can't give her real live gestures justice with a few words."

"Just like he describes Philadelphia to you." Sarah used her elbow to sit up straighter. "He'll use his imagination."

Elizabeth smiled, genuinely moved. Here was her friend setting aside her own pains and worries to settle Elizabeth's concerns. If only Sarah knew her real, deep ache for Sarah's condition, and her true rejoicing over her own baby. In time. But for now, Elizabeth determined to share in Sarah's afternoon without adding anything about herself that could bring emotional pain to her friend.

Although she couldn't tell Sarah her news, Elizabeth had to tell someone. She retrieved Harriet from Amy's care once she returned home. "We will be at Anne's this afternoon." She stopped. "I have an idea. Will you go find your mother and bring her here?"

"Yes, ma'am." Amy scooted off. Ellen had to have been in the next room, for they were back in thirty seconds.

"I want you to take the afternoon off and don't worry about supper. I can have one of your meat pies. Relax or go window shopping, have coffee, and I'll treat you to a meal at the Grand. I want you to enjoy the rest of the day."

Amy and Ellen turned big eyes to each other and back to Elizabeth. Ellen rubbed her hands together. "Thank you. We'll take you up on your offer." Elizabeth could tell Ellen's mind was spinning with ideas.

"Now, I'm off to leave you to your plans." Elizabeth placed Harriet in her carriage and exited the front door into the bright sunlight. The rays pulled her face upward. Eyes closed, she whispered, "Thank you God, for this time of change. Help me use it to be nearer to You." With a deep breath and new resolve, she directed her course to Anne's.

As she approached the gate to her sister's property, she heard distinct shouts from the back yard. Sounds of child's play, not pain or fear. Of course, she knew the boys would be rambling around the shaded garden. She wondered with what game today. Stick horses? Swords? Forts?

The click of the latch didn't disturb their play. Maneuvering slowly around the shrubs, she spied their reenactment of an imaginary battle. Robert, ten years old, pointed his wooden rifle through a bush at the enemy across the yard. Luckily, it wasn't John. She saw the eight-year-old in a tree adjacent to his brother. The enemy was—a tree?

To avoid a stray "shot" from Robert, Elizabeth raised a white cloth from Harriet's bag in the air. "I come in peace."

The boys responded with laughter and noisy exits from their posts.

"Aunt 'Lizabeth."

Now the whole neighborhood would know of her presence. She stooped to accept the boys in her arms. Who would mind the sweat and dirt wrapped up in kisses?

"Oh, Elizabeth, I'm so glad it's you." Anne appeared from the back of the house. Charlotte followed on wobbly legs. Elizabeth moved closer to make the journey easier for the little legs.

"Look at her go. You boys better watch out, she'll catch you soon."

"No, she won't, she's just a girl," John said. He picked up his sword and clambered back up his tree. "Come on, Robert, the battle isn't over yet." The game renewed with vigor.

"They'll be all right. Let's go in the sunroom. I can see them and hear them just fine." Anne reached for Charlotte's hand. Elizabeth lifted Harriet up and followed Anne.

While Charlotte entertained her cousin on the blanket, Elizabeth toyed with a way to wiggle her news into the flow of conversation.

"What have you heard from Louis that might be different from Robert?" Anne continued an ongoing conversation. Elizabeth hoped she didn't miss anything as she tried to wiggle her own piece of information to the forefront.

"Probably nothing. It appears that they attend the same meetings, although Louis did mention something about a navy."

"Robert hinted at that. It might mean he must stay longer. The approval of a fleet has not occurred."

"The only other difference is Mr. Deane wanting Louis as an interpreter with any French contacts. I just hope…" This was her chance, but how to word her surprise?

"You just hope what?"

"I hope he stays home until the baby comes." She paused. All movement ceased. Even the little girls stopped their play, possibly because Elizabeth's voice squealed.

"A baby? You're having another baby?" Anne reached around the babies and hugged Elizabeth. "Oh, I'm so happy. Does Louis know?"

"No, so don't tell Robert. I want to tell Louis in person."

"Another girl for a tea party."

"Or a boy for the battle outside." Elizabeth laughed. Either would be perfect. What would Louis want? At one time, he said Harriet was enough. "I hope Amy and Ellen can handle the addition. We really don't want any more help. But what if Amy finds a better position?"

"That won't happen. What could be better than working for you?" Anne motioned for Sally, her house servant cleaning in the parlor, to bring the refreshments to the table. "Thank you, Sally."

"Anyway," Anne poured some cool lemon water in two glasses. "You send her to school, teach her piano, share your books, and your home. She's almost like family to you."

"She is family. So are Ellen and Tom. We'd do anything for them."

"My point exactly. Amy isn't leaving any time soon. Just keep the boys away."

Boys. Young men. Dances. Military. For now, young men left daily for the regiments. Some had sweethearts, but most were so young, like Tom, where time and work hadn't allowed the option of courting. Soon Raymond would join the ranks. Who could blame him? All his friends from the docks were gone. He bided his time until he turned seventeen in the fall.

"I don't think we'll have to worry about boys this year. They all have dreams of fighting a war." Elizabeth stared at Robert and John, thankfully too young for this war, playing at a grown man's reality.

"I know what you are thinking." Anne's eyes connected with the same vision in the yard. "I'm thankful too. If only Robert didn't…"

"Don't say it. We want this independence from the British stronghold just like our men do. Remember we supported them in the initial stages. We can't wish it all away for their safety out of our selfishness." Elizabeth scrutinized the words tumbling out of her mouth. These words had to have come from her heart, the place of conviction, because any rational woman wouldn't speak them aloud.

Anne nodded. "So, we can pray for their safety and wisdom."

"Yes, pray, but never deflate their purpose and service for this new country."

I must hold to that truth no matter what. Only God had the authority to redirect their course. With Louis in the fray of the body making decisions for their lives, Elizabeth had to dig deep, bringing the roots of her belief to life once again, remembering the beginning didn't have Louis or Harriet as lines of strength. Now, more than ever, she had to find courage to support her words and beliefs.

CHAPTER 23

*R*aymond appeared in Elizabeth's parlor out of breath, hands on knees, and hat askew. "What is it?" Elizabeth asked. The only thing she wanted to hear tumbled forth.

"The *Rose* is pulling in right this moment," Raymond said, straightening his lithe form and adjusting his cap.

She jumped to her feet, leaving her book to topple to the floor. "Louis is here. Oh, Raymond, thank you. Go get yourself a drink."

He pulled in some fresh air and turned to the door. "I can't, ma'am. I must go tell the Wilsons. They are as anxious as you."

"Of course, they are. You run along then." She twirled and brought her arms into a hug. *Thank you, Lord.*

Louis, here. A few days early. He was expected September seventh.

"Ellen. Ellen. Come quickly." Elizabeth moved to the hallway, hand on the staircase rail.

"Yes, ma'am?"

"I need a nice lunch prepared for Mr. Louis, Harriet dressed, and I don't know what else. I'll leave the baby with Amy." She ran up a few steps and embraced Ellen. "He's here."

"He's back, thank God." Ellen clasped her hands in front of her apron.

Elizabeth raced up the rest of the stairs and glanced in the glass. Her cheeks were flushed, but her hair remained in place. A different dress? Or did it really matter?

She decided her pale-yellow dress would do. All she wanted was Louis' arms and kisses. Turning to the side in front of the long mirror, she checked her stomach. Would he notice the ever so slight bulge? Probably not. Wouldn't he be surprised.

At the front door, Elizabeth yelled to Ellen, "We'll be home soon. Bye."

Without the baby carriage, Elizabeth used the alleys and slightly uneven sidewalks to quicken the journey. The tangy smell of the ocean and the flapping of the sails lured her to the active harbor. Elizabeth cared only about the ship pulled close to Christopher's dock. A few feet from the walkway, she halted, straightened her hat and bodice, and pushed stray hairs aside. Would Louis care about her imperfections?

A few more strides. Then, he was there, deposited by an invisible thread. Louis pulled her close and held her like he'd been denied human contact for a year. Well, at least her kind of embrace and touch.

He lifted her off the ground, causing her hat to lose its perch and flop in the breeze, dangling by its strings. "Louis, I thought this day would never come." She caressed his cheeks.

"Ah, *ma chérie*." He captured her hand and kissed her palm, then secured the other in his. His kiss was real, the scent from his morning shave mixed with the salty sea air. The same aroma lingered on his clothes at home. But this was stronger and truer, attached to her living, present husband.

"Is Harriet all right?"

"Oh, yes. I'm sorry. I received the message and made my exit with only a few words to Ellen. I promise the baby and your noon meal will be the first things you encounter at home."

"I rather like having you to myself, even among all these people." He tweaked her nose and returned her flyaway hat.

Elizabeth glanced around at the crowd. "I still expect to see Robert. It seems a little unfair that you can come back without him." Anne wasn't too happy either, but she had this last week to adjust.

"There is so much talk of a navy and Robert wants to be a part of the planning. If he is going to actively participate, he wants to know the details. I've learned more about naval maneuvers and strategies this last month than I can incorporate in my brain."

"I know you are tired of the ship, too. Let's walk a while, perhaps a few blocks out of our way."

"My legs would enjoy, if not demand, the exercise."

Her suggestion was mostly selfish. Should she tell him now? Any advantage in waiting? Once they approached the house, others would demand his attention and time. She took in a deep breath and let it out. Now was best.

The sea wall loomed beside them. The sea gulls performed their dives and antics as they fished. She steered Louis to the ledge facing the blue canvas of sky and sea.

"Louis?"

"Hmm?" He pulled her next to him and trapped her in his gaze.

"I have a surprise for you. Something I couldn't write in a letter."

He raised his eyebrow, just the one as usual. A gesture she had missed. "A surprise?"

"Yes. Are you ready?" She raised up on her tiptoes twice. What if she shouted the news letting everyone share in their celebration? "By the look on your face, it's good and not bad. So yes, I'm ready."

Lacing her fingers in his, she tilted her head and looked at him through her lashes. "We're going to have a baby."

Silence. She released the air caught in her excitement. Her

teeth gnawed her lower lip. Louis' smile met the corners of his eyes.

"Another baby? When? How? Well, I know how. I've been gone so long, I wouldn't have even surmised the possibility."

"It must have been your going away gift." She blushed, somewhat unnatural, she assumed, for a married woman and mother.

"I couldn't have guessed by looking at you." She ran her hand lightly over her stomach. "Are you feeling all right?"

"Yes, Ellen and Amy have taken care of me. Anne knows, but I've avoided telling Sarah or Jeannette or Mother. I wanted you to know before the whole world."

His kiss lingered longer than normal in a public place. Shivers ran up her spine. He really was happy.

"Now we can share the news together."

"Yes." She glanced up into his blue eyes. "You are pleased?"

"Of course, but as I said before, you and Harriet were blessings beyond my belief. Now a third, immeasurable one."

She rested her head against his chest. *Thank you, Lord, for bringing me near to You, so that I can share with this wonderful man all Your goodness.*

Louis couldn't sleep. Roaming the perimeter of the first floor didn't add any solution to his restlessness. Why the unease now? He'd heard rumors before, and he had participated in military negotiations in Philadelphia. But this time it was in his own town, in the dark waters surrounding their peninsula.

Elizabeth slept soundly, hopefully oblivious to his meanderings. All thoughts right now, no action put to the talk. The Council of Safety with the voice of Henry Laurens supplied hints of plans of local royal officials. Louis had sat in the meeting as other concerned patriots did too.

"Beware, Loyalists in the backcountry are joining forces with

British troops expected to arrive aboard British ships of war soon."

What did that mean for his household? Nothing positive, for sure. He listened and wondered how Laurens always seemed to obtain his information in time to plan a counter attack.

Spies.

It was a new career for many, including Louis in a slight way. Correspondence with Silas and André laced with secret terms and phrases. Words like friends for patriots and sympathizers, food for contraband, or social events for secret meetings. Louis wasn't deep in the system, just on the fringe. For now. *Spies, codes, warships.*

Crash!

In the pantry. Louis crept to his desk and returned with his pistol. With shaking hands, he placed the lead bullet in the chamber. *God, please don't let me have to use this.*

He placed his candle on the foyer table and proceeded toward the dim flicker at the entrance to the pantry inside the back door.

"Who's there?" His pistol pointed to the ceiling. He wasn't about to shoot Ellen or Amy or even a squirrel or stray cat.

"Mr. Louis, it's me, Tom." The voice was a whisper from behind the door.

Louis relaxed and lowered his weapon. "What are you doing sneaking around here? Come out. I won't shoot now." His heart bumped back in place, leaving his stomach intact.

"I'm sorry. It was late, and I was hungry."

Louis gave him a huge bear hug. "Welcome home, Son. Let's find you some real food, some that your mother fixed."

They walked to the kitchen. "Why didn't you come here first, to your room and wait until the morning to rob the pantry?" Louis laughed, then noticed Tom's sober strained grin.

"I have to get back to my regiment. We are preparing for action here in Charles Town. I would have left a note about the food I took."

"Sit down." Louis grabbed a plate, cornbread, chicken pie, squash casserole, and apple dumplings. "This should fill you for tonight at least."

"Thank you, sir. You shouldn't wait on me." Tom had cornbread in one hand, a mouthful of casserole, and a fork ready for the chicken.

"I had nothing better to do. I couldn't sleep. Maybe this is why I was up pacing the floors. I knew there was something going on but hadn't figured out what."

"Well, I can't tell you much except Colonel Moultrie ordered the three companies to prepare for action."

"That would be Pinckney, Elliott, and Marion?"

"Right, sir. And I'm with Captain Frances Marion, the best captain around. He knows all about hiding and surprise attacks and living in the wild. But we don't have a good cook. Not like Mother."

"No, not many like her anywhere."

Tom cleaned the last juices from his plate with the cornbread. He downed the cup of milk in one swallow.

"There's nothing more you can tell me?" Louis didn't expect the captain to leak any details to a soldier.

"No, sir. It's all still a secret to us. The captains do a lot of talking with the colonels. It has to do with the harbor and Fort Johnson."

For a minute Louis considered what military plans could be underway. Then he threw the task aside. He'd never sleep if he had to plan a counterattack or any military maneuver. "Can you stay the night and see your mother?"

"No. I've probably stayed too long now. My mission was some flour, sugar, and potatoes, if that is all right." Louis nodded. He grinned, for the young man wasn't asking permission. He acted on command. Fortunately, Louis wished to contribute to the cause. "Please tell everyone I'm doing well, especially now. And you should hear about our mission soon."

"I pray that it is a success."

Tom filled a knapsack with a few items. Louis made a mental note to pass on to Ellen, so she could replace them. Tom shook Louis' hand and disappeared into the moonless night.

Lord, protect him and the others from harm. May Your will be done this night and the days to come. Wrap Your loving arms around my family.

Ellen stood, hands on hips, jaw dropped. "He what?"

Elizabeth moved around the pantry checking on the stock of supplies. Perhaps it was time to increase the staples. "That's what Louis said. He ate a cold meal, took some food, and vanished into the night."

Her head shook under her white cap. "My boy was just a few feet from me and not a word. I should be upset with him, except I'm sure he was following someone's orders."

"You're right. From what I've heard of Captain Marion, Tom would be wise to follow Marion's orders. At least he consumed a good meal and spoke with Louis." He was lucky one of the women hadn't been startled and possibly carrying a loaded pistol.

"The good Lord planned that."

Elizabeth agreed. Louis described his insomnia as an uneasy premonition, one he couldn't turn into a senseless dream. She was glad he was awake last night.

"I need to replace these items today. I hope you don't mind Tom taking the food," Ellen wrung her hands. "I did raise him better." Louis had warned Elizabeth months ago that rations for the army would be an issue, and that he'd do what he could.

"Not at all. This is one way we can help the cause. For now, it's easily replaced. While you are shopping, be sure to buy some extra in case this happens again." How long will there be an abundance of flour and sugar? Would there be a time of ration or worse, no food at all? Louis would tell her not to borrow trouble.

"While you're out, Ellen, pick up some fall material for dresses for you and Amy. It's that time again. The change of season will be upon us."

How would her winter wardrobe fare with a baby on the way? Another project for the afternoon. She knew she'd need a few dresses, since her last pregnancy was not in the dead of winter. And clothes for Harriet? Anne had sent a few of Charlotte's.

"Don't forget you have Christine coming over for the afternoon."

"Thank you, Ellen. I plan for us to be rested and ready. I didn't know what good practice this would be for having two little ones in the house."

"Well, Christine is a good baby. What if you have a rambunctious boy?"

"Hmmm. You forget, I grew up with George, and you had Tom, and it doesn't get more unpredictable than that. Let's pray Louis' son takes after him." Or would he act like George, pulling pranks and causing mischief? What was his childhood really like with his two brothers? She had a feeling he wouldn't confess any time soon.

Ellen smiled. "Don't count on it. Boys have a way of sneaking in worms as if they were prize fish."

Knocking once, Elizabeth entered Louis' library and handed him a letter.

He paused in his correspondence to Christopher.

"This just arrived from a messenger. He didn't stay for an answer." Her hand shook.

"Don't look so worried. Sit down, and I'll read it out loud. I'm sure all is fine. It's from Mr. Laurens." Louis broke the seal.

He scanned it but just seeing pieces of it made no sense. He read in a steady voice, hearing the words echo off the walls.

September fourteenth at seven o'clock. Louis glanced at his pocket watch. Thirty minutes ago.

You are needed at Gadsden's wharf immediately. An urgent mission is planned. The safety council has asked for volunteers to aid the regiments. Keep this quiet. Respond in person quickly. Henry Laurens.

"I wonder how many he sent out." Louis peered at Elizabeth who hadn't moved at all. Fear. Shock. He wanted to convince her that it really was nothing serious. But he had his doubts.

"I have to go." He folded the letter and put it in the back of a drawer.

"I know. But you must be careful."

He retrieved his pistol from the cabinet and placed it in his jacket pocket.

"Don't wait up." He kissed her trembling lips. He sometimes wondered if war would be easier without a wife and child? And would he change his situation? No, he couldn't imagine life without Elizabeth.

"I make no promises," she said. He left knowing she would be restless and possibly sleepless until his return.

Urgent, the message stated. So, he ran through the alleys, making the distance shorter and quicker.

Gadsden's wharf on the Cooper River, basking in the last light of the setting sun, contained a dozen men with more arriving from the streets.

He joined Samuel in the circle surrounding Henry Laurens. The leader waited another five minutes for the group to reach about thirty men.

"Now, I think it's safe to tell you what is happening. Colonel Moultrie has gathered the troops for the taking of Fort Johnson tonight." He paused. Louis looked from man to man, all of them speechless, but expressing shock with similar gestures of shaking heads and shrugging shoulders. It seemed Louis knew more because of Tom's visit than the other men.

"Close to midnight about a hundred and fifty men from the three companies will meet here to embark on the mission. Our job is to keep the way clear. We don't need any wayward Loyalists blocking their departure. We'll break up into pairs and scatter around the area. Report any activity to me. Stay out of sight as much as possible. Any questions?"

What could they ask? Were they in danger? Would the men succeed? Louis felt his pistol close to his side. Would he use it?

"And one more thing. Don't use your weapons, just get the word back to me. This is not our physical fight tonight."

Already the pistol was lighter. Louis wished his racing heartbeat weighed less heavily on him.

Just before midnight, the strike force marched quietly onto Gadsden's wharf. Not one word as they filed past Louis on the boulevard. Tom lifted his hat to Louis and walked on.

In seconds, the men loaded onto two packets that Louis had failed to notice earlier. They pulled off and were gone.

Louis stood with arms crossed with the thirty or so men in awe of the smooth maneuver. Off to James Island to take the British fort. Danger and possible death.

"That's it for now," Mr. Laurens said. "Thank you for your service. We will know in a few hours about the success. Just pray now. It's out of our hands."

Louis and Samuel parted a few blocks away. "I'm sure we'll hear tomorrow," Samuel said.

"Yes, one way or the other, the news will spread. Now home to tell our wives."

"I'm not sure Sarah needs to hear about this in her condition. Today was worse than other days." Samuel's shoulders sagged.

"I'm sorry to hear that. I'll tell Elizabeth to check on her tomorrow."

"Thanks. Good night." Samuel turned at the corner before Louis' street.

Louis couldn't get away with hiding anything from Elizabeth, in her condition or not. Although things were different for Sarah, Louis couldn't imagine Elizabeth quietly sitting by and letting the world explode.

The possibility of finding his wife sound asleep in their bed was slim, but he turned the doorknob in silence, hoping to find a slumbering household. The candles in the parlor sent their yellow halos over the reposing Elizabeth, curled up on the settee covered with her light shawl. Should he wake her or just study her sleeping form for a while?

Her eyes batted open. "How long have you been here?"

"Less than a minute. I'm going to get you to bed."

"What about your meeting?"

He placed his arms under her back and thighs and lifted her close. "Can we wait until the morning?"

She shook her head against him. "No. Tell me the short version."

He added details one step at a time until he deposited her half-asleep body in the bed. "No more until the morning."

Where were the brave men at this hour while he crawled into his comfortable bed?

Protect them Lord, especially Tom.

The breakfast hour arrived all too quickly. Elizabeth barely remembered Louis coming in and didn't even register the hour. She purposed her feet toward the small table and faced Louis and Ellen already in an emotional conversation.

"I will find out right away and come personally to tell you of any news." Louis patted Ellen's hand.

Ellen stepped aside to let Elizabeth take her seat. The distraught woman wiped her hands on her apron again and again. "Should I go to the docks? Will he be there?"

Louis snickered. "That is the last place Moultrie or Marion will take their troops. If successful, they will still be on the island."

Elizabeth cleared her throat. "No word yet?"

"Good morning, sleepyhead. No, not here, but I'm sure on every street corner, there will be news soon. I'll let you know."

"If I'm not here, I'll be at Sarah's. One thing I do remember from last night was your bleak word from Samuel. I feel just awful of my neglect of her since you came home." She paused. "I'll stop by the store first, and hopefully get good news to pass on to her."

"I'm praying it is good news." Ellen poured Louis more coffee. "I know I'm selfish, but my Tom is out there." Elizabeth refrained from the black liquid. It didn't agree with her stomach in the morning. She sipped on her apple juice instead.

"A few more bites and I'll be gone." Louis forked fluffy eggs into his mouth.

What happened in the wee hours to the men floating on the black sea early this morning? Elizabeth nibbled on dry toast contemplating an answer. Before falling asleep in the chair last night, she prayed for safety and success. *Well, I'll know soon enough.*

After Louis kissed her goodbye, Elizabeth dressed in her lightest fabric dress, a pale-blue calico. September seemed to be hotter than August, but the hope of a cooler October pressed near.

Turning the corner onto Tradd Street an hour later, Elizabeth heard street criers spreading the news. "Colonel Moultrie has taken Fort Johnson. The Americans have the fort."

She ran to Wilson's Mercantile. Inside, several women surrounded Jeannette, all talking at once. Elizabeth surveyed the faces and ascertained all were Patriots.

"Is it true? We took over the British garrison?" Elizabeth searched faces and knew the truth before she asked the questions.

"Yes, my dear. And the takeover was bloodless. No injuries or deaths," Jeannette said.

"That's right," Mrs. Singleton continued the tale. "When the troops ran to the fort after unloading, they expected gunfire. But," she paused, "the fort was abandoned."

"What? No one was there?" Elizabeth looked wide-eyed and processed the words. No one was hurt, and Tom was all right.

"No one. Supposedly, the British must have heard about the plan and boarded ships in the harbor," Jeannette said. The other women nodded.

"And picture this. Colonel Moultrie raised a blue flag with a silver crescent design over the fort. No more British flag flying there." Mrs. Singleton clapped her hands.

Raymond ran through the front door panting and calling for Henry. Elizabeth looked on startled by his entrance, not quite the proper form through the middle of a group of ladies.

Jeannette called after him. "What is it?"

He kept his pace up toward the backroom but turned to yell, "Governor Campbell has fled his home and is on the British ship, *Tamar*. Huzzah for South Carolina." He clapped his hands over his head.

Huzzah, indeed. If his information was correct, Elizabeth knew that royal government had ended in the colony.

Louis and Henry confirmed the news. Victory prevailed. Elizabeth imagined the partisan celebration in the streets, the taverns, and the homes. But there was another side—the defeat for the British who were also citizens of Charles Town. Her neighbors. Prominent business owners and doctors and lawyers. Children. And women who hadn't joined either side. What form of retribution awaited the Loyalists?

With a bouquet from her garden and a new book in hand, Elizabeth strolled to Sarah's house just a few shaded blocks away.

Her friend was in bed, pale and weak. Elizabeth often questioned God about why He didn't heal her, why she suffered. No answer, only waiting.

After sharing the news of the victory in the harbor, Elizabeth took Sarah's hand. "I have some good news of my own too. Don't be mad that I didn't tell you sooner. I needed to tell Louis first." She paused. "I'm going to have a baby."

"Oh, Elizabeth, I'm so happy. Our babies can," Sarah hiccupped the next words through tears, "grow up together and play."

"Of course, they can." Tears held steady on Elizabeth's lashes threatening to spill over.

"But I don't think I can hold on to my baby much longer." Sarah sniffled and gained control. "I'm prepared to let go if the time comes."

Elizabeth nodded. Brave Sarah knew the truth and accepted it. Could Elizabeth, in the same situation?

"Oh, I don't want you to have this pain and suffering. I've prayed and prayed."

"I know and for some reason God has determined a different outcome. I accept it. Samuel helped me with that. He's so dear and attentive. He said, 'Having you alone is just fine. I love you first and always.'"

Louis had said the same to Elizabeth. Surely, God would bless Sarah with children. Elizabeth wasn't giving up that hope or prayer.

The hour passed, and Elizabeth raced home to Harriet and squeezed her tightly in her arms. She felt the heartbeat of her precious daughter beat against her.

The next day Samuel sent a note. "Sarah lost the baby last night."

A time to mourn.

CHAPTER 24

*E*lizabeth finally convinced Sarah to emerge from the shadows of her self-inflicted insolation. "What do you think of this material?" She felt the soft wool blend between her fingers then against her cheek. The deep purple reminded her of winter punch, warm and inviting.

"That's fine for the skirt and jacket. Let's find a lighter color for the bodice." Sarah's contribution accompanied by a smile reminiscent of a happier time spurred Elizabeth on in her task.

Elizabeth's hands shuffled through the rolls of material in Wilson's Mercantile. "Look at the purple and cream stripes." She held it next to Sarah's face.

It had taken about a month for Sarah's healthy glow to return. Her eyes sparkled amidst her olive complexion and dark hair.

"Yes. This will be a start. Samuel says I must have three new dresses. He plans on lots of winter entertainment. I keep telling him I'm fine, but he insists on participating in the season more than ever." Sarah picked up a green taffeta.

Elizabeth set a blue satin to the side. The pile of material meant hours of circle sewing. "That doesn't sound like the Samuel of two years ago who rarely ventured out of his office."

"I know." Sarah giggled. "He's full of surprises now. He didn't even balk when I said I wanted to return to teaching."

Elizabeth gasped and dropped a piece of lace. "You miss it that much?"

"I do. I'm not much use just wandering the house. I miss the lively, silly girls."

"Have you spoken with Mrs. Reynolds?"

"This afternoon I have an appointment. I'll want to stick with just a few hours a day. That might quench my desire."

Elizabeth understood Sarah's pull to the school. Something about teaching young girls was rewarding. Even with teaching four girls piano, Elizabeth gained satisfaction in the fact that she made a difference in their development and advancement into society.

Sarah stepped to the window. "Here is the dress for you, right on display."

"Maybe with some adjustment in the middle." Elizabeth didn't mention her condition around Sarah very often.

But today Sarah smiled and said, "With Amy's knack for sewing she could fix it up fine. By the way, you look great, baby included."

"Only you, and possibly Louis, could make me feel beautiful in my roundness." They both laughed. It felt good to have her friend back. Elizabeth thanked God daily for returning Sarah fit and healthy to the land of the living. It didn't stop her from praying that a baby would be in Sarah's future.

They walked to the counter to make Sarah's purchase. Jeannette was nowhere to be seen. Elizabeth shrugged her shoulders as did Sarah. It was unlike Jeannette to leave the shop floor without someone in charge.

"I wonder," Elizabeth began. Loud voices and a slamming door indicated action in the back room.

"You stay here. I'll go see what's happening." Elizabeth lifted heavy feet, not really wanting to walk in on a family feud or an irate customer. Her hand on the handle, ready to turn, Elizabeth found herself face to face with Jeannette. The woman's tear-stained face caused Elizabeth to reach out her arms to hug the ailing form.

"It's Raymond," Jeannette paused and sniffled. "He's gone to join the army," she managed to spill out between snorts and tears.

"I thought he was going to wait."

Jeannette nodded. "We did too. But he turned seventeen last week and…" She held out a note to Elizabeth. "He left us this, delivered by a messenger half an hour ago. Henry just showed me."

After greeting Elizabeth earlier, Jeannette had most likely been called back to face this heart-breaking news. "Perhaps Louis or Henry can look out for the customers, and you go on home to rest."

The weeping woman shook her head. "No, I'm better off here. At home, I'll just be waiting for Raymond to walk in." She wiped her eyes, blew her nose, and straightened her hair and apron. "I knew this day would come. All he could talk about was all the action Tom was experiencing, the taking of the fort."

Elizabeth followed Jeannette onto the floor where a few customers browsed. Jeannette had only had Raymond for such a short time. Was that fair? No, but neither was war. "Well, at least the action hasn't included fighting yet, just a lot of training." Once the words were out, Elizabeth didn't feel comforted.

"Yet, I'm not naïve enough to think shots won't be fired." Stiff backed and chin held high, Jeannette continued to her post. "That day is coming to Charles Town. And now Raymond will be in the middle of it."

Jeannette marched to the counter, pasted on a smile, and calculated Sarah's purchase. Elizabeth motioned with a hand over her mouth and shook her head for Sarah not to ask Jeannette what was wrong. Sarah understood. Package in hand, they waved and left Jeannette tending to another customer. There was nothing Elizabeth could do to take away her friend's sorrow.

Late October in an early morning mist, Louis paced Gadsden's wharf waiting for Robert's arrival. From weekly correspondence from Christopher and Robert, and occasionally from Silas and John Adams, Louis knew Robert had to be exhausted. The political arena steamed up more since Louis departed in late August. Now, the Continental Congress had a navy.

Christopher wrote, "It is absolutely necessary that some plan of defense by sea should be adopted." The debate arose in the summer and finally, according to Robert, John Adams and the rest formed a Naval Committee.

Fortunately, Robert agreed with Congress at least in his letters. "You would have been proud of Christopher. He was like a wild bear, protecting his plan and interest. With John Adams, Silas, and Christopher, along with four others on the committee, progress is being made. We plan to be at war at sea."

And with plans in place for an American fleet to be purchased and outfitted, Robert could return home, for a little while.

Anne ran down the wharf to Louis' side. She grabbed his arm. "How close are they?"

He patted her hand and looped it in his arm. "Don't worry. You have time to catch your breath. About half an hour. I didn't think you would respond so quickly to my note."

She hit his upper arm lightly. "After four months, you thought I could sit at home knowing Robert was stepping off that ship?" Louis laughed at her playful distress.

"No. I knew better. Anyway, I promised Elizabeth I would let you know right away. You Elliott girls sure do attach faithfully to your men."

The mist lifted, as if on cue, when the massive bulk of the ship rounded the bay. Louis stepped back and left Anne standing straight as a rod. How could he disrupt such an anticipated reunion? He felt a little selfish even being there to witness Robert's return. True, they shared their Continental Congress experience and had stock in the wartime endeavors, but right now Robert had a family to get to know again.

Anne looked around just once and caught Louis' eyes. Perhaps his role was of assurance, to confirm Robert was indeed coming home. He nodded and pointed to the figure on deck. Robert was home.

Robert's number one priority was Anne. Louis held a distant second. His handshake minutes later welcomed the captain to shore. "Welcome back. I hope the journey was smooth." Louis grinned. Robert had a hard time dropping his gaze from Anne.

"I'm going to leave you two alone for twenty-four hours," Louis promised. "By then my curiosity will be exploding. Elizabeth has invited your whole family for an early dinner tomorrow night. We'll talk later."

"Thank you, Louis." Anne touched his arm. "For everything."

He didn't quite know what he had done. Besides making sure the Cochrans had everything they needed at the house, he had left Elizabeth in charge of telling him of any troubles. He had spent a few afternoons with the boys, talking ships and battles, and brought them to the store for a few hours. But nothing close to filling in for Robert.

Before leaving, Louis asked the captain a pertinent question. "Is the *Tamar* still off the coast?"

"Yes, sir. She's sitting pretty a few miles out. And the *Cherokee* is close by too."

"Thanks." That wasn't the answer Louis wanted. The British warships posed a threat as long as they sat close to Charles Town's harbor.

On the way to the mercantile, Louis stopped by the *Gazette* office. Mr. Timothy always gathered up the latest tidbits, whether he publicized them or not.

Louis entered the noisy reception area. "Is Mr. Timothy in this morning?"

"Yes, in his office." The young man didn't stop long enough to show him back.

Louis knocked on the half-opened door. "Peter, do you have a moment?"

The man turned sharply and almost dropped a stack of papers. "Oh, Louis. I think I can find a second for you. Have a seat." He indicated a half-vacant chair. Louis moved the books to a shelf nearby.

Peter sat back against his desk, arms crossed. "How is our friend, Christopher?"

"You've probably had more details than I have. Your articles in the paper sound just like Christopher."

"Most are his direct words." Peter took pride in a job he did well. He always wanted truth and a good story and relished the fact that so many of them pertained to the Patriot cause.

"I want to know about our Provisional Congress." Louis crossed his ankle over his knee and steepled his fingers under his chin. "What is the new president, William Drayton, planning?"

"It's public knowledge." Peter moved a stack of papers to another stack, making the papers lean precariously, at least it appeared so to Louis. "He's ordered the blockade of the main channels of the harbor. He and most of the rest of us fear an assault on the town by the warships out there. He's a firebrand, so I'm sure he has a plan and he's not telling me." The editor grinned. "Congress is keeping a watch. He's the only one wanting to go attack the ships. The moderates haven't managed to calm him down too much."

"Again, we wait and see." Louis stood, not wanting to take any more of Peter's valuable time.

"Maybe the outcome will be as easy for the Patriots as the

taking of Fort Johnson." Peter patted Louis' shoulder as they entered the busy office.

"Thank you for your time."

Lots to mull around in his cluttered brain. Drayton. Blockade. Warships. All these spelled a future confrontation. And the Patriots had one armed sloop, the *Defense*. And the British had many.

Boom. Boom. The windows rattled. "What was that?" Elizabeth grabbed Harriet who had cried out loud.

"I don't know." Anne put down the sleeve she was trimming and went to the window.

Elizabeth joined her. "Maybe just soldiers practicing at the fort?" She flattened her palm against the pane still vibrating from the sudden shock.

Again, the terrific booming resounded through Anne's house.

"It sounds closer than the fort. Let's get the boys inside." Anne rushed to the hallway and ran into John and Robert, who were holding their toy guns in their hands. Elizabeth stopped in time to avoid the collision.

"Mother, what is that noise? Is it a cannon? Are the British coming to get us?" John questioned wide-eyed.

"Hush, now. It must be some sort of afternoon drill, practice like you two do outside."

Robert, the oldest, stood still and quiet. Elizabeth didn't think he believed his mother, but it soothed John for the moment.

"Where's Papa?" John asked.

Anne gasped. "At the docks working on the *Rose*." Elizabeth knew the moment Anne connected her words with her fear. Her jaw dropped, and she reached for Elizabeth's arm.

Cannons. Docks. British warships.

And where was Louis? Elizabeth drew a blank. Saturday afternoon, November eleventh. He said he had to work. Hopefully, he was tucked safely in the store not anywhere near the ships. She didn't know for sure.

A closer, deeper boom, one volley after another. It seemed cannons responded to the first round of fire.

The boys clung to Anne's skirt, as the girls buried their faces in their mothers' necks.

"That was closer," Elizabeth whispered. "Possibly from the *Defense*. Every part of me wants to run to find information and Louis." But her protective sensible side glued her to the premises with the children.

"Let's find Cook and some biscuits, and we'll play in the little drawing room," Anne suggested, leading the way.

Situated between the library and dining room, the room had no windows. Elizabeth settled on the floor with the children.

Another rally of cannon fire. Elizabeth recognized a pattern now. Her mind wrapped around only one conclusion—the British and Charles Town fired back and forth. The process repeated itself.

"Boomy, boomy." Charlotte bounced and clapped her hands. The innocent joy at the discovery of a new sound. Despite the irony, Elizabeth smiled and clapped her hands, changing the response to "Patty cake, patty cake".

A shaky tray of refreshments landed without incident on the tea table. "Thank you, Patty." Anne patted her cook's hand. "Don't be afraid. I'm sure everything is fine."

"Yes, ma'am. I just never heard noise like that. It makes my heart pound heavy." The dark woman wrung her hands.

"You take a rest now."

"I'd rather get Mr. Cochran's meal ready. That seems normal to me."

Normal. Certainly not what Elizabeth, her sister, and all of Charles Town, experienced just now.

An hour later Robert and Louis burst into the drawing room,

out of breath but each in perfect condition except for evidence of sweat and grime around their collars.

Louis embraced Elizabeth then Harriet. "Are you all right? No damage here?"

"None at all. We decided a room without windows was best though. Please, tell us what's happening. We know nothing," Elizabeth pleaded.

"We're sorry about that," Robert said. "We couldn't leave the docks not knowing the truth ourselves."

"So?" Elizabeth chose a chair instead of the floor.

"Mr. Drayton chose to sink four rotting hulks of ships from the deck of the *Defense*. The captain of the sixteen-gun *Tamar* opened fire on the hulks. Our ship was ordered to reply with our cannons. So back and forth it has been for two hours."

"Anyone hurt? Are we in danger?"

"No, no. The cannons were not fired toward the city, and so far none has hit a target." Louis bounced Harriet on his knees. Robert filled in details to his boys.

"And all of this means both sides have committed acts of war. I'm afraid the first shots of the war in South Carolina have been fired," Louis concluded.

Shivers inched down Elizabeth's spine. A war in Boston was a distant concern. A war in Charles Town went straight to her heart. *God protect us all.*

By dark, both sides had ceased fire. Louis forced his body to stay with Elizabeth for the evening although his brain wondered to the docks, creating scenarios in a haze of no information. Sleep masked his worries for a precious few hours.

A distant boom woke Louis at dawn. It took a second to register the odd sound. He sat up at the next round of cannon fire. Elizabeth joined his surprise.

"They're at it again. It sounds like the British have more company." Louis toppled out of bed and reached for his trousers.

"How do you know?"

"The fire is coming from two places distinctly apart." He grabbed his shirt. No way could he miss this next installment.

"Where are you going?" Elizabeth rubbed her eyes and stood before him.

"To the docks."

"I'm going with you."

"No, you're not." Last night there was no danger to citizens, but what about this morning?

She grabbed a day dress from the armoire. "I want to see the fiasco in the harbor for myself."

Louis stood with his hands on his hips. "It is five in the morning. The docks are no place for a woman."

"I'll be with you." She already had her dress over her head. She muffled under the fabric. "Your excuse has to be better than my being a woman."

He huffed but conceded. "If you are in any danger, I'm sending you home. Agreed?

"Danger, yes. I'll agree." He watched her twist her hair in a bun and place it neatly under her bonnet.

"I'll go tell Ellen to listen for Harriet, and I'll meet you downstairs." Elizabeth flitted off. No use arguing with her. She seemed to have it all figured out.

Once outside Louis followed others headed to Bay Street. Elizabeth wasn't the only woman attached to a husband's arm. Citizens crowded in front of the wall facing the harbor. Louis had intended to go to Christopher's wharf, but the others had a better plan, at least a clearer view.

Bay Street gave way to a scene that would be etched in Louis' memory forever. He found a place right against the wall with a clear sight of the ships. He turned slightly to face the gathering behind him. Hundreds of citizens, drawn by the canon fire booming across the harbor, lined the area.

Unbelievable. It made him smile to conclude he was not the only crazy man watching a war from a distance.

Elizabeth drew him back to the event unfolding before them. "It looks like two ships, as you said, are out there, and only our one is firing back." She pointed to the objects on the undulating waters.

The early morning light revealed the smoke scene from the canon blasts. "Yes, our sloop is the *Defense*. If I'm correct the British have the *Tamar*, the one involved last night, and the *Cherokee*."

"Will they move any closer to each other or toward the town?" Her voice trembled.

"They haven't since last night. I think they are waiting it out to see what the other will do. The *Defense* will protect the town. No way will either of the warships make it closer into the harbor without major damage or demise."

The crowd cheered the exchange as once again the show began. Spectators of an historic event. One thing Louis hadn't dreamed possible. It was like watching a duel with nothing at stake except the two men fighting. Or a gladiator fight. Except the arena encompassed the dark Atlantic Ocean, and the participants included many men on huge ships with deadly cannons.

And the spectators? Were they in danger? Unlike a duel or a gladiator event, Louis surmised danger lurked if the ships turned toward them and fired on the innocent. But still, they all stood and clapped and yelled. For how long? He had no desire to leave, yet he didn't want any harm to come to him or Elizabeth.

The show ended at seven that Sunday morning when the *Defense* quit firing back. She returned closer to the wharves amidst cheers of "Huzzah! Huzzah!"

Word spread quickly from a messenger sent by the *Defense*. "There were no casualties on our side and most likely none on the

British. Over two hundred cannon balls were fired." All in the ocean. The whole scene was one of warning. The war had reached Charles Town, and perhaps next time it would be a closer exchange.

Elizabeth pulled Louis to a halt with a tear in her eye and a forced laugh.

"What is funny?" he asked.

"It's not funny, just ironic and sad. We go from a battle scene depicting death and hatred to a church service supposedly full of life and love. I just wonder what God is thinking? He can't be smiling at His children fighting."

"No, I don't imagine He is."

CHAPTER 25

*I*n early December, Elizabeth entered the mercantile, intending to replenish some spices for holiday baking. The smell of the enticing baked goods would buoy anyone's spirits with or without Christmas around the corner.

After locking her gaze briefly with Jeannette, Elizabeth focused on her friend's puckered lips and clicking sound from her nails hitting the counter. "Another family just left. The Millers. I wonder if anyone is keeping track of the number who've already gone."

Elizabeth shook her head and leaned on the counter. "Louis and I have talked about getting out of the city, but for now we're staying in Charles Town." She walked to the shelf containing bottles and bins of local and foreign aromatic concoctions perfect to add zest to their goodies.

Jeannette followed with small bags to collect the spices. "Some are living in their houses without family, china, and furniture. Fear is great around here."

Elizabeth stepped closer to Jeannette, dropping a bag of cinnamon in Jeannette's hand. "Well, with the British warships displayed off the coast for all to see, I can understand it." She whispered, "I will admit I've hidden my jewelry and a few family valuables."

"Me, too," Jeannette confessed. "Is Anne staying in town?"

"Yes. Robert is scheduled to leave for Rhode Island this week. If things get worse or she is afraid, she'll move in with us or our parents."

Only a few customers browsed the shelves while Elizabeth visited with Jeannette. "You seem to have lots of good produce and items on the shelves."

"Too much. With so many people gone, the goods are leaving slowly. The regiments in town buy some of the fresh items, but few want any trinkets or household things."

Elizabeth put her purchases in her large sack. She couldn't believe anyone was talking about leaving houses and furniture, and more alarmingly, friends and relatives. "Every place appears to be half full. Many of the homes are empty, most belonging to the Loyalists. And a lot of church members have vanished to the country. Even the school had to dismiss early, so many girls were taken out in November."

"Is Sarah still here?"

"Yes. Samuel wants her someplace else, but the only place she could go is Williamsburg, and that's no better than here. They're staying with her parents for now."

With a slap on an apple barrel, Jeannette muttered, "Well, I know Henry isn't leaving. He'll go down with the town. And I'll be right beside him." They both laughed, letting the release drive away the serious cloud over their lives. And city.

When the office door opened with a screech, Elizabeth watched Louis stroll toward the counter while shrugging into his jacket. He winked at her. "Are you ready for lunch?"

"Of course." Elizabeth put her bag on one arm and her hand on his arm.

Jeannette smiled. "Have a nice time."

Elizabeth grinned. Even after almost two years of marriage, she treasured these moments with Louis, arm in arm, with her big round belly and the number one person in her life.

The restaurant around the corner on King Street still served lunch, although several similar establishments had closed. Owners either closed out of fear of a cannon ball or lack of customers.

Louis chose a table by the warm fire. He ordered vegetable soup before their meal. He took their coats and draped them over a vacant chair before settling in his seat. "How things have changed in less than a month. Are you still all right with our decision?"

Elizabeth ran her finger over the soup spoon in front of her. "I'm sure. Nothing out of the ordinary has happened since the first exchange. At least nothing to the town." She stared out the window. "Except perhaps the view of the ocean." In the past, she had loved watching ships dancing on the ocean. Now, the scene remained menacing.

"Hmmm. Yes. Now four warships and many smaller skiffs."

"That is intimidating, and the continued swapping of cannon fire makes me cringe." But not enough to leave. If they did make that decision, she feared Louis would stay behind to do his part for the cause. She wouldn't say never, but for now her stand proved firm and immoveable. Louis enclosed her left hand in his. "We are doing things to help protect the town. Have you seen the fire brigades?" She nodded and moved her hand from his warm grip when the soup arrived.

"I was with Anne and the boys close to St. Philip's when we saw a few men standing around with hoses, axes, ropes, and ladders. Little Robert asked them without hesitation, 'What are you doing?' Once they answered 'fire brigade,' the boys threw five or six questions at them before we could get them away."

Louis laughed. "Those boys, I guess any boys, are so curious. I don't think they know the seriousness of the fire brigades all over town."

A plate of ham, cheese, and fresh bread arrived, momentarily silencing the conversation. Elizabeth longed for the days when talk was of the school, parties, and the holiday season's festivities. What place did war and bombardment have during Advent? Enough, it seemed, to keep at the forefront of every outing.

Still, she had the power to divert the flow with some effort. She pushed her plate forward and leaned toward Louis. "All is ready for Harriet's party, and so far, all invited have accepted. Oh, how I love the chance to show off the house at Christmastime."

"Well, I'm glad our daughter has given you an extra excuse to celebrate and decorate. Maybe she will surprise us and walk a few more steps." She recognized his teasing, because she never needed an excuse to bring Christmas into her home.

Elizabeth clapped her hands. "That would be a great accomplishment. She doesn't quite know what to do with her chubby little legs."

A group of partisan officers entered the restaurant and occupied a large table by the window. Elizabeth stared, not meaning any disrespect, but curiosity about their dress glued her eyes to them. A true uniform, distinguishing them from the enemy. "Look at the new uniforms. They look as professional as the Redcoats."

"I think that is Colonel Moultrie's addition to the troops. Notice the silver crescent on the front of the hat."

She studied them more, drawn to the sharp-cut blue coats, waistcoats, and breeches trimmed in scarlet. She had to adjust her chair to see the black felt hat clearly. "Yes, I see it. The same as the flag flying at the fort."

"Right," Louis said.

"I wonder if they are wearing the shirts we've made?" she whispered, trying to imagine her work underneath the fancy coats.

"I don't think so. The officers are men of property, not the enlisted men. They can afford their own shirts."

"Oh, at least mine might be good enough for Tom or Raymond."

She would rather that, anyway. With the image of Tom wearing a warm shirt sewn by her hand, she would keep the effort going. If the officers preferred their thin white linen ones, who was she to protest? Her boys would get heavier, warm shirts from her hands.

After their meal, Louis tipped his hat at the officers as they left the building. Elizabeth wondered if Louis would have to wear a uniform one day to fight and protect their homeland. She vanquished the picture to a secluded place and concentrated on the sun peeking out from behind a cloud. For now, her stroll with Louis commandeered her attention.

In front of Wilson's Mercantile, Louis looked around in every direction, and then pulled Elizabeth into his arms. A kiss in broad daylight made her feel like a mischievous girl as well as a cherished and loved woman.

"And that was for?" She let her hand linger on his chest.

"Let's just say I have every right to kiss my wife anywhere I want, and I took it." He kissed the tip of her nose. Her bonnet probably hid her blush. If he kept this up, this half of the town would mistake them for rebellious youth.

She fingered his cravat. "Are you sure you don't want to come on home right now?" she suggested, looking up through her eyelashes.

"Not yet." He captured her hands in his, stepping apart a bit. "I have work to do. Military orders to fill and deliver. Anyway, I thought you had plans."

"I do. In the form of two precious princesses. Christine's nursemaid is bringing her by in an hour. Mother says all hands are needed at her house without a busy little baby around."

"And your mother's special occasion?"

"The family Christmas dinner, of course. How could you forget that?"

"But that's in over two weeks."

Elizabeth shrugged her shoulders. Two weeks wasn't too long to plan and prepare for a party. "A head start, in case company arrives, I guess."

"Well, you have fun and leave some of your kisses and hugs for me."

"Yes, sir." The spring in her step chased away the chill in the air. The distraction of the girls and preparation for the party kept her from missing Louis too much.

Evergreen sprouted out of every niche, all over the house. It draped the front rails, the door, the windows. The rich smell permeated the house since Elizabeth had requested sprigs hung over the mantel, banister, and tables. She heard Louis sigh often at the Christmas wonderland growing in his house, denoting his affection for decorations didn't match hers.

Harriet had to admire the decorations from a distance in the arms of an adult. With one pull on a branch, decoration balls, fruit, and nuts would tumble on her head. The breakfast room and small drawing room, with the door closed, protected her from mishap.

"Today is your first birthday, Harriet." Elizabeth rustled her daughter's light blonde curls. The lively little girl held Elizabeth's knees and bounced up and down on baby legs. "Will you walk today for everyone? Just a few little steps?"

Harriet squealed as if she hid an answer in her laughter. "Papa will be home soon, and then everyone will arrive just for you."

Later that afternoon, Elizabeth stood aside and focused on each face in the room celebrating Harriet. Who would be together with her at Christmas? Who would move to the country? Sarah?

Samuel? Her mother? What if Ellen and Amy left? Was Elizabeth being stubborn and naïve to hang on to a semi-normal life, when a few blocks away cannon balls crashed into the sea wall or old sunken vessels in the harbor's mouth or the fort grounds? If one hit a house, would she regret her decision?

She scrunched her eyes, shutting out the vision of destruction. Louis found her in the middle of transforming her thoughts. He helped dissolve the image. "Elizabeth, it's time to open the gifts." He turned her to him, gently by the shoulders. "Where were you?"

"What?" She shook her trestles of curly hair. "Daydreaming in a negative place. I'm better now. Yes, the presents."

Harriet and Charlotte shared the ripping activity. Brown paper flew from their tiny hands, making a castle of debris around them. A new doll with a green checkered pinafore and a wooden ark with animals succumbed to the increasing paper burial. Louis sat with the girls and rescued the gifts before destruction resulted.

"Who wants cake?" Ellen asked.

Everyone except Harriet and Charlotte, who still wrestled with the mess. Elizabeth laughed. Somehow, this picture needed to remain in the forefront of her mind, replacing any negative ones. Elizabeth and Anne each grabbed a girl and placed them in their high chairs.

"One mess cleaned up, another one started," Anne said.

And soon, Anne gestured to the cake crumbs and icing smeared on the girls' faces, hands, and dresses.

"Well, that's why we only invited family. No one here really cares." Elizabeth looked around. She spotted her mother, in a big chair resting her head on the back of it, smiling but so quiet.

Elizabeth leaned toward Anne. "What is Mother thinking? She seems distant to me."

"Father says she's thinking about moving to the country to her cousin's house with Christine and the nursemaid," Anne said.

Why haven't I heard anything? Have I only looked to my own needs?

"And Father would stay here?" Elizabeth couldn't imagine her mother not being around the corner.

"Yes, for the school."

Mother gone from Charles Town? For how long? Would they visit? Elizabeth wandered over to her mother and took her hand. "Are you all right?"

She sat up straighter and patted Elizabeth's hand. "Yes, my dear. I'm just looking at the children and all the activity."

"Are you really leaving, Mother?" Elizabeth sought a shake of her head but instead received a resolved nod.

Her mother sighed and diverted her gaze to her hands in her lap. "I think so. After Christmas, if things don't improve. Many of my friends have already left. And your father thinks it's best. But we have this joyous season now. Let's not worry about this today."

Elizabeth kissed her mother's brow, then roamed the room, stopping at Sarah and Samuel who were talking to Robert and Louis. Sarah was now a vision of health with energy to spare. At least her miscarriage didn't zap her desire to live and participate in life events. A stronger woman emerged from the trial.

After Elizabeth looked at each face, she took Sarah's hand. "Are you leaving Charles Town any time soon, Sarah?" Elizabeth didn't know if she could take another blow, but she had to ask.

Sarah's brown eyes sparkled with mischief. "Why, no. What brought that on? I can't leave the school and the few girls remaining. I told you that earlier." Her smile convinced Elizabeth something had transpired that she didn't know about yet.

"But will they come back after the Christmas break?"

"I don't know. But I won't abandon them. Samuel finally let me have my way in this. Besides, you are staying, aren't you? And Anne? If you and she can stay with children, I can stay and help with a few girls."

Quiet Sarah had indeed won a battle and stood stronger for it. Elizabeth would love to have seen Samuel's expression when Sarah let her stand be known.

Elizabeth held Sarah's hands in hers and spread their arms out in a childish circle as if making a secret pact. "We'll go through this together."

"Yes." Sarah giggled. "Another adventure to add to our others." How could she call bombardment and war an adventure? Like it was just another dance or party.

CHAPTER 26

Christmas Day 1775 ushered forth as any other day. The celebration of Christ's birth couldn't be delayed or vanquished. A bouncy, chattering one-year-old beckoned Elizabeth to Harriet's bed. One hand on her expanding belly and another on Harriet's rosy cheek, Elizabeth took a deep breath, concentrating for a moment on her blessings. On a chilly morning, she had a warm house. In a time of rationing, she had food. Her family members were still safe and close. A healthy daughter and growing baby. And Louis, always Louis.

As if conjured up, Louis appeared at her side and draped an arm around her. His other arm dipped into the baby bed and scooped up Harriet. Elizabeth leaned her head on his shoulder and sighed.

What more could I want for Christmas, Lord?

"Happy Christmas," Louis whispered.

"Yes, it is."

Harriet squirmed and convinced Elizabeth to move on downstairs to feed the hungry child. Ellen had left a tray of muffins and scones to hold the family until lunch.

Elizabeth didn't expect to hear anyone stirring in the house until later. She jumped when a figure stepped into the hallway.

Louis' quick words prevented her screaming. "Tom, is that you?" Louis asked.

A tall, young man dressed in blue emerged into the light. "Yes, sir. I seem to startle you every time, Mr. Louis."

Elizabeth's heart beat in her throat, but she found her voice. "Oh, Tom. I'm so glad you are here." She hugged his dusty neck. "Does your mother know?"

He shook his head. "No, I wanted to surprise her."

"Well, you go do that and take a muffin with you." He reached for the food without hesitation.

Louis patted the youth's shoulders releasing a cloud of loose particles.

"And, Son, get a bath this morning too."

"Yes, sir." Tom grinned, mimicking Louis' smirk.

Louis put Harriet down, and she immediately wanted to follow Tom upstairs. "No, little miss, you stay with us. Do you have no interest in food now?"

Elizabeth heard the squeals filter down the stairway, first Ellen, then Amy. What a joyous gift for them.

"I wonder if Raymond came home," Louis said.

"I'm sure we'll see at dinner. We can find another seat for him at Mother's big table."

At one o'clock, Elizabeth donned her warm coat, adding gloves and a wool hat. Harriet snuggled into her carriage under blankets. Louis finished his attire with a scarf doubled around his neck.

"You would think we were facing a blizzard, instead of a chilly breeze." Elizabeth paused outside the front door. She placed her hand on Louis' arm stopping his advance.

"What is it?" He bent down to her.

"Listen." She encouraged the silence even from Harriet by putting her finger to her lips.

"I don't hear anything." Louis glanced up and down the street.

"Exactly. Nothing. No cannon fire, no shouting. Peace." The

colonels must have decided a quiet Christmas Day was appropriate with accolades of *Peace on Earth*. It would be hard to sing and praise throughout the day with a lively bombardment in the background.

Once inside the Elliotts', Elizabeth doubted any noise from the outside world could enter in the walls of the old house. Singing, laughing, and playing resounded and crescendoed for an hour before dinner.

Raymond arrived on Jeannette's arm. The boys doted on Raymond, who sported his blue uniform, a real soldier in their midst. That appeared to be better than adding miniature soldiers to their growing toy brigade.

Elizabeth smiled, suppressing her fear of Raymond in danger, and listened to the children demanding details of the war front.

"Please, tell us about the battles. Did you shoot your gun a lot?" Little Robert paused and added big wide eyes. "Have you killed anybody?" His question caught the attention of the adults.

Elizabeth tensed and held her breath. Would Raymond glamorize the war, embellish the battle, or protect their little ears? Although Elizabeth wanted to know the truth, she feared the harm to her nephews' innocent lives.

"Well, those are good questions." Raymond pulled up a chair in front of the boys and looked them in the eyes. "I shoot my gun every day in target practice at a moving decoy. And I have not killed anyone. Basically, I have been at Fort Johnston, and now I'm helping with construction of a fort on Sullivan's Island."

Even though she couldn't see the boys' faces, she imagined momentary frowns. Where were the gloom and doom stories? Raymond told the truth. In fact, the cannon fire from the ships had been the only fighting locally.

"All right, sons, that's enough for now. Let's eat." Robert coaxed his sons toward the dining room. "I'm sure Raymond wants this good hot meal more than anything." They turned their heads back often to view their hero not far behind.

"Do they even realize their own father is a war hero too?" Louis whispered close to Elizabeth.

She shrugged. "I don't know what they have told the children." Would they explain about the navy or let them believe Robert left on a cargo mission as usual?

"He leaves in two days. I'm interested to know the plans. I'll have to find a secure place to do my questioning."

The family held hands around the table, bowed their heads, and prayed along with Mr. Elliott, thankful for Christ's birth, the food, and safety of the ones present. "And please, Lord, keep George secure in your watchful care. Amen."

Elizabeth raised her head and focused on an apparition, a vision as if assembled by her father's prayer. His red coat draped over one shoulder with one arm in a sling. Raymond moved away from the table a step, before Henry pulled him to a stop.

"George!" Elizabeth ran to her brother and hugged and kissed him. Not a ghost or her imagination. No conjuring out of a few words. He was real, alive, and an answer to prayer.

Ten pairs of eyes stared at him, mouths gaping. He kept his arm around Elizabeth and said, "Happy Christmas."

Anne and Mother moved at the same time into the arm vacated by Elizabeth. The men, including Raymond, stood rigid. Elizabeth guessed they couldn't look past the red coat. The boys peeked from behind their father's coat tails. At least they knew now that red was the enemy and not the ally anymore. What fear the other two soldiers had to quench as they reacted to the enemy in their midst—a family member too.

"What is he doing here?" Raymond's voice startled Elizabeth. Of all people to speak first. His agitation pierced the air. Of course, the stark difference between the blue and the red uniforms radiated ill-feelings. Enemies by choice. It appeared George's injury did not soften Raymond's vocal hatred.

"I'm sure he comes in peace," Father said and gestured for

Raymond to be silent. Henry's hand remained on Raymond's sleeve and nodded for him to obey.

"I do." Although there was no way to prove it. "I came in the night and hid in an abandoned house until now. No one saw me." George used a tone Elizabeth never expected to hear from him. Humility? And his chin retained a normal position, not arrogant and haughty. He did seek peace. She had to believe he would not bring the war into his parents' home.

Mother stepped in front of her son and raised her hand for continued silence. "It's Christmas and for this one day, this one meal, we can welcome George home," Mother said. Her son, her only son, brought tears to their mother's eyes and heat to her cheeks.

Elizabeth set a place and a chair for George beside her.

"Then let's eat." Father proceeded to slice the turkey while Louis tackled the ham.

George locked eyes with the curly brown-haired baby sitting in her high chair next to Harriet across the table. "Christine?" he questioned.

Of course, he wouldn't know her, not after six months. Elizabeth's heart tore in two for the child and George. "Yes, this is Christine."

"How do you do, I'm your..." He glanced around the room. Mother nodded at him to continue. "I'm your father."

Elizabeth knew the child did not understand. Her parents were known as grandmamma and grandpapa. No one in her life was Mama or Papa. They had all decided at the first to reserve the telling for George and Victoria, if they ever decided to take their roles.

Father he was not, not in the sense that Louis and Robert were to their children. Elizabeth placed a protective hand on her belly. She yearned to blurt out for him to claim that role, live it, but now was not the time.

Slowly, an awkward normalcy permeated the room. Tidbits of

news made way through the smoke- screened words. Elizabeth felt the shadows hanging from the ceiling, concealing the truth and masking the words from the individual hearts.

Raymond's glare was enough to start a battle. George's gaze never lingered on the young Patriot's face. Before sitting, George discarded his red coat, making the obvious not so blatant.

"What do you hear from Victoria?" Mother asked. She hadn't touched her meal. The yams and corn couldn't compete with George. Elizabeth wondered if shock would be the best word to describe her mother's demeanor.

George choked, then took a sip of water. "Nothing. No one has seen her, not even her parents."

"Really. Since when?" Elizabeth felt caught as a link between two worlds.

George laced his hands on the table in front of his plate. "About five months ago in Philadelphia. Then she disappeared."

"But," Elizabeth stalled, swallowing her words before she said too much.

George turned his head slowly toward her. "But what?" Now she had to say what she had tried to hide. She didn't have the right to keep two lives apart. Her secret did no good hidden anymore.

"I saw her. We saw her in the park." She nodded toward Louis. He winked for her to continue. "Then she came by the house to see Christine."

"Elizabeth, why didn't you tell me? I would have…" Mother's cheeks puffed up and her face reddened.

"I know what you would have done at that time. Perhaps not now. But you would have prevented her from seeing her daughter. I chose to show a little grace. No harm came to anyone and perhaps it helped Victoria." Elizabeth's raised voice returned to normal at the end. *And I wanted Victoria to know the feel of her child in her arms and the love of being a mother.*

George bowed his head and placed his hand over Elizabeth's. "Thank you."

Louis and Robert rescued the remaining portion of the dinner conversation, alternating the leadership role. A few topics were taboo, but honest assessments of the state of Charles Town, the mercantile, church, school, and general weather and health made appearances. Neither George nor Raymond offered any word or hint about the battlefields. George's arm hinted at an encounter, but no one wanted the details over dinner about the possible casualties in the story.

After the Wilsons and Raymond departed, Mr. Elliott asked the men to join him in his study. A few years ago, it would have been for a drink or a cigar. Louis surmised today would take a more serious turn.

"Be honest, Son. Why are you here? Hundreds of miles from your troop? We need to know." Mr. Elliott swung his arm out to include Louis and Robert.

"I know it must seem odd," George stated.

"Odd does not begin to describe it," his father added.

George paced in front of the mantel and stopped to look his father in the eye. "Honestly, after I was wounded in a skirmish, I needed to see my family. Pennsylvania is cold and dreary. The colonel needed a rider to deliver a message to a regiment in North Carolina. I volunteered with a request to continue to Charles Town. I have to return tomorrow."

Louis stood with his arms crossed, peering at the young man. "You risked your life to see your family for one day?"

"Yes. Wouldn't you or Robert have done the same?"

Louis pushed himself from the wall and stuffed his hands in his pockets. He desired to point and prod with his fists on George's chest, if only to bring some sense into him. "Of course, but I have a wife and child as does Robert."

"And I have a father, mother, sisters, and a child. Just because

I've made mistakes doesn't mean I've lost all love for my family." His voice cracked. "If I could I would undo so many things."

Silence. None of them, Louis looked around, could refute the love of family inspiring one to take risky actions. Wasn't he doing that daily?

"Would you undo your loyalty to the British? Would you become a rebel?" Mr. Elliott posed.

George didn't flinch, but Louis did. Hesitating, George pulled his shoulders back. "It's too late for that."

His lack of words spoke volumes. Possibly George regretted his rebellious act of joining the British army. Perhaps his loyalty wavered and possibly changed. But he was in too deep. He risked imprisonment, death, dismemberment, or other atrocities if he switched sides. Anyway, no one on either side would believe or trust him.

It was too late.

"For a twenty-year-old man, you are carrying around lots of regrets. I think you need to straighten things out with God, and maybe other things will look better." Mr. Elliott's words touched on Louis' humility. Why hadn't he put the situation in God's hands? Hadn't he made many mistakes and regrets before placing them all in God's hands? George's problems appeared to be graver, but Louis had lived in the same selfish, self-centered world a few years ago.

Louis knew there was no harder lesson, but no greater return than the freedom it brings. "Your father is right, George. Take it from me. Nothing will make any sense until you come to terms with God." He'd had this conversation with George before he had left for Pennsylvania. George could be closer to acceptance, but even the one step presented a gulf in George's mind. Louis remembered the final step as the biggest.

"Hear, hear." Robert raised an imaginary glass.

"I will think on all you've said. Now, if you don't mind, I'd like to spend the next few hours with Christine."

CHAPTER 27

"It's hard to believe today is the first of January 1776." Elizabeth looked out the frosted window panes into a different world than a year ago. Louis stepped behind her and wrapped his arms around her extended middle.

His hands travelled back and forth, possibly catching a kick or a punch from his baby. "This is a gift we'll receive this year. And with a baby, there is always hope."

"How did you know I was thinking about hope? Sometimes it's so clear that God is holding us all in His hands, and He's bringing us near so He can protect us. Then something will change, and once again I'm questioning or doubting." The war loomed an obvious threat. Yet, so did Grandmamma's illness and death, Sarah's miscarriage, George's choices.

"We all do that." He rested his chin on her shoulder, viewing the same scene "What is it about today that makes you peer out into the dreary morn?"

She turned into his arms. Possibly facing him would focus her dismal thoughts. "Where do I start? I'm facing the New Year with Mother and Christine away in the country, Anne alone with her children, Robert in Rhode Island creating a navy, and Raymond and Tom fighting."

"And me, right by your side." He kissed her pouting mouth, making it pliable and able to smile.

"Well, that is true. Please don't talk about sending us away anymore. I'm staying right here."

Louis flexed his fingers against her sides, as if releasing tension. "I will admit, you are more protected now than three months ago. With the South Carolina navy commissioned and old vessels transformed into warships daily, the British won't enter Charles Town by sea without a fight." Elizabeth ran her fingers through his hair. He pulled her closer. "Don't forget all the Loyalists' houses now occupied by Patriot forces. We have soldiers all around us."

He grabbed each of her hands and kissed each palm. "Promise me you will be careful around the enlisted men. Colonel Moultrie is having a hard time turning the boys into reliable soldiers. He has many who desert, and others who drink all the time. There have been incidents where they've been caught stealing and carousing, even with the curfew enforced."

Elizabeth put her hands on his chest and gazed deeply into his eyes. "I promise. I've already placed a street curfew on Ellen, Amy, and me. You know we're never out after dark without you or a male escort. And they are scarce—you, Henry, or Father."

What kind of world will their children have? Could twenty years down the road be a place of peace, a warless existence? She ran her hand over her skirt, caressing her unborn child and received a tiny kick, as if to say, "You have today, this moment."

The bleakness of the New Year didn't contain all negative scenarios. Louis concentrated on what he could do to help alleviate the strain and stress of many young men in the regiments. Daily, more of the older men accepted new assignments, such as delivery of supplies, taking them away from their normal activities. Commerce had to keep flowing. People needed to eat; therefore, ships continued to come and go. This meant Louis and Henry had to keep their business moving forward, not only for personal gain, but for a community facing shortages and an uncertain future.

The *Rose* made it back into port with a shipment of goods from France and the Indies--items such as spices and coffee, plus luxuries like silk and glassware and everyday commodities ranging from fabric to iron ware.

But as Louis checked the produce, he once again realized that the local goods kept the town and mercantile prospering. Provisions from the farms and plantations nourished the townspeople as well as the regiments. He wondered what would happen if the battles raged in South Carolina's low country or the British blocked the land entrance to the town. All the same questions were asked at council meetings.

Louis knew citizens stored extra food in their secured storerooms. Some had fears of starving or being robbed. All legitimate concerns. The mercantile basement contained crates and shelves of survival materials and food. Just in case. Louis and Henry determined to keep it full and well-stocked. They had restocked arms and ammunition for their own use, if it came to that point.

He prayed the tide would turn, for God to perform a great miracle of peace with the exit of the British ships. To once again stand at the seawall and stare at a crystal-clear horizon devoid of boxlike images dotting his view. Toy ships poised to kill.

In his coat pocket, he carried a bulky envelope. Louis tore into the envelope, since he was alone, for news from Christopher. Not news of peace or withdrawal, but of Christopher's plan to sail home to help protect Charles Town from invasion and destruction. It would be good having his friend around, as an experienced congressman officiating in person for a spell. Talking for now had ceased. The congressional delegates would return to their colonies to implement the new procedures and face the real obstacles in the form of battle ships and food rations.

Before settling in for the evening, Louis visited the harbor, relishing a view of the *Rose* determining her purpose for the good of Charles Town. She would not see battle as other converted merchant ships, but she could receive scars from the open seas as she journeyed back and forth to France. The ship's fate was linked directly to Louis' purpose.

He discerned his investment floated safe and secure at the wharf. The schooners *Polly* and *Defense* along with the brigantine *Comet* and the ships *Betsy* and *Prosper* patrolled off Charles Town's coast, armed and ready.

With practice, Louis had honed the ability to switch from his role as merchant and provider to husband and father as he followed the road home. Church Street had changed little, except for the empty houses deserted for a safer life outside the city. Louis patted the envelope in his pocket before he opened his front door. Grinning as he recalled the second item from Christopher's envelope, he couldn't wait to share it with Elizabeth.

Gone were the days when Louis could yell "Elizabeth" as he walked through the house. At any time of day, Harriet could be sleeping and now with Elizabeth's pregnancy, she could be the one napping. He followed the noise trail, leading him upstairs to the bedroom being converted to a nursery for two.

Ellen, Amy, and Elizabeth held up tiny dresses. Louis guessed they were Harriet's, unpacked for the new baby.

"Excuse me," he ventured, interrupting giggles and sighs. "You seem to all be having a joyful time."

Elizabeth dropped the frilly dress in her possession and turned to his voice. "It is fun. Each piece has a memory, and all of them happy."

Hands on hips, he admired the lace and frills spilling from trunks. How did they even cart them from the storage room?

"Elizabeth, do you think I could steal you away for a moment or two?

"Of course." Elizabeth faced Amy. "Will you watch Harriet, please?"

"Yes, ma'am. She can help us." Amy dropped a tiny dress in Harriet's lap.

Louis laughed. "I'm sure she can." He laced Elizabeth's fingers with his and pulled her to the drawing room off their bedroom. He moved an open Bible off the seat and clutched it in his hands.

Guiding Elizabeth to the settee, he sat next to her and glanced at the Bible. "What were you reading in Nahum?"

She looked at the book in his lap and read, "Watch the road; strengthen your back, summon all your strength." Then she reached over and found a bookmark in Psalms. "But then I read this passage and I'm glad I did. Psalm 121, verse eight, 'The Lord keeps watch over you as you come and go, both now and forever.' So, you see at first, I read about a warning, then a promise."

"God is good at that. Just when we need that bit of hope. That's one reason I wanted to share Christopher's letter and odd gift with you." He reached in his pocket and pulled out the envelope.

Her eyebrows rose. "Odd gift?"

"First, he says he's coming back to Charles Town to help protect the town and speak for Congress. And he sent this item." Louis unfolded a yellow cloth, somewhat larger than a handkerchief and held it in front of them.

"What is that?" Her reaction was like his, surprise mixed with laughter and perhaps a little anxiety or fear.

"This is one of the new continental flags designed by Christopher and unfurled on December twentieth from the main mast of *Alfred.*"

Elizabeth shuddered. "That is a rattlesnake." Her voice shook.

"Yes, a coiled snake. A noble and useful creature who warns his enemies before he strikes. He attacks only in self-defense but is always deadly." He traced a finger around the snake without ever touching it.

"You sound like you're reading a script." She held the cloth up by two fingers and slanted her head.

Louis was sure the angle didn't help the image. A rattlesnake was still a rattlesnake.

"Well, those were Christopher's words in his letter." He paused and noted the color returning to Elizabeth's cheeks and a tiny smile inching toward her eyes.

"It is catching especially with 'Don't Tread on Me' inscribed beneath it." She pulled in her breath and let it out with a giggle. "I think I like it."

"Enough to hang in the nursery?" Louis teased and folded it up. His office was the best place for it.

"Louis, in all seriousness, this war has only just begun, right?"

What was he to say? He could lie and convince her peace reigned close at hand or propose an ending date in the near future. But he knew their hearts knitted together longed for honesty which bound them closer.

"I believe, my dear, the worst is yet to come. But God promises to bring us near, even in the darkest hours."

He held Elizabeth close, cradling her and his unborn child, and bowed his head in silence.

READING GROUP GUIDE

1. Louis and Elizabeth decide to make their home in Charles Town even in the midst of escalating conflict with Britain. Would you be tempted to move and establish your home elsewhere?
2. Louis' friend, Christopher Gadsden, has a powerful, dynamic personality and puts himself out front to be criticized by all levels of society. Do you have a friend like that who you admire even if you don't understand all his/her ins and outs?
3. Elizabeth and Sarah are best friends. When Sarah marries, she immediately wants to start a family. What kind of advice would you give a young wife about the timing of children?
4. Do you think Elizabeth should have told Sarah about her own pregnancy even though Sarah was having difficulty with hers ?
5. How do you think Louis and Robert felt being among all the political leaders in Philadelphia?
6. Young Tom is one of many young men who joined the

militia. As a mother, would you have been proud of him or made more of an effort to stop him?

7. George Elliott and Victoria have a turbulent courtship and marriage. Then they add an unwanted baby. Do you think Elizabeth and her family could have handled the situation in a different way?

8. How does George change in the story? Is he any different or does he stay the same? Do you see any hope for him?

9. Rev. Robert Smith, a dedicated minister, delivers sermons on liberty and patriotism to the American cause. Do you think a minister should ever preach about war especially when he supports separation from the mother country?

10. Obviously, the American Revolution in 1775 has not even touched the levels of casualties and suffering that it will in the next five years. How would you prepare for the possible devastation to come?

MARGUERITE MARTIN GRAY

Marguerite Martin Gray is the author of *Hold Me Close, Surround Me,* and *Bring Me Near– Revolutionary Faith Books One, Two and Three.* She enjoys studying history and writing fiction. An avid traveler and reader, she teaches high school Spanish and has degrees in French, Spanish, and Journalism from Trinity University in San Antonio, Texas, and a MA in English from Hardin-Simmons University in Abilene, Texas. Marguerite is a member of American Christian Fiction Writers, Abilene Writers Guild, Daughters of the American Revolution, South Carolina Historical Society, and Preservation Society of Charleston. She currently lives in North Louisiana with her husband.

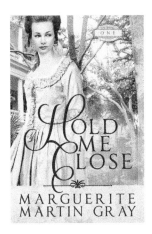
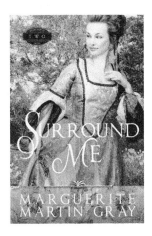

Celebrate Lit Publishing
Is proud to endorse

Roseanna White
D E S I G N S

Finding the pictures to capture your words

http://www.roseannawhitedesigns.com/

Made in the USA
Monee, IL
22 September 2020